# Brotherly Bonds

# Brynn Paulin



Ellora's Cave
Romantica Publishing

## *What the critics are saying...*

ඞ

**ON YOUR KNEES**

**9 Rating** "Ms. Paulin's novella is a completely enjoyable read, brimming with page after page of intimate moments in the BDSM tradition that will have you squirming in your seat. The emotional connection between Jessica and Ryan adds to the D/s theme to make this more than just a sex fest. […] If you are D/s fan and want a nighttime read to put you in the mood, I highly recommend you give *On Your Knees* a place on your nightstand." ~ *Novel Spot Reviews*

**ALL CHAINED UP**

**4.5 Stars** "A sizzling mystical read that leaves goosebumps *All Chained Up* by Brynn Paulin will delight readers while giving them a sensual look into a BDSM relationship. […] This book isn't just about BDSM, although it does play a big role in the whole plot, All Chained Up is also about acceptance and learning that loving someone means sharing everything in your life with them and not keeping secrets that could kill. Ms. Paulin has penned a story not only of hope and closure for those involved but also a romantic tale that only the cards could predict." ~ *Sensual EcataRomance Reviews*

**GENTLE CONTROL**

**5 Angels** "In a word, this story is delicious. […] The Dominance and submission dynamic between this couple is more about the mindset than the kinky scenes and it is this dynamic that works so well for Josh and Tempest. […] *Gentle Control* was the first story I'd read by **Brynn Paulin** but it won't be my last. If you're searching for a quick, sensual, heady read, *Gentle Control* is the perfect story for you." ~ *Fallen Angel Reviews*

### MASTER ME

**4.5 Lips** "*Torrid Tarot: Master Me* is a sensational story about two people who love each other but are afraid to act on their feelings for fear of loosing the friendship between them. All three of these books by Brynn Paulin are exciting and highly erotic. I really wanted to cry at Ana's pain when she thought she lost Max. And Max, I just wanted to grab him by the shirt collar and give him a good shake. This book is very emotional, and the characters are wonderful. I can't wait for Josh's story." ~ *Two Lips Reviews*

An Ellora's Cave Romantica Publication

www.ellorascave.com

Brotherly Bonds

ISBN 9781419958151

Edited by Helen Woodall.
Cover art by Syneca.

This book printed in the U.S.A. by Jasmine-Jade Enterprises, LLC.

Trade paperback Publication September 2008

# BROTHERLY BONDS

# ON YOUR KNEES

# Dedication

*To all the women who have to be in control but don't want to be.*

# Trademarks Acknowledgement

The author acknowledges the trademarked status and trademark owners of the following wordmarks mentioned in this work of fiction:

7-11: 7-Eleven, Inc.

Barbie: Mattel, Inc.

Hotel California: composed of Mike Dimoulas, Roger Lapointe, and Andre Lapointe

Lone Ranger, The: Classic Media, Inc.

*Princess Bride*: Act III Communications, Screenplay and book by William Goldman

## *Three of Wands*

When I chose the Three of Wands for *On Your Knees* I had a plethora of paths to explore. The focus of this card is on new and beneficial partnerships, successful conclusions, fantasies coming to fruition, exploration, having faith and even finding peace with the past. The shadow aspects of the card include wasted efforts and being overwhelmed in delays. Goals are difficult to reach because of failure to work cooperatively with others.

Whew! I could have focused on just one of these but all applied to my heroine, Jessica, who has struggled with her past and as a result, has become a woman obsessed with being in control and proving herself. She feels she must do everything herself. She's swamped in the shadow side of the Three of Wands. Jessica needs the partnership foretold by this card. She needs to explore her fantasies and discover there's more to life than work. Most of all she needs to have faith and trust in someone outside herself. The pressure she puts on herself is eating her alive.

Ryan, the story's hero, recognizes this. In disguise as a dungeon master at Pleasure Palace, he offers Jessica a new partnership in which he will be her Dom and she his submissive. For a long time, Jessica has had fantasies about submitting to a man who would take the power she's felt forced to wield. This seems the perfect opportunity to explore her lurid dreams and exorcise a few demons. At Ryan's hands, Jessica will finally find a happily ever after she's never imagined.

On Your Knees portrays some aspects of Domination/submission and BDSM but is not intended as a true-to-life account of this lifestyle.

## *Author Note*

This book portrays some aspects of Domination/submission and BDSM but is not intended as a true-to-life account of this lifestyle.

# Chapter One

*Please Cum…*

Crass. Jessica Rush wrinkled her nose as she tossed the invitation onto the corner of her desk. A sex toy demonstration.

"No," she told her friend Keera.

"Please," Keera pleaded. "It'll be fun. The whole place is set up for parties like this. I went to one last month. Very erotic. You'll love it."

Erotic. Jess almost snorted as she pulled the latest construction schedule toward her. She'd find it very erotic if her crew could bring in the mall project on time. Until then she didn't have time for anything, not even a diversion like the party Keera had been invited to.

Keera picked up the invitation and dropped it in the middle of the paperwork. "Come on. You need to think about something besides work."

That was easy for her to say. Her job overseeing the administrative personnel wasn't, by her own admission, as stressful as Jess' as Project Manager for Cress Construction. Plenty of people thought Jess couldn't do the job and that she shouldn't have been given the assignment. She was out to prove every one of them wrong, which meant no time for play.

She glanced down at the square of light blue cardboard in the middle of her work. She flipped it over. "*Pleasure Palace, Giving Single Women What They Want Most*. Hmph. It's at Pleasure Palace?" she asked incredulously. She'd heard of that place—and stayed far from it. A sex resort, that's what it was.

"Some of the guys who will be there are hot and available. You could hook up. Blow off some steam."

"Right. You know what I want most? Someone to clean my house."

Keera sighed. "When did you get so boring?"

"Look, let's just go to dinner so I can get home in time to finish my budget updates and get to bed early so I can get here early tomorrow. I'm still recovering from the last party you dragged me to."

"The psychic bridal shower? It was fun."

"Watching the drunk bride-to-be model lingerie? Or that tarot card reader who was a total fraud. I know more about readings than she did." The woman's mystic-tinged voice filled her mind along with the ethereal image of the Three of Wands card. The reader had said it signified Jessica's future. Alliance, exploration and happily ever after, the woman had promised. Past hurts would be healed, she'd learn to trust and her dreams would come to pass.

Right. So far she didn't see a sign of any of that happening and the likelihood of forgetting what screwups her parents had been was nil. Being forced to be the only grownup in the family had a way of shaping one's life and future.

And her dreams?

More like nightmares lately. Good God, she didn't want some of them to occur. That woman at the party had been a charlatan at best.

"Let's just go to a movie or something."

Keera rolled her eyes and snatched away the invitation. "Nope. I'm going. Seriously, I think it's a much better way to spend Thursday night than that." She swept a hand toward Jess' desk. "You've got five minutes to change your mind, then I'm on my way. The party starts at six."

"Party?"

"Hi Ryan, bye Ryan," Keera chirped as she headed out the door.

Jess almost groaned as Ryan Cress, second son of the Cress Construction family, strolled into her office. Not only did his family own the company but he was her boss and frequently in the middle of her business. And her dreams.

Heat flooded up her back as she remembered last night's erotic dream. She desperately tried to focus on him in a strictly work-sense instead. *Business. Keep your thoughts on business.*

At least once a day, he stopped by to check her progress—well, actually the progress on the mall. Still it *felt* like he was checking on her. She would have liked it better if he were checking *out* her. She supposed it was his right. This was his family's company. Rights aside though, she needed space and she didn't need a micro-manager breathing over her shoulder.

She wasn't being fair. Ryan didn't micro-manage. It was just her perception brought on by her need to constantly prove herself.

Still, she didn't doubt he was here to check up on her. While he folded his long frame into the chair across from her, she mentally readied herself to give a quick update of the project. A lock of his wavy black hair drooped over his forehead while he studied her.

She stifled an appreciative sigh. She'd never seen any man wear business clothes as well and as comfortably as Ryan wore his dark razor creased slacks and starched white shirt. They hugged his body as if they'd been specifically made for his lean figure—and they probably had. He was perfection walking.

"What party?" he asked again.

She shrugged dismissively. "A thing Keera's going to."

"You're not going?"

She shook her head. "I've got things to do."

His gray eyes narrowed at her. "Work?"

"Well—"

"Jessica."

A shiver snaked down her spine at his tone. No one except Ryan called her Jessica. To everyone else she was plain old Jess, one of the guys.

He leaned forward resting his elbows on his knees. "You're working yourself to death. As far as our client is concerned you're ahead of schedule. Yet you insist on acting as if you're behind—"

"I am."

"You don't have to prove yourself." He continued as if she hadn't spoken. He knew her too well and that bugged her. "Anyone who had doubts is long convinced that you're the right person for the job."

She bit back a protest. "Thank you."

"Do yourself a favor," he suggested. "Go do something fun tonight."

"I have too much to do."

He stood and leaned on her desk, bending toward her. His warm, minty breath brushed her skin. "Take the night off. If you don't, I'll reassign you. I will not have you killing yourself."

"You wouldn't!" Fighting the image of being reassigned to a position beneath his thrusting body, she glared at him. Her thoughts had gone berserk.

"Try me."

"You can't. I haven't done anything wrong."

He simply watched her, letting her come to her own conclusions. The authority in his gaze set her back in her chair. "Go with Keera. Where is she going tonight?"

"Some party at Pleasure Palace."

Ryan tried to breathe as he realized where he'd ordered Jessica to go. His older brother Theo owned Pleasure Palace and he and Ryan had spent plenty of time there with their submissives. It wasn't exactly the place where he'd expect to find Jessica, as much as he wanted to. He'd stopped fucking other women because every time he did, he saw her face. The disappointment and guilt was too much after a while. Not a good mix for a Dom.

Abstaining until he cleared himself of the obsession seemed the smart thing to do. Until now, he hadn't found the means for striking the fixation from his mind.

He watched Jessica turn away from him to grab her purse from her bottom desk drawer and imagined her on her knees, presenting her ass to him. His cock sprang to attention. He swore under his breath. What the hell was wrong with him? Learning to control his reactions was one of the first things he'd learned as a Dom, still every time he was in the same room with her, he got hard.

If Jessica didn't submit to him soon, he might go nuts.

Of course, she didn't seem to notice *any* man at the office. She was so driven. Her need to control everything and to prove herself colored everything she did from her prim power suits and upswept brown hair to her hard-as-nails attitude. He watched her drive herself into the ground until the wee hours of every night. She left after everyone else, taking home a briefcase full of paperwork which she lugged back into work the next morning. Dark crescents lived beneath her tired green eyes. She never cut herself a break.

No matter how many times he told her not to do it, she continued. He wanted to see her pale skin free of fatigue almost as much as he wanted to fuck her until her slim body collapsed beneath him and they both struggled to breathe again. Actually, he realized, he wanted it more.

Last month, she'd stopped smiling.

As she sat up, she pushed a strand of her long brown hair back into her twist. Her blouse pulled tight against her arm, showing how slim she'd become. It was past time to stop this.

"Did you stop to eat lunch today?"

Gathering papers from her desk, she shook her head without looking at him and missed his pissed off expression. Good thing. He might have scared her to death.

"I was in back to back meetings all day. I grabbed a cola an hour ago."

It sat unopened on her desk. "It tastes better if you open it," he grated and her head snapped up. Ignoring the instant argument in her eyes, he forged ahead, his knuckles against the top of the desk as he leaned forward. "I am giving you two minutes to get your butt out of that chair and get out the door. And I swear if you take one scrap of paper with you—one bit of work—I will fire you before you hit the parking lot. Get moving. Your time started thirty seconds ago."

"You can't do that!"

"Try me. Get in gear and go meet Keera. I want a report tomorrow."

Heat flooded her cheeks turning them bright pink. It was the most life he'd seen in her in weeks. If this is what it took to get a reaction he'd sure as hell keep on. The thought gave him another idea and another reason to hurry her out the door.

He'd bet Theo would be interested in knowing where Keera was planning to spend her evening. Nearly as interested as Ryan was at the prospect of finding Jessica there.

He looked at his watch. "Less than a minute. How much do you value your job?

* * * * *

Okay, Madam Zelda or what ever that psychic's name had been might have been right about her exploring-new-things prediction. Visiting Pleasure Palace certainly qualified as a new experience. If that fraud had been right it was a complete fluke.

Jessica parked in the curved drive in front of Pleasure Palace and surveyed the sprawling structure. Though she'd never been here, she'd always pictured it like Cinderella's castle. There would be towering turrets, a drawbridge and a moat. A dungeon. The very name "Pleasure Palace" spoke of dungeons. Her skin warmed, despite the bite in the fall air and she imagined herself chained and waiting.

"Jessica, you're a pervert." She pushed the thought of dungeons and erotic fantasies from her mind. This was an old-world mansion with double doors and three-story pillars. Definitely no dungeon. What was wrong with her, anyway? Getting all hot and bothered over the thought of being tied up. Damn, next thing she knew she'd be getting off on the thought of being spanked. Her pelvic muscles tightened, sending a tingle through her cleft.

She was a lost cause. She didn't understand it. BDSM was the last thing in the world she wanted, yet she got aroused just considering the scenario. She should just turn around and go home before she got herself into trouble. The parties here were by invitation only. Since she hadn't arrived with Keera, she wasn't even sure she would be admitted. Besides, they'd probably be demonstrating bondage tools inside. Sure she was interested in it but she certainly didn't want anyone else knowing her secret fantasies.

Smoothing her hands down her black slacks, she fought back her nerves. This was only a demonstration. She'd kick back, look at the toys—maybe buy one—and be home in time to finish her project budget. This would just be a bunch of giddy women giggling over huge purple dildos or the like.

It could be fun.

Or it could be as excruciating as a migraine.

Powered by that lovely thought, she dragged herself from her car and headed up the steps to the double doors. She pressed the button on the intercom beside them.

"Name?"

"I'm not sure I'm on the list—"

"Name?"

They weren't exactly cordial here.

"Jessica Rush," she answered. *Please, please, please don't let me be on the list.*

The attendant didn't speak again. The lock on the door clicked. Jessica dove for it before the lock re-engaged. Inside, stood a woman in medieval wench garb. Actually, to be more accurate, it was the gothest, *briefest* wench outfit Jessica had ever seen, rounded out with jagged-cut black hair and black lipstick. Jessica tried her best not to stare at the excessive cleavage. Her gaze flitted about the entry with an eye for the construction and decoration. Pretty standard old money. Several doors, all closed. Expensive wall treatments. Highly polished marble floors. Recently remodeled or exceptionally well-maintained.

"This way," the attendant said. She sighed and shook her head, visibly unimpressed with her duties.

*Oh, I see. Miss Personality here was the one who answered the buzzer.* So far Jessica wasn't thrilled by the service here. Maybe the woman was irritated because she was a latecomer. Jessica thought about turning around and leaving but remembered Ryan's order. He'd probably ask her about this tomorrow and she'd better have answers.

She caught her breath when she stepped through the door leading to the inner portion of the house. The modern façade fell away and she was deep inside a medieval castle complete with wall torches—thankfully an electric simulation she noted—and rough stone walls. Just like a dungeon.

*Oh shut up!* she told her inner voice. *There is no dungeon.*

She jumped as several screams erupted around her, echoing down the hall. *Pleasure? Pain? Holy crap! Where the hell was the exit?*

Her guide turned and rolled her eyes. "Exhibitionists," she muttered in disgust. "Most of the other rooms are soundproofed. Would you like to check in on what they're doing? They won't mind."

"Um, no."

"Okay. This way." She turned the corner and Jessica considered turning around and running for the door. She had a feeling she'd just entered the Hotel California.

The woman huffed and grabbed, her elbow. "You're going to get lost. I'll be in big trouble if you wander in to the wrong room."

She hustled Jessica down a winding hallway and ushered her into another dimly lit room.

Jessica pulled her arm free. "I think there's been some mistake."

"You are Jessica Rush, right?"

"Yes."

"No mistake. This is the package your, uh, *friend* requested for you. Wait here and the, uh, servants will be in to prepare you for your evening." She frowned at a paper on a rough-hewn table beside the door, sighed and shoved it in her pocket. She turned to Jessica with a fake smile. "Happy fucking."

Jessica stared at her aghast. "You don't like your job, do you?"

Another long-suffering sigh burst from between the woman's black painted lips. "No. I've got a busload of transvestites arriving in fifteen minutes and I'm stuck fitting people into the schedule."

"I could leave."

"Hell no. That *would* get me fired." She stomped from the room and slammed the door.

Okay. Now what? Jessica turned around in a circle.

* * * * *

Ryan looked up from the magazine he was flipping through as Francesca stomped through the door and plopped herself into the chair beside the security intercom. "She's here," she said sullenly, glaring from him to where Theo paced.

"Good," Ryan replied.

"Is Keera ready yet?" Theo snapped.

Someone was a little impatient, though Ryan couldn't much blame him. The same edginess had sent him flipping through three magazines and a romance novel already. The sooner he was alone with Jessica the better.

After a scowl at Theo, Francesca checked the schedule tracking system on her computer. "She's waiting for you. By the way, boss man, I want a raise."

Theo darted from the room while she made a fake gagging sound.

*Twerp*, Ryan thought.

She turned on him, arms crossed. When had the little girl who'd planned Barbie weddings turned so militant?

"You know, this is really gross. I do not need to know about my older brothers' sex lives. Any of them. I might need therapy."

"You're already in therapy."

"Oh. Yeah. Right. You know, you look like a dork in that outfit." He looked down at his black leather pants and boots. All the women who'd seen him in this had drooled.

"Only to you."

"Can't you put on a shirt?"

"No."

"What are you supposed to be anyway? Who are you, masked man? The Lone Shirtless Ranger?" She chortled in the way that only little sisters could—and live. Barely. "Watch out ladies, the Ranger rides again."

If he was lucky.

"No hat. I might have a lasso."

"Ew!"

He shook his head and stood. Sometimes his sister forgot she wasn't twelve anymore. "I'm going downstairs."

"Oh man! I *so* didn't need to know that!"

"Shut up, 'Cesca."

She laughed, reaching up his discarded magazine. "Don't rush. I'm sure Finn and Bobby will take their time with her."

A wave of possessiveness stabbed through him along with the urge to kill his baby sister. "You sent Finn and Bobby?"

"Everyone else is busy. It's a full schedule tonight. I had to fit you in."

He tapped his fingers impatiently on his thigh. He'd go nuts if he waited downstairs for Jessica. And his sister sure as hell knew, judging from her shitty grin. She glanced at her watch. "You could go join the masturbation awareness group in 3D. You know, since you have time to kill."

He scowled at her as he left the room. 3D was his private—and empty—room. Masturbation indeed. Why would he bring himself off when he'd soon be inside Jessica's tight little pussy? She'd be right where he wanted her. Hot, ready and panting for his cock.

Hell, he'd been watching her for months, sizing her up. Assessing her. She worked her beautiful ass off, bringing in all her projects under budget and on time, keeping all the contractors in line, never missing a step. She was a formidable force to reckon with and she hated every minute of it. A submissive in wolf's clothing. He hated watching what it was doing to her. Every day she was fighting for power and fighting to prove herself. Fighting to be in control of everything. Every day she became more burdened with it.

She didn't even realize it wasn't control she needed.

* * * * *

This was the weirdest sex toy party ever. So where was the party? She was alone in an empty room, not a toy in sight and someone was coming to prepare her. Prepare her? For what?

She made her third circuit of the room, rounding the massage-style table in the middle. Why didn't this room have any chairs? This was so dumb. She had work to do at home. Gathering her purse from where she'd dropped it on the table beside the room's entrance, she yanked on the door.

It didn't budge.

"Oh, come on! You got to be kidding me." A torrent of prickles leapt down her back. She tried to push her fear aside. This was a public facility with a good reputation. Surely it was a mistake that she'd been locked in. Miss Personality seemed to be more intent on things other than being sure she didn't accidentally confine a patron.

A few feet away, another door opened. She jumped unaware it was there. This place was full of all the bells and whistles, wasn't it? Sulky attendants, doors made to blend into the wall, hulking men dressed in medieval gear… She backed away from the two guys who came through the door. They had to be twice her size. Dressed in hose and tunics, they still looked like wrestlers gone bad.

"The door's locked," she blurted, although as an afterthought she wondered if she shouldn't have said that. "I want to leave."

The darker complected man plucked her purse from her fingers and lifted her onto the table, while his blond counterpart set a canvas bag on the table beside the door.

"There's been a mistake," she protested.

"Miss Rush, just relax," the blond said. "We won't hurt you. It's merely time to prepare you for your evening. I'm Bobby and this is Finn." He exchanged a glance with Finn, who smiled. "He's my *partner*."

He didn't look gay. But really, what did a gay man look like? It wasn't like people wore signs announcing their sexuality. While she stared at him trying to comprehend his statement, Finn managed to remove her blouse.

"Stop!" she shrieked when he reached for the clasp of her bra.

He sighed as he studied her obviously searching for a way to persuade her to cooperate. "Your evening will be more enjoyable if you let us ready you. You can rest and we'll rub you with creams and lotions." He paused, pulling out what he probably considered to be the international persuasion card when it came to women. "We have clothing for you."

She let the clothes remark slide by. "So we're talking like…a massage?"

"Just like."

"I need to be naked for this?"

"It would be helpful."

She considered it for a moment. "And you're, uh, not into women?"

"You're lovely but no, not a bit."

She'd never before disrobed in front of a stranger—or two. If this was what was needed in order to get on with things and meet up with Keera, she'd do what was necessary. Besides, this was one of those forbidden fantasy moments, right? And this *was* the Pleasure Palace.

*Adventure and exploration,* Madam Zelda's voice prompted.

Still, Jessica's fingers trembled as she removed her bra. Slipping from the table, she kicked off her shoes and slid off her pants. Neither man seemed affected by her nakedness. Relief filled her, followed by an irrational spurt of irritation. What kind of a place was this that a naked woman didn't warrant some sort of reaction?

Finn helped her back onto the table. When she attempted to roll onto her stomach for the massage he propelled her onto her back while Bobby opened a hidden cupboard in the wall. Returning to them, he set several jars next to her legs and laid a warm, damp cloth over her mound. Mesmerized, she watched as he coated his hands with lotion. Slowly, he worked the emollient into her foot, then worked his way up to her calf.

Jessica sighed and laid her head on the rolled towel Finn placed beneath her neck. Bobby had enchanting fingers. Her muscles seemed to melt as he kneaded them. Lulled by his touch, she jumped when Finn began kneading her breasts. He worked more quickly than Bobby while smoothing the lightly scented lotion onto her. His hands rubbed to her belly, down her arms, over her shoulders.

"Can I take you home?" she whispered, letting her mind drift as they worked her weary flesh.

"Sorry, not allowed," Bobby answered.

Too soon the soothing touch receded and the cloth over her sex was taken away. She shivered as the air cooled her warm flesh. Her lethargy persisted as she remained still for the men's ministrations.

"This won't do. It will need to be removed," he said. She opened her eyes as he brushed his fingers over the trimmed thatch of curling brown hair hiding her folds. She'd always wondered about what it would be like to have a bald pussy but she'd never been bold enough to try it.

"Okay," she answered although she figured her opinion wouldn't matter. It hadn't so far.

While Finn retrieved supplies from the canvas bag, Bobby spread her thighs and draped her legs over the sides of the table. For the first time, she felt real trepidation. She shifted to pull her legs back together but he held her still. "Relax."

Taking a bottle of cream from his partner, he lathered it over her sex. Jessica lay back determined to enjoy the delicious slide across her already slick folds. When she'd left home this morning, she'd never expected anything like this.

*Thank you, Keera!*

Finn resumed massaging her upper body while Bobby worked the shaving cream into her curls. She tried desperately to stay still as he began to slowly scrape the hair from her pussy. Meanwhile, Finn managed to brush and braid her long hair, binding it into a long plait.

Two strange men. Touching her. Delicious spirals of heat seeped through her.

Decadent.

Her mind emptied. There were no projects, no to-do lists, no responsibilities. There was only the sensation of these delightful hands working over her body.

She sucked in a breath and fought to remain relaxed as Bobby parted her folds to complete his task. The blade scraped over her fleshy mound. Sweet heaven it was making her hot. Her cheeks heated. Could he see how excited he made her while he prepared her? Could he see the way her sheath flexed?

Maybe not. He didn't comment—perhaps he was paid not to—and a warm cloth replaced his fingers and cleaned her smooth skin.

Together the men shifted her to her belly. Bobby's hands became more aggressive, kneading her thighs and buttocks. With her head turned, she watched him unscrew the cap from a jar. He coated his fingers. Lifting her slightly, he slathered the emollient over her folds and rubbed it into her clit. Jessica whimpered as hot tingles enveloped her vagina. They grew stronger by the moment, radiating out to her thighs and up into her belly.

She tried to catch her breath as the strong sensations coiled through her. She tried to twist away. Finn held her down. "Relax," he murmured. "Bobby won't hurt you."

She couldn't. The waves continued to assault her pussy. Bobby applied another coat of his devil-cream, stroking his fingers deep inside her sheath. Finn bent over her. His iron grip on her back held her prone for his partner's work.

Just when she thought it couldn't get worse, Bobby smoothed more of the cream along the tender skin between her pussy and anus. His fingers continued between her ass cheeks.

"Please stop," she whispered, trying again in vain to get away from Finn. No one was listening to her.

Bobby's well-lubricated finger prodded her ass, slowly slipping inside bit by bit. She bit down on her lip to keep from screaming. She couldn't help her hips' movement as she worked against his hand, her body demanding more. Her mind grew dizzy from it. She surrendered to a haze of overwhelming sensation. The two men flipped her over again. Bobby wiped his fingers on a cloth, then continued his ministrations on her folds.

"Please," she pleaded. She tried to control her need and push aside the overwhelming desire but she couldn't. Whatever gel he'd used seeped into her, warming a clawing path into her womb. Even with her most skilled lover—who hadn't been all that skilled—she'd never become such a shivering heap of arousal.

Her sheath clamped and released as it searched for something to fill it. What were the chances those men had a dildo in that nifty bag of theirs? Anything. She needed relief.

Finn roughly rubbed her breasts, applying some of the same emollient to her nipples. Ruthlessly, he pulled them to erect points.

She needed sex and she needed it now.

She barely registered being dressed in the most transparent pink baby doll top she'd ever seen. Three tiny ties held the front closed between her breasts. Her belly was totally bare. Coupled with a miniscule thong that tied on the sides, she was hardly clothed. The fabric chafed her clit and she tried to push it away.

Finn pulled her hands away and lifted her from the table. He guided her toward the secret door. "Come with me," he instructed.

"No. I can't. I need—"

"Your needs will soon be filled," he assured her.

Leaving Bobby in the room, he took her down a flight of stone steps that lead to a long dimly lit hallway. They passed several iron-studded doors before Finn stopped in front of one near the end of the hallway. Moans punctuated the cool air around them.

*Lucky people.*

She had to join a party. No sex for her. Could she just peek in, say hi and dash home to her vibrator? She frowned, knowing she should be more concerned about joining the party dressed in a transparent scrap of lace and drenched panties.

Finn opened the door, revealing a deserted torch-lit chamber. She turned frantically as he shoved her inside. *Now her freaking common sense decided to return?* Chains, cuffs and various whips lined the upper half of one wall, along with several other items she was hesitant to identify. The lower half was a bank of drawers. Hastily sizing up her situation she scanned the rest of the room. An odd bench stood to one side of the room near another iron-studded door. A set of manacles dangled on a thick chain from the center of the ceiling.

Her knees buckled.

A dungeon!

"Wait! There's been a mistake!" she protested.

"It's no mistake, miss." He pulled her toward the chain. She was no match for his strength as he fastened each cuff around her slim wrists. She yanked on them trying to get free. The increased movement served only to amplify the ache throbbing in her cleft and breasts.

"Let me go!"

"You can voice your complaints to the dungeon master."

The *who?*

"What! Let me go!" she demanded. Finn shook his head, wishing her a good night and strolled from the room. The heavy door closed with an echoing thud behind him.

What had she walked right into? She closed her eyes as horrible, scary as hell images filled her head.

*Madam Zelda had better be right about that happily-ever-after part or I'm hunting her down.* Somehow, Jessica couldn't imagine her happy new future beginning in a dungeon.

* * * * *

Ryan almost lost himself—*again*—when he entered the dungeon. Damn he was getting soft. Surveying his woman, he was anything but soft. His cock throbbed against the thick leather pants containing it.

Jessica, unattainable Jessica, whom he'd wanted for months, stood in the middle of the room, her hands bound above her head. Her thighs flexed as she pressed and released them, fighting her arousal.

He frowned. Damn it! Finn and Bobby weren't supposed to use the X-T gel on her. That was the single thing that would have her practically writhing like this. This would be difficult enough for her to accept without being ashamed for her mindless need. Once it was applied, only release would relieve the sensations. No amount of fighting, ignoring or waiting it out would help. The effect from the gel just got worse and worse.

She turned when she heard the door shut, her sparkling green eyes narrowed with anger. "You must be the *dungeon master,*" she spat out derisively.

Yes, this would be difficult.

"Let me go, you prick! I swear if you don't release me, I'm suing all your asses off. This place will be toast."

"Oh, I highly doubt that."

Her anger sent strength through him. Disciplining her would be a pleasure. He crossed his arms over his chest, knowing the muscle beneath the tribal tattoo banding his right biceps would bulge making it more prominent. She wouldn't know the mark was a symbol of his power.

"Try me."

He smiled at the phrase she'd picked up from him. "I intend to."

She yanked on the cuffs, impotent anger making her shake. Well, anger and the arousal.

"Let. Me. *Go!*" she repeated.

He simply watched her without speaking, knowing it would unnerve her quicker than anything he could say. A good master always communicated with his sub but sometimes silence spoke loudest.

She was trying to be so strong, but he could still hear the shudder in her words. Her chest flushed pink, a background to the dark, beaded nipples visible through the sheer lingerie he'd chosen for her.

The muscles in her stomach trembled.

His body tightened at the sight of her deep in the throes of desire. Each shallow breath lifted her full breasts. He'd bet if he touched her cleft she'd be soaked from her need.

"I'll go away," she begged. "I won't say anything. Just please let me leave and you'll never hear from me again."

*Like hell.* He wanted to hear from her as often as possible.

He stepped closer, smoothing his hand over her firm ass. "I don't intend to harm you. And I won't rape you."

"Like I'd stop you right now, you bastard."

His jaw clenched. He'd punish her for that later. "When I take you, you won't be under the control of the gel Bobby and Finn put on you. You'll be fully cognizant of the fact you want me deep in your cunt, fucking you until you scream."

He saw excitement flare in her eyes, before she shifted her gaze away from him. As soon as she was fully his, he'd teach her not to hide from him—even her emotions. He wanted to be inside that pretty head, her thoughts open to him.

She shook her head. "Never."

"We'll see. First you need to come or we'll never get to that."

He reached for her and she shied from his hands. She tried to swing away. The cuffs limited her progress while she yanked fruitlessly at them. He cupped her chin and turned her to look at him. "I *will* touch you. Whenever I want to touch you. You can't control that."

She sucked in a harsh breath. Though she didn't speak, rebellion blazed in her stare. Still holding her so she was forced to watch him, he reached between them to demonstrate his point. He cupped her mound nearly groaning at the drenched inferno that met him. His fingers pressed in, hampered by the thin strip of fabric.

"Do you want me to ease this?"

He felt her jaw tighten and her eyes closed.

"Look at me," he barked in his most commanding Dom voice.

Her eyes snapped open but she wasn't cowed enough by his sharp tone to keep from glaring at him.

His fingers stroked her heated flesh. "Do you want me to help this?" he asked. "Answer me."

"You said you wouldn't."

He chuckled, the sound a thin rattle against the dungeon walls. He'd never been so aroused. Neither had he held himself by such a taut, fraying thread. He'd been a Dom for too long to have so little control. In all that time though, he'd always had subs who'd been broken in and well into the scene. Quite frankly, they'd been more into the scene than he was. Some in the D/s community looked down on him for that. His women had never complained.

"There are ways to bring you to release without using my body," he explained, his mouth a breath from hers. He wouldn't kiss her. His kiss would betray everything he felt for her.

Her breath fluttered across his lips. "How?"

"Trust me."

She tried to shake her head but he still held her chin. He knew she wanted to look away. She always looked away to hide what she was thinking.

"I trusted the people upstairs and look where it got me."

"Right where you need to be. You should be thankful."

She made a disgusted sound. "Right."

Jessica stared at the man who looked like the fucking Dread Pirate Roberts from the *Princess Bride*, only hotter. What was up with the mask and head covering? She should be terrified. Instead, she was pissed. That didn't stop her from noticing his wide shoulders and slim hips. Nor did she miss the black swirling tattoos over his belly button and around his arm. And oh, sweet heaven, the way his ass and thighs filled out those leather pants… If she weren't chained up in such an intolerable situation, she might not be able to keep her hands off him, nor would she be able to keep her mouth off the sharp curve that sloped into his pants at either side of his pelvis. *Man, I could take a bite out of that.*

That aside, she had to admit she was a freaking lunatic. By now, she should be screaming herself hoarse. But no, she was sucked in by his deep commanding voice and those mesmerizing eyes. In the dim light, she couldn't tell the exact color. They were beautiful nonetheless, especially when he stared at her as if he had complete power over the universe.

Damn it! He *and* this situation were turning her on. She was a damned freak. Her traitorous body grew hotter with every word he spoke. Her cleft fairly vibrated with need while it flooded, the cream seeping past her thong. It was on her thighs and now filling his hand.

He had to love that.

She squirmed at the thought of pleasing him. Why did she even care if he was happy? She'd practically been kidnapped yet she wanted this man with every fiber of her being… Well, not every fiber. There was a scrap of her that screamed that this was just that horrible, wonderful gel. She didn't really want him to bend her over that bench over there and fuck her like crazy.

Well, yeah she did. It embarrassed and confused her. This wasn't just the stuff those goons had put on her. It made her hotter than she'd ever imagined to be chained up like this, helpless, in front of a stranger with his hand on her crotch.

As insane as it was, she wanted more. She wanted him to take what he wanted. It was so crazy. This was so unlike her. She didn't get it. And she didn't care. The need inside her grew painful as her muscles bunched and released searching for the cock she so desperately needed. If he lay her on the cement she'd probably spread her legs and beg to be fucked.

She whimpered as he pulled his hand from her. A moment later, she heard several clanks and the chain holding her arms loosened.

"Widen your stance," he commanded. "When you are with me, your feet will always be at least shoulder-width apart."

He made this sound like a long term affair. Was this more than the mistake she'd thought the Palace had made? Was she kidnapped? People knew where she'd gone. She'd be all right. Wouldn't she?

"Move your feet," he growled when she hesitated. He made her tremble inside with the knowledge of the fine edge of danger that lingered in the air around him. If she didn't obey him, what would he do?

"Why?"

He glowered at her and she distantly wondered what he looked like behind his mask. His broad chest was impressive and the tattoos made her drool, but she wanted to see his face. She wanted to know if she met this fine specimen outside this dungeon. Would he even notice her?

This had to all be an act. He was saying these things for her pleasure. None of this was for real. He probably got paid for the sex slave fantasy. Did that make him like a prostitute? She'd kill Keera later. Right now she'd might as well go for it.

"My flog is going to love your ass," he growled.

"You wouldn't!"

"I will. This is your last chance. Move your feet or I'll move them for you."

She moved her feet.

Flog? What the fuck! She'd rarely been spanked as a child, she wasn't letting someone start spanking her now. *A flog is something completely different from that,* she thought.

Well, she wasn't letting this go that far.

Nodding, he went to the wall and pulled down a metal bar, easily a foot and a half wide, with short leather pieces hanging from either end. Her brow furrowed. That was *not* what she thought it was!

He knelt behind her and shoved it between her ankles, quite quickly confirming her suspicion. There was nothing she could do to stop him from fastening the straps around each ankle. She would have toppled if not for the support of the chain holding her arms.

"I wouldn't have to do this if you weren't so rebellious," he told her.

She moaned, unable to halt the sound. She'd never find relief! At least before she could squeeze her legs together. That had helped. Now she was spread wide open, flooding her cream into her panties.

Her fingers clenched. Why did she have to be so excited? Curiosity and lust had edged aside her healthy dose of fear and panic. This was all her fantasies delivered in one power-punch.

She was freaking crazy.

The demand of her body grew stronger. Tremors spiraled through her, demanding she surrender to him. The mere need turning to pain.

"Please," she choked.

"Will you let me help relieve this?" he asked.

They were back to that? She thought her consent had been a foregone conclusion when he'd dragged down this bar. Or maybe that had been to help her make up her mind, in the direction he wanted. Whatever.

"Yes. Yes," she replied, another spasm twisting her.

He smoothed his hands over her abdomen. "Shh. Take deep breaths. I'll take care of you."

She doubted it. No one ever took care of her.

His mouth flattened against her navel, tongue flicking in and out. Her keening wail echoed off the stone walls and probably into the hallway. Anyone could hear. She didn't care. No one save for the dungeon master could help her. She didn't want anyone else. He promised to ease this pain.

Going to the wall, he pulled out what was arguably the loveliest shaped dildo she'd ever seen. Of course at that moment, any dildo headed for her pussy would look good. He tugged the ties on the side of her panties. The garment fell into his waiting hand and he lifted it to his nose.

"You smell good, Jessica."

She couldn't help mirroring his breath as he inhaled again. Dropping the lace beside him, he slipped his arm around her waist. His toy prodded at her slit. It slipped through her juices and easily penetrated her tight sheath. She gasped at the girth of it parting her sensitive tissues. Arching her hips, she tried to take more. He kept pushing, shoving inch by remarkable inch inside her.

"More," she begged.

He leaned into her, his chest pressed to her hard breasts, his heat seeping into her. His lips brushed her ear.

"I lied," he whispered. His midnight velvet voice raked down her skin. "This *is* my body taking you. This dildo was made from a mold of my own cock. Feel me Jessica. Feel me taking your sweet passage. Feel me fucking you." With that revelation he proceeded to claim her with the replica of himself. "Do you like it?" he asked, though surely her cries told him she did. "Do you like me fucking you?"

"Yes," she sobbed, mindlessly working against it the best she could in her position. The cock surged deep, fully demanding her response. Tears streamed down her face at the intensity of it, at the wild tremors exploding through her body. She screamed, she knew she did, but it barely registered as her awareness sank inside her, captivated by the deep digs of that toy. Shimmering heat flooded to every part of her. It pulsed over her rigid body driving her into the jerking rhythm of a shaken marionette. Still he drove on, drawing release after release from her until they piled one atop the other and she begged him to stop as her tortured sheath gushed around the cock.

Weak, she hung limply from the chain, each shallow pant pulling at her body.

The dungeon master pulled the toy from her.

"That was quite possibly the most beautiful thing I've ever seen," he murmured as he helped her to straighten. "A few more moments and your arms will be free."

Crossing the room, he opened the drawer beneath where he'd retrieved the bar and pulled out a cloth. A basin she hadn't noticed sat on a nearby table, almost hidden from view in an alcove. He dampened the fabric and returned to her.

Slowly he dragged it over her swollen folds wiping away the gel that had tormented her. She trembled as he pushed it inside the crease of her ass to remove the excess there too.

"Better?" he asked.

She nodded, realizing she was better. The arousal still tingled through her body like a pleasant buzz. It was still urgent though not as dire. She could make it home now without fucking some hapless pedestrian.

Now that she'd come, he removed the bar from between her ankles. Apparently, he'd only wanted to keep her from pressing her legs together to lessen her need. Left parted, she'd begged to come, begged for him to soothe the itch. Ire wove through her. Tricky bastard. No doubt every move he made tonight would be carefully planned and calculated to bring her to her knees. A vision of her bowed before Ryan shot through her mind. *Her boss*? What the hell! Hastily, she pushed it aside. Ryan had nothing to do with this. And she didn't want to think about subjugating herself before anyone. It wouldn't happen. A, she wasn't doing it. And B, Ryan didn't fit into this scenario.

Remembering what the dungeon master had said, she kept her feet about shoulder-width apart.

"I'd like you to let me go now."

His dark eyes studied her and he tilted his head. "Would you?"

Why did he sound so amused? She yanked on the chains, her anger growing now that the ache from her arousal was greatly diminished. "Yes."

"It's not your decision."

"Look, that was fun—"

He circled her, his glower growing again. "This is all a game for you, isn't it? You don't think any of this is real."

"There's been a mistake…"

"There's no mistake. I know exactly who you are. I know exactly why you're at Pleasure Palace." He stepped close to her and she smelled his deep masculine scent. "And I know exactly why you're *here*. You think you're in charge of this? You're not. You like this, don't you. You wanted this. You wanted to be powerless."

"No." She shook her head, his words both frightening and arousing her. His complete control, the self-assurance, his dominance all nudged up her boiling desire. God, she loved dominant men. Unfortunately, she'd never found one, only read about them.

"Then how did you get here? Like this?"

"I thought it was something else."

"You thought it was something else?" His mask shifted and she knew he was lifting his eyebrows in disbelief. "So you let them touch you? Shave you? Dress you? Chain you here? You were fooled?"

"Yes," she answered in a small voice.

"No you weren't." He stroked his finger down her arm, leaving goose bumps in their wake. "You let them." His finger slid beneath the strap of the baby doll top. "You let them." Over her belly. "You let them."

He cupped her smooth mound before pushing his fingertip inside her still-dripping pussy. "You *let* them." He lifted his hand, heavy with the scent of her arousal, between them. She could smell it as he sucked the juice from his fingers. Even more collected between her legs, seeping onto her thighs.

"Please, don't..."

"You *let* me."

She could only shake her head as the deep need started again, a need that had nothing to do with any stimulant. A need he'd predicted and she couldn't prevent. Every word he said was true. She'd let them because it was her deepest desire. It was a fantasy that lurked in her darkness, coming out to play every time she found pleasure in the quiet of her lonely bedroom.

Suddenly, he stepped back, breaking the disquieting intimacy building between them.

"Let, let, let... It's all about power for you. Isn't it? It's all about you being in control."

She didn't want to hear anymore about herself. He couldn't delve into her psyche and pull out her secrets, putting them on lurid display.

"Let me go!"

"Let?" he mocked. "Doesn't it get tiresome for you? Always being in control of everything?"

Her lips pressed together as she fought her emotions. She sucked in a breath through her nose. "There's nothing wrong with being in control."

"There is if you hate it. You hate it, don't you?" He stepped back into the intimacy and a warm protected feeling, totally incongruous to her situation, enveloped her. "You resent it. I can see the unrest seething inside you."

"No one else is going to take care of things. No one else ever has."

"I would," He replied, his deep velvet voice wrapping around her. He released the ties on the front of her top and it gaped open. Within the security of this moment, she didn't think to protest.

He tapped her chest. "What about in here? Don't you want someone else to be in charge?"

"Sometimes," she admitted, half-heartedly. Sometimes she hated it. She resented always being the responsible one. Sadly, there was no one in her life she could trust to take the weight from her shoulders.

"You don't like power."

"Yes, I do," she lied, unwilling to give over everything.

"No. You embrace it. You try to control everything even though you don't like it." He lightly drew his thumb over the shadow beneath her eye. "These circles testify to how much you don't."

How did a stranger know her so deeply? "I do what has to be done."

"Do you? You don't trust people. You think they'll betray you. They'll fail you…maybe even hurt you, as I suspect you've been hurt before. Someone hurt you badly and now you think you always have to be in control."

She shook her head blinking back tears. He couldn't know that. He couldn't know about her childhood and the pain she'd endured.

His dark gaze captured hers and he gently cupped her chin, not letting her look away from the knowledge in his eyes. "I won't betray you. I won't hurt you. I will never fail you."

She sucked in a shuddering breath that sounded a whole lot like a sob. He'd stripped her soul bare in a so few words.

"You don't want control, do you?" he continued. "You want nothing more than for me to rip off what's left of your clothes and fuck you until you scream. Don't you? This turns you on. You don't want it to, but it does."

She couldn't deny it.

"Please stop."

"And you want to know why you feel this way? Because for once, you have no power. You don't want control. You don't want responsibility. You want to let go."

She nodded. He knew everything. If he knew this, he'd seen to the deepest part of her being. She hadn't even told Keera about this secret resentment.

"Say it," he prompted.

"I don't want control," she admitted.

"Do you trust me to give you what you want?"

Did she? Her eyes closed for a second before she looked directly into his eyes. He'd already taken control. He'd already gained her trust by understanding her needs and filling them. He'd patiently brought her to this unbelievably dark place in herself and he hadn't fallen on her like a ravening beast though judging from the enormous bulge in his pants he really wanted to.

There was no question. Her words would only give him permission. "Yes."

His lips turned up ever so slightly. "Then give me what I want."

She hesitated, momentarily unsure. Suddenly, she stood looking over a narrow precipice. She could jump over to the other side and risk dire consequences or she could dance away and pretend this had never happened.

She could give him control tonight or walk away and forever wonder.

"You're in complete control," she whispered.

"Master," he prompted. He reached in his pocket and withdrew a key.

She swallowed. "Master."

Reaching above their heads, he unlocked the shackles and pulled her tight to him when she would have fallen. Her arms screamed as blood rushed back into them. Weakly, she leaned on his strength. His fierce heartbeat thudded rapidly against her breast, revealing she wasn't the only one excited by their play. He pushed her shirt from her shoulders and it fluttered to the floor leaving her naked in his embrace. He pulled back slightly, his gaze again looking deep inside her and connecting to her with complete knowledge of her desires.

"On. Your. Knees."

# Chapter Two

Jessica looked up at him in surprise. Was he joking? Kneel? She'd said she'd give him control but kneel before him? She was reasonably sure she could walk, perhaps even run, now that the effects of the gel had dissipated. This was her opportunity to make a break for it.

And miss one of the most intriguing experiences in her life.

He didn't say a word. His scowl darkening, he waited for her to make her decision. He seemed to know so much about her. He likely knew exactly what was going through her head right now. He was probably poised to pounce on her when she bolted.

She wouldn't. He made her feel safe in a way she never had before. What had he said? He wouldn't betray her?

He was right. She wanted this. She wanted him to have control.

"Jessica?" he prompted, his voice dangerously soft.

Her head bowed, she sank to her knees before him. Whatever happened, good or bad, her decision had already been made. She'd given over control. She had to follow through.

He didn't step away and her breasts pressed to his powerful thighs. She didn't mind the view from here, she thought studying him through her lashes. Her eyes were level with his protruding, strained fly. He wanted her, possibly as badly as she wanted him. If that was true, when they finally came together, they'd crash against each other in desperation. It would be wild, out-of-control sex.

She hoped he hurried.

"Hands behind your back," he instructed.

She nodded although she wasn't sure she could do as he ordered. Her arms burned and barely responded to her brain's orders to move. Realizing her predicament, he crouched beside her and eased her hands into position, helping her twine her numb fingers together at the small of her back. His thumb stroked along her cheek.

"You'll be fine in a moment," he assured her. "You were chained longer than I'd wanted."

Still he *had* wanted her chained, Jessica interpreted, filling in his unspoken words.

Standing, he wedged his boot between her thighs and nudged them apart. "Never together," he told her. Once she was situated, with arms behind her, knees apart, her ass resting on her heels, he gently tilted her head forward.

She studied the toes of his black boots. They were a lot like the kind she pictured most bikers wearing. With his leather pants they looked incredibly hot. Oh God, who was she kidding? Everything about this situation seemed hot to her. At the moment he could be wearing a hotdog suit and she'd find him incredible. His very presence sank into her, drawing her and molding her reactions.

An odd magic wove around them in this place. It pulled forward parts of her being that had never seen the light. She'd hidden so many of her feelings since childhood, locking them away in her own private dungeon. It seemed fitting that they'd surface here, yet strange that it had been a stranger identifying her deep-seated needs.

This position spiked up her needs about one hundred twelve notches. Spread open, waiting. The cool air rising through the stone floor mingled with the heat pouring from her core. Frankly, she was surprised steam wasn't billowing around her.

Holy crap! She was really into this.

"Remember this position," he commanded. "When you are with me, when I tell you to go to your knees, this is what I want."

She nodded, completely compliant.

How long would he make her wait before he took her?

She might have to figure out how to make this more than a one-time deal. Much more. That might not be easy, though. She couldn't imagine trusting anyone else with this power over her. If he hadn't already proved worthy of her trust, she wouldn't be kneeling here either.

She watched her dungeon master again. No, she couldn't trust anyone the way she was trusting him right now. Maybe it was the mask and the façade of anonymity. Who knew? He probably did. He seemed to know her and what she wanted better than she did.

"You have been particularly disobedient and willful tonight."

"I—"

"Silence," he barked.

Her eyes went wide but she held her tongue.

"I have warned you many times, yet you continued to fight me."

She shook her head. If he hit her, she'd flip out. She'd heard about that stuff. Some aspects of BDSM intrigued her but the thought of being beaten into submission sure as hell didn't. She trusted him, just not that much.

In contrast, her body throbbed at the prospect of him exerting further dominance over her. Curiosity and yes, as Madam Zelda had predicted, there was the thought of exploring this new opportunity. That tiny card had predicted an awful lot. Right then, Jessica reevaluated her opinion of the psychic. That woman was a freaking genius. How could she have known this fantasy would come to fruition? The card.

"Look at me." Her Dom threaded his fingers through her bound hair and pulled her head back. "I will not have my slave disobeying me."

*Whoa! Wait a second! Slave?* Her breathing accelerated and she sank her teeth into her bottom lip.

"Do you understand what I'm saying? You belong to me." He enunciated each word clearly. "All of you. I'm claiming you. From here on, you will be mine. You will be my responsibility and offer me complete obedience. I'll see to your needs and I'll teach you. I'll discipline you if need be. You will trust me in all things."

Give complete trust? *For tonight, right?* The dungeon master was deep into this. She almost believed he meant forever, not just tonight. She took a deep breath. She wasn't so sure about this, even for one night.

Her head turned marginally to the right. She stopped herself before she totally denied his claim. Her quivering body spoke of her acceptance. It was only her mind that couldn't embrace his assertion.

He made an amused sound in his throat. "No, I didn't think you'd so easily agree. You will though. In time. You will learn."

"I don't even know your name!" she blurted.

His hand slashed through the air, dismissing her excuse. "Names aren't important. You know what you need to know about me. For the moment, you will address me as Master. I will answer. Your trust and obedience aren't dependant on my name." His lips quirked. "You're not big on obedience to someone else though, are you? Unless it feeds your power."

How did he know these things about her?

He tipped her head up, making her look at him. "Now, my disobedient slave, it's time for your next lesson."

She cautioned herself to stay calm. He'd promised not to hurt her and she was here for the adventure...whatever happened.

"Your first lesson was to trust me. You must understand that I know your needs and I will care for them. Did I care for you?"

She couldn't deny it. She also couldn't deny that the thought of him taking care of her filled her with unaccustomed well-being. She relaxed, confident that everything would be okay.

She *could* trust him.

"Yes, Master."

He pulled her to her feet and led her to the bench.

*Oh crap.*

"On your knees," he said quietly. It was almost as if he didn't want to say it but had to. His care heightened her growing faith in him. How far would it go? What would she do because of the feeling he invoked within her?

She glanced at the bench. "Please..."

He shook his head. "*Now* Jessica."

*Trust,* she reminded herself. *You promised to give him control.*

She complied and he pushed her so that she leaned over the low, cushioned bench. Despite telling herself to remain calm, every muscle in her body tensed. Her chest pressed into the cushioned surface while her fingers clenched at the small of her back, her ass a little higher than her shoulders. She dropped her face onto the seat. Damn it. She didn't want to be here. She didn't want to trust him. Yet she desired nothing more.

He left for a moment. She looked up when he returned. He set three items on the seat beside her head. Her horrified intake of breath was heavy with her fear. Cuffs, a gag and a whip—at least that's what she figured it was. Long, wide strips of knotted leather were bound together in a black handle. A cord wound around it, no doubt providing a better grip. Was this the flog he'd mentioned?

Her cleft immediately flooded aroused by the forbidden desire. Treacherous body. She could have stupid fantasies all she wanted but she wasn't sticking around here. She unclasped her hands and levered herself upward.

Ryan anticipated her fear. Splaying his hand on the middle of her back, he held her still. He couldn't let her run out now, just when they were making progress. If she left, she'd reinforce the walls she'd erected to sustain her control. He'd never be able to breach them.

"Lesson one, trust. Lesson two, obedience and discipline. Return to your position." He emphasized each word. Right now her head would be screaming that she was crazy yet her body would obey. He bit back a smile when she sank back on to the spanking bench and laced her fingers behind her back.

She might not be trained or experienced in any way but she was particularly responsive to his voice inflections. The way she so easily fell into the submissive role and followed his commands pleased him more than any of his past subs ever had. Her anxious and sometimes apprehensive mien separated her from those before her. Their main objective had been the game. Sure, they'd been aroused but they hadn't locked onto anything except how Ryan's performance would enhance their pleasure.

That wasn't what Jessica was all about.

He drew his finger over the crease of Jessica's ass. She trembled with instant reaction. She was deeply aroused. This wasn't the calculated arousal of the women before her. She'd been born to be his. Now that they were together, they'd become a mutually beneficial alliance. She was the other half of his coin. The s to his D. They were made to coexist and were incomplete without the other.

She'd soon realize that as he introduced her to her new world.

With practiced speed he fastened the cuffs around her wrists and stepped back to survey his work. The other items remained where he'd left them. His body instantly tightened and his throat grew dry. Jessica stretched over the bench, completely open to him. Even in the dim light, her cream gleamed on her bare folds. Long stretches of soft, pale skin begged for his mouth, his hands and his flog. If he knelt behind her and lifted her slightly, he could drive his cock straight to her core.

He shifted his stance, trying to adjust the pressure behind his fly.

"How do you feel right now?" he rasped. Did her position make her as hot as seeing her this way made him?

"Sweet heavens, don't make me talk," she begged, her voice muffled against the seat.

He knelt and leaned over her. His lips grazed her ear.

"How do you feel, Jessica?" he repeated. His hands slipped beneath her to cup her breasts. They'd still ache from the gel Bobby had put on them since he hadn't wiped the emollient off. She gasped as he pinched her nipples, tugging, rolling, then pinching harder. Later in bed, he'd lick those delicious points until she begged for release and then he'd lick some more. He'd be willing to bet he could make her come just by tormenting her breasts.

"How do you feel?" He needed her talking so she didn't drift off into sub-space. While they played this game there was always the chance she, like other subs, would move into an alternate state of mind called subspace because of her intense reactions. He needed her here, fully part of everything they did.

"Helpless," she admitted.

"Do you?" he asked. "Why?"

"Cuffed, kneeling and pressed between a bench and a wicked man?" A tremor rocked through her, rippling against his chest as he leaned to her. She shifted beneath him, her ass brushing his tormented cock.

He promised himself that soon he'd be inside her. As soon as she was ready. That was a rule he'd grown up with. The Cress family shunned the use of a safe word. A good Dom was always in charge—of himself and his slave—and a good Dom recognized his sub's state of mind, identifying acceptance or stress.

Right now Jessica was in a mild state of acceptance. She needed to be further along before he took her. He took a deep breath. Damn, how her scent and that dripping cleft beckoned to him to sink to the balls in her sheath.

"I think you're still fighting to be in control." Removing a hand from beneath her, he trailed a fingertip down her back. She arched into it. Good. She'd surrendered to her hedonistic side. Where the body went, the mind would follow.

"No," she denied. "You're in control."

"Glad to know it." He turned his wicked hand and slid it inside the crease of her ass. The cheeks squeezed together as he teased at the tight flesh. "Have you ever been taken here?"

"No."

"Mmmm. It will be my complete pleasure then. How do you think it will feel to have my cock inside you here?" His fingertip worked inside her to the first knuckle. The snug passage was still well-lubed from the early ministrations.

Her body clenched around his finger as she reacted to the thought. "You're too big," she argued.

"You think? We'll see."

"No."

Possibly she well-remembered the replica of his cock and how it had stretched her pussy. Forceful tremors shook her while his finger screwed in and out of her ass. As she relaxed, he added another. This time she rocked into the gentle thrusts.

"Trust," he admonished firmly.

She sighed, spreading her knees a bit further and canting her hips. "Yes, Master."

God, she was beautiful.

"You were telling me how you feel," he reminded. "You said helpless, which I don't believe, by the way. Go on."

It would take more than what he'd done to Jessica to make her helpless. She could eviscerate anyone with that sharp tongue of hers. Anyone but him. He saw through her guise. Whether she knew it or not, he was her perfect match and probably one of the only people she couldn't cow into doing exactly what she wanted. Right now, she wasn't afraid, not even close to it—and he didn't want her fear. If she were scared, she wouldn't be lying docilely beneath him enjoying this.

How could she describe the delicious sensations filling her? Her ass had always been a taboo spot. She'd never let anyone touch her there, yet here was this stranger shoving his fingers in and out of her. And it felt so good.

She couldn't imagine anything more. Frankly, the thought of his cock plunging into this virgin territory petrified her.

"I'm not sure," she admitted. "Unsure, I mean."

"You can be sure of me. I won't fail you. Not tonight, tomorrow, or ever."

"This is just for tonight."

"Is it? We'll need to address that. Right now, do you like what you feel?"

His voice crawled along her spine, nestling in below her heart. While her mind puzzled over his claim, a million answers to his question roared to mind, all of them relating to how badly she wanted him inside her. Anywhere. Any way he wanted. She couldn't say that.

"Um…"

"Be honest with me. You must always be completely honest. For both our sakes."

What was he? A freaking mind reader?

"It's weird. Um…good." Wonderful. Great. If she got much more aroused, she'd have a puddle beneath her. Why hadn't she done this before? Obviously, the right man had never come along for it.

She wondered off-hand if Pleasure Palace had gift certificates and if she could get a standing appointment with this dungeon master. He said he'd never let her down. A thread of sadness cinched around her heart. What would he say if she told him that he'd already let her down by not having an emotional connection to her for more than this short time she was trapped in his dungeon?

Damn, what was with this emotional neediness? She should know better. Her emotional needs weren't ever met. Life had taught her that. Not by her parents, who expected her to be their emotional support, or the men who wanted her to make all the decisions in relationships. She couldn't remember a time when anyone had taken care of her for any reason beyond obligation. Those times had been grudging at best. She'd learned to take what she could get and accept that as intimacy.

Looking at her friends and their families she knew it was a poor substitute. And she knew she didn't know how to ask for or accept intimacy. She pushed them away. The dungeon master wasn't waiting for her to ask for it. He wasn't waiting for her to accept it. He certainly wasn't letting her push him away.

He added a third finger, spreading her and she yelped in surprise.

"Easy," he murmured. His thumb stretched down to rasp over her clit. Ever so slowly, he continued to stretch her while working in and out. His other hand petted her shivering body.

"Just relax," he instructed. "Stop tensing. Stop thinking. Just feel."

She tried to follow his direction but found it damned difficult with his continual flick over her sensitive nub. With her eyes closed, there was nothing beyond the feel of his hands on her, nothing to distract her from riding the waves of sensation.

"Feels good," she said through her teeth. She could barely stand it. Her need was too strong. A need purely for him. This was nothing like the lame love making of previous lovers. No wondered she'd stopped finding time for sex. If they were like this man, she'd find it hard to leave their bed.

"You're good to continue?"

She nodded, without opening her eyes.

He pumped his fingers deeper. Suddenly, she felt a strange drag of stiff fabric over her skin. Her lids popped open and dread settled over her. The flogger was gone and that hadn't been fabric. It was leather. Oh fuck, maybe she wasn't ready to move on.

"Relax," he said. "I told you punishment was coming."

"Don't hit me." She couldn't keep the tremble from her voice.

The whip pulled over her again, the ends splaying out across her back. "I don't hit. The flog is completely different. Hitting only satisfies an abuser. The flog brings pleasure to both master and slave."

"And pain…"

"At first, perhaps." The thick, cord-wrapped handle of the flog dragged over her ass while he continued to assault her tiny opening with his fingers. "Many couples use spanking as part of their sex play. The position, the pain, the dominance of one over the other all enhances the encounter." The handle slipped into her folds rasping across the tender flesh. "Now the flog is different. This is not for play, Jessica. This is because you were willful and disobedient."

She pressed her lips together before she protested that she didn't know.

"The flog is a tool of punishment," he went on. "Yes, it brings some pain. Still in the end it will bring you pleasure, as it does most."

She doubted that. In her head his voice twined with Madam Zelda's telling her to have faith.

Jessica gasped as the corded grip nudged past the lips of her open pussy. Each ridge caught on her tender walls, sending a riot of sensation to her womb. She pressed her face into the bench overwhelmed by the sensation of the handle tormenting her sheath while his fingers filled her ass. She moaned when he pulled them free but she had little time to ponder it as he drilled the handle in and out of her. His knuckles knocked against her clit with each stroke.

Her inner walls grabbed at the corded rod, amplifying the reaction shooting through her. Release coiled inside her, drawing tighter and tighter until she danced at the edge of explosion.

She jerked when he pulled it away and draped the flog across her back and over her bound hands, the damp end cradled against her ass.

"Don't move," he ordered. "The flog will shift if you disobey."

Taking deep breaths while her body rattled with protest against being left at the brink, she listened to him move around the room. How long would he leave her here in this torment?

She heard water running, followed by silence. Straining her ears, she listened and anticipated his approach. When nothing came, she started to lift her head. A leather tail shifted and she froze, planting her forehead in the cushion.

"Naughty, slave," he admonished.

Oh no, he was watching.

"I'm sorry, Master," she replied, her voice muffled by the seat.

"Um-hmm."

Not seeing him, not knowing what he doing, was killing her. And he didn't seem to be in a big hurry to return to her, either. Didn't he need to fuck her as much as she needed to be fucked? For that matter *would* he ever fuck her? Was this some psychological torment to take her to the edge then leave her there without ever giving her what she needed?

He'd said he'd fill her needs. He'd better or that hapless pedestrian was in trouble again. This wasn't easy kneeling here and effectively being put on display. She tried to forget about it but damn it if it didn't turn her on a little. How had she not known this about herself? She'd always had submission-like fantasies still she'd never thought she'd actually *want* to be in the center of one.

Though she was listening for him, she started when he returned to her and moved aside the flog. He walked as silently as a cat.

"Don't move," he reminded her. A moment later, the cuffs were released and he positioned her so her arms draped over the other side of the bench and down to the floor. A metallic click announced one wrist had been attached to a ring driven into the cement. She yanked at it and found there was no give.

"You can leave me loose," she told him. "I won't move."

It wasn't true. She was worried about what was coming. She wanted to be able to dart for the door if need be. If she went screaming for the exit of Pleasure Palace with the dungeon master on her heels, would people help her or help him? Would they think it was just a game and look away?

"I think maybe you might need a little help." His fingers closed around the other wrist and he dragged it to join the other. The lock clicked into place as he fastened the cuff to the same loop as the other.

"Lift up a little," he told her.

She couldn't move. Her breaths came in shuddering pants as she pressed her face into the cushion of the bench. She couldn't do this. She needed to leave. For the first time since entering the dungeon she felt truly helpless. He could do anything and she couldn't stop him.

"Jessica?"

"I'm scared," she admitted. He'd told her to be completely honest. She hoped it didn't backfire on her.

Gently, he lifted her and pulled the bench from beneath her.

"Elbows down," he told her, at the same time he guided her into position. Her arms stretched out in front of her, her ass stretched up in the air as she knelt. He stroked his hand over it and onto her bowed back.

"My sweet slave. This is what you wanted. Total release from responsibility. Total surrender. Total loss of control and power. You are entirely mine. At my mercy."

Oh God! Why did her body have to respond at the idea of being completely at his whim?

He slid a small, thin pillow beneath her head. "I don't want you to hurt yourself against the cement when you jerk. You're scared right now but in a few moments, you'll learn that with the flog comes pleasure. Your body will experience things you've never imagined and you'll never want to leave. You'll crave more. You'll want me to do more."

She couldn't imagine it, yet she'd never imagined being this aroused before. Heck, she'd never imagined any of this—any of her secret dreams—coming to fruition before.

*Dreams will become reality…*

*Thank you Madam Zelda,* Jessica thought. *Duly noted.*

The waiting was the worst part. Regardless of what the psychic had said when she'd scanned the cards, Jessica didn't foresee this going well. Her captor—when she thought about it, that's what he really was—didn't seem inclined to want to get on with things. It was a head game. He was just fucking with her. Putting her in this ridiculous, revealing, unfortunately arousing position. Watching her without really touching. Making her feel totally helpless without her control. Was that all this was about? Playing with her?

Please, he couldn't be toying with her. She needed to fuck almost more than she needed to breathe. Even the air touching her exposed pussy was driving her need higher. She shifted, adjusting the weight on her knees and flexing her inner muscles. If she rushed home her vibrator would help with this relentless need. She wouldn't make any stops—except darn it, she needed batteries. She'd just have to make do without the vibrating function. She was vibrating enough to do the job anyway. The way she was feeling, she could pickup and screw the clerk from the 7-11 right on the counter, security camera running and all.

"If I ask really nicely and tell you I'm done playing and I want to go home, would you let me go please?"

"No."

"I'm serious. I know you get paid to do this whole thing… I'm sorry. I'm done. I won't ask that my friend's money get refunded. I'd just really like to go home."

He sighed and a moment later, his boots appeared in the corner of her vision. His heels tipped up as he hunkered down beside her and touched her cheek. "Poor Jessica, so confused by all this."

"Stop patronizing me and unlock the cuffs!"

"And here I thought we were beyond this… Are you taking back the gift you gave me?" He leaned down so his mouth was near hers and stared directly into her eyes. "I'm not getting paid. I'm only here because of you."

Stabbing his fingers through her braided hair, he turned her and covered her lips. Jessica groaned as his tongue speared into her mouth taking possession of it as easily as he'd possessed the rest of her. Ravenously, she met him, tasting him and feeling the open need in his urgent kiss. She breathed in his spicy scent, losing herself to him as he consumed her soul.

"Shall we continue?" he said unevenly when he pulled back and stood. "Or do I let you go and we both fruitlessly try to forget this ever happened?"

She turned back to the head-down position she'd been in before.

"If you don't work for Pleasure Palace..." Why was that even hotter? "Then I'm chained up and naked with a stranger."

"You were before."

"That was different. It was almost therapeutic, like sex counseling. This is..."

"Wrong? Sinful? Exciting? Arousing? Exactly what you've dreamed of since you were old enough to understand sex?"

Her fingers clasped around the loop of metal holding her cuffs. It was all the things he said. "Yes."

"I won't endanger you, Jessica." His deep, sexy, almost-familiar voice sank through her. He could take her to the verge of orgasm just with his confident tone alone. Every word proved he had complete control of this situation.

She loved how he said her name as if just that was his claim on her.

"You're completely safe with me."

So this was it. Again she was presented with a decision. He was offering exactly what she'd asked for. She could go home unfulfilled. Or the alternative...explore this unknown lifestyle. She wanted both. Her mental pendulum swung back and forth like a wind chime caught in a tornado. She should reassert that she wanted to leave, yet she didn't really want to leave. She wanted to see what happened. Wasn't it true that the only real reason she wanted to leave was because she was scared of the flog? Jessica Rush, who wasn't afraid of anything?

"I want to go on," she said, tightening her fingers on the ring.

She yelped as the flog thudded against her ass before she could beg him not to hurt her. Much. Deep down, if she examined her hidden fantasies, all those dominations, all the captures, all the force, this was in there too.

"Let it out," he said. "Scream if you must. Personally it makes me hotter for the frenzy that will take you."

Tears welled in her eyes and the sting spread against her buttocks. Frenzy? Hah!

"Again," she whispered. The flog fell, the knots biting into her tender flesh and she bucked unable to hold back a loud cry. He didn't give her time to react before another caught her thighs, another on her back, on the crease where her leg met her ass so perilously close to her needy cleft.

Her mind went fuzzy as she anticipated another stroke and the backslap as the ends ricocheted and connected again. She angled her hips toward it. He ignored her silent plea and let it fall on her upper back.

"Please, oh Master please," she begged, widening her knees and dropping her shoulders to the floor. This time he gave in to her but the extra strength in the blow made it clear it was his decision and his alone. No amount of angling or begging would sway him from his mission of total power.

She didn't care. He could have it. All of it. As long as he wanted.

Ryan watched Jessica's body quiver as he doled out the promised flogging. He'd purposely chosen a medium weight flog to give her an intense experience without risk of really hurting her. He'd meant to count how many strokes he'd given, but instead he'd lost track, just watching her body and listening to how her screams had segued from pain to intense pleasure. She rocked toward him wanting more.

He weighed his options.

He could go on, give her the release needed by this loss of control and total submission while he denied himself or he could drop his fly and plow his rock hard cock as deep into her as it would go. Either way, their pleasure would continue.

Maybe a few more strokes. He didn't think either of them could take much more. Sweat had broken out on his brow and not from exertion. Just working Jessica, whose body also glistened with her perspiration, drove his temperature up too.

Drawing back, he angled the flog, letting the tails fly down toward her delicate folds. Jessica jerked and he knew one had connected. He suddenly had the urge to kiss it better while he drove her straight over the edge with his mouth.

He'd never had a slave affect him like this. Each thud of the flog jerked his cock, pulling her toward him and waiting oblivion.

"Again," she begged, her body sagging with the extreme pleasure attacking it. She felt his discipline everywhere—he'd seen to that—and now it overwhelmed her. She cried out passionately even when the tails weren't connecting with her. Her hips rocked in search of someone to fill her.

Him.

Not one more stroke. He flung the flog aside and reached for his zipper. He shoved down his pants just far enough to expose his cock. Jessica looked over her shoulder, her face tearstained and her eyes dazed.

"Oh thank heaven," she whispered when she saw what he was doing. Quickly, he rolled on a condom and knelt behind her. Grasping her hips, he drove into her with one powerful stroke.

"Yes!" Jessica shrieked, straightening her arms and shoving back into him. Her molten passage branded him, the burning honey of her extreme arousal coating him and dripping down to his tight balls. He moved just to relieve some of the pressure of her clutching walls, only to find he needed that tight squeeze more than he needed to breathe. Urgently, he rammed back inside, giving everything over to her. She thought she was helpless? Her writhing body had the power to give or refuse what he'd desired for so long. Her sharp little tongue honed his need. He couldn't survive without both of them.

Reaching between them, he rasped his thumb over her exposed nub. Her cry echoed off the stone walls and back into his ever-tightening body. He wouldn't last long and he wanted her flying with him when he finally erupted inside her.

She bucked under him almost throwing off his wild rhythm as he pistoned in and out of her cunt. Her "Yes!" and "oh God!" alternated with "Please!" and drove him on. Her fleshy walls convulsed around him.

"No! No!" she wailed, going rigid while he continued to pull her back onto his erection. The tight grip closed around him. He drove on, fighting the release until the last moment when she was spent in his arms and a ball of vibrating nerve endings. Knowing it would drive her to another orgasm, he dragged his fingers over her clit again, coaxing another explosion.

"Take it," he rasped, knowing it would complete this scene in her head. She needed it. She needed his command over her. "Yeah, squeeze my cock. Milk it."

She made a strangled sound and her body shuddered beneath him. Another wave of release tore through her, even stronger than before. It pulled him with it. Urgently, he made one last drive and blasted inside her.

"Mine!" he bellowed, filling her. She was his and he never intended to let her forget it.

# Chapter Three

Jessica slowly became aware she was curled on the cool stone floor with a very male body wrapped around her. Sometime in her haze, he'd released the cuffs holding her. Her arms were crossed over her chest with his crossed over them.

"You did well," he murmured. "I was proud of you, my little slave."

She nuzzled her head back against him, warm with the praise. It pleased her inordinately that she'd pleased him. "Thank you for convincing me not to run."

"Hmmm," he replied. He sounded distracted as he pulled back slightly. She winced when he touched his fingers to her back. The flog didn't feel so good now. She smiled, despite the pain. This would be a constant reminder the next few days of the intensely perfect time she'd spent in the Pleasure Palace dungeon. Every time she moved, the dungeon master would be with her.

Getting up, he carefully lifted her in his arms. He kicked the pillow toward the bench.

"On your knees. On the pillow," he told her. "Then lean over the bench."

She immediately complied, though she couldn't stifle her groan. She didn't know if she could take any more quite yet.

He'd had somewhat kind moments before but now he was almost tender while still commanding her. He smoothed his fingers over her brow. "There won't be more right now," he promised, somehow knowing her thoughts. Why should she be surprised? He'd known them up until now.

She didn't move as he left her and crossed the room. She heard him open cupboards and run water but didn't look at him. Slowly, she took measured breaths while she leaned her head on her crossed arms. The dichotomy between earlier and now made her head spin.

"Master?" she asked, figuring she'd better continue to use the title. Especially since she still didn't know his name. She had a feeling he still wouldn't tell her, either. Not tonight. "Can I ask you a question?"

"Ask me anything."

"How did you…um…when did you…"

He returned to her side and sat on the bench beside her, a square bowl on his lap. He'd completely removed his pants while he'd been away from her. "How did I get to be a Dom?"

She flinched as he dabbed a warm, damp cloth over her bruised skin. "Yes. I'd imagine you don't just say one day 'I think I might like to be a Dom. All I need is a submissive'. There has to be some process."

"There wasn't really." He dabbed cool cream onto her back, carefully rubbing it in to each mark. "I was raised in a D/s family. My father is a Dom and my mother's a sub."

That surprised her. She'd never thought of this in a family setting. "How does that work? I mean with kids and all."

"It was subtle. My mom didn't run around naked, wearing chains. We never saw our father do anything that any other dad wouldn't do. Sometimes they'd disappear to their room, even in the middle of the day." He shrugged continuing his ministrations. "My father was always in charge and Mom mostly complied with what he said. That didn't mean she was weak. She's extremely strong and successful in her own right. Just like you are. I have total respect for her." He lifted her chin so that she looked into his eyes—she still wished she could see their color. His thumb smoothed over her swollen bottom lip. "And believe it or not, I have total respect for you too. Submitting doesn't make you weak. You have to be very strong to do it."

She'd never thought of herself as particularly strong. Actually, she spent every day trying to prove herself. Maybe she didn't need to do that.

"My screams weren't very strong."

"That's a matter of opinion. While I flogged you, you didn't swear at me. You didn't cry and beg me to let you go. You let your body adjust and take it and sink into pleasure. I know men who couldn't handle as much. You were so beautiful."

"I bet you say that to all your slaves."

"There are none. I don't do polygamous relationships. If I had another partner, I wouldn't be here with you."

Bending over, he kissed one of the stripes crossing her shoulder blades. Warm threads of awareness started through her middle again. Again? She wanted him again. She couldn't possibly. New need building low in her belly argued her body wasn't nearly as broken as she might think. She moaned and dropped her head to her arms. No, she couldn't take more. Physically or mentally. She liked his hands on her body but she was done in right now.

Then his firm fingers moved to her ass. Oh man. He seemed to know just how spent she was though. Gently, he worked the cream into the marks, unknowingly easing her desire. Was it crazy that she wanted him to take her to bed somewhere and press her into a firm mattress? Wouldn't Keera have a field day with this? She'd say, "I told you so. And you doubted Madam Zelda?"

Okay, so she should have had more faith. How could she? She wasn't really a tarot believer—not like her friend. Keera lived by the cards she'd inherited from her mother.

Her weak faith was growing fast, both in what Madam Zelda had said and in this man rubbing his hands down her thighs.

Silence fell between them, the only sound their breathing and sporadic groans from her as he occasionally touched spots already more sore than others. It wasn't long before her body practically dissolved into jelly. If not for her increased awareness of this man, she could have slept he had her so relaxed. Overall she just felt good.

She couldn't rouse the energy to move when he left her again. Again she heard water and she wondered if he wasn't the cleanest Dom in the world. She smiled turning her head and watching him move. For a guy, he had a graceful manner about him. He really did move like a cat, his frame working in unison in a lazy assured roll as he walked.

The scarf tied around his head had hiked up a little in the back and short strands of hair peeked out. In the dim light she couldn't tell if it was brown or black, just dark. She knew a ton of built dark-haired guys—she worked in construction for God's sake. It could be anyone. She was swiftly coming to the conclusion that she knew this man. The familiarity about him…the things he said…how well he knew her. And why else would he be here if he wasn't getting paid?

The realization that she must know him should have troubled her. It didn't. She only hoped he'd introduce himself later, without the mask, and they could continue this in the bright light of real life. She wouldn't push the issue now. Her brow furrowed when he turned toward her and her gaze dropped to his tattoos. Perhaps she didn't know him after all. She couldn't think of a man she knew who she hadn't seen without a shirt or at least with sleeves short enough that they would have revealed the wide band on her dungeon master's arm.

So she was back to square one.

"What do your tattoos signify?" she asked when he returned and sat beside her. She sat back on her heels, wrists at the small of her back and winced only slightly when her ass connected with her ankles. "They look like some sort of words."

"Hmmm... well, in a way."

He cleaned the inside of her thighs with the new cloth he'd brought, wiping away her sticky cream. The way he cared for her made her all shuddery inside. She looked into his mesmerizing eyes, enveloped in his intense gaze. Her lips parted.

She wanted him again. Her eyes dropped closed on a tiny moan as the warm cloth pressed to her folds. She heard the wet slap of the cloth on the cement as he tossed it away and he cupped the back of her head, pulling her to him. His mouth covered hers, feasting at her parted lips and sending tremors once again shooting through her. She lifted up at his urging, meeting him chest to chest and feeling his jutting erection against her belly. Being pressed to him, complying with his will like this, filled her empty spaces as nothing ever had. He tilted her head and drove his tongue in for more. She sucked at it, taking his taste, showing him what she wanted to do to his cock if she ever had the chance.

They were both gasping for breath when he pulled back.

"Tattoos?" she managed, trying to regain some level ground. She wanted to know everything she could about him, but maybe that wasn't allowed in this lifestyle. He'd tell her. Maybe after another flash-fire of passion.

Every action, every look, every little word seemed to be a match in a drought-stricken forest for them. Any one of them could start something they both wanted to finish. Right now she didn't care about the stripes across her back. She needed him again.

"Nearly every man in my family has them. It's sort of a ritual. When you turn eighteen, if this is your chosen lifestyle, you go see Uncle Tony to get the marks." He pointed to the one at his navel, partially blocked by the tip of his erection. "This one basically says 'control your belly'. It's about always remembering to control yourself during any situation, sexual or otherwise, involving your sub."

She had to admit, he'd exhibited more control than she would have. She was writhing and begging and given the chance she would have pounced on him without a second thought. Something, she had to admit he brought out in her. She'd never been so desperately needy for any other men.

He held out his arm, displaying the band of black figures on it. "This one says 'keeper of the temple'." He touched her forehead. "And 'owner of the treasure'." He cupped her mound and she tilted into him, making a needy sound when his finger slowly dragged over her clit. Pulling away, he flattened his hand between her breasts. "And 'protector of the spirit'."

She swallowed wondering if eventually, she'd get a mark that said temple, treasure and spirit. Even if this was really just for tonight as she suspected, she'd look into it. She was all those things and even if he didn't claim her, he'd touched those parts of her marking her as indelible as any tattoo.

"What now?" she asked. She didn't want this to be over yet.

"How does your back feel? There was lanocaine in the cream."

"I'm okay." She would have said the same even if she felt every bruise. "I'd like to continue."

He was silent for a moment and from the corner of her eye she could see him studying her. "I don't think you can. Not as we've been so far."

"But—"

"Don't argue with your master. I'd hate to top this with a spanking which, I think, is about all you'd be able to take right now."

"All right," she said sadly.

"I didn't say we were finished…just finished like this."

"We didn't even try—"

"Another time."

Ryan lifted her into his arms and headed for the door that connected to the room beside this one—room 3D, the other half of his private quarters here at Pleasure Palace. He'd already pulled back the blanket on the bed and it stood ready and waiting for the next step of Jessica's seduction.

Carefully, he laid her on the satin sheets, conscious of her back. She wasn't really hurt, just aching in the aftermath of something to which she wasn't accustomed.

"This is nice for a dungeon," she commented, lifting up on her elbows.

"This isn't the dungeon. It's my room when I stay over here."

"So does that mean you'll tell me your name and I can stop calling you Master?"

"No." If she hadn't guessed it was him, he wasn't really ready to tell her. She'd know soon enough. He'd have liked to have said he kept the secret because he was unselfishly providing the stranger fantasy for her, that he was seeing it out until the end. Truly, it was more dread of the look on her face when she realized everything her boss had done to her. He hadn't thought that part through very well.

He had plenty of experience with women rejecting him for his lifestyle. Even though she enjoyed this scene, Jessica might reject him too. He didn't know how he'd take that. Everyone outside the scene thought a Dom was so always strong, almost impervious to life's arrows. He was human, just like any other man. Jessica had given him her power but she still had the ability to eviscerate him with a few words.

One word in particular. Goodbye.

She looked up at him with her huge green eyes. Excitement swirled in them without a lick of fear. Despite the mask and the intensity of what had occurred the other room he'd managed to win her over. There might be hope for him yet.

"So, slave," he said, purposely reminding her of her position. "We're going to play a little game."

She shifted sinuously on the sheets, looking for all the world like Aphrodite come to seduce the mere mortal. The little minx. "Is this a game I'm destined to lose?"

"Depends on your point of view." The way she was taunting him, he'd definitely see she lost while they both won. "This game is called 'Can Jessica stay still?' Ever heard of it?"

"No but I don't like the sound of it." The aroused edge to her words belied her statement. This wouldn't take long. She was already squirming with desire.

"Now in this game, I don't cuff you."

She took a shaky breath. "Uh-huh…"

"And I get to try out some of my favorite toys on you."

"What happens when I lose?"

He noticed she didn't say if. It wasn't like her to give up already. Her legs shifted apart inviting him inside. Soon enough. He had a short list of toys which would be introduced to her lovely pussy in a few moments.

It would be better for her if she tried to fight the need to move…

"I get to claim my prize. And if you win… I'll take off my mask."

Presented with a dilemma, she sank her teeth into her bottom lip, tormenting the flesh he'd like to suck on. She sighed. "So, this doesn't seem fair. Do I get a chance to see if you'll stay still?"

"Is the name of the game 'Can the Dungeon Master Stay Still?'?"

She shook her head. "What constitutes a move?"

"Anything more than a gentle tremor."

"Shit."

He shook his head, clicking his tongue at her. "Do I need to wash my slave's mouth out with something?"

Her eyes narrowed growing dark as summer leaves. "Depends on what you want to use."

"Generally, a flogging makes a slave less sassy."

"Am I an ordinary slave?"

"No." He held up a hand to forestall whatever mouthy response was about to spring forth. "The game starts now. Moving your mouth is considered movement."

God he loved playing with her and sparring with her. Years and years of this would be wonderful.

She pressed her lush lips together but he ignored it. Opening the drawer beside the bed, he withdrew a few of his favorite tools and realized he'd left the ball gag in the other room. Damn, he needed it. Unlike the dungeon this room wasn't soundproof. He didn't want to share Jessica's cries with anyone else.

He held a blindfold before her. "Did I mention that you don't get to see what I'm going to do?"

She growled her displeasure, fury burning in those fiery green eyes as he slipped it over them and eased the elastic bands behind her head. She obviously had things to say but didn't want to lose. Her frustration level would have her literally shaking for release soon.

Leaving her waiting he went to retrieve the gag. She might as well get used to the mouthpiece. Some situations required its use. This one didn't. He wanted to see the dark blue ball pressed between her lush cherry lips, stretching her mouth as wide as his cock would when he fucked her mouth. There went his control again. He closed his eyes, clutching the oral restraint in his fist.

He had to regain himself before he returned. He went to his supplies, considering what else he could use to taunt her. He'd left a small vibrating egg and a two-sided whip on the bed. He didn't intend to use the whip portion on her but the other end was tipped with feathers. Jessica wouldn't hold out long against them.

He knew exactly the thing that would drive her insane. Opening a refrigerated drawer, he removed a heavy glass dildo and a tube of gel. Perfect.

She hadn't moved when he returned. Good. She was invested in winning the competition. Not that she had a prayer. But he wanted her to try. He wanted to watch her fight her reactions to him and lose. She'd discover she had no power here either.

Setting the dildo and the lube on the bed, he pressed the ball to her lips.

"Open your mouth," he instructed.

She sucked in a breath through her nose, not moving her mouth.

"I won't hold it against you," he added.

Her brow furrowed and he guessed she was deciding if it was a ploy to make her lose the game. Slowly, she opened. He jammed the ball between her teeth and fastened the leather strap. His cock jerked. Seeing Jessica bound before, seeing her modeling his preferred paraphernalia made him hotter than the summer sun.

He'd never thought he'd see her like this…naked in his bed…waiting for him…pert breasts rising and falling on each excited breath. The overwhelming need to reveal himself and see where it led almost distracted him from his course of action.

Afterward. He'd tell her whether she won or not. He almost laughed. What was he thinking *if she won*? As if that would happen. He played dirty. It was his specialty and marked him as a master, in more ways than one.

"It also won't count against you if I move you," he told her. Her fingers were clenched into the sheets at her hips and he gently unfolded them. Her tight, closed up position gave her a false sense of security. He wanted her open and vulnerable with nothing impeding him.

Sliding his hands down her arms, he pulled them over her head and crossed her wrists just above her crown. Dragging his fingertips along the sensitive flesh on the inside of her arms, he made a path down her body. Deliberately, he raked all ten fingers over her tempting breasts then headed over her torso and hips until he reached her tightly compressed thighs.

He traced a line along the crease, from mound to knees. "You are a very naughty slave." Grabbing her legs, he forced them apart. "Never together," he murmured, though parting her increased the throbbing in his veins.

"Luckily," he continued, grabbing the icy cold dildo. "I know just the thing for disobedient slaves." He dragged the tip along her naked, glistening folds and watched her shake as the frigid glass tormented her clit. Pulling it away, he coated it with equally cold lube. "I decided you're right. Your tight little ass is too small and untried to take me right now."

She shrieked behind the gag as he pressed the dildo to her anus. This was one of his favorites. The length and modest width made it a good choice for vaginal activity while the deep groove toward the base made it perfect for this. Agitated, she clenched her muscles, trying to get away without actually moving. He kept it pushed to her while he waited for her to exhale then forced it slightly inside her momentarily relaxed body. She made agitated sounds in her throat, protesting the invasion.

During other play, he might have worried and become more vigilant to her reaction. This was different. With her hands unbound, she could literally reach down and deck him if he really pushed her beyond her limits. Doggedly, he continued the invasion until the entire length of the icy invader was lodged inside her. He checked to be sure it was seated properly and let go, watching her buck as the chill invaded her heated tissues.

Her muffled, unchecked cries yanked at his cock, begging him to fuck her. Leaning forward, he sucked her clit into his mouth and nipped the sensitive flesh. Her taste flooded his mouth. He'd dreamed of this for so long. Languidly, he dragged his tongue through her tangy cream. He looped his arms under her thighs, capturing them as he pressed his hands over her pubic bone and helped her to stay still. It was a battle she'd already lost.

Taking his time, he lapped at her folds. Greedily, he took his fill of her working from the back of her swollen cleft to the front containing her most sensitive flesh. Her protests segued into throaty moans that vibrated through him. He did this to her. He turned her into this warm, sensual creature. She was his.

Grasping her ass, he lifted her and drove his tongue into her supple sheath. It immediately convulsed. He continued his jabbing thrusts while her body jerked into an orgasmic rhythm. Her muscles clenched and she bowed up into him, flooding his mouth with her sweet taste.

Her pleasure entwined with his, drawing him into her sensations. Shaky with the need to be inside her, he knelt between her legs and dragged the feather lightly over her in a path from belly to chin. She trembled as it tickled her over-sensitized skin and she tried to roll away from it.

He pushed the blindfold from her eyes and gazed down at her. "You're not very good at staying still," he laughed. "You lost. I guess I keep my mask."

Her brows drew together, her glare speaking loudly of how unhappy she was with that. If the gag hadn't prevented it, he had a feeling her sharp little tongue would be lashing him with her thoughts of his game. She settled for pointedly sliding her gaze away from him.

"None of that… I won fair and square."

Her eyebrows shot up and her chin lowered as she looked at him in disbelief. She had a very expressive face and damned if it wasn't as sassy as that mouth of hers. She was going to make his life a challenge. Good, he didn't particularly want someone who kissed his feet. Maybe his ass but that was another thing.

"Now, I get to claim my prize." Too bad he hadn't pinpointed what he wanted as a prize… he'd have to punt. "So what shall it be?"

She shrugged.

He trailed his fingers lightly over her shoulder. "A tattoo? No? I think you'd look good with your nipple pierced. No?" He lowered his voice. "I know what I want…"

Slowly, he removed the now-warm dildo. She groaned as the slight ridges caught on her tight flesh. He'd like to leave it. It wasn't flexible enough for what he wanted from her, though. Next he removed the gag and tossed it aside. Without a word, he turned and walked away.

Confused, Jessica dampened her lips and watched him walk away. He sank in a large wood chair with a maroon cushion. Slouching, his chin resting on his hand, he looked like an extremely bored king surveying his kingdom. A naked king. And she was his only subject.

He pointed to a spot between his sprawled legs.

"On your knees," he growled.

Her stomach fluttered, reacting to those promising words. Excited by the prospect of more lessons at his hands, she hurried to comply.

"Master," she said, head bowed as she surveyed him through her lashes. Reaching to the table beside him, he removed a strip of leather. Her eyes went wide as he leaned toward her.

"I want you to wear this—no speaking!" he ordered when she started to open her mouth. "You've given yourself to me and I'm claiming my prize. You get to be my pet."

*What?*

She swallowed hard as he looped the leather around her neck and fastened it. He'd just put a collar on her! Her outraged senses protested. He couldn't. She shouldn't let him. While her body tensed and reacted to the screaming voices inside her, she tried to remain calm. She trusted him. She'd promised to give over her power to him. This was just another part of that. And he had won that damned unfair game of his. Strangely the part that rankled the most wasn't that she had to give him a prize, it was that he wouldn't show her his face.

She panicked, however, when he withdrew a longer strip of black leather. Deftly, he fastened it to the D-ring beneath her chin.

"I wouldn't want you to run away," he explained. She tried to swallow around the intolerable tightness closing her throat. On her knees, leashed and at his mercy… How many more humiliations would she endure tonight?

Once again he leaned back this time giving a gentle tug on the leash. "Now, for my prize—"

This wasn't his prize!

"I want to watch you pleasuring yourself."

Her stomach knotted. She'd never masturbated in front of anyone. She couldn't do this. Years of Midwest morality crashed down on her, reminding her of all the lectures she'd ever gotten about what good girls did and didn't do. Good girls don't touch themselves…

A good girl wouldn't find herself willingly in this situation. Her teeth sank into her bottom lip. Maybe if she closed her eyes, she could pretend he wasn't here watching her. A thrill of erotic pleasure teased her exposed cleft. This was another one of those fantasies—touching herself while someone else watched. Alone in the dark, she'd kicked off her blankets and thought of this as her fingers had reached for her waiting pussy.

Her lids dropped as she unclasped her hands from behind her back.

"And you will look at me."

*Damn it*. Slowly she raised her chin and looked up into his slumberous eyes. It was brighter in this room and they were gray. It again struck her that she knew him and she knew these eyes. Right now, she hoped not.

"Start with your breasts," he said, leaning against the back of the chair. His cock jerked and he reached for it, circling the wide girth with his strong fingers. Mesmerized, she watched him run that fist up and down the shaft. "Touch them in a way that arouses you."

Hesitantly, she raised her hands and cupped her breasts. Her fingers teased over the taut peaks, tracing the wrinkled areolas. Faint strands of bliss inched through her and she sighed. Her hands tightened, molding the mounds.

"Pinch them."

Raising her eyes, she met his gaze and followed his command, immediate pleasure pain streaked through her straight to her waiting womb.

"Harder."

She whimpered. Her head tossed back, pulling at the restraint at her neck. She caught the tips between her thumb and forefinger, pinching hard. She gave a strangled little cry.

"That's it," he murmured. "That's what I was waiting for. Do it again."

Pushing her breasts into her palms, she complied. Her fingers squeezed together and twisted slightly, drawing another cry. She couldn't believe she was doing this in front of him.

"Now touch yourself with one hand."

Immediately, she slid her hand down her belly and into her drenched folds. She licked her lips as she watched a droplet appear on the head of his cock. She wanted to taste him the way he'd tasted her. She almost groaned in protest when he smoothed it into the flushed flesh.

Fine. Well, she hoped he enjoyed the show. Releasing her other breast, she leaned back on one hand while she parted her mound. She wanted him to see her fingers plunging inside. But not yet.

Her hips swiveled as she rubbed her clit, tremors from the tight little knob pricking along her limbs. Here it was. He had her so aroused. It took next to nothing to bring on the tide.

Her cries came in earnest now, growing in intensity as she plowed two fingers into her channel. Oh. God. Yes. She might have said it aloud as she reached deep, surging through gushing folds.

Suddenly, he yanked on the leash, pulling her toward him before her release could take her. "Come here," he commanded roughly, half dragging her as she scrambled to comply on shuddering legs. He lifted her onto his lap, draping one leg over the armrest while the other sprawled toward the floor. An arm behind her back steadied her. She clasped his knee and continued to work her slippery passage. Her head turned into his shoulder as she moaned. The entire scene they played sent fire leaping through her veins. She'd never felt quite so decadent or sensual.

Leaving the leash dangling down her chest and between her legs, he grabbed her hand and pulled it to his lips. He stared into her eyes while he sucked the juice from her fingers. His tongue worked between them, pulling every drop of nectar.

"I want to see you come," he told her. "Can you come with your fingers?"

"Sometimes," she answered, her voice a husky shadow of normal. Right now she thought she might be able to find release by only looking into his eyes. They seemed to look straight to her core and make love to her with just their sultry, knowing look.

He reached into the drawer of the table beside them where he'd had the collar and removed a vibrator with an extra protrusion to stimulate her clit—similar to hers at home. This was almost familiar territory. Oh baby, she could definitely come with this!

He handed it to her. "Use this."

Without waiting for her to start, he caught up the leash, wrapping the excess length around his hand before he gripped her thigh holding her wide. His cock knocked persistently at her hip. He'd managed to put on a condom while he'd watched her performance. She wanted to turn to straddle him and sink onto the burning rod. A vibrator was great but it was nothing compared to wrapping around a real man and touching with all that warm skin.

She couldn't turn. He held her too tightly.

Breathing shallowly, she pushed the vibrator slowly inside and flicked the switch to the lowest setting. A steady pulse worked across her cleft. Mmm…yeah. This was good. Losing herself in the sensation, she rocked it in and out of her clenching sheath pretending it was his cock again.

"Turn it higher," he said.

"Yes, Master," she gasped as she obediently followed his wish. She was really getting into this D/s thing. "Oh!"

Her cries crescendoed as she surrendered to the toy. The pounding vibrations raked over her. It was too much. She had to pull it away. His hand trapped hers holding it in place.

"Take it," he grated.

"I can't. I can't!" Her body twisted straining for more, trying to escape.

"You can." His mouth covered hers capturing her keening wails as the strongest orgasm she'd ever experienced splintered through her, almost throwing her from his lap. His tongue attacked hers with claiming ferocity while she twisted and wrapped her free arm around his neck.

She barely felt him move as he stood and strode to the bed with her in his arms. He tossed the toy away, immediately replacing it with his cock, stretching her wider, slamming deeper. Trapping her arms over her head, he again caught her gaze. "Mine," he repeated with each upstroke. "Mine, mine, mine..."

She struggled to meet him each time, until he slowed.

"I intended to take my time this round," he said against her neck while he sucked at her pulse. "You're so damned hot!"

"I've never been hot before," she managed. Each excruciating long slide took forever and her urgent movements weren't fulfilled. Like this, his girth was emphasized as he slowly pushed apart her clutching tissues. On each slow stroke, her body closed then readjusted as he returned. Her belly tightened, readying for the release winding inside her womb.

"Don't come yet," he whispered, trailing his mouth to her breast. He sucked the peak deep inside his mouth. His tongue rasped over the nipple.

And she wasn't supposed to come? How the hell?

She tried to draw her focus away from her pussy and the exquisite sensation of his cock plunging in and out of it. She still had, uh, *work,* yes work, waiting at home for her. Reports...lots and lots of—oh he felt so good! She panted trying to hold off—

"Now, Jessica!"

She exploded around him, clamping down on his cock and hampering his continued digging thrusts.

"So...tight..." he grunted through his teeth. With one deep stab, he turned and pulled her over to straddle him. Fighting through her release, she rode him, the leash flapping against her chest as he grasped her hips. Reaching up, he wrapped it around one of her breasts before reclaiming his grip on her hips.

She glanced down at the black leather, surprised at how aroused she was to be his slave for the moment. Totally his to control and direct. She didn't have to prove herself to him. She needed only to obey and react. Gazing down at him, she knew she pleased him. She almost heard the clank as the chains that had bound her for so long fell away. Freedom. Because she was his.

"Thank you," she whispered, unable to articulate everything she was feeling even when he tilted his head waiting for her go on. Leaning forward, she brushed her lips over his and rode him with everything in her. She wanted him to explode as hard as she had and in it she was giving him the gift of herself, everything directed at him and this moment.

Tremors immediately started through her as the angle hit her hot spot, setting her off. Adjusting, she kept on for the one who'd mastered her. In moments, his fingers tightened and he shoved her down on him with more force. She might be on top but he was in control. She sat up, palming her breast as he worked her. She couldn't stop her smile as she gazed down at him. Happiness flooded through her.

He surged up into her with a ragged bellow, his cock banging into her trigger point. Jessica let go, riding the riptide pulling through her. They both froze, captivated by the moment as they tried to catch their breath.

Gently, he tugged her down into his embrace. His lips feathered over hers.

"Well done, love."

She snuggled into him, pleased with herself, pleased to be in his arms and pushing the next morning from her thoughts as long as possible. Pragmatic Jessica desperately hoped that somehow Madam Zelda's prediction for a successful conclusion would include a real life happily ever after. She couldn't expect every aspect of the Three of Wands card to be fulfilled, though. So much of it already had been.

A buzz blurred her thoughts and she focused on the sensation of his powerful arms holding her as if he'd never let go and the slight possessive pull at her neck. His lips pressed to her mussed hair. She must look a mess by now. She couldn't rouse enough energy to even care.

Her brow furrowed as the buzz went on, then she laughed.

"I think the vibrator's screwing the floor." Absolute giddiness filled her spirit. Somehow tonight, she'd changed at his hands and peace filled her.

# Chapter Four

Jessica woke slowly, disoriented by the light shining in her eyes. Where the heck was she? She blinked then opened one eye. Mmm...yeah. She was in the dungeon master's bed. They'd made love again last night—despite the situation, that's what it had been. Sweet. Tender—then they'd fallen asleep. Neither of them had had the energy to switch off the torch lights.

It had to be near morning. A rock settled in her belly. She had to get moving so she wasn't late for work.

She wrinkled her nose. Work. There was no way she was going back to being the person she'd been before. She'd figure out a way to handle the pressures without destroying herself anymore.

Turning, she glanced at the man who'd done so much for her. The leash she yet wore was still wrapped around his hand and pulled at her throat. Carefully, she unhooked it. She didn't want to wake him. She couldn't bear the final scene when he sent her on her way.

His mask was hiked up slightly on one side but not enough to reveal his identity. Her fingers flexed as she fought the temptation to push it up and see what he looked like. She didn't dare. Sliding from the bed, she contemplated how she would get her things from upstairs and almost immediately found them folded on a chest beside the door. Padding to them, she quickly removed the collar and dressed, not bothering with her panties and bra. She shoved them in her purse and pulled out a pad of paper.

Hastily she scratched him a note, left it on the chest with the collar she'd been wearing and slipped from the room.

In these early morning hours, Pleasure Palace's hallways were brightly lit. She had no problem finding her way outside and locating her car. All the way, she fought the need to cry. It seemed as if she left part of her soul behind in the dungeons of the Palace.

Would he be angry when he woke and she was gone? Would he be relieved that he didn't have to gently give her a push off? Worst, would he find her note needy?

She almost regretted leaving it. There was no way she could turn around and retrieve it. What was said was said and she'd given him her cell phone number.

* * * * *

*Thank you. If this can be for more than one night…call me. J*

Ryan watched the green-eyed minx settle gingerly into the chair across the conference room from him and forced back the need to order everyone else from the room. Anger he'd been shoving down since he'd woken alone this morning, pathetically clutching that leash, simmered just below the exploding point.

And that damned note. If this could be for more than one night? How had she missed his point and the many times he'd alluded to this being long term?

She glanced at her cell phone, burying a frown, then smiled at his brother Max. Smiling, damn it! She should be smiling at him.

"Jessica!" he snapped. "Do you have something you want to share with the rest of us?" *Hell, Ryan,* he chided himself. *What is this? The third grade?*

Startled, she spun toward him, wincing as her clothes slid against her stripes. She serenely smiled again, humor flickering in her eyes. "Sorry, Ryan. I didn't know we'd started."

She opened her planner and popped a piece of chocolate in her mouth as she scanned her notes.

"Don't mind him," Max said. "He and Theo have been in bad moods all day today. I don't know what the hell crawled up their asses but I hope it's not contagious. We artist-types are broody enough without that."

Ryan glared at his brother. Max…brood? Right? He was surprised his brother had been serious long enough to make it through design school.

And he really didn't like the way Max was edging toward Jessica.

He glanced at his phone before he jumped his brother for showing her conceptual designs for the upcoming subdivision project they'd just won.

"Sorry," he lied, looking at the committee he'd gathered to discuss the upcoming work. "I have an important call I have to take. Let's go ahead and reconvene on Monday." He waved his phone ignoring how relieved everyone looked. "Sorry, it's one of those life or death responsibilities."

His life. Max's death if he didn't get out of here fast.

Stalking from the room, Jessica's tinkling laugh followed him as she agreed to have coffee with the co-workers gathered there—all men. Damn it, he had to get her in hand quickly before he lost it.

All day, he'd watched the creature he'd unleashed—he almost groaned. She was magnificent. Beautiful and so full of life. And suddenly a magnet. Every time he'd ventured from his office, he'd seen her with some man or another glued to her side.

How the hell was anyone getting any work done? He sure wasn't. All he could think of was how to get her to his side. He should have called her this morning when he'd woken. He should have told her who he was last night. He should not have—No. No matter how many times the thought came that he shouldn't have done what he had last night, he shoved it away. There was no way he'd ever regret what he'd done.

Jessica was his.

Now he just had to tell her. He didn't want to wake up again without her in his arms.

* * * * *

"Jessica, something's different about you today," Max said, studying her as they stood beside her office door. "What happened to you last night? It's like you're a new person."

"Wouldn't you like to know?" she laughed, ignoring how his gray eyes sent a tremor through her. She wanted to shove up the sleeve of his sports shirt and look for that commanding tattoo. That was silly. Max's voice, his demeanor, even his build were all wrong to be her dungeon master. Close yet not even within sight.

"I have to get to work," she said, entering her office. A few more minutes and she could leave for the evening. God, she felt good today. A little out of control. How many men had found reasons to talk to her today? "Have fun at that thing you're going to tonight."

"The club? Wanna go with me? You'd have to wear a collar—I'm sure you'd manage okay."

Heat flooded up her cheeks. God if he only knew. "Um..." she stammered, backing into her office. "Maybe lunch or something another time. I'm...ah...kind of taken."

Not really. She couldn't ignore how conspicuously silent her phone had been today. A few times she'd even checked to be sure it was still on. If he didn't call, she'd go on, strong in the discoveries she'd made last night. It wasn't power inside her. It was strength. She didn't need to prove herself to anyone, including herself. She was just great as-is. And in that alone, she had power—not control, keep that away. She was strong and in that she gathered power.

It was incredible and it bolstered her great mood. Who'd have thought? A submissive having power? She'd never understood the possibility before. But the Dom from the Pleasure Palace had taught her. She had worth and great power in her femininity. She had inner strength she'd never imagined.

Confidence flowed through her and today she'd handed over work to her administrative assistant, work the assistant was supposed to do anyway. Jessica had just never let her.

She didn't have to oversee *everything*. She'd never understood that before.

The discipline and pleasure she'd received at Pleasure Palace last night was never far from her mind. She reveled in and wanted more. She liked belonging to the dungeon master. It had been a mistake to leave. She should have stayed to see what he said. Maybe negotiated something for the future… Now what? She didn't even know his name. How would she ever find him and throw herself at his feet, if need be? She suspected that might be necessary. The fact that her phone remained ominously quiet said to her that he was pissed. This wasn't a blow off… this was anger.

He'd shown her so clearly that she craved being beneath him. She needed to be his—charge and control taken from her. The relief she felt today was unbelievable. Though she'd spent the night strenuously fucking, she was more rejuvenated than when she'd returned from her vacation last month.

Of course on that vacation, she'd worried constantly about her projects. The mental vacation at her master's hands was refreshing. Except it wasn't just that. Knowing the pleasure she gave with her obedience to him, knowing she had the power—yes, the power—to fill his needs with only her willingness to literally and figuratively go to her knees healed years of poor self-worth. She didn't fool herself into believing all her self-image problems had miraculously disappeared. Some things took more time. Hopefully, it could be with his tutelage.

Swinging around her desk, she decided to look up Madam Zelda on the internet and see if she could get another reading. Accidentally, she came across a site on tarot card meanings. Well, maybe before she scheduled that reading, she'd verify what the psychic had said. When looking for answers, meanings could be attributed to anything.

Hadn't she learned to have faith by now?

Shaking her head at her persistent pessimism, she opened the web page for the Three of Wands. It was all as the woman had said…learning to have faith, okay she was working on it. New partnership, well hopefully. Exploration, was there ever. Peace with the past, emotional calm…

She stared at the last two interpretations, again reminding herself that no card stood alone—that's what Keera said—and that it wasn't common for every possible meaning of the card to be fulfilled. *Successful conclusion and informed courage to make a difficult decision.*

She needed informed courage to achieve the successful conclusion she wanted most. And she might need a little luck too. Closing the website, she reached for her purse and a card she'd snagged from Pleasure Palace. She'd contact them and find him. Yes, he was probably angry about how she'd gone but she'd beg forgiveness. She'd do whatever he ordered because she knew he wouldn't do anything to harm her. She'd given him everything, even that power, when they were alone in private. She'd do it again.

He'd forgive her. She knew it in her core.

Pulling out the card, she lifted the phone to dial Pleasure Palace.

The sound of the lock on her office door engaging startled her, quickly she hung up the phone. Ryan stood just inside the closed door, his hands on his hips as he stared at her with his mesmerizing gray eyes. A bolt of recognition shot through her and she started to tremble.

Ryan! Her dungeon master was Ryan. Her psyche threw a triumphant fist into the air as joy flooded her. Yes!

A slow smile curved his full lips as he realized her reaction. His eyes smoldered.

"On your knees," he growled.

She hesitated. Oh God, it *had* been Ryan in the dungeon? What the hell must he think of her? Her boss? She'd fucked her boss. How had she not known it was him? Confusion speared through her happiness. What had she done? Yet given the opportunity, she'd do it again.

Wasn't this the opportunity?

"Jessica," he prompted. "Do you want to earn another punishment?"

Another? What had she done? Well, yeah, he was pissed about her leaving. There was that.

Without regard for where they were, she left her chair and knelt before him, her hands behind her back and her head lowered as she knew he wanted. She stared at his black wingtips.

Slowly, he circled her. He prodded her knees further apart with his toes, forcing her skirt to ride up her thighs. The lacy tops of her stockings peeked from beneath the hem. Much higher and he'd discover she'd forgone panties this morning. Even a thong had seemed too much for her swollen flesh.

"You've been a very bad girl today," he told her. How had she not recognized his voice?

"I haven't," she replied.

"Did I give you permission to speak?"

She shook her head absolutely bubbling with joy that she knew who he was and *he'd come to her*. He wanted more, otherwise he wouldn't be here, demanding her obedience.

"You *have* been bad. I've watched you tease every cock in this office today. They all want you." He caught her hair in his hand and tilted her head back so she was forced to look into his eyes. "But you're mine."

She nodded. *Yes, yes, yes, she was his!* How could he think any differently?

"So what should your punishment be, hmm?" He released her hair and circled her while the possibilities filled her thoughts. Would he flog her again? Surely not *here*. She wasn't sure her body could withstand it. She'd try, for him, if he insisted. Heat flooded through her and she fought the urge to squirm.

"No, not after last night," he continued, once again on the same page with her thoughts. "I had intended to take you to dinner tonight. Perhaps I should take you to the Palace and let you be dinner for the crowd. Either way, you'll spend tonight shackled to my bed. I was not impressed by your disappearing act."

Her eyes went wide and her fingers clenched where they were joined behind her back. Resolutely, she kept her lips pressed together to keep from protesting. She didn't want anyone other than Ryan but she'd given up her power to him. She knew if she said the word, he'd stop. He wouldn't force her to let other men touch her. She could stop it.

If she really wanted to. She wanted to please him. She'd already failed in that this morning. Whatever his choice, she'd comply. Her insides trembled knowing she was at the mercy of his decision.

Quietly, she waited while her breathing accelerated. Her heart pounded. Her cleft flooded. She was so wet for him. The scent rose around her and she was sure he could smell it too. More than anything, she wanted him pounding into her like he had last night. Bent over, impaled from behind. All day, she'd thought of little aside from the ways he'd touched her and the ways he'd fucked her.

"Stand," he instructed.

As gracefully as she could with her hands laced behind her, she complied, thankful for strong thigh muscles. She kept her feet the requisite shoulder-width apart. In her heels, with her arms in this position, her breasts pushed forward slightly straining the buttons on her blouse. The thick silk concealed enough that it wasn't apparent that she wore a demi-bra which lifted and cupped the underside of her breasts but covered nothing. The brush of fabric over her nipples had kept her on edge all day.

Ryan flicked open the top button. His finger stroked the upper curve of a breast, nodding when she sucked in a breath. She loved his hands on her.

"So sensitive. Good." Going to her desk, he pulled something from his pocket and set on the surface. She tried to see around his shoulders but couldn't without moving. She didn't dare. She quickly returned her focus to the geometric patterns on the carpet when he turned.

She wouldn't worry. Ryan wouldn't harm her. She knew that and she trusted him.

"Take off your clothes," he instructed.

She looked around. The office door was locked. That wouldn't stop the cleaning crew nor did it obstruct the view from her huge outside window, though she was fairly sure no one could see inside.

"Stop delaying," he ordered sharply.

She swallowed hard, knowing she was close to earning a second punishment. She bit the inside of her cheek to keep from smiling. Would another punishment be so bad? It had turned out well for her last night.

Her fingers went to the buttons on her shirt. In moments, she stood in only her bra, stockings and shoes. His eyes turned smoky as he surveyed her. "Perfect."

Taking her hand, he led her to the desk. He'd laid out a jumble of wires, a remote and a tube of gel. "Do you know what this is?"

She shook her head.

He unscrewed the cap on the gel and dabbed a bit beneath each nipple. She gasped at the icy cold sensation when he applied it to her burning clit. "These are electrodes," he explained holding up the wires. Studying the y-shaped wires, her stomach sank as apprehension filled her. Each end had a small, flat metal tip.

He watched her, obviously waiting for her protest. She refused to give it. She controlled herself enough to keep still but she couldn't slow her breathing.

Rolling a tip between them, he tilted his head to meet her eyes. "Answer me aloud. You realize what this is, don't you? You understand what it will do?

She nodded her head, belatedly remembering to speak. "Yes…Master."

"Are you afraid, slave?"

"A little."

He pressed a flat-tipped electrode to each of the gel locations, then tilted her chin so she looked at him. "You are my treasure. I will care for you always."

Her peace returned. He would treasure her always… He forgave her for leaving. It wouldn't get her out of this yet things would be all right.

Once again pocketing the remote, he moved to one of the arm chairs and pulled her to straddle him, her knees bent beside his hips. She fought back a groan at being so close to his cock, yet so far from it. She wanted him free of his clothes so that she could take him inside her and relive last night. It surprised her that she wondered if he'd brought the collar and leash. That alone had been strangely erotic.

"I must also punish you when you are disobedient."

"I haven't disobeyed," she protested. She sucked in a breath, knowing she shouldn't have spoken. His stormy gray eyes narrowed slightly as his jaw tightened.

"Leaving my chamber without permission. Flaunting what is mine today… Perhaps I can't fully hold that against you. I didn't place my collar on you yesterday. You thought you might not see me again, didn't you?"

She nodded, though she wanted to argue that there hadn't been a bit of flaunting. His irritation had obviously colored the way he'd viewed her today. Still, he was right on the other counts. Her cleft flexed at the thought of the collar he'd mentioned…his collar. Would he give it to her now that she'd disappointed him? He'd said she was his.

She squirmed against her arousal. He was here with her. She could still barely believe it and being able to look at him without that mask was wonderful. It was so strange to look at Ryan, the man she'd silently lusted after, and know he was her dungeon master. He'd said he was there at Pleasure Palace for her. If only she'd known. They could have saved themselves months.

She arched closer to him. The wires for his device draped down her abdomen, shifting with each breath and reminding her they remained secure.

"Stay still."

She tried, oh she tried. Her pussy opened as the small muscles begged to be touched and filled. The gel tingled, sending vibrations to her womb.

Ryan reached in his pocket and withdrew a heavy fall of gold links. A necklace. Glancing at him and the tension in his face, she knew better. This was no ordinary necklace. It was a collar.

She swallowed around the tightness in her throat. Would he put it on her and make her completely his?

"Will you give everything over to me, Jessica?" he asked. He pressed his finger to her lips to keep her from immediately answering. "Your heart, your body, your soul? Will you be completely mine? Think about it."

Think about it… He wanted everything. She wanted to give him everything too. She just didn't know if she could.

He laid the strand of thick links on the table beside them and removed the remote from his coat. "This has quite a few settings. We'll start with the lowest power. I can choose which electrodes activate or set it to random."

He showed it to her as he flicked the switch to random. Her eyes went wide at the dial settings. Oh man. Ryan said he start with the lowest and she trusted him to know what she could handle. If he thought she could take this, she would, even if it pushed her limits. He'd never taken her past what she could take last night. Her trust was in him.

"Look at me. Don't look away. Don't close your eyes." He slid his thumb along the side of her face before he pulled the oh-so-familiar ball gag from his pocket—what the hell else did he have in his coat? "You'll need this," he said.

*Oh hell, how bad will this be?* Fear gripped her. She couldn't hide her apprehension. He disregarded it and jammed the ball inside her mouth, quickly fastening the strap. "If you close your eyes, I will stop. Nod if you understand."

Against everything that bellowed no, she did.

"What you did was unacceptable. This is your punishment. Nod if you understand."

Slowly she complied.

He flicked a switch on the remote. Setting it on the table next to the collar, he grabbed her hands, holding them together at the small of her back as the first jolt rocketed through her breasts.

Taken by surprise, Jessica yelped. Pain laced through her, pulling her nipples into tight knots. Another immediately followed before the first had completely receded. This time she screamed, writhing above him, trying to pull her hands free and rake away the offending electrodes.

"Easy," he whispered, his gaze never leaving her. In the back of her sensation-fogged mind, she realized he was watching for distress. Watching to be sure he pushed her only as far as she could handle.

She loved him. What a time to realize it.

The next pulse surged into her clit. She groaned, tears pooling on her lower lids. Her hips jerked up and bumped into his groin, drawing a muffled groan from Ryan while the pulses twisted her into a maniacal lap dance. Suddenly, pleasure erupted through her dragging her toward the dark spiral of release. Her eyelids drooped.

"Careful," Ryan rasped. His grasp tightened as the jolts continued, moving intermittently between her nipples and clit, the initial pain long gone.

Her eyes snapped wide at his command. The intensity in his gaze twined with the throbbing waves building inside her middle. The continued jolts shoved her closer and closer to the edge. She sobbed behind the ball trying to hold back her release as it clawed across her womb.

"Let go," Ryan commanded as a series of quick pulses tormented her. She exploded, her vision dimming though she fought to keep her eyes open. Her scream crowded out everything else in her head. Driving her higher while her cleft gushed around the empty space she needed filled so desperately.

Boneless, she collapsed on him. The muscles in her arms and legs burned while a sheen of sweat coated her, trickling between her breasts.

Reaching over, he turned off the remote as her orgasm subsided. He removed the gag. Carefully, he pulled the metal tabs from her. Without regard for the expensive material, he used his suit coat sleeve to wipe away the gel from her rock-hard breasts. Gently, he kneaded them before trailing his hands to her mound. His fingers slipped through her drenched folds, seeking her aroused bud.

"Well done," he murmured, gently kissing her. "Don't leave me like that again."

"I won't." She lifted into him and opening to his probing tongue, wishing he'd give her permission to use her arms and wrap them around his neck. She settled for worshiping his mouth. She moaned, sucking him inside.

She jumped a moment later when someone pounded on her office door.

"Ryan!"

Oh no. His brother Theo. And she was basically naked.

"Just a minute!" Ryan called. "He wouldn't be shocked by this, you know. He owns Pleasure Palace."

Standing, he set her on her feet and shucked off his suit coat. Her eyes widened as he wrapped it around her. The jacket, which smelled distinctly of Ryan and the cologne he wore, enveloped her, hanging past mid-thigh and wrapping around her with plenty of room to spare. He adjusted the top so her breast didn't peek out of the gaping fabric.

He smoothed the line that must have appeared on her forehead. "Contrary to what you may have read about this scene or my idle threat earlier, I don't want anyone else to see you naked. And I certainly won't share you. Even with my brother."

Good to know. His possessive nature prompted warm fuzzy feelings to worm through her. The feeling swamped her. She needed his arms around her again while he dragged her to the carpet and fully *possessed* her.

Still she moved from direct view of the open door when Ryan went to let his brother in.

"Is Jessica with you?" Theo demanded, barging past Ryan.

*So much for hiding.*

"I'm here," she answered already feeling the blood rush to her face. There was nothing quite like getting caught fucking the boss by *his* boss and brother. Theo didn't seem to notice her lack of attire.

Worry etched his face. She'd never seen him worried. In line to take control of the company from his father, he always had everything completely under control. He ignored Ryan and stared at her.

"Where's Keera?" he demanded.

"She's not here," Ryan answered, coming back to Jessica's side. His arm locked protectively around her waist. "Look Theo, I like Keera but I've got my own woman."

Theo made a sound in his throat and waved Ryan's words away. "I know that."

"I haven't seen her since yesterday," Jessica said.

"She was with me." He glanced at Ryan. "I gave her my collar. Today she's gone with no word or explanation."

"She called in sick."

Theo shook his head. "That's the word I spread. She quit."

"What!" Jessica exclaimed. What could possibly have happened between Keera and Theo that had made her run like that? She couldn't believe he'd be any less attentive than Ryan had been. They'd received training at the hands of the same man—their father.

Leaving, Ryan's side, she dashed for her cell phone and dialed her friend.

"Hello," Keera answered hesitantly after several rings. She sounded frightened but healthy.

"Keera, where are you?" Jessica exclaimed, relief filling her that her friend was okay. "What's going on?"

A few feet from her, Theo growled. A pissed off frown replacing his worry.

"Is Theo with you?" Keera gasped as the sound filtered through the phone connection.

Jessica glanced over at him. "Yes."

He snatched it from her hand and stomped from the office. "Where are you?" he snarled. The door slammed shut behind him.

Jessica turned to Ryan. "He took my cell phone."

"You'll get it back, or I'll get you a new one, with my number programmed into it."

She snorted. "It's already programmed into it."

"As number one?"

"Of course, Master."

He yanked her to him. "Don't ever run away like Keera did. Having you leave today undid me enough."

"Do you think she's okay?"

"Just scared. Don't worry. Theo won't harm her. His feelings run almost as deep for her as mine do for you." He slipped off his shirt, then his shoes and pants.

Jessica swallowed her reaction to his well-developed chest and the tribal tattoo on his arm and belly. Their meaning would never leave her unaffected. She was his temple, his treasure and he owned her spirit.

He lifted her into his arms and carried her to the chair.

"Reassure me," he murmured, pulling her onto his lap. His eager erection prodded her mound. He needed inside her as much as she needed him in her.

"Condom?" she asked.

"In the pocket."

So there was more in there. Fishing inside, she grabbed out several foil packets and tossed all except one on the table. Tearing it open, she smoothed the latex over him, running her fingers over every throbbing inch.

"Jessica..." he warned. Quickly he shoved the suit coat off her and cupped her breasts. With long fingers he kneaded the peaks and pulled at her nipples, dragging fervent groans from her. His wide cock prodded at her cleft. Reaching between them, she guided him inside her hungry pussy and sank down him until her naked flesh rubbed against the crisp hair circling his manhood. She loved the sensation of it against her bare skin and the feel of him impaling her, spreading her wide. She grasped his shoulders and slid up his shaft, her thick juice spreading over him and easing her way.

He grunted as she shoved back down him, eager to please him. "Yeah, love, ride me. God your pussy's so hot! Faster."

He grasped her ass drawing her harder and angling her wild movements. A moment later, he tipped them both from the chair and onto the carpet. Lifting her hips, he pounded into her.

"Yes!" she cried, losing any restraint. "Oh! Fuck me. Harder, oh please, harder."

After being parted from him, even for just this long, she needed him deep inside her, branding her with his rod. There was no holding back, no control for either of them. Ryan stiffened, shoving into her. His movements jerked as he brought her along with him. His thumb rubbed her clit until she screamed, arching beneath him and squeezing the cock still lodged deep inside her.

They collapsed in a sweaty heap. Ryan rolled to the side, drawing her with him. "I love being in your pussy," he managed between heavy breaths.

She pressed her face into his neck. "I love having you there."

"How much?" He reached behind them on the table and brought down the collar. Contemplatively, he fingered the heavy links. He looked far from confident when he met her eyes. She couldn't blame him after what had happened with Theo and Keera.

Keera was a jumper. Unlike Jessica, she leapt without asking, then she got scared.

"What would you expect of me?" she asked, sitting up and wrapping her arms around her knees. Her position left her pussy open to him and he slid a finger inside her, stroking her engorged tissues.

Her breathing shuddered. If he continued, another orgasm would be crashing down on her. She wouldn't be able to think.

She knew he wouldn't allow her to tell him to stop without a punishment. He added another finger and she braced her arms behind her, moving her thighs apart.

"I'm not asking you to give up your life. You will, of course, live with me. I think that's a given. I need you in my bed."

"I need to be in your bed," she replied. No need to leave him out on a limb all by himself. He was her support, she could lend acceptance.

"In public, I'll expect you to go toe-to-toe with me just as you always have. In private, especially in the bedroom, you will regard me as Master. You will defer to me."

"Yes," she gasped as he jabbed his fingers in and out.

"Still, in public, you will never forget who you belong to even if our relationship isn't made public."

She nodded barely able to think over the sensations rioting through her. What did he mean, their relationship wouldn't be public. Wouldn't he claim her in any way that people could see?

"You'll let me choose what you wear, if I decide to."

"Will you wear your leather pants, then?" she asked.

"Only at home." He rose over her and knelt between her legs to further their negotiations. "You'll still make plans, be with your friends and family, but you will check with me first."

That sounded normal. She nodded her understanding. She fell back on her elbows. The muscles in her belly rippled as she listened to his guidelines for their relationship. How was it possible she already wanted him in her again?

"My family will of course know what you are to me but you will not discuss the full nature of our relationship with anyone unless I give you permission."

Jessica bit her lip and Ryan softened his tone. "At all times you will remember you're mine. You will not behave as you did today. I will have your complete devotion. The world *will* know you're mine, even if they don't know the extent."

*No problem.* She almost smiled. She lowered her gaze to where he'd spread her wide. The lips of her pussy glistened with her slippery juices. "Yes, Master."

He blew out a breath. "One last thing… Be very clear on this. I'm not asking you to be a mindless sycophant. You are an exceptional and extraordinary woman. I don't want to change that about you. You'll always be the friction that drives me farther at work. Even when we're alone, I'll want your opinion. I'll expect discussion and for you to speak your mind even if you don't think I'll agree with your conclusions—outside the bedroom. In the bedroom, I will always be your master."

She glanced around, refraining from raising her eyebrows. "Bedroom" was apparently a situational term for him. This was far from a bedroom still there was no doubt who was in charge.

She pushed anyway.

"And if my opinion is this?" She pulled away from his hand and turned to her knees, ass in the air and shoulders to the carpet. She swayed, tempting him. Eyes half-closed, she glided her finger across her clit. Ryan's nostrils flared and he dived on her, impaling her with one solid thrust.

"You're aware you'll be punished when we get home?" he rasped bending over her.

She sure hoped so.

He dragged the cool metal collar between her shoulder blades, letting the wide clasp scrap lightly over her spine. Drawing back, he smacked the links across her ass. Jessica yelped.

"Yes, Master." *Yes, yes, yes, yes, yes. Fuck me until I can't walk straight. Yes.*

Reaching between them, he coated his fingers with her cream and smeared it across her anus. She trembled, waiting for what she knew was coming. The slight pain and, oh, so much pleasure. She'd protested before that she wanted him like this too. Claiming every part of her.

The wide knob of his cock prodded at the entrance. She relaxed, letting him plunge in until he'd slid to the hilt. She winced at the pull on her inexperienced muscles. Still, this was easier than she'd thought.

"You're so tight," he grunted. He plowed in and out in shallow digs, resuming his finger-fuck of her cunt. Filled, Jessica bucked, crying for her release, begging. When it came, she fell to the floor blanketed by the man she loved. How did she get so lucky to end up in his dungeon and to end up as his?

It was all so much to comprehend. He made his proposal sound so much like a marriage between a loving couple. She wasn't fooled into believing that was what he wanted. He wasn't looking for permanent. A collar was removable. Even now, she knew she'd crumble when he removed it. He'd shown her she was strong. Alone, she wasn't so much. He strengthened her. What she sensed between them was more than last night. It was more than today. This had been building for over a year.

Ryan knew her.

And she knew him.

In the past year, he'd had women. None had lasted longer than three months. She thought of what she felt for him and wondered if those other women had been devastated.

She eyed the collar. She'd never seen any of them wear it, or anything like it. Was this new for Ryan? Hadn't he ever offered his possession to another before? He must have.

Ryan got up and disposed of the condom, then slipped on his pants. He draped his coat around her again, then sat on the floor, leaning against the chair. Roughly, he pulled her to him. "You're naughty to distract me. I can't stop wanting you. I want to possess you and know you're mine for my pleasure."

She glanced at the gold chain beside them.

"For how long?" she blurted.

"Forever."

She blinked in surprise and turned to face him. "Not just a few months?"

"No. Is that all you want?"

Was that a faint tinge of hurt in his voice? "Of course not!"

Forever? As his slave, taking his instruction, receiving his punishments, sharing his pleasure? Tough gig. She almost chortled as happiness bubbled inside her. She needed him as her master. She needed to be his slave. She'd soothe the need and emptiness inside him in a way only she could. And he'd keep her from letting control overwhelm her ever again.

Jessica met his eyes. "I love you."

She lifted her hair in silent answer to the growing plea in his gaze and the tension vibrating from him. His triumphant smile filled her. "Mine."

He slipped the collar around her neck and it snapped shut with a distinct click that shot a shiver down her spine. *His.*

"Well done, my love." Gently he kissed her, worshiping at her mouth, reminding her that she was indeed his treasure and he'd guard her and care for her always. As he saw fit. She could trust him and give him her control.

Sitting back, he looped his finger through the necklace and pulled her forward. "I love you too. Now... On. Your. Knees."

Her new favorite phrase.

She was tired from their exuberant activities but it didn't slow the excitement that rushed over her. She hurried to comply. Pleasure waited moments away. She was ready for it, ready for whatever life with this man brought her. Ready to be his.

# ALL CHAINED UP

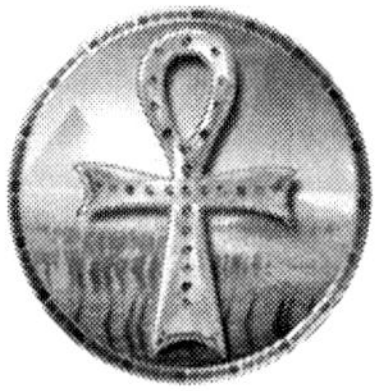

# Dedication

*To Bronwyn, who never lets me give up.*

# Trademarks Acknowledgement

The author acknowledges the trademarked status and trademark owners of the following wordmarks mentioned in this work of fiction:

Coke: Coca-Cola Company

Oreo: Kraft Foods Holdings, Inc.

Three Stooges: Comedy III Entertainment, Inc.

## *Four of Wands*

Dear Reader,

I consider myself incredibly lucky to have been able write a story for the Four of Wands. Traditionally, this card is considered one of the most positive in the deck. My heroine, Keera, is stunned when she draws it. After all, she is on the run from a stalker who's repeatedly threatened her life. She doesn't see anything positive on the horizon. Yet this card promises that seeds already sown will lead to her happily ever after, she will find completion of the journey she's been undertaking and she will enjoy the mutual support of another. Even more, she will find freedom and refuge from the bondage that has kept her on the run for years.

Keera made an alliance with the hero, Theo, on the night before she ran once again. She doesn't realize this union has set the foretold events into action. When she accepted her position as his submissive, she gained protection and a way to eliminate the threat from her life. And if she believes in the romance often associated with the Four of Wands, she might even find an unexpected happily ever after.

## *Author Note*

This book portrays some aspects of Domination/submission and BDSM but is not intended as a true-to-life account of this lifestyle.

# Chapter One

"How are you feeling about this?"

Keera Thornton snuggled into the arms of her lover of five hours and looked up into his gray eyes, captured by her devotion to him. Theo Cress. He owned every part of her and didn't even know it.

He fingered the heavy gold links he'd placed around her neck earlier tonight. It looked like a necklace but in actuality, it was a collar. She wanted to be with him but the thought of agreeing to be his submissive did make her a little panicky.

"I'm okay," she answered. She was sure the few worries she had would disappear soon. She trusted Theo and she knew him well. After all, they'd been friends for six months. She smiled. And she'd been in lust with him since about five minutes after she started working for Cress Construction. Still, she never expected to discover his involvement in the Dominant/submissive community when she came to Pleasure Palace tonight to attend a sex toy party. Heck, she'd never expect to run in to him either.

She grew warm and fuzzy when she remembered how he'd separated her from the others and pulled her to another room where he'd pressed her to the wall and kissed her breathless. She'd been stunned. Since she'd first met him, they'd gotten to know each other, often sharing lunch or dinner. While she'd sometimes caught him regarding her with a strange look on his face, he'd never expressed outright attraction. Last night, right now, it was apparent Theo was out for sex.

His palm slid over her shoulder and down to cup her breast. "You know, the collar is a serious thing in the D/s community," he said, massaging her erect nipple. The sensitive flesh still throbbed from the nipple clamp she'd had on earlier. Still the flesh hardened to his touch while the rest of her body softened to him. Her insides just melted for him.

"How serious?" she asked, realizing she should have asked this before. But this was Theo, the only man she really felt comfortable around, protected. She'd give him everything.

*Not everything.*

She flinched as the familiar voice of her tormentor entered her thoughts. She would not sink into the fear that man roused. With Theo, she was safe. *He* couldn't touch her while Theo stood watch.

Worry flickered in Theo's eyes. He rolled her beneath him, his body settling between her thighs. His dark curls fell forward around his face while he gazed earnestly at her. "We should have discussed this before."

That hardly seemed feasible while she'd been bent over the end of the bed, calling him Master and begging for his cock. A fresh flood of arousal warmed her cleft. Mmmm. Yeah. She needed him again. Eagerly, she rubbed against him. "Tell me now. How serious?"

"Wedding ring serious."

Her eyes went wide. "Oh."

"Forever serious."

"Oh," she whispered, barely able to force the air from her lips.

Oh no. What had she done? How long could forever be when a stalker continually sent her running? *He* wouldn't allow Theo to have her. But *he* hadn't caught up with her in six months. If he didn't know… Maybe he'd given up. Maybe she could be with Theo. She had no question in her mind that she wanted to be with him.

"What is it?" Theo asked. "Do you need to think about this? Change your mind?"

He sounded certain that she'd leap from the bed right now. Sure, she hadn't anticipated "forever" but stalker aside, it settled well inside her. Belonging to Theo? Oh yes. And maybe if he fucked her hard enough he'd drive her stalker permanently from her thoughts.

She shook her head, trying to smile. "No. I need you."

"I need you too," he admitted.

She lifted her knees to bracket his hips the way he liked and pressed her wrists beside her head, offering herself to him. She wasn't the only one with demons. She sensed his unspoken pain in his caution. He was a man full of power—in charge of his company, in charge of his world and in charge of her. Yet he needed reassurance.

"Then take me. I'm yours. I accept what you offer," she whispered. "We'll work out the rest later. Just be patient with me. I'm…ah…new to this slave thing."

"You're mine and right now that *is* all that matters." His lips covered hers, devouring her mouth, claiming every part of it. Immediate fire leapt through her. If she ever had any doubt his kiss drove worry away. To think, after years of running, she'd stumbled into the ultimate protective embrace tonight. Theo would never let anyone touch her.

"Yes. Yours. Please don't make me wait." This entire night was foreplay enough.

His cock surged through her drenched folds and stabbed into her sensitive channel. How many times had they done this tonight? Yet every time had been different. How many times had she hovered at the edge of release while he ordered her not to come? Not yet. Not until he was ready and as if he had complete control over her body as well, her orgasm always receded but not far. He'd kept her perched on the precipice of release. Not this time.

Theo drove into her claiming every part of her pussy with the same ferocity as he'd taken her mouth. His wide cock surged through her swollen tissues, branding her as his.

"Yes, Theo," she cried, lifting into him. Already tremors erupted in her sheath as it clutched at him, holding him and claiming him as he claimed her. There was no holding back. Pleasure shot through her and a moment later, Theo stiffened above her on a deep groan, his cock throbbing inside her as he followed her into release. His face dropped to the curve of her neck as they both tried to breathe.

"Quick," he muttered.

"Wonderful." She threaded her fingers through his damp hair. Smoothing her palm over his head. She was so lucky to belong to this man.

"I'm sweating all over you."

"I don't mind."

"Hmm. Well, I'm going to go take a shower and then draw a bath for you."

"You don't have to."

He looked down at her, the intensity in his gaze making it clear that there wasn't just a bath involved and there was no "have to" on his part. This was something he desperately wanted to do to reward her good behavior. "Get some rest. I'll be back in a few minutes."

Rolling on her side, she watched him walk into the bathroom and enjoyed the sight of his muscles dimpling the side of his awesome ass as he went. She turned over hugging the pillow. How did she get so lucky?

She had a hard time squashing the giggle bubbling up her throat. She had to tell Jessica. As soon as she heard the water start, she swung from the bed and pulled her cell phone from her purse. Frowning she realized the display read one in the morning. Oh, that wouldn't matter. Her best friend was a working machine. Chances were good she was still up to her neck in reports.

The phone chirped signaling a missed call. Still smiling, she dialed up voice mail by rote. She had a minute before Theo returned.

"Hello, bitch. Have fun fucking? You probably still are since I have to leave a message. You know I don't like that."

*No. Oh God no.*

As soon as she heard the voice through the phone, her blood went cold. Any joy or peace she'd achieved evaporated like water in the desert.

Cary, her stepbrother, had found her again. And apparently, he'd been watching her for a while.

"I want my money, bitch."

She hugged an arm around her middle. "There isn't any," she whispered to the message. If there were some fortune left by her parents, she'd give him every bit just to be free of him.

"I know what you're going to say. Don't bother. If you won't give me what's mine, I'll take my payment in the hot little cunt of yours. And don't think that man you just finished fucking will help you. I'll take care of him if he tries."

*No.* She had to run. She had to run as fast and as far as she could. Now. Quickly dragging on her clothes, she spared one last look toward the bathroom where Theo whistled cheerfully off-key and took off the collar he'd put around her neck.

He couldn't afford to claim her. And she could never bear the pain of seeing him hurt.

* * * * *

Theo left the shower with his spirit soaring. Keera was finally his and better, she accepted him. Quickly, he ran a towel over his body while he started to run Keera's bath in the garden tub then set about gathering items to assist them in the "bathing". He had a feeling, he'd end up in the tub with her.

He grinned. Life would be good with Keera in it.

He turned off the water and silence surrounded him. Too much silence.

"Keera," he called, going to the doorway. She must have fallen asleep. He couldn't blame her. They'd had a strenuous evening so far.

The bedside light seemed to cast a spotlight on the middle of the bed, reflecting off the gleaming gold in the center of the sheets. *Rejected again, you fool.* No…

No.

She couldn't desert him. She'd wanted to be with him and be his. This didn't make any sense. Keera had never lied to him before. Why would she lie now? Storming to the door, he threw it open as anger flooded him.

The hallway was empty. Stopping long enough to grab up a pair of pants, he started down the hall while he tried to pull them on, finally having to stop a moment before he fell on his face. His fingers were clumsy with impatience. Even a small delay was too long. He needed to talk to Keera before she filled her thoughts with all sorts of irrational reasons for them not to be together.

She wasn't anywhere on this floor.

He headed to the main floor of Pleasure Palace but it too was deserted. She couldn't have gone already. He dashed for the security room, shoving open the door. He'd had surveillance cameras installed throughout the main areas of Pleasure Palace when he'd purchased it. He should be able to find Keera through them.

Inside, his sister Francesca jumped away from where she was sucking face with some guy he didn't know.

"What the heck are you doing here?" she demanded, shoving a strand of goth-black hair over her shoulder and wiping excess black lipstick off her partner's mouth. "Shouldn't you be molesting some unsuspecting woman?"

"Shut up, Cesca. I need to check the cameras." He didn't have time for his sister's antics or sarcasm.

"Whoa wait a sec. Was there some sort of crime?"

"Depends on your point of view."

His sister, the bane of her existence, turned indignant. Her black-tipped fingers planted on her hips. "Did she run out on you? What kind of an idiot is she?"

"A missing one. I need to see the main floor and outside cameras."

"Marco?" she said, turning to her friend.

Theo squinted at the young man. He must work for Pleasure Palace. Theo bit back a growl. He'd discuss Cesca with the boy later. First he needed to locate Keera.

None of the cameras showed her.

"Go back ten minutes," he said.

He immediately found Keera tearing down the hallway from his room as if Satan himself was on her heels. His stomach lurched. Why did she look so scared? She hadn't been scared at all when he'd gone into the shower. He knew he hadn't scared her. The tears streaming down her face didn't look like fear, though. They were distress. Sorrow-filled distress as if she didn't really want to leave.

None of it made sense.

Watching her progression across the cameras, he saw her dash across the entry hall then freeze at the front door looking around in panic. She wasn't looking behind her. She wasn't afraid he was chasing her. She was afraid of someone outside...

What the hell?

Apparently deciding the coast was clear, she dashed for her car. A moment later, she sped away.

"What on earth was that?" Francesca asked as confused as he was.

He shook his head. Keera was gone. Now he had to find out why.

*****

Keera snapped awake from a nightmare in which the two halves of her reality crashed together in a disturbing mimic of her life. Theo and her stalker had both battled for her—the stalker was stronger.

Anxiously, she reached for the matches on the table beside her bed and lit the three fat candles there. The flickering flames cast eerie shadows around the dusty, one-room cabin. It was the only light. She hadn't expected to be here, so she hadn't had the power turned on. She wouldn't either. By the time arrangements for electricity could be made, she'd be long gone.

Cary was on her heels again. She couldn't stay.

Finally being with Theo was everything she'd hoped it would be. And surprising. She'd never imagined he'd be into bondage and domination. She'd never known she would be into it too. Submitting to him was a relief after these five years of running and fear and fending for herself. His powerful arms around her erased her fear—at least for the short time she found herself in his arms. He wouldn't let anyone hurt her. She was his.

She touched her bare neck. Already, she missed the collar he'd placed on her. If only she could have stayed with him. Should she have told him about her troubles? Tried to stay with him? Surrendered to Cary?

She shuddered and tried to push away those thoughts. She had to focus on her future and her plan, not her past and what could have been. The darkness made her question her decisions. She couldn't afford regrets. Regrets led to dark places she didn't want to visit.

The phone call had set her on the run again. How many times had she run and restarted in the last years? Too many to count. This six months in Brandywine working for Cress Construction was the longest she'd been without Cary's shadow looming over her. She'd actually begun to believe she was free of him.

The very psychotic nature of his personality should have told her better. He wouldn't give up. He'd spent five years chasing her. Why would he stop now? He wasn't capable. The money was his obsession. In the last year, she'd discovered, so was she.

She cast a worried glance around the darkness. Getting up, she walked the perimeter of the spacious open floor plan cabin and checked the locks on the door and windows. It wasn't that late, only early evening. If she opened the heavy curtains, sunlight would pour inside and fill the space. She didn't dare. Anyone could look through the windows. Like a stalker. Her stomach knotted as she remembered the last time he'd caught up with her and attacked her. As she took a moment to watch Lake Superior's waves crash on the beach behind the house, she ran her fingers over the long pink scar on her arm.

She'd barely escaped.

The heavy drapery fell into place over the window. Enough. She wouldn't remember that. Angrily, she shook off the fear. Cary had manipulated enough of her life without giving him more power over her by letting him fill her thoughts with terror. Still, there was no way she was going back to sleep even though she was tired from driving most of the night. Too many jumbled emotions kept her awake.

Since she'd left Theo just after one a.m., she'd been unable to shake the feeling of his strong arms around her. His commanding voice still rang in her ears. She wondered if she'd ever be able to take another lover in the future and not have Theo with them in bed. It was his bed she wanted to be in. Wearing his collar…like a wedding ring.

"Forget it, Keera," she ordered. She couldn't have him or he'd get hurt.

Returning to the bed, she huddled in the blankets and reached for the small cloth bundle beside the candles. Carefully, she unwrapped a worn deck of tarot cards. Her thumb rubbed over the familiar green and black Celtic knots decorating the backs.

These were her only wealth but Cary didn't want these. He wanted her parents' nonexistent fortune. If there had been any money she would have given every cent of it to him but there was none. All she'd inherited was this cabin and a few nominal personal articles. They were all worthless except for their sentimental value. They were precious to her. These cards represented so many cherished moments in her past.

She never knew when she'd have to run. She always carried these with her in her gargantuan purse. They were her touchstone to the past and her source of hope for the future. That hope was growing as frayed as the edges of the well-worn cards.

She shuffled the deck by rote. Over and over she dropped them from one hand to the other, letting them mix as they fell. The quiet slide of the cards against each other wrapped around her to momentarily block out her worries. How many times had she heard this sound when she was growing up? Hundreds. Her mother had been a tarot reader. These had been her cards and the strongest connection Keera had to her.

When the cards stopped shuffling easily, Keera cut them into three piles then gathered them into one stack again. Swiftly, she dealt them into the simple three-card spread she'd chosen. It was a quick look at the past, present and future. Right now, she didn't have the mental fortitude for anything else. She needed answers and guidance. Too bad, this reading would probably blow. She couldn't focus on her question. Despite the comfort brought by the cards, chaos filled her thoughts and crowded out everything else.

She was screwed. Well…yeah screwed. Literally. Last night she'd surrendered to a night of passion with Theo. That in itself was foolish but when she'd discovered he dabbled in the D/s scene she hadn't run for the hills. No, instead she'd knelt before him, giving her promise to serve him. If she belonged to him, she couldn't belong to the other man who wanted to own her. She and Theo had always been careful not to cross the fine line defining their relationship as friendly colleagues. That was until Theo had stormed over that line last night.

It had seemed so right. Instead she'd managed to derail the entire life she'd built over the last six months. She just hadn't realized it until too late. Cary knew what she was doing. When he'd promised to punish her for it then go after Theo, she hadn't considered her next move. She'd moved by instinct rather than actual thought, running while Theo showered. She hadn't even stopped at her apartment. Nothing there was as important as protecting the man she now called Master.

Again regret pushed at her. Theo wouldn't understand but there was no way she could involve him in this. He didn't need to be a player in the macabre soap opera underscoring her life.

Pushing a long strand of dark brown hair back over her shoulder, she slowly turned over the three cards one after another. The first card, her past, showed the Black Tower. Well, that stood to reason. Her life had pretty much blown up and been under a black cloud for the last five years.

She flipped the next card, her present and found the Five of Cups. It indicated disappointment over loss and blindness to an existing support system. Absolutely true. She wasn't just disappointed by her loss of Theo and everything she'd worked toward. Devastated would be a better description. As for her supposed support system…there wasn't one. Still the card was mostly right. Maybe she was getting better at reading.

Finally she turned the remaining card. Her eyes went wide as she stared at it. What? Surely this was a mistake. The Four of Wands? A thread of hope wavered through her. The Four of Wands was considered one of the most positive cards in the deck.

What was it doing in her reading?

Tentatively, she picked it up, surprised by the slight tingle that went through her fingertips. Goose bumps shot up her arm. What did this mean? A new beginning, joining with someone else, completion, a trip… She remembered those things. Her hope faded when she realized completion could also mean death, although that wasn't the commonly accepted interpretation of the four. Okay, it was *never* the interpretation but she had to admit she might be lot happier in the afterlife than she was in this one.

For the last five years since her parents' death, a death she found questionable, she'd been in hell. Stalked and threatened. Whenever she settled in, Cary reappeared and she ran again. Last night with Theo was the first time she'd let anyone close to her in all that time. To be so close, to feel his touch…

If not for the voice mail message she'd received, she'd likely still be in Theo's bed, submitting to whatever he wished. Her lip trembled as she took a final look at the Four of Wands then gathered all the cards together. She'd miss Theo and always regret they hadn't had a chance to explore their newfound relationship.

Setting the cards aside, she blew out the candles and curled into the middle of the bed. Beyond the window, the waves of Lake Superior continued to crash onto the rocks lining the shore beyond the cabin. She'd enjoy the sound for a few more hours and let the memories from her happy childhood wrap around her. She'd leave in the morning and never return. She couldn't. It was only a matter of time before Cary discovered she'd come here and followed her.

She had to run before then. She wished she could get help but she knew no one would help her. *Theo would,* her inner voice chided. Keera ignored it. She couldn't endanger him. She knew firsthand what Cary could do. She had to go this alone.

Even law enforcement wasn't an option. The few times she'd gone to the police it hadn't helped. One officer had even suggested she buy a big dog. Unfortunately, that had been the best assistance she'd received. Even though she knew the identity of her stalker they'd looked the other way, so to speak. Cary was related to her, therefore the situation was deemed a domestic problem. Her report immediately lost its credibility. They refused to further investigate her parents' death too. To them, it was an accident, plain and simple. Case closed. After a few fruitless attempts, she'd given up on the men in blue and resorted to running.

And now she had to run again.

*****

Theo knew he was having a sulk worthy of a toddler, complete with occasional outbursts. This wasn't good. He was a grown man with a company to run. He still couldn't manage to stop slamming things around his office—although he'd confined that to when he was alone—nor could he remove his scowl. More times than not, he'd snapped when forced to speak. All day he'd been given the same wide berth people would give an ogre. Fitting. He *was* being an ogre.

This was more than anger, though. He was worried about Keera. He'd watched the security tapes over and over until Francesca had begged him to give it a rest and then he'd taken them with him. The more he watched, the more concerned he'd become. Keera wasn't just frightened. She was panicked.

And he was convinced that while she'd run, she hadn't really run from him.

So why had she gone?

That's what he wanted to know and was working to discover. He'd called in favors but so far no one had been able to locate her. The more time that passed, the more his own panicky feeling built in his middle. If anything happened to her…

He paced, shoving back the possibilities. His gaze repeatedly darted back to the phone, willing Keera to call him. She'd given herself to him. She couldn't just disappear.

Shoving his hand in his pocket, he closed a fist around Keera's collar, a stab piercing through his heart. Last night she'd promised herself to him, her trust, love and devotion clear in her shining green eyes. Then she was gone. It didn't make sense. If she needed help, it was his place as her Dominant to provide what she needed, physically and emotionally. He'd have to make that very clear when he caught up with her.

His jaw tightened. Tomorrow, she'd be back in his bed. Tied to it if necessary. Then they'd work out whatever had her so scared.

He fingered the gold links. She intended to make her disappearance permanent, something he couldn't abide. This morning when he'd come into the office, he'd received her phone message saying she was quitting her job effective immediately. The hell with that. Even if her voice hadn't been heavy with sorrow, he wouldn't have accepted her resignation without an explanation.

He'd spread the word that she'd called in sick.

By Monday morning, he intended to have this straightened out and she'd back at her desk, well recovered from "the flu" although her bottom might not have recovered from the spanking he intended to give her. Were all subs so difficult? He knew they weren't but he'd never had a collared submissive before. Having grown up in a D/s family, he knew the rules and he knew how things were supposed to go. The submissive in a relationship didn't take off for parts unknown without consulting their master.

He took a few deep breaths as he felt his fury returning. He'd deal with Keera calmly and rationally when he found her. She'd know his disappointment and his displeasure but not his anger. It was the burden of his position to remain calm and rational when dealing with his sub and a burden he didn't take lightly.

Where was she? And what was she so scared of? She wasn't at home. When she hadn't arrived this morning, he'd immediately left Cress Construction's office and gone to her apartment. There'd been no answer when he'd pounded the door. His concern level had skyrocketed, especially after he'd bribed her landlord to let him inside for a handful of hundred dollar bills. She hadn't been home since the day before. The clothes she'd worn to the office yesterday still lay discarded across her bed.

That's when he'd started calling in favors and his fear for her safety had quadrupled. If she'd been harmed, he'd hunt down the person who'd done it and be sure they never hurt anyone again.

His rage surprised him but his not protectiveness for the little brown-haired siren who'd declared herself to him.

Impatiently, he snatched up the phone and punched the extension for his brother Ryan. No answer. He slammed down the receiver. His brother was probably in Jessica his submissive's office. Hopefully, he wasn't fucking her. Theo needed to talk to her. At this point, if anyone could help him find Keera, it was probably Jess.

Storming down the hall, he cut a wide swath through the horde of departing employees. He didn't care that they were all afraid of him. He'd give them an extra percentage in this year's Christmas bonus. By then he should be feeling jolly. What man wouldn't, with Keera in his bed every night? His scowl deepened. Good lord. He didn't need to think of her in anyone else's bed, even theoretically. He was already too grouchy and worried. He couldn't even stand himself.

Muted moans filtered through Jessica's door as he lifted his hand to knock. He let his fist drop to his side. Damn it. Now he'd have to institute some sort of fucking-at-work rule. How on earth would that fit into the employee handbook? A muffled female scream assaulted his cock as he thought of all the ways he'd break that rule with Keera. What the hell was Ryan doing to Jessica? Probably something similar to the things he considered for his own woman.

After a moment, the sounds died down and he pounded on the door.

"Is Jessica with you?" he demanded, barging past Ryan when he answered. She wasn't in sight but he knew she was there. Ryan certainly wasn't the source of those moans he'd heard.

"I'm here," she answered. Turning, he saw her standing to the side where she couldn't be easily seen from the door. Ryan's jacket engulfed her and she appeared decidedly flushed. In the past, the sight might have affected him. Now he had only one thought.

"Where's Keera?" he demanded, verbally slapping away the afterglow. He was an ass of epic proportions, a determined and worried ass. He knew it but he couldn't suppress his need for immediate answers.

"She's not here," Ryan answered obviously taken aback by the question. He crossed to Jessica's side and locked an arm possessively around her waist. "Look Theo, I like Keera but I've got my own woman."

Theo strangled a growl and waved away Ryan's words. As if. He'd kill any of his brothers if they'd tried to make time with Keera. And Ryan knew it.

"I'm aware of that," he bit out.

"I haven't seen her since yesterday," Jessica said.

Theo drove his hand through his hair and stared at the ceiling as he tried to push down his feelings. He didn't need to wear his fucking feelings on his sleeve.

"She was with me," he admitted. "I gave her my collar. Today she's gone with no word or explanation."

"She called in sick."

He shook his head. "That's the word I spread. She quit."

"What?" Jessica dashed for her cell phone and dialed—Keera, he hoped. His tension cranked up several notches. Why hadn't he thought to have Jessica call her earlier? *Stupid, stupid, stupid.* It hadn't been necessary to go through this hell today.

"Keera, where are you?" Jessica exclaimed after a moment. "What's going on?"

A few feet from her, Theo growled. Jessica glanced over at him.

"Yes," she answered. Keera had obviously asked if he was there.

He snatched the phone from Jessica's hand and stormed from the office. "Where are you?" he snarled, slamming the door behind him as he went.

"Theo..."

*Who the hell else would it be?*

"Where are you?" he demanded already heading for the parking garage. As soon as she told him, he'd be on the way.

"That doesn't matter. Look I made a mistake—"

"Yeah. You left my bed. You belong to me. Mine. Got that?"

"Theo—"

Why was she delaying? His slave needed a crash course in obedience. At the moment, he'd gladly mete out the discipline but not until he calmed. He'd never risk harming her.

"Last time, Keera. Where are you?"

"Nowhere. I'm sorry." He could hear her crying. Her voice faltered as she spoke. "I left the collar behind. I'm not yours... I can't be."

Before he could protest that she'd always be his, that this was more than a piece of gold, she hung up the phone. He tried to call back but went directly to her voice mail. She'd turned off the phone. Obviously, she'd been unclear about the warning implied by "last time". As soon as he found her, she'd be made very clear.

The tremor in her voice confirmed his worries. This was more than her changing her mind. If that had been the case, she'd have shown up this morning, thrown it in his face and walked out. Then he would have followed her, locked the door of her office and bent her lithe body over the desk. God knew he'd fantasized about that enough in the past six months. He wouldn't need much of an excuse to make it happen.

If he didn't care for her as much as he did, he might have been able to let this and her go and move on. But he did and he couldn't. He couldn't let her face whatever demon haunted her alone. And if the pain in her voice was any indication, she cared for him too.

If only he could track her… What if…didn't phones have GPS capabilities in them now? Doing an about-face, he marched to his brother Josh's cubical. Josh complained about being low sibling on the totem pole and about only having a cube, with no door. As resident troublemaker, it was far safer that way and less likely Josh would get the company in a fix with his amazing and sometimes deviant computer savvy.

"Josh," Theo said by way of greeting.

"I didn't do it," his brother muttered as he typed code into his laptop.

*He's probably hacking into the Pentagon.* Theo knew he should care but he didn't, not right now. Later when he received the hefty fine, he'd have a cow. Then Keera could soothe his pain. She'd have a lot of soothing to do. He usually scooped Josh out of trouble once or twice a month.

Josh hit enter a few times before looking up. "I've heard you're on the warpath. Don't take it out on me. I didn't do it this time."

He ignored everything but the fact he had Josh's fleeting attention. If something shiny or shapely flitted past, he'd be gone. "I need a favor."

"Of course, you do." Josh crossed his arms over his chest, looking like Theo's twin but younger with piercings—six that were visible. Theo, *unfortunately,* had heard about two more that made him squirm. Gray eyes that matched Theo's filled with accusation. "Why else would you visit my hovel?"

Josh's huge cube was hardly a hovel. It was larger than all the others on the floor and had heavy executive-quality furniture. The same that Theo, Ryan and their remaining brother, Max had in their offices, as a matter of fact.

"I need to find someone."

"Have you though about going to Pleasure Palace? They probably wouldn't charge you since you own it."

Theo gritted his teeth. He always felt like one of the Three Stooges when he talked to Josh—the one that didn't have a sense of humor. "I'm serious. I need to track down someone."

"There's software for that on your computer." Josh returned to his hacking, making it clear the conversation was done. He had little time for anyone he deemed below his technical level. "Put in the name, social security number, address or phone number. It should come back with quick results."

Theo shook his head. That wouldn't help him find Keera. He already knew where she supposedly lived. "I need her tracked using the GPS in her cell phone."

Josh laughed. "*Her?* Now I understand why you're a bastard today. Sorry. No can do, man. Cell phone GPS is for 9-1-1 purposes only."

Theo snorted. Like that restriction meant anything to Josh. "But you can hack in."

"Well, duh. Of course I can."

"Then I need you to do this." Keera was as good as found. He tapped his foot, impatient to reclaim her. She was already his, always would be but she would be back in his hands before he knew it. And he had a bag with his portable Pleasure Palace packed in the trunk of his car. It might come in handy for persuading her to trust him with whatever it was that had made her run.

"Illegal, bro," Josh warned, closing whatever he was working on and opening another application.

"Probably. I'll make it worth your while."

Josh's eyes gleamed as he calculated what he'd get from this deal. "How worth it?"

Theo knew the perfect price. He'd regret it later. "An office. With a door."

"And a couch."

*Oh hell*. "Done."

"Give me the number and fifteen minutes."

* * * * *

Keera jerked awake. Pain immediately shot down her arms at her startled movement, yanking a cry from her. Her arms were tied above her head and her blanket had been ripped away. In an instant, panic overrode the discomfort. Any residual haze from her sleep disappeared and she frantically looked around.

Why had she fallen asleep? Why had she come here? She'd never thought Cary would find her so quickly. Not within a day anyway.

She sucked in shaking breaths. In this position, her chest thrust upward with each intake. Her eyes flitted back and forth, searching but she couldn't see anyone. He was there, though. Somewhere in the midnight shadows. Something had woken her…

Fighting hysteria, she shook her hair from her face and she tugged at her wrists. A disheartening clang rewarded her effort. Not tied. Chained. She'd never get away this way.

"Please—" she muttered, working her fingers up the chain to where it was wrapped around the iron-spindled headboard. If it was a weak spindle, maybe she could yank it loose.

"I'm irritated, slave, so hold your tongue."

*Theo.* She wilted into the pillows, instant relief filling her.

A match flared and he lit the candles beside the bed, the tiny flame briefly illuminating his granitelike features. Lines bracketed his mouth and the space between his slightly narrowed eyes. Oh man, he was pissed. He might not be Cary but she might not come through this unscathed.

Despite Theo's anger, his presence bolstered her. He might be intimidating but she knew she was safe with him. Far safer than if she was alone. They were both still in danger, though. Yes, it had been a mistake to leave him last night without an explanation. He deserved to know the threat posed by Cary. But if Cary found Theo here with her, he wouldn't think twice about harming, or even killing, Theo.

She closed her eyes, shuddering when she remembered the gun Cary had pressed to her temple the last time he'd caught up with her. She'd been lucky to escape when he'd gone to another room to "prepare". She'd always known she wouldn't be able to evade him forever. She'd also known if she allowed anyone close to her they could be in danger too. That's why she'd never taken a lover…until last night.

Longing twisted inside her as she gazed up at Theo. The threat to him was only present when he was with her. As much as she wanted to trust in his protection, she couldn't burden him with her issues. This wasn't something small like a tire blowout. She'd been dealing with a whole life blowout for years.

His hand traveled over her abdomen and up to cup her breast through the T-shirt she'd worn to bed. She arched into him, catching her breath as he pinched her nipple. Desire throbbed through her. She'd never thought she'd be this close to him again.

As her body called to him, she knew she couldn't stay with him. She'd hurt him before when she'd run and she'd have to hurt him again. The pain of desertion was far better than death. He'd get over it. After all, they'd only had one night together. Why should he die at a psychopath's hands because he'd made the mistake of wanting her?

"I'm sorry," she whispered. If she could erase the pain her presence had caused, she would.

"Are you sorry because you think that will convince me let you go? Or sorry for the pain and difficulty you've caused your master?"

"I didn't want to hurt you." Tears formed in her eyes. She knew he couldn't see them because of the dark. That didn't matter. She wasn't trying to play on his sympathies.

"You thought I'd be unconcerned that you took my collar then disappeared?"

"I left it."

He swore under his breath and flicked the links he'd refastened around her neck while she'd slept. "I'm not concerned about this damned strip of gold, only about she who wears it." He climbed on the bed, caging her with his huge body. His knees clamped on either side of her hips, holding them still. When he leaned down, she saw the fury in his gray eyes. "You belong to me and I will not let you go. Run as far as you like, I'll always come after you. Hide, I will always find you. I will always bring you back to me."

A liquid jolt leapt through her and pooled in her center. If she didn't trust him, if she didn't care for him as much as she did, his words might have frightened her. They didn't. She knew he only said them because he'd worried so much. He cared for her too.

"Theo, I—"

"Master."

So he was in that kind of mood. She took a deep breath. "Master, I made a mistake."

"You did." Sitting back and straddling her hips, he pulled off his shirt, revealing a field of rolling muscles. Her eyes were drawn to his two tattoos, one banding his arm and the other over his navel. He'd told her that almost every man in his family who'd chosen the dominant lifestyle had them. Her mouth went dry at the sight the marks. Most of his family might have them but more personally to Keera, she remembered tracing the marks on Theo's belly with her tongue before taking his generous erection deep in her throat.

She'd never think of his tattoos without remembering that.

He pointed to the one at his navel. "You need to know a few things," he said.

That he was hotter than a starburst and she reacted even quicker?

"These symbols are part of the vow I took when I became a man and chose my path in life. They've been handed down through generations of my family for over a century and I take them seriously." He tapped his belly. "This one is a warning to me to control myself when I'm with my submissive. This is the one on which you can build your trust." He moved his hand to his arm. "This one is more complicated. This one charges me to be the keeper of the temple. To be the owner of the treasure. And to be the protector of the spirit."

He leaned down so he knelt over her body again and dropped his head so that the ends of his hair tickled her forehead. "Protector of your spirit," he said. "Keeper of your temple. You are my treasure. Now," he bit out, his intimate tone changing. "Why did you leave?"

"I..." Presented with this crossroads, she hesitated. Either she told him about Cary stalking her or she fought the battle herself. She wanted his protection, even if it was just his presence at her side. She'd fought for so long. She was weary from it.

Desperately, she wished her hands were free so she could touch him. She couldn't surrender this battle to him. It wasn't his to fight, no matter his vow and she didn't know how to let someone else help her. Cary wanted her for himself. She couldn't trust him not to hurt whatever man she was with. She knew he would. He had it in him. He'd spent too much energy pursuing her, not to be psychotic enough to kill Theo.

When it came down to it, she couldn't risk Theo even if she wanted to trust her entire being to him. This wasn't about whether she surrendered or not. This was his wellbeing. When she'd given herself to him, she'd agreed to fill his needs. He needed to be alive and she couldn't guarantee that while she was with him. Quite the opposite was true. In order to serve him and her love for him, she had to leave.

"Keera?" he prompted.

She shook her head, unable to come up with a suitable lie to cover her real reason for running. In the shadowy light she saw his lips press together. He knew she was hiding something.

"Very well. We'll begin with your discipline then. Then maybe you'll decide to stop concealing the truth from me."

Her heart beat double time while her cleft warmed to the idea of his punishment. She'd been "punished" last night and it had been the most erotic thing she'd ever experienced—quite far from what she deemed punishment. If he began that it might be hours before she could escape—or even remembered to—and Cary might be upon them.

"Wait," she begged. Her wanton thighs parted as far as they could with his knees beside them. Arousal and need flowed hungrily through her, preparing her swelling folds for his entrance.

"Yes?"

"I...ah..." She pulled on the chains. "I...well, I need to go to the bathroom. Can I please before you do whatever you're going to do?"

He nodded and her heart caught. His compassion never failed even when he stared down at her with that forbidding, stern face. Reaching into his pocket, he withdrew a small key. Quickly, he unlocked the cuffs that held her and moved so that she could leave the bed.

"Don't delay," he growled. She wondered if he couldn't read her intent. Sometimes he seemed almost able to read her mind. Last night he'd told her it was because he'd been measuring her for months. Learning her. Gentling her. Readying her.

She'd been his all that time and hadn't even known it.

She rubbed her wrists and glanced over at the tarot cards piled on the bedside table. The four of wands was flipped over, winking at her. Regret filled her. This time she was leaving everything. Theo. Her only refuge. Her most precious keepsake from her mother.

She glared at that card. Romance, freedom from what bound her and refuge from the turmoil in her life? Yeah, right. Obviously, her mother was the only one with any card reading ability. Keera had gotten it all wrong.

She looked at Theo, knowing if circumstances were different, he could be the man to provide all the things promised by the tarot card.

"I'll be right back," she choked.

*Liar, liar, liar.* Someday, if this was ever over, she'd explain to him.

Before she melted into a wallowing spineless heap, she headed for the bathroom on the sure feet of one who'd walked these floors hundreds of times. She couldn't be weak. Despite the dark, she closed the bathroom door and shut out the illumination from the flickering candles. She didn't need it. The window here didn't have a curtain and moonlight flooded the bathroom. Slowly, she turned the door's lock, careful to keep it from clicking.

Immediately, she went to the glass and looked outside. She knew this beach and the surrounding woods well enough. If she got a head start on Theo, she'd be well hidden before he discovered she'd escaped.

Unlatching the window, she pushed up the wood. It creaked. Loudly. Urgently, she shoved it up and dove through the unscreened opening. Hopefully, he hadn't heard the screech. Yeah right. His yell, followed by the pounding on the door and the rattle of the doorknob, confirmed her fear.

She'd better run fast.

Rolling to her feet, she dashed across the sucking sand. Behind her Theo bellowed her name, the sound caught in the wind and nearly drowned by the crashing waves. She didn't slow as she headed for the trees beyond the rise of sand. Dodging a stand of rocks, she hit firmer ground and gained speed.

She didn't dare look back and hoped her head start would be enough. Damn that swollen wood for announcing her departure.

Suddenly, Theo crashed into her back, arms locking around her waist. He twisted as they went to the ground and took the brunt of the impact. In one smooth motion, he flipped her onto her back and rolled over her.

"Ow," she griped.

He glared down at her, the moon reflecting on the fury flicking in his eyes. "You have no idea."

He didn't wait for her consent or cooperation. Angrily, he pushed her long T-shirt over her head and tossed the garment toward the waves. Her panties immediately followed. The waves worked with him, pulling the pieces of clothing out into the lake where they became irretrievable.

Panting she lay naked in his arms while he stared down at her. Lake Superior's spray speckled his bare chest, reminding her of what it had been like when they'd both been damp after he'd fucked her repeatedly. Every remarkable inch of his muscled form pressed into her, reminiscent of what it had been to have him straining over her while they both rushed to completion. Her middle went soft and fluttery. Why did she have to want him so badly? Unconsciously, she lifted into him.

With a groan, Theo captured her lips. His tongue plunged deep inside, dominating her mouth as he dominated her body. His hands were everywhere setting her on fire. It seemed years since they'd parted, not a mere day. Urgently, he ripped at his clothes.

"You will not escape me," he promised. At that moment, it was her last thought.

"Please, I need you," she answered.

What was it about Keera that drove him to the edge of his control? Hell, he'd been a Dom for fifteen years. Even when he was younger than that, he'd taken command of his relationships. Still here was a slip of a woman stealing his control and throwing it to the wind. It might as well have been pulled into the lake with her clothes the way it had deserted him.

She didn't try to squirm away while he ripped at his damp pants. She pushed at them, freeing his cock from his briefs. While he tried to push down the wet denim, she reached into the pocket and withdrew the condom she knew he kept there. He'd revealed last night that he always had one available so he could fuck her at the spur of the moment. She'd remembered.

Need blazed in her eyes, supporting her claim to want him. This wasn't a ploy.

She didn't waste time caressing or teasing as she hastily smoothed the condom over his erection. Spreading her thighs and digging her heels into the sand, she pressed her wrists on either side of her head and stared up into his eyes.

"Master," she murmured.

His groin knotted. Oh God, he'd explode the second he dipped inside her.

He slid his fingers along her naked folds, running his thumb over the bare skin that hid her sweet opening. He needed to taste her and feel that wonderful honey flowing over his tongue.

His nails scored down her body as he licked his way to her center. Keera's ass lifted off the sand as she anticipated his intent. This was why they were perfectly matched—the way she made him wild, the way she anticipated his needs and intentions. Keera didn't play. She fully engaged. So why the fuck was she running from him? She'd tell him before this night was out.

Her cry swelled around him when he flicked his tongue over her clit. Beside her head, her fingers flexed. Her hips jerked. Clamping his hands around them, he pressed her into the sand and stabbed his tongue through her gathering heat. Her body pawed at him as he licked and feasted on her cream.

"Feel what I do to you," he ordered. "Close your eyes. Give me your hands." He slid his arms beneath her thighs so her legs draped over his shoulders. Reaching down, she twined her fingers through his. Her scent filled his nostrils and he breathed deeply, intoxicated by her.

Beneath him, her waiting cleft opened like a flower revealing her treasures for his mouth and later his cock. Both would love her until she screamed her release. Once she came the first time, he'd carry her into the house and tie her to the bed and fuck her until she begged never to be parted from him.

He dragged his tongue from the front of her pussy to the back, teasing the delicate flesh that led to her anus. His teeth scraped over her and she quivered, whispering his name like a benediction. There was no blessing here. They were both too deep into their own hells and desperately trying to find a way out.

He decided not to let her have release after all… Not just yet.

"Don't come," he commanded when she started to convulse around him. He rose over her, knowing he couldn't enter her delicate sheath with the sand-covered condom. "Don't come."

Her teeth sank into her plump bottom lip while her fingers squeezed his.

"Don't," he told her.

"Theo, *Master*, please."

"No," he answered firmly. Standing, he yanked his pants back up then lifted her into his arms. She melted into his chest, compliant where before she'd wanted only to run. He wasn't sure about what had changed between them. Perhaps she'd changed her mind. Perhaps she'd decided to quit running when she'd realized he'd always outrun her. Perhaps she just wanted him more than she could admit.

Shouldering his way into the cottage, he slammed the door shut and headed across the unobstructed floor plan, following the flickering candlelight. He deposited her on the bed on her stomach and refastened the cuffs. Keera immediately crawled to her knees, hopefully presenting her ass to him while he shucked off his wet jeans and the sandy condom.

His bag lay at the end of the bed. He lifted it onto the mattress, then crossed his arms and waited for Keera to realize he'd grown still.

# Chapter Two

She was so fucked. Well, if she got lucky, she was. Looking up at Theo, she began to doubt it would ever happen. He stared at her with a forbidding scowl, likely meant to have her shivering in her slave shackles. Instead she found it damn hot.

"Are you going to explain why you ran?" he asked.

Regretfully, she shook her head. She wanted to… She just couldn't. She knew what would happen. He'd get all protective and wrap her in metaphorical bubble wrap while he went gunning for her stalker and made himself a great big Dominant target.

He drew his hand over the curve of her ass, trailing his last finger deep inside the crease. It scraped over her anus and she shivered. His manner worried her. He had something planned. He was far too calm.

"You know that it's not acceptable for a submissive to keep secrets from her master?"

She looked away, unable to meet his eyes. She'd tell him almost anything. In the past she had. However this was one secret she couldn't share, even if she wanted to. Theo's safety was on the line.

The silence grew heavy between them while she stonewalled and he waited.

"Do you know the history of ginger?" he asked suddenly.

*What the –*

Her head snapped up and she stared at him. "No."

What on earth was he on about? Ginger? She was chained to a bed, ass in the air and hotter than hell for him. Who cared about the history of ginger? It was good in stir-fry…and had no bearing here.

Theo reached into the bag he'd placed at the end of the bed and withdrew a long finger of the root.

"Are you planning to cook?" she snarked.

"You have a smart mouth, slave. You might want to curb it."

Not hardly. She couldn't believe he'd hurt her. If she had so much as a suspicion he would, he wouldn't have been able to chain her to the bed so easily.

"Couldn't I do something else with it?" she countered, drawing her tongue over her bottom lip before she drew the plump flesh between her teeth.

"No." He turned away and reached into the bag again, this time withdrawing a small knife. Her brow furrowed as she watched him start to carve away the outer skin of the root and shape it.

"Briefly," he began, "ginger was used as a tool of punishment in the Victorian days."

*Punishment? Oh no.*

"Because of its strong scent?"

"Ah no, darling slave. It was used in conjunction with caning."

She sucked in a harsh breath and he drew the back of his knuckles over her ass. "Don't worry. I don't plan ever to cane this pretty ass."

Somehow, that didn't reassure her. He had other plans in that brilliant mind of his and that worried her. He wanted to pry her secrets from her. From the look on his face, he thought whatever he intended would have her talking. "What are you going to do with that?"

An eyebrow lifted.

"In time…"

"For what? Dinner? The kitchen's over there. You can stick that in the fridge." Who cared that the appliance didn't have power and probably smelled funky. She didn't want that ginger anywhere near her… Theo knew things about sex that she couldn't dream of. From what she'd experienced last night, she'd wager he hadn't become a Dom without learning his share about discipline and punishment.

She wanted warm and caring Theo, the master who ruled over her and pushed her sexual limits. She was frightened of this disciplinarian side of him.

"You wouldn't want that," he replied as he continued shaping the ginger. "It would only get stronger. For your first punishment, I think this strength will do."

"Theo, please," she begged.

"All you have to do is tell me. Why are you running?"

If only she could tell him and know he'd just let her go. She closed her eyes and took a shuddering breath. Fruitlessly, she tried to swallow back the trepidation soaring through her.

She didn't have a high pain tolerance. It wouldn't take much more than a tiny swat to have her screaming. He'd think she was a total baby.

He held the root near her face, the pungent scent flooding her senses. "What does that look like?"

She stared at the slim tip that widened into a bulbous middle before narrowing and widening again. "A…ah…a…plug?"

"Exactly. I can't thin it as much as I'd like and I've purposely widened it in the end to keep you safe. We don't want any accidents. 'Safe' does not mean punishment-free. Do you understand why you are being punished, slave?"

She nodded sure she'd be unable to speak around the stone lodged in her throat.

"Aloud."

"For…ah…running away."

"And?"

"For not telling you why."

He parted her ass and rested the root against her anus. "Do you want to tell me why?"

Her eyes squeezed shut. "No."

He sighed, though he didn't seem particularly distressed. She looked up at him while he pressed the ginger forward. Disappointment filled his eyes. She'd disappointed him. She had no choice.

"Lube," she squealed.

"No, that would ruin the effect. The juice will help it slide right in."

"What effect?" she gasped.

"Wait."

She tried to breathe as he slowly pushed it inside her until it seated within her. She was full but not too full. It wasn't bad. What exactly was the punishment?

Theo got up and went into the other room. The water turned on and splashed as he washed his hands.

Then the fire began.

"Theo!" she screamed, yanking on the chains that held her. Her whole ass burned, radiating down into her middle as she writhed. Her body clenched and the heat increased. She'd kill him. Who cared that she was the slave? She'd fucking kill him, if this didn't kill her first.

So surrounded by the sensations rioting through her, she didn't realized Theo had returned until his hand pulled down her spine from neck to ass.

"Relax," he said gently. "The burn is worse if you tense."

"Take it out," she cried. She couldn't take it. It was too intense.

He smacked her ass.

"Stop gritting your teeth. You'll hurt yourself." Digging in his bag, he came up with a small ball and shoved it into her mouth before fastening the attached leather behind her head. Tears filled her eyes and she squirmed trying to get away from the sensation assailing her bottom half. It only grew worse as she moved. She tried to relax. If the intensity continued to increase, she'd die. She just knew it.

Sweat coated her body as her muscles trembled. She could barely remain on her knees. She tried to breathe, slowly becoming aware that while she'd fought, the burning she'd classified as pain had morphed into a coiling, dripping sensation inside her.

It couldn't be. Yet she couldn't mistake the tremors exploding in her sheath. Her sheath clenched as it searched for her mate, needed to be filled as the warming sensation cruised through her. Her mind tripped into another space where there was only her body and the shocks shoving through her. She could do this. She could take this. She was one shimmering puddle of arousal.

Gently, Theo removed the ginger plug and discarded it in the wastebasket beside the bed. The burn didn't recede. She knew some juice from the ginger must have remained.

When the first lash fell, she jumped, her ass clenching and fire searing. Her eyes went wide and she saw Theo draw back. Another blow thumped across the top of her ass. The stands of his flogger splayed across the small of her back and she arched shoving her behind higher in the air. She welcomed another blow. Unbelievable pleasure surged through her. She wanted to scream "More. Oh please more." Tears streamed down her face at the unbelievable mix of sensations. The cream from her arousal dampened her upper thighs. She needed him.

The next fall of the knotted leather caught the crease between her butt and upper thighs. Overwhelmed by it, she screamed, the sounds muffled by the pillow and the ball in her mouth. Two, three, four more lashes fell, each rocking her as the stings raked across her shuddering flesh. Another fall and the flogger's tails smacked dead center on her ass, a few stray ends curling down to smack against her clit.

She was lost. Out of control, her body convulsed and shuddered, a soul-stripping orgasm crashing through her. Her body clenched, only to be thrown higher by the increased burn from the ginger's juice. Unable to support herself, she collapsed into the blankets, tremors still rippling through her.

She sank toward oblivion, unconcerned about anything for the first time in five years.

"Keera?" He turned her onto her back and stroked her cheek. "Sweetheart? Keera?"

Her eyes opened as he pulled the ball gag from her mouth and she distantly realized his concern. She winced as an unexpected pang tingled through her. Her body wasn't done yet even if her mind was traveling to la-la land. She lifted her back from the mattress pressing her breasts toward him.

"Please," she whispered. Raising her gaze, she stared imploringly into his gray eyes and added, "Master. Don't punish me anymore. I'm sorry. I'm sorry." His mouth covered hers. "I'm sorry," she murmured as his lips stopped all words. Gently, he kissed her, thrusting his tongue in and out as he stroked hers. With a groan she sucked him inside. His kisses completed her and told her she hadn't fallen completely from his grace. He still needed her as desperately as she needed him.

He made love to her mouth, cupping her breasts and molding the firm flesh into tight peaks. She twisted upward into his hands.

"Take me," she begged while he plucked and rolled her nipples. Her breath shuddered in her chest. She whimpered. "Please. Oh please."

He bent and rasped his tongue over one rigid point then caught the puckered tip between his teeth and tugged. She couldn't think. Agitated she yanked on the chains. She might come from the sensations threading from her breast to her core. Why was he waiting? As he moved, long strands of his dark brown hair fell around his face and tickled her skin.

She needed to touch him. She writhed beneath him, her lips moving with unspoken words. She'd never felt so wild or needy. Theo was the center of everything she desired.

He covered her, his mouth settling against her ear as he insinuated his hard thigh between her legs. "Did I forget to tell you…?" he murmured, sheathing himself with a condom he'd left on the nightstand. "The juice from the ginger root is an aphrodisiac."

Well, no he hadn't mentioned that. It didn't really matter. She didn't need an aphrodisiac to want him.

His fingers trailed over her belly and into her folds. She bit her lip, knowing he'd find her drenched. She couldn't stop the cream that flooded her whenever she was near him. All he had to do was speak and her body got ready. She'd been like this for months—before he'd even touched her. As she'd predicted, his fingertips slid easily over her, the sensuous glide pulling a moan from her. Frantically she tried to squirm closer.

His heavy cock pressed against her as she canted her hips toward him. Theo surged forward. With a bellow of triumph, he buried himself to the hilt. His girth stretched her but she quickly adjusted to it, thankful she got to feel him inside her one more time.

He slid his arm beneath her to control her jerking movements. She flinched as the hair on his arm abraded the skin that still throbbed from his lashes.

Theo froze.

"I'm fine," she assured him through her teeth. She rose against him, refusing to let him quit now that he was finally inside her. "Don't. Stop," she panted.

With a groan, he began his easy slide in and out. He shoved her thighs wide and held her open to his plunder. Oh hell, yes. She was captured and unable to control anything he did. Surrendered.

"You're going to come this time," he promised. His growl plundered her senses, drawing another gush of arousal. "You'll come once for every hour I searched for you. Once for every hour you forced us to be parted. You'll come until you pass out from the pleasure of it with my name on your lips."

Her body clenched around him. How did he know exactly the right things to say to wring a reaction from her womb? Because he was her master. She was his slave.

"Please," she moaned. Wanton agitation drove her and her release wound tighter and tighter. She couldn't stand it. Her fingers clenched around the chain holding her and she used it as leverage as she moved her body with his.

She whimpered desperate for all he promised, even as the beginnings of release tightened around his driving thrusts.

"Yes, sweetheart, like that. Just like that," he groaned. "I love the sounds you make."

"Oh God…" she gasped, bending. Her mind blanked, assailed by the continual contractions flung down her body, stealing the little control she'd retained. She writhed as the cycling tremors overwhelmed her and tore cries from her.

Theo's satisfied growls were counterpoint to her high-pitched sobs. He rotated his hips, sending more cataclysmic spasms down her limbs. Goose bumps followed in their wake. Bigger and bigger and stronger. Each climax built upon the last, tying her insides in tension-filled knots and stealing every thought she'd ever had.

Finally, she wilted into the blankets, weak from the exertion. She panted, desperately trying to grasp an anchor to reality. Theo wasn't ready to let her.

"Now. One more time," Theo ordered. "Come now, Keera."

Before she could react, he slammed deep. She shoved right over the edge and into black oblivion.

"Theo!" she screamed, plummeting into the orgasm faster than her body could adjust. What she said, what she screamed, how she shook under him was all lost to her as she lost her grip on everything but the cock still plowing into her and the earthquake rocking through her.

His bellow barely pierced the darkness wrapping around her. She sank bonelessly into the mattress. She'd never move again.

His lips pressed to her temple. "You're so perfect."

Perfect? Yes, this was perfect.

Damp strands of his hair fell over her shoulder as he kissed her neck. Slipping to the side, he carefully wrapped her in his arms, mindful that she was still restrained. The chains offered enough leeway for her to turn. She pressed her face into his chest while he played with the specially made gold collar he'd placed around her neck.

"Why did you run?" he asked quietly. "Were you scared?"

Why had she—what? Her brow furrowed as she tried to comprehend his question. Right now she wasn't scared of anything. She sighed, letting sleep edge in. She'd answer later when she understood him.

"Keera." He shook her gently.

"What?" she groaned. Why wasn't he one of those men who fell asleep right after sex? She struggled up to consciousness.

"Why did you run?" he asked softly.

That again. All the reasons flooded back to her—the reasons she'd run and the reason she couldn't be with Theo. Cary.

"Theo..." she began.

"You know I'll always take care of you, don't you? I won't harm you. You might be my submissive but I'll cherish you."

He retrieved the key to the cuffs from the bedside table and released her restraints. Pulling her hands toward him, he rubbed her wrists.

"Everything between us went too fast, didn't it? I didn't give you time to consider what you were doing before I bound you to me. I didn't make sure I had your trust."

"Trust? I trust you. It's not as if I didn't know you before yesterday. You were my friend Theo. Last night, even what you just did—which by the way, how do you *know* these things?—that didn't deplete my trust. I might not completely understand this lifestyle but I know you."

Sitting against the iron headboard, he pulled her onto his lap. She rested limply against his chest, really just wanting to sleep. Curled in his arms she felt safe. Cary seemed so far away and unable to hurt her.

Theo's heart thumped solidly beneath her ear while he ran his fingers through her long hair. "Sometimes I forget this isn't a way of life for everyone. I grew up with this. My father and mother are two halves of a perfect coin. You can't have a Dom without a sub. When two people fight for control, there's war and someone always loses. In a D/s relationship, who makes the final decision is a given. There's no war because both parties have already agreed that the Dom has control. He will always do what is best for the two of them."

"So one side always gives in?"

"My mother isn't weak. I have complete respect for her—and sometimes fear." He laughed. "She speaks her mind but yes, she does defer to my father. Only to my father. That woman can be fearsome. I've seen her in action, just like I've seen you in action. You're not weak either, but you are mine." He tilted her head up and kissed her. "Don't fight this Keera. You know what's between us is right. You're meant to be mine."

That had never been the problem. She took a deep breath. Here was that crossroads again. She didn't want to tell Theo

about Cary. To even say the man's name would in some way taint her relationship with Theo.

Thinking, she traced the tattoo on his belly with her fingertip. It was the hottest damned thing she'd ever seen. She wanted to investigate it everyday while she straddled his chest. She didn't want to run anymore.

Therein lay her answer.

Theo had power over her—because she'd given it to him—but he was also powerful. Did she really need to continue alone? He wanted her trust, shouldn't she trust him with this?

"Theo, when I ran, it wasn't because of you. I've been running for the past five years."

Theo nudged his nose into her neck, drinking in her fragrance mixed with the heady scent of their sex. He tightened his hold on her. She wasn't running anymore. Not from him.

She pulled back to look into his eyes, her brows pulling together. "How did you find me?"

"The GPS in your cell phone." He drew her back. Absently, he nuzzled his cheek over the top of her head, fighting the tension building inside him. What the hell kind of secret had sent her on the run in the first place? What was she hiding from? An ex-boyfriend? A not-so-ex-husband? The law?

His stomach knotted. He couldn't imagine Keera committing a crime that would have her on the run. It might be the middle of the night but he'd call his lawyer and get him started on her case now if necessary.

She looked over at where her phone lay on the table beside a stack of weird, beat-up cards. "You can do that?"

"Not legally." He wanted her to get to the point and tell him what was behind curtain number three. He had a feeling it wouldn't be the big prize. It was gonna be a nightmare.

"Josh?" she asked. She knew his brother's skills, having listened to him lament about Josh a few times in the last months.

"Who else?" he said impatiently. He needed her to get on with it and she was stalling. He explained the rest of how he'd gotten here, before she could ask about that too. "Then, I used the information he got, flew here in the Cress plane, found this place…and you. It's amazing what you can do with an old lock and a credit card even if you're not quite sure what you're doing. Still, I'm surprised you didn't hear me swearing."

"Maybe that's what woke me up," she laughed, the sound brittle.

"No, it was my kiss, sleeping beauty. I had you all chained up, mine for the taking but I needed you awake. I was dying for your pretty lips around my cock again. Still am. But mostly, I want to know what the hell is going on. What are you running from?"

He couldn't help her if he didn't know.

With a sigh, she pulled from his embrace. He let her go. She wasn't going far, not after what they'd just done. She settled cross-legged between his bent knees and looked up at him with tormented green eyes.

"Just tell me," he urged.

"This cabin… It was my parents'. We came here for vacations in the summer. After they—" She paused, closing her eyes for a moment. Pain vibrated from her. He wanted to reach out and grab her to him and soothe it all away, make her forget it all, but he sensed she was holding herself together with a brittle cord right now. If he touched her, she'd lose it.

"Well, they died five years ago. Car accident." Her voice wobbled. "It was suspicious, at least to me. At the funeral my stepbrother Cary cornered me. He's the son of my mother's first husband. I barely knew him. I didn't even remember the last time I'd seen him. Cary said he wanted his portion of the money. I didn't know what he was talking about. My parents barely had any money. Everything remaining plus a lot of my savings went to paying funeral expenses. I got a few keepsakes. This place. He insisted there was more. Some windfall they'd gotten from one of my father's relatives. If there was I don't know about it and I don't know how he did"

Theo tilted his head, trying to understand. "So he wanted money? Is he suing you for it?"

"I wish. If he sued me for it, I could prove there was nothing. Even if there is something, I can't see that anything would be his. I'd give it to him though just to make him leave me alone. I couldn't find any information in my parents' things about the money and I really had no idea how to track down this fictional windfall. I was working full-time and trying to get their affairs in order. All the while, he hounded me, calling at all hours, showing up at my apartment, harassing me at work. The police wouldn't help me since he's my stepbrother. They looked the other way. It was a domestic thing, you know. In the town where I lived, it was really low on the roster of importance."

Suddenly, he saw where this was going. Leaning forward, he pulled her back against him and shifted so they were lying chest to chest. He had to work hard to keep from crushing her to him and to keep his voice even. "He's stalking you."

She nodded. "He started threatening me. I ran after he attacked me the first time."

After the first time? The *first* time? "What do you mean 'the first time'?"

Staying calm might be an impossibility.

"He broke into my apartment. I got away before he could really hurt me. By then, I'd given up on getting help, so I just ran. I left everything except those cards from my mother. I would have left them too if I hadn't been able to grab them easily. I just drove and drove, until I found myself in a little Podunk burg in the middle of nowhere. I figured I'd be safe. At the time it wasn't as easy to track someone with the internet and Cary didn't have the connections to have me found. I didn't even try to pursue the inheritance. To do that, I'd have to give information about my whereabouts so I could be contacted. If Cary had so easily discovered the money what was to stop him from also getting my location? I thought if I lie low, he'd forget about me and I could move on with my life. I was wrong. He found me three months later. I ran again. It's been the same over and over. Six months ago, he tried to kill me."

Theo's blood went cold. "The scar on your arm?"

She nodded as he ran his thumb over the six inches of puckered, pink skin. "He stabbed me. His knife slashed my arm while I was turning away from him. I'm lucky he fell or he would have—"

She pressed her face into his chest and he tightened his arms. He couldn't do anything else. She could have been killed... He'd still be walking away with an empty space inside him...and she'd be dead.

"Surely the police helped you after that." Well, obviously they hadn't. She was still running.

She let out a sound that could have been a laugh, if it wasn't so full of disgust. "You'd think, wouldn't you? Cary apparently has a connection I knew nothing about. A drinking buddy, who's also a cop. He was kind enough to let slip that that was how he keeps finding me. His friend who 'has his back'. So, I ran again. I patched myself up with hope and a lot of tape. I didn't want the hospital to ask questions and draw attention to me—Cary's friend might have poor taste in companions but he's good at finding people."

Theo gritted his teeth and fought back the torrent of curses that threatened. This guy's ass was toast. So was the cop who'd helped him. No one messed with what was his and Keera most definitely belonged to him. "Then what?"

"I drifted. The wound made it hard to work. Thankfully I had money to sustain me for a while because I never bought anything... Why bother when it will be left behind in a few months? I've even kept most of my clothes packed in the trunk of my car. Eventually, I ended up in Brandywine. And I met you. I felt safe for a while. It was so long without any contact from Cary I thought maybe, this time, he wouldn't find me. Maybe he'd finally lost interest...given up..."

"Then he found you again."

She pulled from his arms and left the bed. Despite his confidence that she wouldn't run, he tensed as he sat up and watched her. She was in so much pain and he only wanted to take it away. If it took his last breath, he would end this. She wasn't fighting alone anymore.

She wrapped her arms around her middle and paced a few feet away. "I got a voice message from him last night...um...while you were in the shower."

He ignored the irritation that revelation roused. It was insignificant compared to his rage at what she'd endured. Still, she should have told him and she shouldn't have run. Now was not the time to focus on that, however. They'd deal with her mistake later, after he'd dealt with her stalker.

He could only guess what her stepbrother had said to terrify her. After stabbing her, "Hi" might have done that.

"I don't know how he found me this time. He couldn't track me by my social security number...I...um...lied and gave my mother's number. I figured that's how he'd been finding me. You know, with his cop friend's connections. As soon as he let that slip, I started trying to outthink him. Would he expect me to come back to Michigan? What identification was he looking for? I didn't know any legal ways of blocking him. You can't just go by a different name and still be able to function in society. It's a lot harder than they make it look on TV."

"I'd imagine." He'd known she was strong but he couldn't believe what she'd gone through. He'd get her social security number corrected when they got home. Cress

Construction could forgive her deception but he wasn't sure the federal government would. They preferred names and numbers to match.

"So... your name really is Keera?" he asked cautiously, wondering if he'd have to relearn his lover's name. He favored using the right name in bed.

She grinned at him, wry amusement lighting her pained eyes. "Yes, it is. Keera Jean Thornton."

Soon to be Cress. Every one of his brothers would protect her.

Desperately, he rattled through the problem in his head, looking at different angles. Problem solving was what he did. Yes, he might be the oldest Cress boy but he'd earned his position through skill not nepotism or birth order.

"You said he left you a message...but you got a new cell phone two months ago. How did he get your number?"

"I don't know how. Maybe he traced me the same way he did before. I wouldn't have gotten the phone if I hadn't needed it for work. I put it off as long as I could."

Theo ran his hand over his face, Cary's method growing clearer. "Is there anyone back home, from five years ago, that you keep in touch with? Anyone who would have had your cell number or would have had your number come across their call log?"

"No one who would have given the number to Cary."

"That's not what I asked."

"You mean he stole the number." Horrified realization dawned across her features. "Yes. I called my best friend to check in last week. I check in once a month..."

Theo climbed out of bed and started pulling on his clothes. "He's tracking you through your phone, just like I did. His lackey has access to the police GPS system. Get dressed. We need to leave."

"Wait, Theo. There's more." She turned to him, panicked and looking for all the world as if she was ready to run again even though she was stark naked.

He tensed, ready to stop her. "What?"

"I can't go with you. He said if I was with you, he'd hurt you. He implied he'd kill you. Theo, please. I couldn't bear that to happen. Just go without me."

*Like hell.* "Get dressed. We're leaving."

"But—"

"No buts. Listen to me. You're done facing this alone and I'm sure as hell not leaving you behind." He gripped her shoulders, drawing her close to him. "You're mine. Get that through your head, once and for all. You stay with me."

Turning from her, he snatched up the jacket he'd removed before she'd woken and removed his cell phone. It might be the middle of the night but he needed to get the ball rolling on this now.

Keera sat on the bed and watched Theo pace. Knowing him as well as she did, she shouldn't have been as shell-shocked by his all-fired, take-charge attitude but she was having trouble adjusting. This was just an extension of the Theo who stormed her senses in bed and the Theo who took no prisoners in business. Still, it had been so long since anyone had fought her battles or been on her side.

More quickly than she'd have imagined, he had his lawyer on the phone and set him to work on her situation. A few moments later, he'd dialed up his pilot.

"I don't care what time it is or how much it costs," he snapped. "Get whatever officials need to be there. Have the plane fueled and ready. I need to take off within an hour." Flipping shut his phone without waiting for further argument, he turned to her.

"You're not dressed."

She glanced at the jeans tangled beside the bed. Her behind was beginning to sting where the flogger had landed. She couldn't imagine putting the stiff denim over them. "You threw my clothes in the lake. The rest of them are in my car."

He too, glanced at the jeans. "Stand up and let me see your back."

She stood, feeling the pull of the stripes. She didn't mind them. They reminded her she belonged to him—and they'd felt good at the time. When she'd agreed to this D/s relationship, she'd agreed to the punishment and, in retrospect, she shouldn't have run—though she wasn't sure she wouldn't do the same thing again.

She knew people who would see her back and cry abuse but she knew it wasn't. Theo would never hit her in anger. She realized from experience that he watched her closely to know if he was pushing too far. He'd even stopped last night at the height of her pleasure to check her status. She smiled remembering when she'd told him she was fine but he might be dead if he didn't continue. That was definitely the wrong thing to say. He prolonged her path to release until she thought she'd go out of her mind for need of it.

That was the difference between this and abuse. He cherished her and she knew it. He never pushed beyond the limit of what she'd allow and again she knew it. With Theo, she'd never doubt her worth and she'd never sport a black eye and broken bones. He bolstered her self-confidence and courage.

Theo dug in his bag and knelt behind her.

"Don't we have to leave?" she asked in confusion. She twisted to look over her shoulder.

"Stay still. We do but you'll never make it through the flight if we don't do this first." His hands trailed over her sore ass. She shuddered at the pleasure of his fingers again sliding over her. Cool relief followed their course in stark contrast to the warmth seeping through her.

He pressed a kiss to the small of her back.

"I will always take care of you, Keera. Never doubt that."

"I don't." He'd always care for her if he could. What would he do if that choice was taken from his hands? That's what she was afraid of, because she knew he'd never willingly let that happen. It terrified her that he might get badly hurt or killed because of her.

"But you still doubt I can stand my own against this stalker of yours."

She stood silently and he sighed, shaking his head.

"You trust me," he said. "Perhaps you could muster a little faith."

He picked up her jeans and shoved them in his bag. He slipped off his white shirt and left on his T-shirt. "Put this on, then gather up your things. We're leaving."

"I could just go and get something from my suitcase," she replied as she put on the garment. The tails hung to the middle of her thighs, covering her, yet exposing her in a sensual way that heightened her awareness.

She breathed deeply as his masculine, woods-tinged scent enveloped her. God she loved his smell. She might never return his shirt…or keep stealing them. Theo might soon have a shirt shortage.

He studied her. "I think wearing that is fine. It's not that I think you'll run. It's just not safe here and until we're safe, I want you close to me where I can protect you if necessary. Besides," he said, trailing his finger along a flog mark on her thigh. "I like you in my shirt… It says you're mine."

*And leaves me vulnerable to anything you plan on the way home.* She didn't mention that and he left it unspoken but clear as he traced a line upward to her cleft. She drew a shaky breath, her body ready for him again.

"But your pilot—"

"Like I said…mine. I want everyone to know, especially those close to me." His finger slipped into her drenched folds. He groaned. "I want you again."

"Yes."

"Can't risk it." He pulled his fingers from her, watching her as he sucked her essence from them. Her insides clenched with need.

"Please."

He shook his head, regret clear in his eyes. "As soon as we get home… You might not leave our bed for a week."

She liked the sound of that. She liked *our*. It reminded her she was part of something special and permanent. Safe and secure in Theo.

The chirp of her cell phone broke the spell and she automatically reached for it, answering before Theo could stop her. She realized her mistake immediately.

"I warned you, bitch. You think I don't know he followed you. Now he dies."

"No," she cried. Any peace she'd achieved ripped from beneath her, leaving her again wallowing in fear.

Theo wrenched the phone from her numb fingers. "Listen asshole… Damn it," he swore. "The bastard hung up. Get your things."

She couldn't move. "He said…he said he'd kill you."

Other than a slight tightening of his jaw, he appeared unmoved by the revelation. He shrugged. "Threats to scare you. Now, gather your things. We can't stay here."

Hastily, she wrapped the tarot cards in the cloth in which she stored them. She ignored the Four of Wands winking at her. The card lied. She wasn't any closer to the end of this horror than she'd ever been and now an innocent person had been dragged into the mix.

She wouldn't be able to forgive herself if he was hurt.

She'd barely slung her purse strap onto her shoulder and tugged the shirt back into place when Theo pulled her toward the door. Cautiously, he looked outside then hustled her to the SUV he'd driven from the airport.

Drawing back, he hurled her phone into the lake's roiling waves.

"Hey," she protested when it disappeared into the black water.

"I'll get you a new one. Give me your keys so I can get your bags."

A moment later, he had her luggage stowed in the back of the truck and he peeled out of the driveway, a rain of pebbles behind them.

"My car," she protested weakly.

"I'll get you a new one."

That was getting to be a theme. It would be interesting to be a rich man's submissive. She hadn't given a thought to that when she'd said yes to his collar. She didn't want all these things from him but she wouldn't argue since he'd abandoned her car and destroyed her phone. Of course, leaving her without a car—even temporarily—cut off one of her escape options. She suspected he knew as much too.

She shifted on the leather seat, pulling the shirt beneath her as well as she could. Despite the cream, the slightly raised welts stuck uncomfortably to the seat. It was a good thing they weren't traveling the whole six hours back to Brandywine in the SUV. She'd never make it. She sucked in a breath as the seat seemed to adhere to her skin and Theo cast a glance her direction.

"I'm fine," she said through her teeth.

"No you're not." Pulling to the side of the road, he reached behind them and grabbed his jacket off the seat where he must have discarded it on the way from the airport earlier.

"Lift up," he commanded.

She lifted her hips and he spread the jacket beneath her, with the fleecy side up. She sighed as it softly cradled her skin.

"Better?" He smoothed a hand over her thigh.

"Yes."

"Good. Now, I've been lax as you've been explaining yourself but now, is this how you're to have your legs when you're alone with me?"

She blinked at him in surprise then remembered the instructions she'd first received from him when she'd agreed to become his submissive. Thighs never together…

"No," she answered and moved them apart. She was immediately rewarded with his fingers stroking into her cleft. She moaned, rocking her hips toward him. Her head tilted back against the seat and she enjoyed the sensation.

"Just so you know," he said as he flicked her throbbing clit. "You're not coming until we get home."

*Oh God…*

* * * * *

So this was the home of a Dom. Keera had seen all but the bedrooms when he'd given her a quick tour. While he took her bags to his—their—room, she wandered Theo's enormous living room. Early morning sunlight flooded the space, reminding her how little sleep she'd had in the last twenty-four hours. Theo had slept less. She suspected when they finally fell into bed, sex would become their third priority behind sleep and safety.

She yawned, looking around. The living room was neat, while stark and done completely in black and white, with nary a whip or chain in sight. *What were you expecting, Keera? Shackles hanging from the walls?*

It looked like any of the homes she'd seen in interior decorating books. Despite the starkness, the room still managed to look inviting. She could picture Theo slouched on the couch with his feet on the coffee table, while she curled up beside him after a day of swimming in the pool that lay beyond the double doors behind her.

She took the two steps down into the large sunken portion of the room and crossed to the far wall. Floor to ceiling, black wood bookshelves stretched from one wall to the other. She sighed in appreciation. Theo apparently shared her fondness for books, an addiction she'd been forced to curb in the past years. She loved reading great stories over and over. She drew a finger along the spine of one of her favorite books. It appeared he had the same taste and habit with reading material.

"My vice," he said behind her. She turned to find he'd discarded his clothes. Books weren't his only vice. Thank goodness.

He'd managed to keep her on edge for the entire flight home. After a brief call to Ryan and Jessica to let them know she was okay, he'd focused his sole attention on her. Holding her, caressing her, touching her intimately while the pilot was mere feet away yet hopefully oblivious to what occurred behind him. And the naughty things Theo had whispered to her… They seared straight through her, keeping her moist and wanting.

Seeing him naked now gave her a second wind unrivaled by the strongest caffeine. She didn't need sleep. She needed him.

The shirt she wore tickled her thighs while she placed her wrists together over her ass and spread her feet to shoulder width. She wanted him to fuck her now and she figured this waiting pose was the quickest path to a screaming release.

Surely release was coming now that they were safely ensconced in his home, security alarms engaged. Theo had made it clear she wasn't venturing from beyond these walls until her stalker was out of the picture. She had a feeling Theo wouldn't be opposed to drowning him in the pool and burying him in the massive woods crowding the back edge of the property.

She looked through her lashes at him. Theo had also made it clear he'd keep her adequately occupied while she was sequestered. She didn't know if she could take much more of his sensual torture. She might go out of her mind.

He took in her stance, a slight smile tilting his full lips. "Come with me."

He turned, heading down the wide hallway she knew led to one wing of bedrooms. Her pussy gave a cheer. Bedroom equaled sex. Theo equaled hot sex. And he'd ensured she had a one-track mind. If she didn't have him soon, she'd dissolve into a puddle of seething need. Toward the end of the passage, he swung open a door and stepped back, motioning her inside.

She should have known he'd seemed too eager. Here were all the whips and chains missing from the living room. She looked around caught up in the sex-store extravaganza. Her mouth fell open at the array of equipment.

"This is your bedroom?" she gasped.

"No. This is the playroom and now that you're here, my collection's complete. I have the perfect companion to explore all these possibilities with." He gestured at the collection filling the room. She eyed the assortment. She wasn't so sure she was up for all the exploration he obviously had planned.

He kissed her gently. "Don't fret. If you absolutely don't like something, we won't try it. Samples of all the products we sell at Pleasure Palace come to me first. After a while it accumulates. I'm trusting you to help me sort through it." He ran his hand over the stocks near the door. "Of course there are some things I'll insist we keep."

Her mind screamed no while her body thought trying it would be a good idea. "There might be some things we need to negotiate," she hedged. She didn't want to say no outright and she didn't want to disappoint him. Pleasing him had somehow niggled its way to the head of her priorities.

As an independent woman, who'd relied on herself for so long, it seemed foreign. She hadn't had to think about how anyone else felt in years—she hadn't let herself. Knowing she might be leaving a trail of worries and sadness when she disappeared hurt too much. It was better not to connect, not to get involved. Theo hadn't let her do that. Neither had many of the people at Cress Construction. Leaving them behind had hurt immensely. Being able to come back—with Theo at her side—filled her with unbelievable joy, because he wanted her at his side.

She tipped back her head and looked up at him. "How can I please you?"

Unidentifiable emotion swirled through his gray eyes. "Never leave me again."

"Never." As if she could. Without him, she felt like flotsam caught upon stormy waves.

He pulled her to him, his hand slipping beneath where she held hers securely behind her. His rigid arousal thrummed against her belly while her tender breasts pressed to him. He worked his free hand between them to loosen the buttons on her shirt while she stood carefully still in his embrace until he revealed his desire.

It was almost more control than she had.

How could she please him? Didn't she know having her secure in his arms almost undid him. He gazed at her ripe lips and imagined another way. He wanted to fuck her sweet mouth until he lingered on the edge of explosion and wasn't sure if he could stop before flooding down her throat. Her mouth was dangerous and he wanted nothing more at the moment than to tempt fate.

He wanted to see her in chains again too. He had a thing about them, though to most it would have embarrassed him to admit. Maybe it was the reality she couldn't up and run away when he had her bound—hell, he didn't know. It wasn't as if he'd fuck her if she was unwilling. He wasn't that sort of sick asshole. All he knew was her knots undid him.

Walking her to the center of the room, he gathered himself. He slipped the shirt from her and kicked it aside. "Kneel," he ordered.

"Yes," she replied, going to her knees. For a moment, he looked down at her, her firm breasts lifting with each excited breath, the pretty nipples begging for his mouth. Before he succumbed to temptation, he strode to the bed where he'd laid out a set of ankle and wrist cuffs and a fine but sturdy, chain. He jangled them in his hand to let her know what was to come and watched the resulting tension draw her body taut. Yet she didn't break her pose or try to dissuade him.

Warmth built in his chest. This woman, this spectacular woman, knew what he needed and was willing to give it, no matter the cost to herself. She had to know by now that he wouldn't bring her harm. Her fingers flexed against one another while she waited. Quickly, he squatted behind her and fastened the first strip of leather around her slim wrist and repeated the procedure with the other, then secured both ankle cuffs—for later. Her breathing accelerated as he clipped the two wristbands together, catching the chain in the clasp. He drew the links down and threaded them through a loop hidden within the thick carpet before bringing the end back to her wrists and connecting it.

He leaned forward until his lips were at her ear. "Try to get away."

She complied, yanking on the chain. It rattled but didn't budge.

Perfect.

Gently, he pushed her forward. The chain kept her upright while it crept between her ass cheeks. His cock grew unbearably hard. He wanted to take her there but not yet, not before he fucked her sweet mouth. But first, one more thing…

Returning to the bed, he retrieved the tiny clips he'd left there. The tiny bells on them tinkled as he swept them into his palm. They'd shake and chime as she strained for him. Watching Keera's eyes, he clamped a clip to the base of each of her nipples. She cried out at the first then dug her teeth into her lip. She groaned working against the chains that held her and shaking with the sensations taking her. Her eyes squeezed shut, her lips moving in silent words as the tiny bells jingled frantically.

He squeezed his hand up his shaft while he watched her, imagining the feel of her around him.

"Keera," he growled. Her eyes flew open at she stared up at him, her eyes glazed from her arousal. He stepped toward her. "Take me," he ordered. He didn't help her, knowing she was close enough to reach him. She strained upward, moaning and fighting the chains as they stimulated her. Her lips closed around him.

"Yes," he groaned as heat flooded up his shaft and into his groin. His fingers threaded through her hair as he guided her, needing her heat surrounding him. She sucked her mouth tight around him, flattening her tongue on the head of his cock. Swirling, flattening, sucking she tormented the tip, refusing to take more even as he fought for greater access. Suddenly, she tilted her head and took him deep, ripping a groan from him as she clamped around his length and drew backward. She scraped her teeth lightly along him, heightening the sensation as she immediately soothed him with her tongue.

His balls drew tight as he fought his building climax. He'd waited too long for this. He should have jerked off while she'd waited in the living room, then maybe he'd have a grasp on his reputed control.

His fingers tightened in her hair as he drove in and out of her mouth, the helpless aroused sounds she made vibrating along him. The bells on the nipple clamps rattled in a wild frenzy. He couldn't hold out much more. His muscles twitched as he fought to prolong the agony. It was either pull out or explode and there was no way humanly possible he could force himself to leave her warm, damp mouth even for the promise of her burning pussy.

"Keera…I…" he gasped.

"Yes," she moaned around his cock, clamping down harder and pressing her tongue along the vein at the underside of his shaft.

Damn, where had she learned to give head?

"Keera!" he bellowed, letting loose in an eruption that blasted the back of her throat and jolted through him, hollowing out his being. His knees nearly buckled.

Keera calmly continued to suck and lick his rapidly depleting staff, draining him of every last drop. Finally, she leaned back and licked her lips, her expression completely self-satisfied.

"Witch," he rasped.

She blinked at him innocently, looking as smug as if she were free and he was in chains. "I was only following directions, Master."

"I think you might need another flogging."

That struck fear in her eyes and she looked away without protesting. He didn't say anything to relieve her worry. When would she learn to completely trust him?

Unhooking the chain that held her to the floor, he freed her hands, leaving the cuffs around her wrists. Carefully, he lifted her into his arms and carried her to the bed. Her creamy flesh stood out in stark contrast to the black satin sheets and though he wasn't a photographer, he knew someday he'd take pictures of her like this. Despite her worry, her arousal was evident. She shifted restlessly on the sheets, pressing her thighs together as she tried to fight her need.

His cock stirred. While she writhed, he slipped on a very special cock ring he'd kept on the table beside the bed. He had to get it on quickly before she sent him out of control again and it became impossible.

"What is that?" she breathed as he slid the seven rings into place, locking the last around his balls. He adjusted the leather holding the custom-fitted array together. The pain as he engorged would be exquisite and the pleasure for both of them unbelievable.

"The gates of hell," he answered.

Her eyes went wide. "For which of us."

"Perhaps both."

"Sweet heaven…"

"Can't save you now." He attached her wrist and ankle cuffs to the restraints on the four corners of the bed. Already, his staff swelled against the titanium rings circling him. "Now about that flogging."

Her slightly parted folds and upper thighs glistened with her arousal. "Please Theo, no. I can't take another flogging."

"How badly do you want me to fuck you?"

Her lips parted as she struggled to breathe around her need. "I need you. Please. Theo."

"Then you'll take it. Close your eyes."

She whimpered but complied, even as she went stiff. He almost took pity on her. Almost. Opening the drawer in the bedside table, he removed the "whip". He trailed it over her stomach, letting her feel the soft slide of fabric. This toy, a bundle of silk scarves gathered into a handle, would torment her but wouldn't come close to hurting her, which was exactly his plan.

She trembled, yanking on her restraints. He brought back his hand and flung the silk over her breasts. Her nipple clamps tinkled. Much as he loved their sound, it was time for them to come off. He pulled off the first and caught the rapidly plumping flesh in his mouth as she cried out from the sudden pain of blood rushing to the area. Her cry soon segued into a moan as she strained toward him. He paid meticulous attention to the hard little bud, then repeated the procedure at her other breast.

His focus divided between her pleasure and the pressure building on his cock. The rings that once fitted almost loosely now started to bite into his growing flesh and ready him for the long session ahead. He wouldn't find relief until after she'd collapsed beneath him and he removed this thing.

He plied the flogger to the inside of her thighs, each time dragging it across her cleft. The silk grew damp with her juices. It connected more solidly with her skin but he took care to build her arousal with the sensation. There would be no pain for her, only unspeakable craving. Abandoning the simulation of punishment, he climbed onto the bed and straddled her hips. His metal-clad cock thumped her belly as he trailed the ends of the silk over her chest and up her neck. Her arms trembled as he teased her sensitive inner arm.

"Please, Theo," she begged.

Silently, he slithered the fabric over her closed eyes. Her nose quivered and he pulled the ends over her mouth and nose. He leaned forward, smelling her on the cloth. Gently, he kissed her through the thin silk, urging her lips apart, almost tasting her. He met her veiled tongue, plunging his against it.

Need superseded all else. Never ceasing his kisses, he grabbed a condom from the drawer where he'd kept the silk flogger and rolled it over his tormented cock. Shifting between her thighs, he slid a hand beneath her and lifted her hips. Slowly, he slid into her clenching sheath, his teeth gritting as she squeezed his already squeezed flesh. It really was the gates of hell. He would die.

"Oh God, Theo," she cried, as each ridge slipped inside her.

"Call me Master," he rasped through his teeth. Oh God, it was too much. The burn of his release surged up his shaft, going nowhere. Spasms racked him, while little release occurred. He moaned in blissful agony. This could go on for an hour more.

"Master," she gasped as he plunged forward. He had to be completely inside her, only inside her tight sheath did any relief occur. "Oh please," she begged twisting beneath him.

"Fight me," he whispered. "Try to get away."

She immediately contracted around his tortured cock. Twisting beneath him she yanked at the chains holding her, the metal rattling against the iron bed. "Let me go," she demanded. Urgently, her hips surged into his as he fucked her. "Let me go. Let me…oh Master," she wailed, arching beneath him. Her legs fought the little give in her restraints and clamped against his. Relentlessly, he plunged into her fisting channel, taking whatever relief he could.

"Theo," she wailed, going stiff. A few heartbeats later, she rejoined his rhythm. Her broken cries joined with his grunts to fill the room. Slowing, he laved her breasts. In turn, he sucked each peak deep in his mouth. Her fight renewed. "Let me go so I can touch you."

"You're my slave," he managed. "You are for my pleasure. Giving you pleasure is my pleasure. Feeling your body squeeze me is my pleasure." He bit the upper curve of her breast. "Milk me, Keera. Pull my come from me. Now Keera. Take it now."

She screamed as he drove deep, her body erupting around him as her muscles became a vise. "Milk me," he whispered again as the metal rings caught on her muscles yet didn't budge from their positions around his cock. The ring around his balls seemed to tighten as they fought for release and locked the cage tighter around him. An unbearable burn rocketed up his cock while a corresponding explosion scalded down his legs and up his back.

Breathing hard, he knew neither of them was finished. "Again."

"No," she moaned, canting her hips up even as she uttered her denial. He squeezed her over-sensitized nipples, reveling in the shuddering cries wrung from her. He barely had to move, as she flexed beneath him taking him in and out with her confined movements. Kneeling up, he reached down and unclipped her ankle restraints. Her legs immediately wrapped around him as she slammed her pelvis up to him.

Mesmerized, he watched the play of muscles beneath the smooth skin of her belly as she worked. He trailed his hands over them before he clasped her hips. One more time… She was already spent. Perspiration covered her body like tiny translucent pearls. Her hair clung to her face and neck in wild, wet curls.

His sweat dropped onto her belly, streaming over her undulating muscles toward her breasts as she worked. He'd never had a partner who could meet him so perfectly in his personal battlefield. She wasn't the least put off by any of it.

"Fuck!" she screamed as her heels dug into his ass and her cleft flooded around him. The tip of his cock blazed as his body begged for release. Driving deep, he sought it, knowing relief was found only in Keera, perfect Keera.

# Chapter Three

Keera stirred, looking around the unfamiliar room where she'd slept. Theo had carried her in here sometime after he'd pried that wretched wonderful device off his cock. She was a little fuzzy on that and a little less fuzzy on the gentle way he'd loved her body once he'd brought her into his bedroom. Good Lord, the things that man knew. He wore her out. She'd always laughed about people's claims to passing out after sex but she had to admit, that's what she'd done. She didn't remember him removing his condom or pulling this thick down comforter over her.

She giggled. He really had fucked her senseless.

Her stomach growled and she carefully eased her way from beneath his heavy arm. Pulling on his T-shirt, she headed for the kitchen. Her body ached in places she didn't even know she had. She wasn't so sure she'd be able to walk comfortably for a week.

Absently, she rubbed her wrists vaguely remembering Theo removing the cuffs from around them and rubbing lotion into the chafed skin. He'd kissed the insides of her wrists and mentioned getting different cuffs with fur inside them. Hours later, the skin still appeared raw.

A huge smile bloomed across her face. She and Theo had been a little vigorous. No wonder she was starving.

Grabbing an apple from the bowl on the counter, she opened the huge refrigerator and surveyed the contents. She took a bite of the apple and shook her head. He was rich, had a kitchen any chef would die for and he still managed to stock the place like the typical bachelor. They'd have to go shopping for food. Two people couldn't live on beer, questionable condiments and stale-looking cheese. She wasn't sure she wanted to chance the contents of the take-out containers either.

Well, at least there was fruit and a lone pair of Cokes in the back of the fridge. She pulled out one bottle and cracked it open. She might survive for a couple more hours. Discarding the apple core, she hobbled into the living room with her drink and considered taking some aspirin before her aches segued from pleasant reminder to nagging annoyance.

She dug through her purse, searching for the pills. From necessity, it was a voluminous bag, holding more than any purse should. She never knew when she'd be on the run again. Carrying personal provisions with her was important. She pulled out the tarot cards and set them on the table to get them out of the way while she hunted for the bottle. Finally, her fingers closed around the container. She threw back to of the aspirin with a fizzy Coke chaser.

Setting aside her purse, she focused on the cards. Would a reading be different now that she was with Theo? She leaned forward and folded back the cloth. The Four of Wands stared up at her. She hadn't reshuffled it into the deck before she and Theo had left the cabin. It wasn't a sign, just an oversight. She flipped the card over and pulled the worn stack into her hands. Deep in thought, she shuffled.

* * * * *

His arms were empty. Panic rifled through Theo as he snapped awake, Keera's name on his lips. No. She'd run again. This morning—the playroom—had been too much. He'd driven her over the edge.

Throwing back the comforter, he stumbled from bed and yanked on his jeans. He couldn't let her go. He just couldn't. Even if he had to change. His eyes squeezed shut. He didn't know if he could.

He dragged his hands over his face. He needed to calm down and think. Where would she go? How would she go?

Her car wasn't here. She could have called a cab. Well, he'd call and find out where it had taken her. Money talked. He'd get answers and she'd be back at his side and under his protection before her stalker found her.

What if she didn't want to be with him? Running spoke clearly—especially this time. Could he let her go? Could he take the chance her stalker would hurt her? His stomach lurched. If that bastard hurt her, he'd kill him.

He dodged around her luggage—she'd been in that big of a hurry?—and rushed down the hallway, haunted by the memory of carrying her down it a few hours ago.

"Keera, where are you going?" he muttered as he headed for the front door.

"Hey, I'm right here," she said quietly.

He jerked around, finding her curled in the corner of one of the couches, a drink beside her and those weird cards in her hands. She set them on the table and stood.

"I'm sorry. I didn't mean to scare you. I—I was hungry and then—"

He tugged her into his arms, kissing her as if he hadn't seen her for a year and never would again. His mouth devoured hers while she touched his cheeks, stroked her hands into his hair. He needed to taste her, he needed the contact and reassurance. Neither of them had showered and the smell of their sex rose around him, enflaming him for more. Mostly, he needed to hold her until he was sure she'd never want to let go.

He'd never been so needy. He ruled his world, wielding his power over hundreds of lives and she broke him in half.

"I'm sorry," she whispered between kisses. "I promised I wouldn't go… I don't want to go. God, Theo, I don't ever want to be without you."

"I thought I'd scared you away. What we did—"

"Are you kidding? Your chains don't scare me." She bit his bottom lip and rubbed against him. Holding him tightly, she looked up at him with her soulful green eyes. "They're hot. They make *me* hot."

The pain of rejection that had filled him for years crumbled under the furious truth written on her face. He'd barely realized he'd had that feeling. Sure, he'd always known he didn't quite fit in. Too many people had left him, too many people had rejected his way of life, for him to believe otherwise. But he'd always stayed strong and accepted it as his reality…until Keera. He didn't care how weak anyone believed him. He craved her acceptance and yes, her submission to him, more than anything else in his life.

"What were you doing?" he asked.

"Eating an apple. Then I took some aspirin—"

"A little sore?"

She smiled, kissing his jaw. "Pleasantly. Then I was mostly waiting for you to wake up." She sniffed and wrinkled her nose. "I didn't even shower because I didn't want to bother you."

"I would have loved waking to the sound of you in the shower. I would have joined you." He could have guaranteed washing wouldn't have been the only affair taking place. He slid her shirt up enough that he could cup her naked ass and pull her toward him. "So Ms. Thornton, it's the middle of Saturday afternoon. What are your plans for the rest of the day?"

"Well, you know, I've met this guy—"

His fingers tightened even though he knew she was talking about him. "Should I be jealous?"

"Nah. But it might be over between us real fast if he doesn't feed me. That apple isn't gonna cut it. I'm a real woman and it takes some effort to maintain these curves. I need more than fifty calories to sustain me or I might expire."

"Well we can't have that," he laughed. "Will pizza do and we can buy groceries tomorrow?"

"Extra cheese?"

He nuzzled her ear. "Only if you sleep with me tonight."

She made a "well duh" sound in her throat. "I thought that was a given. My stuff is in your room."

And it would stay there.

Her stomach growled and he stepped back, laughing. "I better order that pizza. Anything you don't like?"

"Delays. I get cranky when I'm hungry."

"Really? I hadn't noticed." He tilted her head up and kissed her, then swatted her ass and stepped away. "Don't get cranky with your master, slave."

"Yes, Master." Her lips twitched. He thought maybe she was debating whether or not to bite him. D/s aside, if she didn't eat something soon, he was in big trouble. He'd seen this side of her before…right before she'd fired off an email to his father telling him exactly what he could do with his monthly personnel reports. That had taken some smoothing. Theo had taken her to lunch and gently recommended she forget about her current diet.

If her stalker were to show, now would be the time. She'd eviscerate him.

"I'll order breadsticks too. Play solitaire or whatever that was you were doing. After the pizza order, I'll call my lawyer and see if he has any updates." He backed away, unbelievably happy to have her in his life, even with her hungry moods. "Drink your Coke."

Solitaire? How hard was it to recognize tarot cards? Keera took a deep breath, forcing back her irritability. She hated when she got like this, especially when it came on suddenly. If she kept it up, Theo might consider chaining her for an entirely different reason.

She sank onto the couch and started shuffling the cards again. She'd seen Theo's look. He was remembering that crazy incident with his father. She'd never live that down. She'd been a complete beast. Rabid. Thank God, Theo had gone to bat for her. She didn't know what he'd said but Mr. Cress had sent her a box of chocolates that afternoon.

Her stomach growled again and she chugged a few gulps of soda. Theo appeared from the kitchen and jabbed a package of Oreos her direction while he "Um-hmmed" into the phone. She hardly needed the *whole* package. She took two. Theo frowned and handed her two more.

"Trust me," he mouthed.

*Whatever.*

He made another I'm-listening sound into the phone. It was his lawyer, she supposed. Good. That meant pizza was on the way since Theo had called them first.

She twisted open a cookie. Looking pointedly at his fly, she flattened her tongue over the cream filling and swiped upward. Theo's eyes narrowed and he swallowed. Dropping the package on the coffee table, he plucked the cookie from her fingers and tossed it over her shoulder. *Uh-oh.* His eyes intent, he shoved her against the back of the couch. Straddling her legs, he reached for his zipper, all the while listening to his lawyer.

Her breathing caught. No. He *wouldn't*. Not while he was talking on the phone. She shoved his hand aside and pulled his cock free. Cupping his ass, she pulled him toward her and he braced his free hand on the wall above her head.

Gently, she licked his hardening length. The abused flesh was still red from that hell thing he'd put on it. Damn, that had felt good. Looking at his shaft, however, she wondered if they shouldn't rethink ever using it again. It wasn't up to her. She was the slave. There for his pleasure and all that…

Geez, she was cranky. She cradled his balls in her hand, running her thumb along the underside of his arousal. Could she make him come again before the pizza arrived?

"Okay, well, I'll let her know," he said into the receiver. Clicking the off button, he tossed it onto the couch.

"You didn't say goodbye," she laughed.

He prodded her lips. "Stop talking."

She laughed, biting him gently. "Mmmm, yum. A Theo kebab."

She sucked him into her mouth, swirling her tongue over the head of his cock. She squeezed him lightly and weighed his balls in her hand. How she loved them slapping against her, especially when he took her from behind. If she bent across the couch, would he do it again? She wasn't so sure she could take anything but the gentlest loving right now.

Detouring from his cock, she nibbled her way to the base of his arousal and across his groin to the sharp curve over his hip. He had the most beautiful body and this part of him turned her on every time she saw him without a shirt. She opened her lips along the hard ridge, investigating it with her tongue.

He dug his fingers into her hair. "Keera," he warned.

She moaned as her cleft began to tingle. Her legs drifted apart and the T-shirt rode up around her waist. Her fingertips plowed through her dewy folds as she worked her mouth back across his abdomen. She dipped her tongue into the indent of his navel at the same time she worked two fingers inside her pussy.

*Mmmm…yes.*

The doorbell rang and he thunked his head against the wall. "Damn it," he swore, under his breath. He sighed. "I paid extra for the quickest delivery they could get me."

"That was fast."

"They're a minute down the road."

She sat back, pulling her fingers from her cleft and tucking his cock inside his unzipped pants. "Thank goodness. I'm starving."

He grabbed her hand. Watching her, he licked her juice from her fingers while the doorbell rang again. "You know you're gonna pay for this later?"

"I sure hope so."

Standing her looked down at her. She knew what he'd see. Her shirt hiked around her hips, thighs sprawled open. She started to close them but he stopped her with a palm on either knee. "Don't move an inch," he commanded.

"But—" The delivery person might see her if Theo let him inside.

He pressed a finger over her mouth. "Are you arguing with your Master?"

She pressed her lips together and shook her head. Well maybe she was… She wasn't so sure she wanted some pimply-faced kid eying her up and going back to the shop to tell his friends. She flexed her fingers into the couch as Theo went to the door. This pizza had better be damned good.

The door swung open before he reached it.

"Theo, for God's sake what's taking so long? Are you okay? I heard from Ryan—Oh, hello… Oops."

"Damn it, Josh," Theo swore.

She closed her eyes, not moving despite her intense humiliation. Theo couldn't even shield her body, since he was halfway across the room. Josh got a huge eyeful before he looked away.

"Uh, hi Keera."

"Josh," she said through her teeth. She sighed and opened her eyes. It was too late to hide now, though hightailing it into the other room seemed like a really good idea.

"Don't move," Theo said over his shoulder, reading her thoughts or perhaps hearing her shift as she prepared to flee.

"Theo," she breathed. He shook his head, stalling her protest with a hard look. Oh right…he was the master and she was his…to display if he wanted. Anger seethed inside her and she considered options for retribution. Her biggest option stood just inside the doorway. She wasn't sure she could. She knew without his saying so that Theo would be pissed if she invited another man's attention.

He stepped between them. A huge brick wall hiding her from Josh wouldn't have been enough to make her feel better. It was one thing to be like this with the man she loved, it was another to have his brother covertly checking her out.

Theo crossed his arms and stared at his brother. "Don't you have a computer to hack? Why are you here?"

Josh crossed his arms and glared back. "You weren't so upset about hacking yesterday, when you needed to find Keera."

Theo lifted a shoulder. As much as he was making her stay still, he was apparently furious at the intrusion. She hated when she got this make-me-care attitude. It meant an explosion was sure to follow, unless he was defused. Poor Josh…

It might be good for her though.

The tiny ring in Josh's eyebrow vibrated as he stuffed back his own anger. "I was worried when you didn't answer your phone. Some guy's been skulking around the office. After what Ryan told me, I thought you might want to know and since I know your security code so I thought I'd buzz over and fill you in."

Theo's arms dropped. "What do you mean 'skulking'?"

His entire demeanor changed and Keera could almost believe he'd forgotten she sat mostly naked behind him. *She* almost forgot.

Cary was snooping around Cress Construction? That meant he probably knew who Theo was. Fear shot through her. If he knew Theo's identity, Theo was in more danger than she'd thought. Disregarding his order, she stood and wrapped her arms around his waist, pressing her face into his back. Theo reached behind with one arm and held her to him.

"Tell me what you know," he told his brother.

"I was working—not hacking. *Working*—and the security warning went off on my desktop. I figured someone had forgotten their ID to get into the building but I'd never seen the guy on the camera. Big guy, long stringy hair, a little wild around the eyes...maybe, you know him Keera?"

Theo's arm tightened. "And?"

"Well, duh, I called the cops. Seemed the thing to do given the situation and his claiming to be you."

"What?" Keera exclaimed.

"Yeah, he must think we're real idiots. Unfortunately, he got a clue and took off before the police showed up. I've got him on camera trying to break in, though and the cops are on the lookout for him." Josh reached around Theo and stroked his hand over Keera's hair. "I was afraid for you and your treasure. We all are."

She looked up at him in surprise.

"Don't look so shocked. You're part of our family now. Our ways might be foreign to you but we'll all protect you. No matter what. You belong to Theo, you belong to all of us." He grinned. "In a platonic way. I don't think Theo will let any of us sample that tasty clit of yours, though I could recommend a guy who'd be good at piercing it."

"Josiah," Theo growled giving his brother a shove. He turned slightly and kissed her. "Welcome to my dysfunctional family."

"I'm not dysfunctional. Everything works just fine," Josh laughed, heading for the door.

"Wait." Theo called. "Be careful. If he's after me, he might be out for anyone who can get to me. It would take him three seconds on the internet to find my family connections."

Keera stiffened. She hadn't considered the danger would extend beyond her and Theo. His whole family could be a target. His parents, his brothers and sister, her best friend—

"I'll warn everyone. Although...I don't think Ryan and Jessica will come up for air before Monday."

"I should go," Keera whispered.

"Like hell," both men exclaimed, demonstrating how very alike they were despite their contrasting appearances. Theo pulled her around into his embrace, locking his arms around her. "You're not going anywhere. Even if I have to chain you to my bed. Am I clear?"

"Yes," she answered, though running was number one on her to-do list at the moment. She wouldn't. Not after she'd seen Theo's reaction to her supposed departure earlier. It would rip him apart. What she should do and what he needed her to do warred within her. It was a short battle. She was bound to what he needed and what he commanded. She'd given her pledge.

"Yes what?" he prompted.

She bit her lip and looked over her shoulder at his brother. She didn't want to do this in front of him.

"Don't involve me in this," he said, holding up a hand. "I'm on his side."

She looked back at Theo. His gray-eyed gaze had never left her. He waited so patiently, she almost believed he'd wait forever while those eyes devoured her.

"Master," she added quietly.

A brow lifted. "What was that?"

"Yes, *Master*."

"That is so hot," Josh breathed. "I need to get me one of those."

"Get out," Theo ordered without looking at him.

"I'm gone. Watch your backs."

"I will, you know," Theo said after Josh had left and the security alarm was reengaged. "You're safe with me. I'm not going to let Cary hurt you."

"I'm not worried about me." She wanted to hit him. Didn't he get it? "He wants to hurt you. He wants to hurt the people I'm close to. He wants some nonexistent money I don't have and can't give to him."

He shifted, glancing to the side. "It exists."

"What?"

"My lawyer… That's what he was telling me earlier. He discovered your parents had inherited some money from a relative in England. They never claimed it for some reason and it's yours. A lot of money, Keera. Over a million."

Excitement thrilled through her. Maybe that tarot card was right. Her problems *would* soon be behind her. "Then I can give it to him and he'll go away."

"No, you can't. Jerks like him never go away. He'll only want more."

Her hopes shattered at her feet. Theo was right. Cary wouldn't be so easily dissuaded. He'd chased her for far too long to be satisfied with a few paltry dollars—that's what he'd probably call it. He wanted more. He wanted his pound of flesh. Her flesh.

She stared at the floor, her arms tight over her middle. So what if she gave herself over to him? It would be one person's life for many lives. What could he do to her that would be so much worse than what she'd been through the past five years? Her eyes closed. Hundreds of things. She'd have to chance it. For Theo. For the others.

"Theo, I—"

"Don't even think it." He lifted her chin, forcing her surprised gaze to him. "Don't you think I know you well enough to sense what's going in that head of yours? You can't save the world. And you can't give yourself to him. You're mine, remember? Mine to protect, mine to keep." He dragged his thumb over her bottom lip. "So stop thinking that way. This will work out. Your stepbrother is doing a fine job of digging himself into a hole. His stunt at Cress proves that. We've had a restraining order issued and Tom—that's my lawyer—has two investigators digging up information. Cary and his cop friend will be out of commission soon. Meanwhile…" He grinned a wicked grin that made her toes curl into the carpet. Her belly trembled with the unspoken promises on those lips. How did he do that?

"Yes?"

"Meanwhile, you'll be safely chained to my bed." He curled his finger beneath her collar and pulled her closer. "And completely at my mercy."

"Now?" she asked hopefully.

He shook his head. "We have to wait for the pizza. You've got cards. We could play strip poker… Winner answers the door."

She had a feeling he'd make sure she lost her clothes pretty quickly. "They're tarot cards."

"For telling the future?"

"Among other things."

He sat on the couch and pulled her to sit between his spread legs. She picked up the cards and leaned back against his chest. She shifted slightly to the side so he could easily see over her shoulder. He immediately took it as an invitation to feast on her neck.

"I was shuffling these when you came in earlier," she told him, trying her best to ignore the feel of his mouth nibbling toward her ear and his hand creeping up her middle.

She gave the cards one last shuffle, her fingers shaking and lifted up the top card. *Not again…* She sighed, the sound completely disgusted.

"What is it?" he asked.

She lifted up the card, showing a wedding celebration. "All the cards have different meanings. This one is the Four of Wands. I've been getting it a lot lately."

"It doesn't look bad."

"It's not. Generally, it means a celebration is in order. The cards have different meanings whether they're right side up or upside down. Usually good one way or no so good the other way. Not necessarily *bad*. It's just usually… Well, I guess sometimes it, can be bad… Or a warning."

He cupped her breast, rolling the nipple through the thin cotton. "And what does this card mean?"

What did it mean? How did he expect her to think when he was making her wet with her need of him? She pressed her thighs together and almost moaned at the intense zing that went through her. It wasn't supposed to work that way.

She stared at the card. "It's…um… This card is good whichever direction it's in. One way is better than the other but both are very good."

The card was kind of like sex. She thought of Theo bending her forward and taking her from behind, then sighed and remembered the way he'd taken her later from the front. Didn't matter if it was up or down, it was good either way.

He ran his tongue along the edge of her ear. She squirmed. Her fingers clenched around the deck while she tried not to crush the card she held up. The couple on the card blurred into one as Theo continued to mold and twist her nipple.

One. Unified.

If only…

"And which way is this card?" he whispered. He took the extra cards from her and set them aside. His free hand traced the crease between her tightly clenched thighs and she felt him shake his head. Grasping one knee, he pried her legs apart and pulled one over the top of his. "Is it down?" he asked, slowly trailing his fingertips along the inside of her thigh. "Or is it up?"

His hand didn't move nearly as slowly as it made a quick path toward her cleft. "Up or down?" he murmured mimicking his movement along her folds. His thumb flicked over her nipple in the same rhythm.

Up or down? She didn't care. It was in she wanted, as in his fingers plunging inside her. She moaned and tilted her hips. "Up," she managed. "It's always upright in my readings. The better of the two."

"And it means?" He traced the rim of her opening without dipping his fingers inside. The man was adept at driving her crazy. He stopped tormenting her breast and grabbed her hand as it traveled toward her clit. He held it against her belly.

"Still waiting for your answer, love."

Love? It was just a name. An endearment. No need to go all squishy inside—although his touch was doing that to her. "It doesn't mean anything," she said. "It's a mistake."

"A mistake? Why would you say that?"

"Supposedly, according to this…" She flicked the card onto the coffee table. "Everything's supposed to fall into place and I'll have cause for major celebration. I've already set the groundwork for life to be grand. I'll have freedom and yet a binding commitment."

Theo turned her in his arms, his liquid silver eyes burning her with their intensity. "Shouldn't you have a little faith? An ounce of hope? I don't think there's a mistake at all. This thing with Cary… It's ending," he ground out. "I'd end it today for you, if I could. And then everything will fall into place. That card is not some distant future. It's coming soon."

She wanted to believe him. She wanted it so badly she had to blink back her threatening tears. Freedom from the terror of the last five years danced just beyond her reach. If she willed it hard enough, would it come close enough to grasp?

"I never pictured you quite so mystical," she laughed. She couldn't deal with the possibility that she'd never regain her peace. "You believe in tarot cards."

"I believe what I know. I know you're not alone in this and Cary's going to trip up and he's going to be stopped. Your days of running and hiding are behind you forever."

"What if he tries to hurt you? What if he goes after someone in your family?"

"Then we deal with it. You're not running anymore." He tipped her sideways on the couch and lay over her, wedging himself between her legs. His parted fly rubbed her naked cleft, the friction prodding her need higher. How could she need him so badly at a time like this? Shouldn't she be planning how she'd move on and protect him? Instead she wondered if he could make her come before the pizza guy arrived.

Theo was her reassurance. He was the marble pillar supporting her while she endured the lashes from her world. Somehow, he'd become her shining knight, ready to wield his metaphorical sword against her enemies.

She rubbed her pussy against his groin. Right now she wanted to forget the metaphorical sword. She wanted his fleshy sword impaling her while she forgot everything but his hard body over her. She couldn't contain her needy cries as he reached between them to pull his cock from his pants. His knuckles brushed her folds and a burst of sensation shocked through her womb.

He stared into her eyes as he seated his cock at the mouth of her trembling channel. "As for that commitment—"

The doorbell rang.

With an agonized groan, he dropped his forehead to her shoulder. "The pizza's here," he muttered.

"Fuck the pizza," she growled.

"I'd rather fuck you but unfortunately—" The doorbell rang again. "He's not going away."

Keera rolled into a hypersensitive ball while he got up to get the pizza and pay the delivery person. She heard the sad sound of his zipper as he made himself decent on the way to the door. Why was his house just this side of Grand Central Station? At this rate, a plumber, a minister and his parents would show up before she and Theo could get on with it.

Practically yanking the box from the boy's hands, Theo returned quickly and tossed the pizza box on the table, smiling at her. "Now where were we?"

His hands went for his fly but Keera was distracted by a shadow moving from the hallway behind him. She screamed but it was too late to warn Theo. He collapsed while she sobbed his name. The man behind him laughed, lunging for her.

"No!" she screamed, scrambling backward across the couch. The corner of the wood table beside it gouged into the back of her leg. She kept moving. If she could get to the double doors, she could get help. Cary tossed aside the heavy object—a sculpture of some sort—he'd used to strike Theo.

*God, please let him be all right.* She'd never forgive herself. Tears blurred her vision as she ran for the door. Cary's fingers closed around her arm, his nails biting into her skin. The stench of his unwashed body surrounded her as he pulled her against him.

"Oh no," he chortled. "You're mine now, bitch."

"No," she cried, fighting as he dragged her across the living room and toward the hallway. No. She hadn't run for so long to have him take her like this. "Let me go. Please. You want money? I can get it. I know where it is now."

"Too late. I don't want the money anymore." He pressed her against the wall. His fingers dug into her breasts as he covered her mouth with his. She gagged at his putrid breath, tasting blood as her teeth cut her lip. She clawed at him. Fruitlessly, she shoved at his throat, tried to kick her knee into his groin, smashed her foot into his instep. He seemed impervious to any attacks.

Drawing back, he slammed his hand across her face. Stars erupted before her eyes and he started dragging her down the hallway again.

"You people are so stupid," he muttered. "Did you think I'd come in through the front door? All I had to do was wait.

As soon as the doorbell rang and the alarm was turned off, I came through the window. You know…the one in your lover boy's sex room. I bet you had fun playing in there this morning. Will you make that much noise with me?"

He'd listened? Revulsion and fury warred through her. He wouldn't get away with this. She realized suddenly that he was pulling her into Theo's playroom. In an instant the room turned from adventure to horror.

"Imagine my surprise when you two actually showed up at the house I'd been watching. That room is a sadist's palace. I never realized you were into that, Keera. We'll have some great fun together."

"No," she begged, letting her weight sag away from him. "You won't get away with this. Just let me go. I'll give you the money. I'll go away.

"Stop it," he yelled, shoving her into the doorframe. The hollow thunk of her head against the wood pulled on her stomach. She was going to vomit. Yanking her around, he threw her backward toward the bed. Her arms windmilled as she desperately tried to get her balance and run. Cary was on her in an instant, forcing her onto the bed and shoving up the T-shirt. "I'll show you who you belong to."

He would not rape her. She punched him as hard as she could and his blood showered down on her, the burning droplets like fire on her cheek. He was stronger than she was but she wouldn't comply with anything. She tried to twist away from him and he wrenched her onto her stomach, pressing her face into the mattress. She screamed, sobbing as she tried to pull her hands from where he held them above her head and do anything she could to keep him off her. His body was heavy on her back. She couldn't breathe—

A bellow of rage thundered across her senses. Suddenly, Cary was gone. As she struggled upright, she heard a crash behind her followed by grunts and wet, meaty smacks. She turned to find Theo straddling Cary, his fists pummeling into him.

"Theo," she gasped. She stumbled toward him. She dropped to her knees beside him and reached toward him. He'd kill Cary if she didn't stop him. "Theo. Stop. Please. Stop."

He didn't listen, shaking her off when she tried to grab for him. She dove for him, pulling him backward. He turned, wrapping her in his arms. His eyes cleared a moment before he buried his face in her neck. "Keera. Oh my God. Are you all right? I'm sorry. I— Are you hurt? When I saw him— When I saw—"

A stampede sounded behind her before he could finish and she could answer. Four police officers flooded into the room, followed by his brother.

"Freeze!" the first yelled, leveling his gun at them. Keera furrowed her brow in confusion. Shouldn't they be stealthier? Why the hell was he pointing his gun at Theo?

Theo stood slowly, holding out his hands.

"She's hurt," he said. "By him. He broke in."

"Who are you?" the one in the lead questioned.

"Theo Cress. This is my house."

The gun shifted to Cary and Theo crouched beside her again, gathering her to him. The questioning officer called in the report and requested an ambulance. One cuffed Cary, while he muttered incoherently.

"Are you okay? When I came to and heard him… He didn't— You are okay, right?"

She'd never seen him so undone. He trembled as he held her, his body a protective shell around her. Aches were blooming across her body and she drew a shaky breath. She'd been acting on adrenaline. How badly had Cary hurt her?

"I think—" She struggled to breathe, her torso burning where she'd been slammed into the doorframe.

"Look at this place," she heard. Another officer made a noncommittal sound.

"Mr. Cress, I'm afraid you'll need to come with us as well."

"Theo," she cried, wrapping her arms as tightly as she could around his waist. One seemed a bit weak. She grasped it with the opposite hand, holding it around him.

He slid his hand into her hair and pressed his forehead to hers. "Call my lawyer. My brother there will get the number for you. I'm going with her. If you want to talk to me, talk to me at the hospital."

Fear wound through her. She knew how the room would look to an outsider. They couldn't arrest Theo. He hadn't done anything wrong. He'd saved her.

Theo tried not to crush Keera as he held her to him. Thank God, the windows were on a different alarm system from the doors and the police had been alerted immediately.

"I need you with me," she whispered. He wasn't going anywhere. Nothing would drag him from her side before he knew she was okay. He could barely catch his breath after the terror that had gripped him. Hard as he tried to calm down, his heart still raced inside him.

Everything had been fine, then Keera's scream. Pain had flooded through him, exploding at the base of his skull. When the darkness cleared he'd heard Keera's cries from the back of the house. Rage had driven him. He barely remembered tearing Cary from her and tossing him to the floor. Had he killed the man? No. The asshole was moaning. He scowled unsure whether or not that made him happy. Cary had been about to rape Keera. Theo had snapped.

His chest constricted again.

"Josh, call Tom," he instructed. He might need his lawyer. "Call the doctors' emergency line."

His brother nodded, his piercings dark against his ashen face.

"I'm going with her," Theo bit out. "I'll sue every one of your asses if you try to stop me."

No one would stop him from going with her. Keera needed him there. She shuddered in his arms, her tears still flooding over her cheeks while she clung to him. Gently, he ran his hand through her matted hair. Damn, she was just *covered* with blood. He wanted to wipe it from her and drag her into the shower to erase her stalker from her. He didn't dare. It could be evidence.

The officers looked at one another. "We do need her statement."

In the distance, he heard the ambulance blaring down the road. So did Keera. "Don't leave me."

"I won't. Josh, will you go get her a robe from my bedroom?"

Josh nodded and disappeared down the hallway, skirting around the pair of officers escorting Cary from the room. The man swore profusely and tried to yank away. A picture slammed to the floor in a crash of glass as they redirected him.

Theo held Keera a little tighter. He'd almost lost her.

"I don't want to go to the hospital. I'm fine," she muttered. "I just want everyone to go."

Theo ignored her assertion. She was going to the hospital whether she liked it or not. He helped her into the robe Josh brought back then lifted her into his arms. "We need to be sure you're okay." He leaned close to her ear and whispered, "I'd be a poor master if I let anything happen to my slave."

She went still then turned her face into his neck. "Okay," she murmured. "Whatever you say."

After a brief negotiation with the ambulance technicians about who would ride in the vehicle and where—Keera refused to lie on the stretcher no matter what he said but finally, the EMTs forced her onto it—they sped to the hospital, arriving less than fifteen minutes later. The hospital staff tried to bar him from accompanying her to the room but Keera raised such a fuss, they let him. He immediately dismissed her earlier willful behavior, pleased that this bout worked in his favor.

Unfortunately one of the cops accompanied them as well. Theo answered questions relating to Cary and the break-in as well as several questions about his home that in his opinion shouldn't have been asked. Whose business was it that his sexual practices leaned toward BDSM? Still, he carefully skirted the subject answering only enough to keep from being deemed difficult and outright lying that the equipment was for Pleasure Palace. The cop wasn't buying it and kept asking questions.

The physician, Dr. Manning, entered just as the questions turned to Keera. Keera started answering the same inquiries about Cary, going more in depth about the background of the situation. The officer's pen flew over the paper, his frown deepening as she elaborated on the lack of help she'd received and Cary's means of finding her.

She trembled with the emotion of it, though she was stronger than Theo would expect from anyone else who'd gone through such a trauma. He longed to go to her and wrap her in his arms and make her feel safe. Would she actually feel safe? He'd let Cary get to her.

A knot twisted his stomach. He'd failed her.

"Did Mr. Thornton mention this individual's name?" the officer asked.

She shook her head. "No. He just told me it was his drinking buddy who was a cop."

"And how did you come to know Mr. Cress?"

She looked at Theo and her green eyes like damp moss. She bit her lip then winced as it started to bleed again. Hastily she wiped away the blood with the back of her hand. Watching her so hurt and unable to fix it was tearing him apart. He forced his gaze away.

She drew a harsh breath and he knew suddenly he'd unintentionally hurt her. Damn it. He was an ass. A weak foolish ass. He looked back at her but it was too late.

She stared at her hands. "I work for Theo—um, Mr. Cress—at Cress Construction. For six months."

"And in that time, have you ever had reason to fear Mr. Cress?"

Keera stared at the officer, aghast. When had Theo become the bad guy?

"No," she answered indignantly.

"Has Mr. Cress abused you in anyway?"

Her gaze frantically flew to Theo. My God, how could this man ask this? Cary had hurt her, not Theo. Some people might misunderstand what was between them but—

"No."

"You hesitated. Are you sure, Ms. Thornton?"

"*Yes*, I'm sure."

The cop looked unconvinced. He tapped his pen on his paper and looked slowly at Theo whose face was slowly filling with fury. He turned back to Keera. "Are you afraid in any way to answer these questions with Mr. Cress present, ma'am?"

"That's quite enough," the doctor snapped.

"Would you feel more comfortable if Mr. Cress left?" he continued.

Keera's fingers curled into the edge of the table. She'd feel more comfortable if they'd all allow her to go home. "No. I want Theo here."

The cop sighed. "Ms. Thornton. Does Mr. Cress have any sort of hold over you?"

Her brow furrowed. What? Why were they asking all these things? Theo wasn't the bad guy here.

"For God's sake," Theo swore, obviously just as irritated as she was. He crossed his arms over his chest and glared at the police officer. "Is this really necessary? I'm not the one who attacked her."

She needed to end this before Theo lost it and plowed his fist into the cop's smug face. She searched for the right words. She needed the cop to believe and leave them alone.

Deliberately, she studied Theo, her face tight with feigned distaste. She gave a little shake of her head and turned her head away. "No, Theo doesn't have any kind of hold over me."

She glanced back at him in time to see him briefly close his eyes, looking for all the world as if she'd slapped him across the face then crushed his balls beneath her foot. He quickly gathered himself and gave a single nod. He looked at the doctor.

"Take good care of her."

"Yes, sir," Dr. Manning answered.

He turned to Keera. One side of his mouth tried to lift in a smile but failed. He raised a shoulder. Her strong, powerful master was gone, leaving behind a desolate shadow. She saw a thousand words race across his face but he said nothing before shaking his head and turning away.

"Hey!" the cop exclaimed as Theo slipped from the room. He followed spluttering about questions.

"Theo," Keera whispered. He was deserting her? Now? Now when they could finally be together without the threat of Cary hanging over her head? He wasn't supposed to believe what she'd just said. The cop was. Didn't Theo know her better than that? What had she done? The bottom was falling out of the world she'd only just discovered. For the first time she'd been whole and oh God she loved him. Yet she'd managed to drive away the man she loved.

She levered herself up to jump off the table. She had to stop him.

"Ms. Thornton, please stay still so I can examine you."

"I need him here. He's my—" What could she say? Master? Not hardly. Not after the cop's interrogation. "Um…boyfriend. I need to go to him."

Dr. Manning raised an eyebrow and held her still, her cool expression melting into compassion. "Boyfriend? Stay put."

"But—"

"Stay." Leaving Keera's side, Dr. Manning peeked out the door. "It doesn't look like he's going anywhere. He's just pacing like a madman. Now let's check you out and get you out of here. So…" She picked up the clipboard. "Josh tells me you were thrown about a bit. At least your attacker's been arrested, huh?"

"Yes." She tilted her head. "You know Josh?"

"He called me. My partner and I treat the Cress family." She pushed the robe off Keera and lifted away her shirt. She didn't say anything for a moment. She reached out and lightly drew a finger over one of the stripes running horizontally across Keera's buttocks. It had been so long since the flogging, Keera had almost forgotten them. She winced—here came the questions.

"He did a nice job on these," Dr. Manning said quietly.

Keera looked over her shoulder in shock as the doctor palpated her back, looking for other injuries. The woman shrugged, amused.

"He's not your boyfriend. He's your Master."

It wasn't a question but Keera nodded. After the way Theo had left, though, she wasn't so sure. "How do you know?"

"I have stripes of my own. It's amazing isn't it? Unexpected?"

"I never thought I'd like it."

"It's the endorphins kicking in. They turn pain to pleasure, as long as you're mentally in the right place when it begins. I'm guessing your master had you properly warmed up."

Heat rushed through Keera as she remembered the ginger. Warmed up? Definitely. She'd never experienced anything like it. And later in the playroom… That man could warm her up like no other ever had. Or ever would. "Oh yes," she sighed. She glanced at the door. "I guess it's over now, though."

Dr. Manning made a disgusted sound. "Men are dumb sometimes. Yes even our masters. What did he expect? You couldn't say 'He's my master' and not end up getting him arrested on some charge like attempted slavery or something. That cop was itching for another arrest. Go home. Supplicate him. He'll be fine."

Keera wished she could believe it.

Dr. Manning helped her back into the robe, then handed her a card. "Things get sticky in the scene sometimes. If you ever need help, medically or otherwise, call me. I'll be happy to help you with questions. Now… I think you're just badly bruised. Let's get a few x-rays to be certain. I think a CT scan is in order too. I want to make sure there's no concussion from your impact. Then I think you'll be on your way and tucked safely back in your master's bed."

The x-rays and scan proved the doctor's opinion but didn't make her feel any better, especially when she found Jessica waiting for her instead of Theo.

He'd gone.

Black spots rushed before her vision and she gripped the back of the nearest chair. Silent sobs gripped her chest and she shook while her mind screamed, "No". He hadn't left her. It wasn't over. She was finally free. No one was chasing her, no one was threatening her, she could do whatever she wanted and all she wanted was to be in Theo's chains.

How would she survive?

"Keera," Jessica whispered, folding her in her arms. Keera held back. If she hugged her friend, she'd collapse. She wasn't the one she wanted to hug.

She tried to smile. Jessica looked...different. She also wore a necklace similar to her own. She reached out and touched it, wondering if she'd have to give hers back.

"Ryan?" she asked.

"Yes." Her slight grin mixed with her concern. "At your Pleasure Palace party."

"Gee, I must throw one heck of a party." She pushed her hand through her hair. It caught in the matted curls. She needed a shower. She needed a whole lot more than that. "Where's Theo?"

"He wouldn't tell me, just asked me to come and get you. Ryan's looking for him... We're both worried. Theo wasn't— He didn't sound like himself. I'm sure it will be okay." She sounded neither sure nor reassuring.

Keera sighed wearily. "Let's go then."

Where to? Her apartment? She wasn't sure she could face that emptiness. Even though she was happy for her friend, she couldn't face Ryan and Jessica's togetherness either. She needed to face Theo. There was only one place she could.

"Will you take me to Theo's house?"

Jessica hesitated. "Keera, I don't know—"

"I have to," she interrupted. She knew his code. Everything she wanted or needed was there. If he wasn't home, she'd wait. Then she'd convince him she didn't want to be anywhere but in his arms.

* * * * *

Theo wearily let himself into his house, disengaging the security alarm before it summoned the police again. He didn't want to deal with a return engagement. He didn't want to deal with anything. Except Keera and that was out of the question. That look in her eyes… Suddenly in the triage room it had all been clear. She'd needed his protection. She'd done what was necessary to get it, but she hated his lifestyle and was disgusted by him.

She'd rejected him, just like others had rejected him before her.

He'd driven for hours, unwilling to return to his empty house. It was a disaster too. Black dust coated the surfaces where the police had checked for prints and there was a gouge in one of the walls. The statuette Cary had hit him with must have bounced off it when he's tossed it aside.

Keera's cards were scattered over the couch. His heart twisted. She'd want them back. Even without her explaining why they were so important to her, he knew they were. He'd make sure to give them back to her… Maybe by then she'd have changed her mind—

He didn't deserve for her to change her mind. He'd failed her. He'd let Cary get to her and almost rape her. She'd seen the light and decided she didn't want such a horrible master, even if he did treasure her more than his own life. She had money now. She could travel or do whatever she wanted. He wanted to go with her and show her the world.

Slowly, he picked up the cards and put them in a pile on the coffee table. He stared at the Four of Wands for a long while before setting it aside. A good card either way it fell, huh? It had turned out well for her.

He ran his finger over the figure of the male celebrant. Lucky devil was uniting with his woman. Theo scowled. He wanted to be the one joining with Keera at the celebration.

Stupid fanciful thinking.

She'd made her decision. He'd thought she'd be the one who wouldn't ditch him like those others had. *Wrong again, Theo.* This sucked. He hadn't liked the desertions but he'd bounced back with barely more than a shrug. With Keera, he'd turned to concrete and shattered.

Maybe he'd take a trip, get someone to clean up the house, maybe even make a few changes. Keera was imprinted on the living room…the playroom…his bedroom.

He grabbed a beer from the fridge, circled back and grabbed a second and headed for his bedroom. Two beers wouldn't get him drunk but they'd give him a healthy buzz before he grabbed a few more. Avoiding the glass in the hallway, he stepped into his bedroom and almost dropped both bottles.

He set them on the dresser before they slipped from his fingers.

Keera knelt in the center of his bed, facing the door, rumpled silk sheets a nest around her naked body. She looked up and his heart caught. Bruises covered her face, matching the ones that mapped across her ivory skin. They angered him but it was her tear-ravaged eyes and swollen lips that killed him.

The pain on her face was unmistakable. It wasn't bodily pain. It was heart pain—emotional pain.

"What are you doing here?" he asked quietly, afraid to ask, afraid to hope but knowing he had to find out for sure. Her damp hair hung down her back—she couldn't be long from the shower. She'd been busy. Leather cuffs circled the wrists resting on her thighs and he could see the matching cuffs around her ankles.

She fingered the chain that draped across her thighs.

*I'm not afraid of your chains.*

"There's nowhere else I want to be." She swallowed and let out a harsh breath. "I'm finally free of Cary. With the money I have and the money I've apparently inherited, I can go anywhere. I'm free to do whatever I want."

She looked down, pulling the chain in her hands taut. "I don't *want* anything but to be with you. Am I a fool?"

"No." He practically dove for her, remembering at the last moment to slow before he hurt her. "I thought you were ending it."

Her lush curves pressed into him and she hugged him none too gently. "I know you thought that. It's not what I meant. You misunderstood—"

Kneeling in front of her, he cradled her head and brushed his lips as tenderly across hers as he could. He knew her lips hurt but he needed to kiss her. He needed her taste on his mouth. Keera moaned, opening. She darted her tongue against his and enticed him to take more. When he drew back, still holding her head, she smiled up at him. Blood pounded to his cock.

Her fingers curled into his waistband. She pulled him closer.

He cupped her ass and tilted her back onto the mattress. He needed inside her—to reassure himself she was still his. This was stupid. She was too sore for even a slow session. As long as she was in his arms, he'd be all right.

Keera had other plans. Her legs wrapped around his waist and she ground her mound into him. He groaned as she opened his fly and shoved down his pants.

"Are you trying to control me, slave?" he laughed, all the joy returning to his universe. His cock prodded her folds while her molten juices coated him.

She shook her head, denying it even as she shifted upward on his staff and took the head inside.

"Condom," he said under his breath. He wanted nothing more than to lose himself in her clenching passage and feel her flesh against his. But not if she wasn't ready for that.

She shook her head again.

"I love you," she said. "Forever."

"All of me? Chains, punishments and all? I'm not likely to change, even if I'd try for you." He sank to the hilt. It was dangerous but if he had to, he'd pull out and put on the rubber to lessen the damage.

Her eyes closed and she smiled, pleasure across her face. "I like you the way you are. Just the way you are. There's a lot more than chains and flogging and those are exciting, idiot. Master. I love all of you."

Life with her would be an unbelievable adventure. She was his. Forever.

"Insubordinate wench." Reaching between them, he pinched her clit. She clenched around his cock as she cried out, arching against his groin. Her heat flooded over him and straight into his heart. "I love you," he gasped. "I love you, Keera."

She filled all the empty spaces inside him and made his darkness all right. He turned so she was over him and she rode him, one hand pressed over his navel, the other clasping the place where the tattoo banded his upper arm. She was claiming those promises, fulfilling them and giving them new meaning.

She was his to protect. His treasure, his to own, his to keep…and his to make free. Forever.

# MASTER ME

# *Dedication*

*For Chuck*

# *Trademarks Acknowledgement*

The author acknowledges the trademarked status and trademark owners of the following wordmarks mentioned in this work of fiction:

Bollywood: HisKarma Productions, Inc.

Greyhound: Greyhound Lines, Inc.

## *Six of Pentacles*

Dear Reader,

The Six of Pentacles traditionally signifies generous giving and the resultant balance of power between the giver and receiver. It is often represented by a wealthy benefactor handing gold to beggars. Because of this, the card is most often interpreted in a financial sense. The significance of the Six of Pentacles in an interpersonal relationship, however, is on adjustments in thoughts and attitudes. It is also on giving and receiving kindness, knowledge and love. I have focused on the relational meanings of this card—after all, isn't the relationship the core of romance?

On the shadow side of this card is accumulated debt, greed, selfishness, underhandedness and exploitation. Again, these apply to both monetary and interpersonal relationships.

For years, Max has stood by and watched his friend Ana search for the person who will meet her emotional needs and though he's had the means to help her, he's protected his secret lifestyle rather than damage their friendship. While Ana is strong, she senses that there is a hole inside her that needs to be filled. She's vaguely aware of what she wants but is trying to fill her need with all the wrong men. Now she's chosen a man who will leave her even more emotionally impoverished and Max knows it's time to step in. Both Max and Ana have been experiencing different aspects of the shadow side of this card. Max has been selfish and even envious of the men in Ana's life. Ana has been accumulating one bad relationship after another, each stealing more and more of her soul.

Once Max decides to take their relationship to another level, the two are also the perfect embodiment of the upright Six of Pentacles. He is the benefactor and she is the beggar. He is the Dominant and she is the submissive. He will teach and she will learn. He will give and she will receive. But as with all giving, the beggar isn't the only one who receives. Gifts are bestowed on the benefactor as well. In accepting Max's power over her and taking what he offers, Ana will give him the fulfillment he has searched for all his life and satisfy his needs as only she can.

## *Author Note*

This book portrays some aspects of Domination/submission and BDSM but is not intended as a true-to-life account of this lifestyle.

# Chapter One

"No. I'm not at home. I'm at Max's." A laugh followed. "*Max*? No, he's not like that."

Max Cress frowned at the closed door separating him from his friend Anastasia Cooper. They'd been friends for years, she'd been to his house a million times yet she didn't know he could hear her conversation through the door? Or maybe, she just didn't care that he heard. After all, he was "just Max" who wasn't "like that". Wasn't like that? For fuck's sake. She always managed to make him sound like he didn't have a penis.

Not like that, indeed.

Brooding, he slouched back into the couch, his tense mood tipping toward bad. His frown deepened into a scowl. Ana was searching for a dominant man. Wouldn't she be surprised if she discovered exactly how "like that" he was? Wouldn't she be stunned by his carefully hidden nature?

"Sorry 'bout that," she said, coming through the kitchen door and flipping shut her cell phone. She shoved a long hank of curly black hair behind a slim shoulder, the dark, silky length a striking reminder of her gypsy heritage. Her black knit shirt lifted away from her matching skirt to reveal a thin strip of creamy belly. "Keera worries about me. After the message I left her last night, she wanted to check up on me."

"What about last night?" Max asked sharply. Ana seemed to be on a long string of dates with a parade of Mr. Wrongs. He tried not to interfere but it was damned difficult, especially when she went out with jerk after jerk. She was looking for the proverbial bad boy and instead just found bad.

"I was with Tyler."

Speaking of bad. Max's lips compressed. Tyler Awkes. The man traveled in Max's circle. Unfortunately. The man's behavior was notorious.

"And?" he asked. He'd tried to discreetly warn Ana away from the man but she'd seemed disinclined to listen. Tyler was just what she'd been looking for or so she'd said. Yes, he was a Dom and she was a submissive but Tyler was sadistic. He didn't care for his slaves. He took things to extremes that gave BDSM a bad name.

Ana, on the other hand, was new to the whole scene. She didn't know the ins and outs. She didn't know Tyler was little more than a bully. And how would Max know? To her he was just her friend, the laid-back artist. He'd had about enough. Ana was going to get hurt if she kept up this way and he wasn't about to let it happen. It was time someone took her in hand. Someone she could trust. Someone who knew the ropes. He smiled, cementing the decision he'd avoided for years. She'd enjoy his ropes. He'd show her exactly what she should look for in a man. And when they were done, she'd be prepared to kneel to a new master who was worthy of her devotion.

"And?" Max repeated, pulling out his most commanding Dom voice. It was time. It had been for a while yet he'd ignored the call, not wanting to damage their friendship. This superseded any worry. Ana was playing a game where she didn't know the rules.

"You know I agreed to be his slave—"

"No, I did not," he ground out. This was far worse than he'd thought. God knew what Tyler had done to her this week. Max knew the man's MO. He tricked unsuspecting women, being deceptively nice until they were sucked into his web. Then he crushed them, destroying their spirits.

Max curled his fingers into the couch. He took a deep breath through his nose as he controlled his temper. Tyler would not destroy Ana.

"Well, I did." Her fist clenched around the phone she still held. "Anyway, he wanted to take me to this club he goes to. He told me wanted me to prove my devotion to him by letting anyone there fuck me if they wanted to. In whatever way they wanted to."

Max's blood turned cold. Not his Ana.

"You didn't do it, did you?"

"He wanted me to—"

"Anastasia. You didn't do it, did you?"

"No. Of course not. I mean, I can accept he has other slaves. I don't like it but I can accept it. But I'm not doing that. He got really mad and tried to make me. He forced me into his car."

Max swore under his breath. Next time he saw Tyler he might kill the man.

She sank into the chair across from where he sat and shoved her cell in her purse. With a sigh, she gave a wobbly smile. "I told him I'm no longer his slave. I broke the contract."

She'd signed a fucking contract with that bastard? That would make it difficult for her. A slave couldn't just break an agreement. There were discussions…mutual arrangements. Of course with Tyler, Max could see a discussion would be pointless. Regardless, any future Dom would be leery of taking on a sub who theoretically belonged to someone else.

She swallowed. "Then he told me I'm not really a sub, that I'm just playing around. Maybe I'm not a sub if I can't even do something like this to please my master. If this is what it is—"

"The scene doesn't have to be like that."

"I guess I'm just not submissive material."

Right. And he didn't have a cock. The flesh in question shoved against the fly of his jeans making its vote known and telling him it wanted to sink deep inside Ana. Big surprise there.

"Either you are or you aren't," he said, looking straight into her sky-blue eyes. "You are."

She looked at him in surprise. "What would you know of it?"

He sat up. The master didn't explain himself. His temporary slave would soon learn that and much more. "First, Tyler isn't your master. He doesn't deserve to be called that by anyone. Second, in any D/s relationship, the submissive is allowed boundaries. Hell, *I* know your boundaries. He should have taken the time to find out what you like and what you don't. Before either of you agreed to anything, he should have known what you might do and what you absolutely won't. Did he ever ask?"

"No."

"Push up your skirt a little," he said suddenly, his tone relaxed as he eyed the black flippy skirt that she'd smoothed into place when she'd sat. He both loved and hated when she wore it. The light fabric danced around her legs when she walked, giving him teasing glimpses of her creamy thighs.

"What?" she exclaimed. His order visibly startled her, her eyes going wide. Nervously, she pulled her hem toward her knees. It was inches from touching.

He lowered his brows and added bite to his command. "Push up your skirt."

"No."

"No? Now, see? This is the kind of thing we've discussed. This is not on your boundary list. Pushing up your skirt for the man you're with is something you'd actually find sensual. Refusing to do it when it's something you've deemed okay is disobedient." He clamped down on the excitement unfurling inside him. This was where he'd cross the invisible line he'd placed between them all these years. "Now, come here."

"Max?" she whispered uncertainly.

"Come. Here." He spread his knees slightly and waited, striving to appear casual despite the blood pounding past his ears. There was nothing casual about what was about to happen. The days of ever-searching Ana and laid-back friend Max were over. Either he'd ruin a long-standing relationship or he'd take it to a new level.

She looked confused. Still, she got up and slowly walked toward him. He smiled as she again smoothed down her little skirt. That was unnecessary. He was about to get it all out of place.

Clasping her waist, he pulled her between his knees. She resisted too late, a flush creeping across her cheeks.

"Now bend," he told her.

Her brows shot up. "What?"

"*Bend*." He stared into her turbulent blue eyes, daring her to disobey.

"I don't—"

"Do it, Anastasia," he growled.

She jumped slightly then started to bend toward him. Quickly, he turned her, ignoring her shriek, positioned her across his knee and trapped her thighs between his. He held her in place with an arm across her back.

"Max. Let me up," she protested, twisting ineffectively.

"You see," he began. "I know what you've been looking for and I know the thought of this turns you on."

"Not with you."

"Oh, really?" He pushed up her skirt until it was bunched on her back, leaving her white panties visible. Hell. Prissy, white cotton panties. Nothing got to him, yet they nearly undid him. Unbelievable.

Ana went still as he smoothed his hand over the perfect globes of her ass. He'd wanted to spank her for so long—probably since she'd casually mentioned she thought it might be her fetish. As if she actually comprehended what a fetish was.

He inched down the cotton, revealing the upper swell of her ass. Now he, *he* had a fetish. It was called Ana's ass and he'd had it since the first time he'd seen her in short shorts, his freshman year of college. She'd still been a junior in high school. Untouchable. He'd let her remain that way all these years.

No more.

"Max, please don't," she whispered.

"You want me to, don't you?" He tightened the arm braced across her back. Tugging on her panties, he revealed another inch of perfect ivory skin. He hardened at the thought of it pinkened by his mark.

"Yes," she admitted. "But…we shouldn't."

"I disagree. I should have taken you in hand a long time ago. It would have saved me a lot of headaches while you've run around." At the thought of her with other men, he yanked the cotton to her upper thighs.

"Max."

Sweet heaven, her ass was beautiful.

"Silence, slave," he ordered.

"Max," she protested again.

"Silence!" He accompanied his order with a resounding smack across her firm buttocks. Ana cried out in surprise and immediately tried to squirm away. He held her still, leaning slightly on his arm and tightening his legs to keep her from kicking.

"Stay still and take your punishment for not listening to me." Smack. "You could have been hurt." Smack. With each fall of his hand, she muffled her cries. He rubbed his palm over her swiftly reddening ass. Pulling back, he again slapped her behind. This time, her groan broke loose. A distinctly aroused groan. Good. That was where he'd been heading with this. Pain was not his objective with this punishment. Soon, the heat from his spanking would travel from her rear and into her cunt. Then she'd be moaning her need as her cleft dampened his thigh. He resisted the urge to slide his fingers between folds and find her molten honey.

"Did Tyler ever spank you?" he asked, clapping his hand on her again.

"No," she managed around her groan.

"Has anyone?" He caught his next blow in the crease where her thighs met her ass.

"No. Oh God, Max. I—"

She needed him to touch her, probably as much as he wanted to. Not yet. He gave her ass a few more swats until she was sobbing her arousal as strongly as if he plowed his cock into her pussy.

"Did you fuck him?" he demanded.

She didn't answer. He tilted to look at her face but found it hidden behind a curtain of hair. His belly tightened, yanking at his groin. The sight of her inky locks pooled on his white carpet captivated him. He wanted to see her curls spread around her head as he laid her on that carpet and sank into her.

"Anastasia?" he prompted. He stroked his hand over her reddened buttocks. Heat radiated into his hand. She'd remember this every time she sat for the next few days. Good. He didn't want her running to another jerk. She needed someone who'd take her in hand. Someone who'd take care of her submissive needs.

For now, it seemed that task fell to him.

Reaching into the drawer of the table beside the couch, he removed balm to rub over her bottom. It wouldn't soothe. Instead, it would intensify the heat flooding her body without hurting her.

"Did you fuck him?" he asked again as he spread the balm over her.

"No," she breathlessly admitted.

"No? I thought you'd been his slave for a whole week."

"I was—Max, what the hell is that?" she demanded as the burn sank into her skin. She whimpered, making gasping little cries that drove him insane. He'd bet her cleft was flooding. The sheer temptation to check was almost too much.

"You were telling me about Tyler," he reminded.

"He didn't fuck me." Her bottom quivered as her body lifted and fell with her aroused pants as he smoothed the balm between her ass cheeks. One hand clenched around his ankle. "He preferred to subjugate. I knelt and waited while he rested his feet on me. Sometimes, he wanted to watch while I played with myself. He seemed to really get off on that but it didn't do much for me."

Now that would have been fucking hot to see, not that it made Max happy. Of course, he was thrilled she hadn't fucked that bastard. Hell, with her sprawled across his leg, he didn't know what he thought.

Her fingernails bit into his ankle as she remembered. "He had two other slaves, too. We weren't allowed to speak or even look at each other. Their unhappiness should have been my first clue. But I didn't go. I think he meant to sleep with me last night—after God knows who else did."

He scowled at the undesirable vision of her body dripping with semen. Tyler didn't bother with using protection and Max was fairly certain he didn't enforce it with others either. Max circled her puckered anus with his fingertip. He wasn't sure Tyler would even make them use lube.

Ana shied away from his caress. "Damn it, Max. Stop."

He frowned. Pulling his hand away, he gave her one last swat across her ass. This time combined with the balm, the stroke would skyrocket through her. She screamed, going up on her toes and clawing the carpet.

"Again. Oh please, again," she begged.

He pulled up her panties and straightened her skirt. He didn't want her to come just yet. Tomorrow would be soon enough. Tomorrow, after work…if she accepted his proposition.

Guiding her upright, he turned her to face him and cupped the back of her supple thighs. Her tear-stained cheeks tightened his balls.

"There's something I haven't told you about myself. Something I've hidden all these years," he told her.

Not at all cowed despite the spanking, she gave him a look that clearly said "duh". She'd be the perfect submissive for some man. Spunky and full of spirit, yet willing to bend to her Dom's needs.

"So I gathered," she replied, her dry tone in opposition to her shuddering arousal. "Why, Max? I've told you everything."

"It's not something I share with many people. I'm not ashamed of who I am. I grew up this way. For me, for my family, this way of life is normal. Most people just don't understand."

"You thought I wouldn't understand. Damn it, Max."

"Anastasia," he warned.

"Sorry." She bowed her head, then her gaze snapped up full of pained betrayal. "You didn't think *I'd* understand this?" she hissed. "I told you I thought I was a sub. I told you the deep desires inside me. What I *needed*. And you hid this?"

"You said it earlier, 'but not with you'. You didn't want me to be this person. To you I'm just Max. Laid-back, nice-guy Max. You never wanted to see me any other way. Instead you fell for every asshole who crossed you path. I've watched it long enough. It's time you start thinking of me another way."

Defiance flashed in her eyes. "And how is that?"

"You need training. I'm the most obvious person to give it to you before you dig yourself into a situation where you'll get hurt." He curled his fingers into her lush ass, drawing a moan from her as he pulled her close enough to smell her heady arousal. "To you, I will be Master, at least temporarily. You are my slave. When the time comes, I will help you find a Dominant who will fit your needs."

"Do I get a choice in this?"

He dropped his hands, sliding his fingertips down her thighs on the way. "Of course you have a choice. Kneel. I'll talk."

Indecision filled her eyes, along with confusion.

He stared at her impassively, waiting. She had to make this decision on her own. It was the first of several to come and he wouldn't influence it.

Slowly, still looking unsure, she backed away from him and dropped to her knees, her arms crossed over her chest. He eyed her stiff closed-legged stance and fisted hands. Just as he'd suspected. Tyler hadn't taught her anything.

Max stood. He prodded her knees apart with his foot. "When we are alone and I tell you to kneel, your knees will be apart. Likewise when you sit. When you stand, your feet will be shoulder-width. Do you understand?"

One finger uncurled from her fist and tapped on her arm.

"Yeah," she replied.

"You will refer to me as Master unless I give you permission to address me otherwise."

The finger tapped a little faster and she made an unimpressed face. "Yeah. Master."

He sighed silently. She would be difficult—if she decided to let him train her. That remained to be seen.

He crouched in front of her. Gently, he unfolded her arms and pushed them behind her back so that her hands rested on her beautiful ass, her right hand holding her left wrist. Now she could tap that damn finger all she wanted and he wouldn't see it. Unless he was behind her. Suddenly the thought of mounting her from behind punched a hole in his middle. Yeah, he needed to do that.

Standing, he squashed the need to bend her forward, shove up her skirt and take her right now. Not until tomorrow…not until she'd thought about this.

He tipped her head slightly forward. If she raised her eyes she'd still see him clearly. She kept her gaze militantly focused on his toes. Ugly trepidation clawed up his spine. Max suspected maybe he might have totally fucked up their long-standing friendship.

He couldn't hide his nature anymore and watch Ana continue to hurt herself. Silence surrounded them while he waited for her acceptance. He suspected she was waiting for something from him as well. An apology? He wouldn't apologize for what he'd done. This was who he was.

Swallowing his misgivings, he stepped from her line of sight. He was a Dom. He naturally took charge and she was a natural submissive. This is how it was supposed to be with them, how it had always been on some levels. The sooner she accepted that the sooner they could open their relationship to levels she'd only imagined.

He trailed his fingers over her silky curls. "When I tell you to kneel, this is the position I require."

Ana didn't reply.

"When I tell you to kneel, you will immediately comply."

She drew in a shaking breath, holding it for a moment before she released it. Again, she said nothing. Anger rolled from her, yet she held herself in check and maintained the position he'd dictated.

Ana fought the urge to clench her fists as Max watched her. She couldn't see him now that he'd moved just behind her right side. Nevertheless she could feel him. Watching her. Her mind raced as she tried to catch up with the events of the past minutes. Max—laid-back, funny, kind *Max*—was a Dom? Everything she thought she knew about him said no way, yet the past half-hour didn't lie. He wasn't faking this. There was no role-playing. Max had emerged and shown her his true nature and revealed a skin far more suited to him than that of the man she'd always known.

Whether she wanted to admit it or not, it rang true to what she knew. Bits and pieces of their past settled into place. Max took gentle control of every situation. He wasn't pushy or obnoxious about it. He had an air of authority to which people, men and women alike, naturally deferred.

Even her. Especially her. She'd wanted him since she was a sophomore in high school. He'd been a senior forced into tutoring math because of some prank he'd pulled. It soon became evident she was better at math than he was, still, they'd become fast friends. She'd learned to hide her desire for him in order to retain hold of her prized position at his side. As one of his closest friends, she'd always had more pull with him than any of the sundry girlfriends who'd waltzed in and out of his life.

Yet he'd hidden this.

Betrayal and anger fought inside her before aligning in a single-minded frenzy of hurt. She had to hold back her reaction or she'd explode in a flood of recriminations. Had he been sitting back and laughing the whole time she'd been rhapsodizing about thinking she'd really be into the D/s scene?

"I'm leaving," she said, lifting her head and flexing her toes into the carpet in preparation to rise.

"Stay still."

She ignored him and started to get up. He pressed his hand to her shoulder. "Anastasia, stay where you are or I swear I will restrain you."

Restrain? She almost swore at the rush of moisture to her cleft. Damn it. She couldn't be aroused by him. He was an asshole. A freaking asshole who'd lied to his friends.

She tried to shrug off his hand but he tightened his grip.

"Let me go."

He crouched behind her, his knees bracketing her sides and trapping her arms between them. Damn it. Why hadn't she moved them when she'd decided to go? He slid his around her, one around her middle and one over the top of her breasts. She found herself wrapped in Max, enveloped by his deep woodsy scent. His lips brushed her ear. "You don't give the orders here, slave."

"I'm not your slave," she murmured, unable to place much conviction in her words. A wicked part of her had wanted that from the first time she'd encountered writings on Dominant/submissive relationships. For years she'd squelched that desire. She'd thought Max wasn't into that so she'd explored her own options. Damn him.

His presence elicited long-suppressed responses in her middle. If his hand was to drift down a few inches, she knew he'd find her pebble-hard nipples. She struggled to hide her arousal and the moan that threatened when his equally hard cock brushed her trapped hands.

"That remains to be seen," he replied, tightening his hold when she tried to squirm from him.

She had to get out of here.

"Max, let me go. I mean it. I'm pissed at you and this isn't helping. How could you keep this from me all this time? I've told you everything. And you knew what I was searching for. You could have helped me but you didn't. You let me flounder along and make a fool of myself."

He nuzzled her cheek, unaffected by her tirade. "And here I thought you were most pissed because I spanked you."

Embarrassed heat flooded up her neck. She should be angry except anger hadn't even entered that equation. What was wrong with her? She couldn't even think straight with him this close.

"I want to leave."

"Then I guess we're at cross-purposes. I want to hold you. Since I'm the Dom, that means I win."

She closed her eyes in frustration, trying to figure her way through this. If she threw a big enough hissy fit, she knew he'd let her go. She didn't want to throw a fit. Besides, would he even believe her? Max knew her and knew her well. She wanted him. He'd sense it even if she protested. Really most of all she just wanted to pelt him. He'd hidden this from her. And now, by showing her... Their relationship would never be the same again. So this was what it felt like to lose your best friend. He held her, the bands of his strong arms burning pleasure into her, yet a new hollowness inside her echoed with her pain. She'd always told him everything...

He pressed his face into her shoulder. "Relax, angel. This isn't as bad as you're making it."

"And how's that?"

"You want to learn this lifestyle. I can show you how. I'll still always be here for you. I'll catch you if you fall, although your new master, whoever he turns out to be, might object to that."

New master? She couldn't fathom it. If she let Max teach her—and she knew that would include sex—she'd completely lose herself to him. She'd never been able to fully commit herself to any relationships because Max already owned most of her. She doubted that after him she'd recover enough to move on.

His hands splayed and he moved one to cup her breast while the other spread on her belly. She'd never realized quite how big his hands were. They seemed to cover her, although she knew they didn't really. It was the bliss radiating from his touch.

She was lost. Very, very lost.

"Max, I can't..."

He sighed. "You need to think about it. I can help you explore what you're looking for, however, I won't force you. I won't ever harm you, Ana. I don't think you can say that about the guys you've been hooking up with."

He was right. Her dating history read like a Who's Who in the Loser Parade. It didn't make the thought of submitting to Max any easier.

"Do you like the feel of my hands on you, Ana?" he asked, the deep rumble of his voice stroking her womb.

She tried to stay still. She wouldn't admit it.

Helplessly, she nodded, her body overriding her mind.

He rewarded her with a nip on her shoulder. A tremor ran through her. She had to get out of here before she sank to the carpet and begged him to fuck her. His insistent arousal prodded at her back, proving he'd be fully able to fill her need.

Slowly, he stroked both hands up and down her parted thighs. His thumbs repeatedly bumped against the damp cotton covering her pussy. How humiliating to have him know how aroused this made her and how weak she was to him. It occurred to her that he no longer held her captive. She could scramble away now that his arms weren't around her.

She didn't move.

As if he'd sensed her aborted thought one of his arms again locked around her waist. She immediately realized her notion of escape had nothing to do with it. She whimpered as one big hand slipped beneath her skirt and into the waistband of her panties.

He groaned as he slipped two fingers into her slippery folds. She erupted at his first touch.

"Max, no," she pleaded. "I can't. Not with you."

"Of course with me. Oh God, Ana, you feel so good. I want to feel you fly apart in my palm."

Insidious ribbons of delight stole through her, lifting her hips into his strokes. She couldn't surrender to him. She couldn't do this, yet her body seemed intent on giving him exactly what he wanted. Her cream flowed as the sensations continued and grew stronger.

"Max," she groaned. Her fingers flexed where they were trapped behind her. Inadvertently, she caressed the hard ridge in his jeans. Her hand didn't come close to spanning its length. Mercy, he had to be impressive. Right now, she didn't care about his size, she just wanted him in her.

"Call me Master," he murmured, giving her aroused flesh a sharp tap.

"Master," she gasped.

He leaned against her back, silently urging her to bend forward, then pulled away just enough that she could pull her arms free. "Down on your elbows," he commanded. "Rest your head on your forearms."

She did as he said. All the while his caresses continued to claim her needy cunt. As soon as she'd assumed the position he'd ordered, he dipped a finger inside her clenching channel. He shoved her panties to her knees. A surge of cream followed.

Right and wrong, can and can't disappeared. This was Max. With Max she was safe. At least, she always had been. She rocked against him as he added two more fingers to the one plowing into her channel. Her belly tightened as her release grew closer. He'd get his desire. It would be fast and hard. She'd wanted for too many years.

Her breasts tingled, growing harder within their confinement, her bra suddenly feeling a size too small. She wanted his mouth on them. She wanted his mouth everywhere. Her thighs burned with the need radiating to them.

"That's good, angel," Max said as he leaned over her and she frantically worked her hips. "Milk my fingers. Show me how much you want me. You do want me, don't you? You want my cock inside you, showing you who you belong to. Don't you?"

"Yes," she groaned. "Yes, Master. Please fuck me."

Her release coiled, ready to explode. He had to feel it tightening around his coated fingers. Slowly he pulled them free, taking time to drag his fingertips over her exposed clit. Then he was gone.

She peeked over her shoulder to find him sucking her essence from his fingers. "You taste fantastic, angel."

She blinked in surprise when he didn't come back to her. He moved to sit in the chair she'd earlier vacated.

"Kneel."

What the hell?

She scooted around to face him, taking the position he'd guided her into earlier. She knew the picture she must present. Breasts heaving, skirt bunched at her waist, panties tight around her spread knees. Yet he watched her dispassionately as if nothing had happened between them. The way his cock strained for release was all that comforted her and kept her from calling herself a thousand times the fool. She settled for nine hundred ninety-nine. Stupid. Stupid, stupid, stupid. What was she doing? She knew she couldn't invest in anything with Max, yet here she was half-naked on her knees before him.

His jaw clenched.

"You will not come today."

He got that wrong. She was coming as soon as she got home to her vibrator.

"You are not to bring yourself pleasure," he continued.

Damn it.

"I know you too well for you to lie to me. I'll know if you've orgasmed."

His words brought a fresh wave of arousal flooding into her pussy. She distantly wondered if he could see it glistening on the inky thatch of curls between her legs. He'd think of it when he masturbated later and she knew damned well he would. Max was the most sexual being she knew. He thrived on pleasure.

That didn't stop her ire. She glared at his cock, trying to summon one of the gypsy curses her grandmother had taught her. He deserved a virulent case of crotch rot. A tiny voice inside her whispered not to do it and against her desire she reluctantly listened. She really didn't want the karma that would accompany her curse. A naughty part of her whispered that he deserved it… A curse would assist the universe in punishing him.

No, a curse would just be Ana being vengeful.

She clenched her fingers behind her, reining in the temper that had gotten one of her ancestors burnt at the stake. The universe—unfortunately—would have to do its own dirty work.

"Why are you doing this?" she muttered, knowing full well she shouldn't snap at her self-appointed master. She bit back a wry grin. Another spanking wouldn't be so intolerable.

"I want you to have something to think about. Every time you sit, probably every time you move, you'll think of me."

Like that was ever in question. She thought about him all the time anyway.

"I'm offering you a proposition, Ana. I'll train you. I will be the Dom you've searched for and you'll be my sub. At least, until you're trained. Tomorrow, if you accept my proposition, you will present yourself here and give yourself into my keeping. Think about it. Think hard, Ana. Once you accept, I won't allow you to turn back."

*****

Max's words followed Ana home. She realized after he'd left the room and she'd gathered her things that he'd never given a scenario for what would happen if she didn't accept his proposition. Could they continue on at work together? They worked in different departments of Cress Construction, she as the company's equipment coordinator and he as the head of Conceptual Designs. Their paths rarely crossed professionally. Still, it wasn't a huge company. They'd see each other.

Perhaps she should take the position she'd been offered at Cress' competitor, Sissek. She wasn't fully utilizing her degree in project management. At Sissek Construction she'd oversee several of their supermarket construction projects. When the headhunter had contacted her, loyalty to Max and to Cress was the only thing holding her back.

Shoving a hand through her hair to push it off her face, she worked her key into the sticky lock on her apartment door. Max hated this place. He didn't think it was safe enough. The apartment building was too run-down and the neighborhood was dangerous. She could almost hear his voice as he griped.

She pushed open the heavy wood door and flipped on the light, listening as it buzzed to life. She happened to think the building had character. Yes, the door stuck and the windows liked to swell shut in the summer but you didn't find woodwork like this in modern construction. All around her, dark wood trimmed the walls and ceilings of her spacious apartment.

She knew it worried Max that crime was higher around here. Correspondingly, the rents were lower. Worked for her. Besides, not everyone could afford a sprawling four-bedroom-three-bath ranch house with all the comforts of wealth. She didn't begrudge Max his nice house. She just wished he'd stop picking on hers.

She wandered though to her bedroom, the rooms lit only by the hall light and the neon from the store across the street. Max needed to stop worrying. Her cards would have told her if she needed to be concerned.

Absently, she pushed the button on her answering machine as she pulled off her clothes. Her body still throbbed with the aftermath of his attention. She could barely imagine trying to sleep tonight with this rampant arousal thrumming through her. Would Max really know if she relieved the tension knotting her belly? Did it matter?

She wouldn't say yes to his plan.

"Slave, answer this phone."

Ana jumped at the nasty voice echoing through the machine's speaker. What had she been thinking to align herself with someone so malevolent?

"You will call me immediately when you return. I did not give you permission to go anywhere. You will call me."

A harsh noise broke the air of her quiet apartment as he slammed the receiver down. Four similar messages followed.

Ana made a face.

*You will call me.*

Not. She didn't belong to him. She'd broken their contract, though he was choosing to ignore it. As far as she was concerned, if she never saw him again, it would be fine. She'd never had an emotional connection to Tyler. It had been just sex—even though they'd never actually fucked. It was nothing like her connection to Max.

Ending their friendship would cripple her.

Naked, she flopped down on her bed, hoping she'd jolt some of her arousal from her system. Instead, her thighs rubbed together, stimulating her drenched folds. She needed to come. Badly. Rolling on her back, she propped one leg on the mattress while the other dangled over the edge. Slowly, she ran her hands over her ribs, cupping her breasts then gently squeezing her way up to her nipples. She moaned softly as she ran her palms over the points and imagined it was Max's hands on her.

Picturing his hard body kneeling over her, she continued to massage one peak while her other hand drifted over her belly, in search of her cleft. She splayed her fingers through the springy hair covering her pussy and thought of his large fingers, one pushing inside to slide between the inner lips.

She'd wanted him so badly earlier. Needed him to fuck her. Oh God, she wanted that impressive cock parting her and driving deep inside. She gasped as she pressed her finger to her clit and wobbled it from side to side. Mild ripples of pleasure skipped through her yet nothing as strong as when Max touched her.

Still, she closed her eyes and enjoyed the sensation.

Max would be angry if he knew what she was doing. It didn't matter. He had no hold over her. She hadn't agreed to anything and she wasn't going to.

Little by little, the sensations built, stacking upon each other until her control threatened to topple. One more second, a few more strokes. Her lips parted. Oh, Max...

The harsh jangle of her phone ripped her from her daze and pushed back her release. She groaned, turning to her side and hugging her pillow. She just couldn't get a break. All she wanted was a fucking orgasm.

"Ana, please pick up the phone."

Max.

Fumbling for the portable receiver, she clicked it on and brought it to her ear. "Hullo?"

Please don't let her sound as breathless as she thought she did. She struggled to slow her breathing so she wasn't panting in his ear.

"What are you doing?" he asked, his low, knowing tone sending heat rushing through her.

"Nothing."

"I forbade you from pleasuring yourself."

"And you would be...God?" she snapped angrily. He was badgering her about this and keeping her from a lovely release?

"To you? Close enough. Remember, that's Master to you."

A flash fire of fury raged through her, storming away with her tongue and leaving her helpless to stop the words spewing from her. How dare he? How *dare* he? "First of all, you are not my master. Second, you can't tell me what I can and cannot do. Third, what the fuck, Max? Why are you harassing me about this? What happened tonight…it was a mistake. It was nothing more than a mistake. We shouldn't have—"

"Give it a chance, Ana. Don't refuse before you've even given it any thought."

"We can't do this."

"Why not?"

Why not? A million reasons. The number one being she was sure she'd get hurt. Number two, she'd end up hurting him in the process. Her job, his family…the list went on and on.

"Because I can't."

He sighed and she heard every ounce of his frustration with her. "So you're not even going to think about it. You're going to say no to a wealth of opportunity, a relationship that could change your life, because you're scared."

He would pull out the fear card. Low move. Max knew she wouldn't back down from a blatant dare like that one. Valiantly, she fought her instinctual reaction. He would not goad her into this.

Defiantly, she slid her fingers along her cleft, listening to his breathing. "Mmmm," she hummed.

"Ana…"

"It feels so good and I'm thinking of a big strong man, Max. A man who'll fuck me hard." She smiled. She wasn't the only one who couldn't back away from a dare. She wouldn't be surprised if he was on his way to his car as he spoke.

She clutched the phone as she plowed two fingers into her needy passage.

"You need to stop," he growled, she heard distinct rustling as he settled onto his bed. Okay, he wasn't on his way. "You know I'll punish you for this."

A ripple went through her. *Yeah, keep talking*.

"No, you won't. You aren't my master."

He released a short burst of laughter. "I have a flogger with your name on it."

"They personalize those things?"

"All my toys have your name on them. The plugs, the clamps, the whips..."

"You're trying to worry me." She chuckled, tipping her head back as delicious ripples worked through her. "Sticks and stones may break my bones but whips and chains don't scare me."

"I don't want you scared. I want you to obey."

Every word pushed her awareness higher. He wanted her to obey him. Why did she get off on that? Yet her body thrilled at the thought of being at his mercy. She wanted to give him control. She couldn't. They'd been friends too long. He knew too much about her. And look what had happened when she'd given control to Tyler. She shuddered. What he'd intended was awful. Max wouldn't expect that of her, would he? She was sure he wouldn't. Almost.

He hadn't shared this part of himself. She couldn't forget that. If he'd hidden this, what other darkness might he hide?

She wanted to explore it.

Her fingers squeezed the phone. What the hell was wrong with her? Wasn't it enough to be burned once? She wanted to go jump right into the flames?

She yanked her hand away from her pussy.

"Max—"

A dial tone answered. Shit. She'd hung up on him when she'd squeezed the phone. Disgusted, she tossed the receiver to the side and pulled a pillow over her head. She should just take her vibrator and move to...to...Timbuktu. Maybe there she could forget the disaster she'd made of her life and escape the phone that was again ringing insistently beside her.

She blindly grabbed it up, clicking it on as she brought it back to her ear beneath the pillow. "Look, Max, I stopped, okay?"

"Who the hell is Max?"

Tyler. Fuck. She tossed away the pillow and dragged her thick comforter around her. Any residual arousal from her encounters with Max shot away, leaving her naked and vulnerable.

"A friend."

"Have you been with him tonight? Fucking him?"

*Almost.*

"It's not your business," she retorted. She wouldn't let him bully her. He wasn't in charge of her life. She'd been stupid. She knew it. He wasn't pushing her around.

"You are my business, slave. You belong to me."

Her chin wobbled as she listened and she started to tremble. She steeled herself against it. She wouldn't let him take her.

"You signed yourself away to me. You're mine, don't you forget it."

"No, I broke the contract."

His harsh laugh sent a shudder through her. How unlike Max he was. "A slave can't break a contract. You gave your rights away to me. Tomorrow we'll start training that knowledge into you."

"No," she whispered.

"Oh yes. Are you scared? You should be."

Scared? No. Terrified was more like it.

"I want you here at five sharp. Naked under your trench coat and ready."

"No, Tyler…"

"If you don't show up, I *will* find you and you *will* be punished."

Her hands shaking she hung up the phone, her finger trembling so badly she missed the disconnect button on her first attempt. She leapt from the bed and raced to the kitchen and her only corded phone to take it off the hook. It wouldn't keep Tyler away but at least he wouldn't be able to harass her all night.

What the hell was she going to do?

She sank into a kitchen chair and dropped her head to the table. In the stark light of hindsight, she recognized the crushed spirit in Tyler's other two slaves. How foolish she'd been. She'd thought they'd been angry he was taking another slave. They were abused. Mentally and physically. She'd studied enough about the culture of the scene to know there was a vast difference between pain for pleasure and pain that was abuse. Yet, she'd been so desperate for the right man—the bad boy who'd fill her fantasies—that she'd blindly committed herself to a devil.

# Chapter Two

Max scowled as he watched Ana talk to one of their coworkers, her back partially turned to him. Purposely turned. When she'd seen him she'd angled herself away from him.

It shouldn't surprise him. She'd avoided him all day, even canceling the lunch appointment they'd had every Friday for the last ten years. No matter who was in their lives, no matter what was going on, neither of them canceled. The first time he'd been out of town she'd surprised him for virtual lunch. They never missed. Yet today she'd canceled for what? The sniffles? His secretary had taken the call and he'd never gotten a straight answer.

And Ana had blithely managed to avoid him all day. That was his answer. She wasn't accepting his proposition and, worse, she was ending their friendship.

So she thought…

Max swung around and headed back to his office. Ana had until tomorrow morning to accept. It killed him to wait. He *hated* waiting. But he would. If she didn't come to him, he'd make a stand. She wouldn't shut him out.

He knew perfectly well the flimsy lock on her apartment door wouldn't keep him out—not that her resistance would stretch that far.

He stopped just inside his office, letting the door swing shut as he realized the direction of his thoughts. What was he thinking? He'd stop her from making her own decision? Because he thought she was wrong? Yeah, she was his friend and he was sure she was destroying her life, but did he really know better?

*Hell yes, I do.* He rolled his eyes as his Dom nature instinctively spoke up. He did understand this life better than she did. After all, he'd been raised in it. The D/s lifestyle was deep-seated in his family. It had been for over a hundred years.

Whether he knew better or not, he needed to get his thoughts together before he confronted her. He needed to know why her training was so important to him. There was no leaning on the friend crutch... He certainly hadn't been thinking of friendship last night when he'd gripped his cock and visualized himself surging in and out of her silk-walled cunt.

Shit. He wanted her. What the hell was his problem? It had had bugged him that she'd run around searching for Mr. Right in guy after guy. He'd shrugged off his discomfort as knowing she was barking up the wrong trees. It horrified him that she'd been in Tyler's clutches. Still, he'd put his feelings down to friendship. Now he'd offered this harebrained idea of training her? He really was a masochist.

He jabbed a hand through his hair, knotting his fingers at his crown as he thought. He really just wanted her in his bed. Not forever. Just until he got her out of his system. However long that took. An extended training should cover it.

Punching the call button on his phone, he told his secretary to hold his calls then sat at the drafting table in front of the large window overlooking Lake Michigan. The waves crashing to the shore echoed his peace of mind... He had none.

Pulling out a soft-leaded pencil, he started to sketch on the large piece of paper taped to the slanted surface. Long graceful lines flowed from his pencil as a figure emerged. It wasn't work, though he did appreciate the concept in its design.

A likeness of Ana quickly formed beneath his strokes. Ana naked and kneeling, her wrists and ankles in cuffs, her face wreathed in ecstasy as she tipped it toward the ceiling.

"Now that's something I wouldn't mind seeing."

Max jumped at his brother's voice. He glanced at his watch. Great. He'd lost track of time and the meeting they were supposed to start ten minutes ago. Apparently, his brother cared for their subject as much as he did. Actually, Max knew the truth in that. His brother's favorite phrase for describing the computer-assisted drawing program was "pain in the ass".

"Josh. You're late," he said, turning from his drawing to face his younger brother. Josh didn't care that he worked in a professional environment. He'd cashed in on nepotism and his talent with computers to forge his way into a position heading the IT department at Cress, a position that would have been out of his reach at any other employer. While Josh resembled his three older brothers with the same muscular build, strong features, dark brown hair and gray eyes, the similarities stopped there. He shunned office attire, opting instead for jeans, running shoes and untucked shirts. He apparently shunned the barber as well. His hair hung just past his shoulders and he seemed to have a thing for piercings. Six that Max knew of.

Max forced back a shudder at the places he knew needles had gone. Aside from the piercings, he saw himself in Josh—ten years ago. Unfortunately, his baby brother was only two years younger, not ten.

"Somehow, I don't think you care that I'm late," Josh said, examining the drawing.

"I do. I have things to get done."

"Hmmm. Yes, I see that." Shaking his head, he slouched into a chair across from Max's desk. Max took a final look at his rendering, experiencing a tug in his gut when he thought of Ana. Reluctantly, he returned to his desk. He'd wasted too much time this afternoon. It was time to get back to business.

*****

Ana loved lists. They were all over her desk, reminding her of what she needed to complete. None of them said worry about her situation with Tyler or obsess over Max. Yet it was what she'd done all day. If it wasn't one, it was the other. Her head hurt from it.

They both wanted her, she didn't want either. Well, actually she did. She wanted to be with Max. She just couldn't see her way to it.

She knew she couldn't surrender to Tyler's demands. He'd hurt her, physically and spiritually. Max would cherish her—she knew that—but loving and losing him would destroy her soul.

She rested her forehead on her hands, glad her desk was in an out-of-the-way spot where she had few interruptions. It wouldn't do for anyone to find the supply Nazi at odds with herself.

Okay. Tyler would show up at her place tonight when it became apparent she wasn't coming to him. She could deal with him, even if she had to call the police. She could ask Max for help—

No, she couldn't. He'd drawn the line last night. Either she chose him or she didn't. Her side seemed awfully lonely and empty right now. That wasn't a basis for a decision. The tarot card that had come up last night was.

After Tyler had called, when she couldn't sleep, she'd done a gypsy card reading that had come down the ages through her family. An hour later, the final result had lain before her, a strong suggestion for her path. The Six of Pentacles. She didn't want to believe it.

The card signified the balance of power, one person giving the other person taking. It could be her and Tyler. She knew it wasn't. The person who gave, the person who had power, was benevolent. They gave kindness, knowledge and love. That wasn't Tyler. It wasn't her—she didn't have the knowledge about which she worried. It was Max. There was no question. And she was the receiver. Max would teach. She would learn. He'd give her what she'd sought.

Could she really trust herself to Max like this? She didn't need Max to help her with Tyler. She just needed him. Period. As he'd claimed, he could teach her and guide her. He was right. Who better than the man who'd been her friend for so long? The thing was, she didn't want to accept that. She wasn't ready for things to change and she'd battled it out inside herself all day. She'd avoided him. He knew her so well. He'd see the questions and desire in her eyes. He'd see her internal fight.

She stood, her silky skirt sliding over her bare ass. Thoughts of Max had kept her panties constantly damp all morning. She'd stripped them off at lunch, fed up with the moist cloth stimulating her aroused flesh. Commando wasn't much better. Every shift of fabric reminded her of Max's hands sliding over her skin. In a few minutes, if he hadn't changed his mind, she'd feel him touching her again.

A slight smile curved her lips as she headed toward his office. Her decision firmed as each second passed. Soul destroying aside, being with Max would fulfill so many long-held fantasies. The pain would come, yet she had to believe that somehow she'd survive it. The cards said she would.

"Miss Cooper, can I help you?" Max's secretary, Rebecca, intoned through her nose as Ana approached. The ice princess didn't like her and she made no bones about hiding it.

"I'd like to see Max."

Rebecca wrinkled her nose at Ana's familiarity. She didn't seem to put any account in the fact Ana and Max had been friends since before either of them had worked here. "Mr. Cress is in a meeting with his brother."

"Well, great. Josh will want to talk to me." She started skirting the desk. The icy gatekeeper wouldn't keep her from Max. This was important. Especially since she'd avoided him all day.

"It's a private meeting. You can't go in there," the secretary exclaimed.

"Look, Bec." She knew Rebecca hated being called that. "Josh has known me since…well, forever. Max needs to see me and neither of them will care."

"Miss Cooper—"

Ana ignored her protest, heading for the door. "Thanks. I knew you'd understand."

Two dark heads turned toward her as she stepped inside the office and closed the door on Rebecca's protests. Leaning against the door, she met first one set of laughing gray eyes, then the intense gray of her master. Max's gaze seemed to devour her. Caught in his web, she froze unsure what to do or what to say.

Her breathing quickened as she stared at him.

"You wanted something, Ana?"

*You. I want you.*

She swallowed around the lump in her throat. Of all the scenarios she'd envisioned she hadn't included anyone else. Even barging in here, she hadn't thought through what she'd do with Josh in the room. Her eyes closed for a brief moment and she shoved away from the door. It didn't matter that he was here. Max and Josh were close. Josh would know the lay of the land with his brother.

She ordered herself to stay calm as she approached. This was right. This was Max. Her cards supported this. She stopped a few feet from the desk. Fastening her gaze on the carpet, she lowered herself to her knees and clasped her hands behind her.

"Holy shit!" Josh exclaimed.

Max stood. "Shut up, Josh."

"Man, I didn't know this was how it was with you two."

He ignored his brother and rounded the desk, coming to stand before her. Reaching down, he tilted up her chin. "Are you sure?"

"Yes."

He raised an eyebrow and she closed her eyes, taking a breath. "Master."

"Josh, leave."

A rustle of papers followed. She sensed rather than saw Max's brother leave. Her eyes never left Max. Desire blazed in his gaze as he regarded her.

"You were very bad last night," he said when the door clicked shut. She hoped Josh had locked it.

"I—" she stopped, unsure whether she could speak.

"Go ahead."

"I didn't...um...come," she confessed, unable to believe she'd discuss this with him. "I stopped."

He studied her, his brows coming together. "Tell me again."

"I stopped. Like you said." She bit her lip. "And I really need... Well, I hung up the phone by accident. Not because I didn't want you to hear. And...and well...I just stopped."

"You really need? What?"

She sighed. Had she thought this would be easy? "You. I really need you."

He nodded and moved away. "Good."

Good? That was all? *Good*?

She struggled to keep her body relaxed and her breathing calm. A display of her temper wouldn't get them anywhere. Against all reason, warmth seeped into her pussy, making her want to squirm.

"That still leaves the question...why didn't you call me back?"

"Tyler."

"What?" he asked sharply. "He was there?"

She shook her head quickly. "No. He called. He was a jerk. Demanded I show up at his place today or else. I kept the phone off the hook."

Silence followed. It was broken suddenly by the slap of a hand on his desk.

"I would have come for you. You should have called me," he rasped. "He could have shown up and decided to hurt you. You know that, don't you? Do you realize the danger you were in? I will not allow that. You're mine now."

She nodded, unsure what to say.

His now. It shouldn't have made her all trembly inside but it did. Her tongue darted out to wet her lips. When Tyler had staked his claim, a heady excitement had filled her. Excitement at the unknown and the forbidden. This was different. There was excitement, but with it was an unbelievable calm. Sharp-edged curiosity and fear twined together, yet she knew she was safe. She'd never really felt safe with Tyler, just completely out of control. She didn't like that. It scared her.

Still, Max had the control here. More power than Tyler had ever had. This was different. Unlike her experience with Tyler, she didn't feel *out of* control. It took strength to kneel here before Max and accept what he offered. An underlying comfort supported her. If she said no, she knew he'd stop. Max wouldn't harm her.

She trusted him. Even as the tension rose around them, dredged in deep silence, fear wasn't present. Arousal was. Her position drew her shoulders back and pushed forward her breasts. The thin layers of lace and silk did nothing to disguise the thrust of her hard nipples against the fabric. She could barely stand their confinement. The need to rub them or have Max roll them between his fingers sent liquid heat rushing to her barely hidden pussy. It inflamed her beyond belief. Her skirt pulled across her thighs and if it shifted just an inch, he'd know she was bare beneath it.

He stopped before her and leaned back on the front of his desk, his ankles crossed. Glancing up, she saw his arms were crossed as well, his face closed as he regarded her. Sheesh.

"Have you eaten?"

Her head snapped up in surprise. What? That wasn't what she'd expected. "No…"

"Me either." He raised his eyebrows at her. "My lunch date canceled on me."

She winced. "Sorry."

"Hmm, well, you'll make it up to me. Why did you cancel?"

"I was still trying to decide."

"I want you naked."

She blinked at him. Naked? Here in his very professional, perfectly decorated office? Challenge glinted in his eyes. He was trying to keep her off balance. He might know her well but she knew him too. He was testing her.

She glanced over her shoulder at the door then back at him.

"Don't worry about the door. It doesn't matter who sees. You're mine, at my command. Nothing else matters."

Heat prickled up her back and her stomach knotted. Slowly, she reached for her buttons. She pushed one pearly button after another free of the holes that held them. Her blouse gaped open, revealing her bra. Her breathing growing shaky, she pulled the tails free of her skirt. Shrugging her shoulders, she let it slide free, to pool over her ankles.

Max sucked in a breath at the sight of the bruises marring her shoulders and upper arms. "Did he do that?"

She nodded. "It's not a big deal."

"That bastard," he growled. His face hardened, his eyes flinty. "Keep going. I want to see what else he's done."

Her womb jerked at his proprietary demeanor. Why hadn't she seen this in him before now? He'd always been like this. Perhaps he hadn't hidden as much as she had. After all, she'd lusted after him all this time.

"This is it."

"I want to see for myself."

If she were in his position, she'd want the same thing. Biting her lip, she reached for the front clasp of her bra. A moment later, her breasts spilled forward and the garment landed atop her blouse. Her breasts settled high and firm against her chest.

His lips parted when he discovered she hadn't quite told the truth. Five mottled circles marked one breast, testament to Tyler's anger when she'd refused to go to the club. Max's hands dropped to his sides in fists.

"I'll kill him." Max struggled to hold back his rage as he advanced on her. Ana was his woman and Tyler had done this to her. It didn't matter that he'd just staked his claim. She'd been his since high school. Shit. This sucked. And he'd just offered her the proposition of training her. Being her *temporary* master. He couldn't just change gears now.

What the hell was he going to do now? Yesterday, he'd truly only wanted to train her. She needed to be shown how to behave in the scene and how to navigate through the lifestyle. Staring at the blotchy purple marks on her creamy flesh, he realized he'd subconsciously had another agenda. He wanted her to be his.

Unfortunately, not only did Ana have a penchant for selecting losers, she had a commitment problem… She couldn't make one. He'd been completely shocked to find she'd made a contract with Tyler. Max had never thought she'd do it. A contract meant long-term and as far as he knew the only long-term relationship Ana had ever had was with her pet turtle, Loki, who'd died several years ago. Ana didn't do commitment, therefore he couldn't come right out and say "I want you…forever". If he said that, she'd run…forever.

"I'm fine," she whispered as he crouched in front of her.

"You call this fine? Angel, in this scene, bruises happen but not like this. This is…" He trailed off, shaking his head. He reached out and stroked the back of his finger over the marks. Her skin was soft against his knuckles. He circled her wrists with his hands and pushed them behind her as he leaned forward and drew the nipple of her battered breast into his mouth. Gently, he suctioned and flicked his tongue over the hard peak.

Ana moaned, bowing into him. He tipped her back onto the carpet and settled between her parted thighs, easing his body upward until his cock nestled against her cunt. God, she felt good. She smelled good. This was just…good. Balancing his weight on his arms, he leaned down and brushed his lips over hers.

She squirmed against him, rubbing her groin against his. He'd come in his damn pants and lose his hard-won control if she continued. He'd not been a Dom all these years to lose himself at the first heated frenzy of his sub—even if she was the sub he desired to take permanently.

"Stay still," he commanded, working hard to keep the signs of his arousal from his hard tone. She needed to know he meant business. These first encounters were paramount for setting the tone of their relationship. He would not let her try to dominate him from the bottom.

"I can't," she replied.

"You can. Stay still or I stop." He trailed his lips over her collarbone and dipped his tongue into the indentation. She shuddered and he suppressed a smile. Lazily, nipping and licking, he worked his way up her neck until he reached her ear. "You were very naughty last night and you must be punished."

"I didn't come," she protested.

"Was there pleasure?"

He pulled back to look into her revealing gaze. She couldn't lie to him. She bit her lush lower lip and he was tempted to pull it free with his own teeth. Slowly she nodded.

"Then you disobeyed."

She closed her eyes as she nodded yet not before he saw a glimpse of fear in them. He didn't want her fear. There would be punishments between them from time to time, perhaps spanking, perhaps flogging, perhaps something else, but still, she should never have cause to fear him. Obviously she didn't trust him nearly as much as he'd believed she did.

"Yes, Master," she sighed.

"In light of circumstances…traditional corporal punishment seems a poor choice. So instead you will endure."

Her eyes went wide in surprise. "Endure?"

"Whatever I give you. Still and silent."

"Whatever you wish," she replied.

"I *wish* to taste your mouth. Open for me," he murmured before covering her lips with his and consuming her. He stabbed his tongue inside, tasting her until she moaned and tilted her head to receive his kiss more fully. Methodically, he set about exploring, glorying in each suppressed sigh. Good lord, he wanted to feel the damp warmth of her soft mouth enveloping his cock as he worked in and out of her lips. To feel her sweet sounds vibrating down his length. His cock jerked in agreement.

He palmed her breasts while he kissed her, pulling at the hard tips and envisioning them clasped in the jeweled nipple clamps in his dungeon. Tonight he'd introduce her to that special space, the only part of his house she'd never seen.

She took shallow breaths the sounds turning to whimpers as he pinched and rolled her nipples. She was trying to comply…and failing. Miserably. He pulled back just enough to speak.

"Silence," he reminded.

"Max," she mouthed, then released a soundless sigh. Her breath feathered along his skin.

He had to move. At this rate he'd be reaching for his fly and plowing into her, control be damned. Shifting his hips away from the burning heat at her center, he slid down her body. His cock protested being pressed to the industrial carpet but that damn dick was getting him into trouble. A little discomfort wouldn't hurt his situation.

Ana jerked as he laved his tongue over her pearled nipple, her fingers clawing the floor beside them. Damn, he loved that she had such a reaction to him. A knot formed low in his groin and pleasure radiated through him. She reacted as if she were the other half of him—

He shoved the thought away. Ana thought he would train her for submission. He might as well proceed on that path. If he failed to win her, she'd go to another.

Fuck the thought of her with another. His stomach lurched, twisting at the idea. He would not fail. He would train her for himself and his pleasure.

"Be still," he reminded her. He spread her arms out to the side and laced his fingers through hers. Determined to torment, he returned to his feast, sucking her breast deep inside his mouth and pressing his tongue hard over the beaded peak.

"Hey, I thought you might need this."

Max yanked away from Ana, his head snapping up to find his brother standing just inside the door staring at them. Heat flooded his gaze, his lips parting slightly as he surveyed the scene. "Damn, you guys work fast."

"Damn it, Josh."

Unabashed and drawn to the encounter he'd interrupted, Josh slowly walked toward them, a bulge growing behind his fly. "Don't worry," he said, his tone distracted. "Wonder assistant left her post. She didn't see me come in here." He gestured a hand at them. "She didn't see this."

"Stay still," Max warned Ana. He levered himself up and sat back on his heels, staying between her splayed legs. Looking up at his brother, he saw an important lesson for Ana to learn.

What was he doing to her? Ana squeezed her eyes shut. Staying still when he'd touched her with his hands and mouth had been nearly impossible. Now with his brother standing over them, he wanted her to stay still? Her first instinct was to fling her arms over her breasts and turn away. This was Josh, Max's kid brother, the same one who'd hooted at her when she'd go out on dates during high school. Letting him see her half-naked almost seemed perverse. It didn't matter that he was years over the drinking age.

"Ana," Max growled.

She opened her eyes and looked at him, almost afraid of what she'd find there. This was the same as Tyler...almost. Max wouldn't hurt her but for all intents and purposes, it appeared to her that he intended to share her with his brother. Her stomach churned. It appeared he'd let another man fuck her.

He certainly wasn't ordering Josh to get the hell out. Instead, he reached for her hand. "Stand up. Let Josh look at you."

Without waiting for her compliance, he pulled her to her feet. He guided her hands behind her back, placing them over the top of her ass in the same way he required when she kneeled.

"Hands like this. Feet apart," he told her, standing behind her and whispering in her ear. He trailed his fingers lightly over her arms. Goose bumps rose in their wake and she struggled not to tremble. Other than standing, he hadn't said she could move. Feeling Max so close behind her while his brother stood before her looking tenderly into her eyes sent a confusion of sensations racing through her. Her nipples tightened painfully, begging to be touched…by either of them…while a rush of arousal flooded into her cleft.

Josh's gaze dropped to her chest and his brows drew together as he lightly touched the bruised flesh. Ana sucked in a tremulous breath though he didn't notice. His focus shot to Max, his expression askance with disbelief. "You didn't—"

"Tyler," Max said, his voice a deadly rumble.

"That bastard."

Ana wanted to scowl. Or better, scream. Okay, already. The man sucked. She was standing here practically naked and no one seemed to really notice—except for the damn bruises. Well, Max had noticed when she was on the floor but come on…

It wasn't that she wanted to sleep with Josh and so far Max wasn't asking her to prove anything. However, her master's lack of communication didn't instill hope in her that she'd know only his possession. Her thoughts dissolved as Josh lifted her chin with two fingers and kissed her. Really kissed her with a gentle sweep of his tongue into her mouth. He tasted of coffee and sugar. Completely Josh. The piercing on his tongue pulled across her sensitive inner lip.

Max's hands clamped on her hips and he pushed against her back, a hard wall demanding her surrender. She couldn't retreat. Still, his body reassured her, reminding her of his protective presence. Max wouldn't leave her to fly alone through the disorienting emotions tensing her limbs. He buried his face in her hair, whispering how beautiful she was while Josh plundered her mouth, finding portions that Max hadn't touched. Aside from his mouth on hers, though, Josh didn't touch her.

She knew how sexual he was. She'd watched him in action for years. So why didn't he touch her? Was there something wrong with her? She locked her hands together to keep from covering herself or shoving him so she could dive away. Of course nothing was wrong with her, physically anyway. She wasn't ready to tackle the ghosts haunting her inner psyche. If there was something lacking in her she wouldn't be sandwiched between two wonderful men.

Her pussy tingled as she gave her all to the kiss, ever aware of Max holding her.

She'd run from relationship to relationship, never finding what she needed. Never trusting any union to last, especially when the guy discovered her needs—needs considered perverse by bland middle-class standards. Her need for bondage and discipline even scared the bad boys who liked to play at being tough but really weren't. They didn't understand she didn't want to be abused. She wanted—

Max splayed his hands on her abdomen, holding her still and exerting his control over her. He had the power. She'd given it over to him and now he was giving her exactly what she wanted. *This* was what she wanted. Being mastered. Losing her control…willingly.

With Max all the crap in her past ceased to matter.

From behind, he dragged a palm up her body until he cupped a breast. His long fingers toyed with her taut nipple, drawing tight the nerves that yanked at her womb. She whimpered into Josh's mouth as her release drew closer from her lover's touch alone.

Max's other hand traveled down her thigh, slipping beneath her skirt. He brushed across the top of her lace-topped, thigh-high nylons.

"So hot. For me?" he whispered, fingering the lace. Unable to answer, she made an affirmative sound in her throat. Heat built in her center. She wanted to scream "touch me, give me the release you denied me". She couldn't without releasing Josh's mouth. At that moment, unless Max would immediately begin kissing her, she'd rather have stopped breathing.

Frustration building, she waited. Her fingers curled around the cock pressed to them. Deny her, would he? Slowly, she stroked up and down his rigid length, dragging her thumb over the clearly palpable head and wishing two layers of cloth didn't separate his flesh from her palm.

"Oh, angel," he murmured, thrusting into her grip. Abandoning her thigh, he snaked his hand toward her pussy. She sighed in relief, widening her stance and fisting his arousal.

Max sucked in a breath when he encountered her uncovered curls. "You are a bad, bad girl."

And she hoped she'd be punished appropriately. And soon. She was so wet for him, she was sure he'd find an ocean when he finally entered her. She squeezed him, envisioning the hard length stretching her needy channel.

Max groaned. He worked one long finger inside her slick folds. The touch alone, so long coming, triggered a wave of jagged tremors. Ana cried out, the sound absorbed by Josh's mouth. He stabbed his tongue in and out of her mouth, simulating what she desperately needed Max to do to her sheath. Locking her knees, she endeavored to stay still and not rock against Max's hand.

Josh stepped back and she barely noticed it. Her sole focus was in the way Max rubbed up and down her clit. Unbearable tension circled upon itself inside her, drawing tighter and tighter until she gritted her teeth. She needed him inside her.

"You want release?" Max growled. His fingers shoved along the length of her folds, tracing her opening while Josh watched, his eyes intent on his brother's movements. Unsatisfied by the way her skirt disguised the movement, Max released the button and zipper holding up her skirt. He pulled his hand away only long enough for the fabric to cascade to her feet. Heat crept up neck and into her face while evidence of her arousal flooded onto Max's hand.

"Yes," she whispered.

"What was that, slave? Did you address me?"

Oh right. What was she supposed to...

"Yes, Master," she replied. Yes, she wanted to come. At her master's hands. She needed it and she didn't care if Josh was watching or not. Shame crimped the edges of her consciousness. She not only didn't care if he watched...she wanted him to.

Max plowed two fingers hard into her already convulsing sheath, his thumb pressing her clit. He'd waited too long. She'd needed release too long. She came on a muffled scream, her body clamping around his surging digits as she held Josh's stare. Her knees buckled. However, Max caught her, his arm tight around her waist.

She'd never shared such an intimate moment with anyone.

"Fucking beautiful," Josh commented. His thumb traced her parted lips. She drew it inside, watching his eyes go dark as she sucked it the same way she would have if it had been the cock trying to shove out of his pants.

Suddenly he pulled free and backed a few steps away, visibly shaken. "I'm—" he broke off staring at Max's fingers buried inside her pussy. "I'm going."

Ana stared at him through a haze, almost unable to comprehend. He was going to what?

"Lock the door this time, baby brother," Max growled.

"I'll hardwire your office to the paging system if you ever call me that again," Josh muttered. He looked at Ana again, his hand drifting toward his cock before he fisted his fingers and forced his arm to his side. It didn't erase the need in his face.

"Get. Out," Max rasped. He'd barely borne it to see his brother at Ana's lips, to know she'd kissed him so passionately. It shocked him that he wanted to punch his little brother for his presumption. It was childish and beneath him and more fucking possessive than he'd ever been in his life. He'd lashed out, reminding Josh of his position in the family. He'd apologize later.

Josh gave a mock salute and left, the door thudding behind him.

"Why did he—"

Max spun her around, stroking his fingers into her once more. "He wants you. He wants to fuck this tight passage that belongs to me. He wants to taste you. I won't let him. Cresses don't share, angel. It's practically our credo. *I won't share*. You need to remember that. Josh knows it. That's why he left. I couldn't just tell you. It was for you to learn." He lifted his soaked fingers to her lips. "Taste what he wants, angel."

Obediently, she parted her lips and sucked her essence from his fingers, her eyelids closing as she moaned. The erotic sound sliced through his restraint, cutting away the precious few pieces of control he still commanded.

"I might let you be tasted," he managed. "But I will never share you. Not like Tyler wanted. Josh wouldn't dare touch you. He knows you're mine."

Her eyes opened and she studied him. Questions filled her passion-glazed gaze. Questions he didn't want to answer. Not yet. She wasn't ready.

"For now," she murmured.

*For always.*

Without answering, he stepped back. Right. Training. She expected him to train her. "One of the first things a submissive must learn is that her Dom's pleasure comes first. His pleasure comes from your obedience. His pleasure comes from your willingness to meet his needs. Finally his pleasure comes from your pleasure."

*My pleasure comes from you, angel.*

"Your pleasure has always given me pleasure, Max," she confessed quietly. The hundreds of times she'd done nice things for him, made him smile or just been there filled his mind. Ana had been submissive to him for years and neither of them had realized it. Even now, she dropped to her knees without him asking and reached for his fly. Hands poised above the closure, she looked up at him, silently asking permission. *Oh God, yes.* He nodded and prayed he wouldn't lose himself the second her lips wrapped around him.

He toed off his shoes and socks while she slowly lowered his zipper.

"What made you change your mind?" he asked, needing a distraction.

Her hands paused in the act of pushing down his pants and underwear. She glanced up at him in surprise.

"I know you were going to say no," he continued. "Why didn't you?"

"Last night, after Tyler called me, I did a reading."

A tarot card reading, he surmised. He liked to have her do them for him. Not because he necessarily believed but because he loved the husky, mystical tone her voice took on as she explained each card and its position. How many boners had he hidden while she'd shared her gypsy heritage with him? Hell, the one time she'd let him sit in on an incantation, she'd sounded as breathless as if he'd been driving into her sweet body. He'd nearly lost it in his jeans.

"And," he prompted, shoving off his shirt. She finished pushing his pants over his hips and he kicked free of them, his cock standing proud and ready for her. She sat back on her heels, her tongue gliding over her bottom lip. It didn't escape his notice that she'd automatically reverted to the position he'd taught her.

"They told me to accept your offer."

"Really? As easy as that, they said 'take Max's proposition to train you'."

She made a face and pulled him between her parted knees. "Something like that," she muttered as she ran her fingers over the tattoo surrounding his navel. Tilting back her head, she dragged her tongue along the bottom of his penis before stretching upward and engulfing the sensitive head between her soft lips. It took all his power to keep from driving deep as the damp heat closed around him. How much better and more difficult would it be when he finally filled her pussy?

His hand caught the back of her head, tangling in her hair and he pulled his cock free of her mouth. He caught it in his other hand and guided it back toward her. Slowly, he traced her lips with the tip while her tongue flicked out to gather the tiny droplets marking his intense need for her.

"Did the cards tell you to let me fuck your mouth?" he asked.

"Yes," she replied, her voice so husky it scraped across his most primal needs, waking the beast within him. There was no stopping now. He'd take her before they left here, with Ana likely screaming out her release for half their office to hear. And he just couldn't give a damn. She was his and he wanted everyone to know it. He wanted her to know it. She would soon enough.

"Did they tell you to let me tie you to my bed and fuck you until you can barely walk?"

Her eyes were almost black with the desire swirling through them. "Yes."

"I don't want to be in your mouth. Not right now," he added when embarrassed disappointment filled her expression. He took a step back. "Stand up."

Agilely she came to her feet and he saw her as Josh had in the last minutes before he'd left. Josh had more strength than Max had ever given him credit for. Surveying her gentle curves and long expanses of creamy skin, broken only by the thatch of ebony curls hiding her damp folds, he wasn't sure he'd have been able to walk away.

Turning, he walked away, beckoning for her to follow him to his drawing table. "Come here, Ana," he said when she hesitated to come close to the wall of windows. "Do you really care if people see you? Do you know how exquisite you are?"

"I work with them."

"Very few people wander onto this side of the building," he told her, taking pity on her. "The chances of anyone looking up here are slim. No one looks at the building when they can look at the lake."

Taking a deep breath, she stepped to his side. She glanced at the table, then did a double take and stared at the drawing on the table, her lips parting slightly.

"I told you you're exquisite," he whispered. "Do you see how beautiful you are when you submit?"

"Max," she breathed.

He carefully removed the picture and rolled it, placing it in a protective tube. He intended to hang it on their bedroom wall as soon as he framed it. After setting it beside his briefcase he retrieved a condom from an inner pocket of the bag. Slowly, he rolled it over his tight flesh. God, she was beautiful. He'd never been so satisfied by his foresight as he was now as he returned to her and bent her over the tilted surface. Before Ana could question him, he lifted her hips, positioned himself at her entrance and plowed inside her. She cried out at his hasty invasion and whimpered when he pulled back. There were no more preliminaries… They'd been dancing around this moment since last night.

Just as quickly, he surged back into her, holding her hips while her fingers grasped the edge of the table, her knuckles turning white. Her honey flowed around his cock, coating him with her sweet nectar while her walls tightly hugged him.

Suddenly, he couldn't believe he was inside her after all these years. It was completely right and there was no way he'd let her wriggle away from him. Temporary master, his ass.

This was not temporary and this was most definitely his ass. Forever.

He changed his angle until her toes barely touched the floor. Her breasts pressed to the drawing board. She rested her cheek against it, letting him see her passion-filled face. He'd draw this moment and put it on the wall beside the other. He'd never seen anything more beautiful than Ana in ecstasy.

"Yes," she gasped.

She felt so good.

He pumped hard, reaching deep inside her. Her molten folds milked him, drawing him closer to the explosion looming before them. He couldn't stop the sensations washing over him… He couldn't…

"Yes," Ana groaned. "Fuck me harder, Max, fill me." The thought of Max's scalding release inside her aroused her to the point of frenzy. Her breasts rubbed against the table's smooth, cool wood, sticking and catching in mind-blowing friction. And the way he'd lifted her… The position stole nearly all her control over their encounter. She could only receive and react to his primal demands. Helpless, she watched the muscles in the arm she could see flex and release as he held her. The wide black tattoo banding it seemed to do a victory dance as he claimed her.

She loved his tattoos and his rock-hard body. And his domination. She loved his power over her.

"Call me Master," he growled.

"Master," she keened, biting her lip to keep from begging for even more. He was the master with full domination over her. And for the first time in her life she wasn't scared, unsatisfied or resentful with it. How easily he'd just stepped in and taken over.

He pistoned through her channel's soft tissues as if they'd been designed for him. For his satisfaction. Unfathomable pleasure coiled through her, tighter and tighter until she thought she'd fracture when it flew loose. Her arousal burned down into her thighs, signaling her impending release a moment before the spasms clamped over her. She bowed and thrashed. Her heated flesh clutched Max's cock as he drove into her, his grunts exploding through gritted teeth.

"Yeah, take me, Ana. Take all of it." A moment later, he stiffened behind her, shooting inside her. She collapsed against the table, for the first time feeling the molded ridge at the bottom bite into her thighs. She didn't care. Euphoria blanketed her, filling her with well-being. Max leaned over her and kissed her. "Well done. I've never had a sub do better."

Pride welled inside her, mixed with the heavy knowledge that she was no more than that to him. A submissive.

"Thank you," she murmured. This was what she'd wanted, wasn't it? And they were friends too. She couldn't forget that even though she couldn't comprehend how their friendship would survive this.

Pulling her up into his arms, he cupped the back of her head and kissed her lightly. Slowly, he parted her lips with his tongue and delved inside her mouth. Unlike Josh, Max tasted of the hard butter candies he kept in his desk. She sucked that flavor from him, growing aroused again as he continued to tangle his tongue with hers. Good lord, the Cress men could kiss. She'd never had her mouth worshiped like this.

He lifted his head, bright desire burning in his eyes. "Let's go home."

"Yes," she replied. The sooner they were home, the sooner she would be in his arms again.

They quickly dressed and in minutes, aside from kiss-swollen lips and dreadfully mussed hair, looked for all the world their normal selves.

Rebecca looked up at them, her face flushed and horrified as they exited the office and Ana knew the secretary had heard far more than she'd ever wanted.

"I'll be out for the rest of the day," Max, aka Mr. Oblivious, told the woman while her lips worked to form words.

Ana raised an eyebrow and smiled. "See. I told you he'd want to see me."

# Chapter Three

Max insisted they stop at her apartment on the way to his home. As far as he was concerned, Ana wasn't staying alone in her low-security apartment until Tyler was out of the picture and Max was confident she was safe. With his help, she packed most of her clothes in three large suitcases. He carried them to his SUV while she gathered her toiletries. At the last moment, he plucked her tarot cards from the kitchen table and tucked them into side pocket of her bag.

"Are you ready?" he asked, taking her final bag and hustling her outside. "I want you out of here before Tyler discovers you're not complying with his demand and comes looking for you."

"This isn't necessary. I'm sure I'll be fine," she protested as he pushed inside the vehicle and slammed the door.

He climbed into the driver's side. She could see his anger simmering just beneath the surface. His knuckles went white on the steering wheel. "Fine? Have you taken a look at yourself? You're not staying."

"Because you're the Dom? And what you say is law?" she spouted.

"Well, if nothing else, you're comfortable enough to speak your mind," he muttered. "No, this is not about our D/s relationship. Not fully. You're not staying because you're my friend and I don't want you to get hurt. And I don't relish a prison sentence for killing that asshole."

He started the car and shot off down the street, while she gripped the armrest. His fingers tapped on the steering wheel until they got onto the highway and he'd accelerated to seventy. He didn't speak, his firm lips pressed together.

Now she'd managed to piss him off. This was just like with Tyler. She was a rotten sub. "This isn't going to work, Max. I'm just no good at this. If you don't want me at my apartment, fine. Take me to a hotel."

"Like hell. I want you where I know you're safe. Besides, the sooner we're home, the sooner I can introduce your sweet little body to my dungeon and toys."

Ana went all hot, her mind considering all the possibilities. It both worried her and sent excitement flying through her. "You have a…dungeon?" she asked.

He nodded, not taking his eyes off the traffic. She studied his hard profile, loving the look of his chiseled jaw and stylishly cut hair. The man was beautiful and, for the time being, hers. She snuggled into the seat, content with that knowledge. She wouldn't consider the day when it would end.

As soon as she'd slouched slightly, he slid his hand up her thigh. His fingers stole beneath the edge of her short skirt and played with the edge of her thigh-highs. The muscles in her pelvis flexed as she anticipated him touching her again.

"God, I loved these. I want these beautiful legs wrapped around me again as soon as possible. Slide off your skirt, angel."

Here? She glanced around at the passing traffic. "But…"

Max slanted her a glance. "Are you arguing with me?"

Biting her lip, she unfastened her waistband and shimmied the garment down her legs. The soft leather against her ass sent decadent pleasure through her. Never in her wildest fantasies had she imagined this—speeding down the highway with her bottom naked as the day she'd been born.

"Spread your legs for me, angel. When we're together they should never be pressed together. I should always have access." She stared at him while her thighs instantly parted on his command. Where had he learned these things? Cool air from the vents touched her heated folds, cooling the cream gathered there for him and tickling the sensitive flesh. She bit back a moan as she enjoyed the secret pleasure of the blasting streams from the cooling system.

Letting her eyes close halfway, she imagined it was his breath. Any moment she'd feel his lips and tongue.

Max passed a slow-moving vehicle before he went on. "Now because you asked *so nicely* earlier… Yes, I expect you to defer to me because I'm the Dom, especially in the bedroom. I don't want a servant or a carpet. I can't abide a sub who simpers at her master's feet. I do expect obedience and when it comes to making the final decisions on matters that affect the two of us, I will decide."

"I won't have any choices?" she asked, still caught in the sensation building from the puffy lips hiding her sex.

"Of course you'll make choices," he replied impatiently. "I'm not taking away your free will. You'll choose how you will submit. Damn, I'm doing a piss-poor job of explaining myself. I've always had subs who knew their way around the scene."

Idly, he caressed her thigh, moving his hand close to her center. She really didn't care how he explained as long as he touched her. He didn't, always sliding his hand away when he got close.

"Look," he began again. "I know your limits and I'll expect you to participate in anything that falls in that area. Don't expect that I won't push your boundaries. I will. And you will obey me."

The spell holding her broke and she realized what he was saying.

"And be naked whenever we're alone," she added wryly, staring out the window. That's what Tyler had wanted. His slaves were to be naked and ready whenever they were in his presence. The act had been foreign and uncomfortable. The first time it had seemed a little naughty, but after that, as he sat fully clothed reading the paper while he rested his feet on a slave's back, it had struck her as demeaning. The feeling never receded.

Being naked and ready for Max didn't seem so bad. The appeal ricocheted around her belly, melting her resistance to the idea. This was Max not Tyler. Max didn't want a footstool. Her cleft called for him. It demanded her attention with wet pleas. She wanted little more than to grab his hand and press it to her center.

She needed to get a grip.

"As appealing as that sounds, it's a bit inconvenient and unrealistic. What if someone stops by unexpectedly?" He grinned and rolled his eyes at her. "Or if I want to go out to eat or to a movie. I'd have to wait for you to get dressed and we both know how long that takes."

She scowled and shoved at his hand. His fingers tightened on her thigh. "You. Will. Not."

Her eyes widened in surprise. As easily as that they were back to Master and slave and he had total control. Her body knew it. Immediately a tremor quivered through her belly. Her nipples went hard. How had she ever imagined she could have a vanilla-equal-ground relationship? A rush of fresh arousal flooded her naked cleft, readying her for him to take possession again. Soon.

She took a shuddering breath before she begged him to pull to the side of the road and fuck her. This was why he was a Dom and she wasn't. She was weak to the needs assailing her body. As if to contradict her thoughts about his being in control of himself, he stabbed his finger deep inside her.

"So wet, so hot," he murmured, working in and out. "This is my cunt. You will not deny me it."

"Yes…Master," she stuttered.

"Don't come," he ordered. "Talk to me. Find control, Ana. Don't come."

He asked the impossible. How could she not with everything surging through her, with his fingers spiking in and out of her pussy, exposed to anyone who passed them. Black spots peppered her vision as she struggled to follow his command.

Her thighs twitched, ribbons of pleasure beginning to unfurl. Her hands fisted and she purposely dug her nails into her palms and focused on the pain.

"How did you get into this?" she gasped.

"BDSM?" he asked. His thumb massaged her clit. Damn him. He was testing her, making it as hard as possible. His fingers never ceased their press into her. He scissored them on alternate strokes, stretching her and catching pleasure spots. "This is the lifestyle I was raised in."

"You mean your parents are into it?"

"Into it?" he mused. "It's more than that. For all of us. I mean, my brothers and sister and I didn't witness how the politics of it worked in the bedroom for our parents—that's just sick—but they were very open. Our sex education was different from that of our peers. That's for sure."

And he was well educated in it. Ana took shallow breaths as she tried to counteract the knotting need twisting in her belly. She wasn't sure how long she'd win.

"When most kids were watching the films about how boys and girls are different, I was already learning how to implement the D/s lifestyle into my life. And when kids in high school were starting to experiment in the back of cars, I was learning at the hands of a trainer chosen by my family."

She bit the inside of her cheek. Experimenting in the back of his car sounded like a great idea. Would he punish her if she came? Oh. Wrong thought. *Stop. Stop. Stop.* She begged her body. Her breathing was harsh in the quiet vehicle.

"It's strange," she panted, trying desperately to focus on his words. She couldn't stop the tidal wave surging toward her. Any second it would slam over them both.

He shrugged and added another finger into her pussy. "It's been like this for my family for over a century. Kind of a tradition."

His thumb scraped across her clit, pushing, drawing a reaction that pulled at her scarcely held control. "Come, Ana. Come now," he ordered. "Scream for me, angel. Fill my fingers with it. Now, Ana."

Suddenly, her body arched off the seat, her head pressing backward as a blinding orgasm shredded through her. Mindlessly, she worked on his fingers, the waves cascading over her, her hands splayed on the soft leather seat.

"Yes, like that," he groaned, encouraging her. She whimpered as he pulled his fingers from her. He brought them to his lips. "I've wanted to taste you since last night but earlier I was too interested in fucking you."

She collapsed against the seat, realizing for the first time that they were driving neck and neck with a Greyhound bus. Embarrassment flooded her. He'd brought her off in front of a busload of strangers. She turned to stare at him, aghast.

He smiled, finishing his feast. "They're from out of town."

She shook her head. "You must have thought it was hysterical when I started waxing on about thinking I was into bondage."

"No, I just desperately wanted to be the one to train you."

"Then why didn't you?"

"For the same reason you hesitated to take my offer. I didn't want to ruin our friendship. But here we are." He stroked his finger over her clit, gathering more cream and sending a chain reaction of shudders through her. It wouldn't take much for her to explode again.

She breathed a sigh of relief as he signaled and pulled onto the off-ramp. A few minutes later, he pulled into his garage. The automatic door slid closed behind them, leaving them alone in the dim enclosure.

Max watched the shadows play over Ana's face, reminded of the last time they'd gone camping together. The wind blowing the tree outside the garage window made the sunlight flicker on her face much like the campfire had that night. When she'd finally snuggled into him, too cold not to, he'd been hard-pressed not to show her a new use for their tent tie-downs.

His cock throbbed. There was a tie down in her near future.

"Let's get inside," he said, opening the door and going around to open hers. She looked surprised. Max grinned. She might as well get used to being treasured. A true master cherished his slave.

Taking her hand, he led her inside, telling her that they'd get her bags later. "Do I get to see the dungeon now?" she asked. Trepidation trembled in her words. She wasn't ready for the dungeon yet.

Unbuttoning his shirt with his free hand, he guided her down the hall to his bedroom. "No, not yet."

She looked around his room as they entered. It was clean and he'd actually pulled the blanket back over the bed this morning, still there was nothing to see here. Almost all his toys were locked up in the dungeon so that they didn't shock the maid who came in three times a week.

"Kneel," he said as he headed for his dresser. He didn't look to see if she complied. He knew she had. And he couldn't look at her. He was about to do perhaps the most devious and foolhardy thing he'd even done—even more so than showing his true nature and spanking her yesterday.

Pushing aside a pile of underwear, he lifted out a velvet-covered box and set it on the top of the dresser. His stomach tumbling with misgivings he opened the lid. Carefully, he lifted out the heavy gold chain inside. This was the collar used by his family to signify a Cress sub. A permanent sub. Though the collar, comprised of thick links, appeared decorative, it had several hidden loops handy for bondage.

Each of his brothers had identical bands for their subs. If any one of his relatives saw this on Ana, they'd know he'd permanently claimed her. He might have a whole lot of explaining to do to them and Ana. Hopefully by then she'd know how he felt and be ready to stay with him.

*Dangerous thoughts, Max.* Ana had always been the love 'em and leave 'em sort. Due to her father's job, she and her family had moved continually while she'd been growing up. By the time she'd met Max she'd said goodbye to so many friends, she'd stopped investing herself to any sort of relationships. She hadn't had much of a choice with him though. After they'd been thrown together by school officials, he'd crept under her skin. Eventually, she'd opened up to him. However, it had taken months of ignoring her rebuffs.

Refusing to commit was still such a habit for her. He wasn't sure she'd allow him to take their relationship to the next level. He was fairly sure the only reason she was kneeling on the floor behind him was because she knew this was temporary.

Turning, he caught his breath, the sight of her punching him in the gut. Her hair fell in wild ebony waves around her slim shoulders and down to her waist. The top three buttons of her white blouse were open, exposing the upper swells of her breasts while the tails of the shirt hung between her spread thighs. With her arms pulled behind her, the tails hiked up, revealing several tantalizing inches of silky black curls and pink aroused folds.

The blood feeding his thought centers deserted him, rushing for his cock. Ana was the most beautiful sight he'd ever seen. Hell, she looked like sex waiting to happen. She *was* sex waiting to happen, who was he kidding?

"While you are with me," he said around the rock in his throat, "you will wear this."

Her brow furrowed.

"It's not a necklace, not really," he continued. Holding the links in one hand, he showed her the hidden loops. "It's a collar. This will signify that you are under my protection."

Her tongue darted out to dampen her lips and she nodded. Raising her arms, she lifted her heavy hair and straightened her neck. He held the necklace so she could see the ends and its strange fasteners. After his brother Theo's sub, Keera, had blithely removed her collar and taken off, all four brothers had had the collars altered. "Once this is on you, you won't be able to remove it," he told her. "The fasteners must be in a particular position to open. Like a combination lock."

Her position didn't falter. The threat of permanence didn't seem to affect her. That was promising. The boulders knocking around in his middle settled slightly. A moment later, the collar was locked in place and Ana lowered her hair.

He ran a finger over the gold. "Beautiful."

"It's like Keera's and Jessica's," Ana ventured with more calm than he'd have expected. She eyed him curiously.

So she knew his sister-in-laws had similar collars. "I don't just want to train you," he admitted. Shit. Where had that come from? "I'm afraid you'll never be properly trained and in all good conscience I need to take you on permanently. I can't set you loose on the world like this."

She lowered her head, staring at his toes. "You'll have to. Eventually. This morning I accepted an offer to be a project manager for Sissek Construction. I'll be in their Chicago office. I have to report in four weeks."

"What?" he exclaimed, the bottom ripped from his world. Of all the scenarios he'd thought of, he hadn't envisioned this. Rebellion and argument. Yes. Total desertion... He'd always been such a strong Dom with no problem getting his sub to bend to his will with a few words or the occasional punishment. Ana made him feel like a total wuss. It was unacceptable that she made him feel so weak. Damn it. He loved her. She couldn't just take off to Chicago.

"You're not going."

"I am, Max. This is about my life, not sex. Last night when I didn't know about how to handle you and Tyler was threatening me… I had this offer on the table. I called Sissek this morning and took it."

"You're right. This isn't just about sex. This is our lives, Ana. This is about the two of us being opposite sides of a whole. And not just the D/s relationship even though that's part of it. You might find another Dom in Chicago." His whole being protested that thought. "But you will never find what is between us, what has *always* been between us."

She didn't reply and she didn't meet his eyes. Slowly she shook her head, denying him and shaking away some of his hope. They weren't leaving it at this.

"When are you going?"

"Three weeks," she replied.

"Then you're mine for the next three weeks, complying with what I demand. I want you in my bed every night."

When it came time for her to leave, he wanted it to be damned hard. She lifted her head and he saw the tears pooling on her lids and making her blue eyes glassy. It was already difficult for her. In three weeks he'd make it impossible or kill himself trying.

He didn't let her tears weaken his resolve. In fact, they strengthened him.

He tossed his shirt on the bed. He toed off his black dress shoes and pulled off his socks, leaving himself clad only in his black dress pants and leather belt. "Come with me."

Again he didn't look to see if she complied. He led her to the end of the hallway to the stairs leading to the lower level. At the bottom of the steps they entered the family room. His house was built into the side of a hill so that the front of this level was underground but on this side large glass windows and doors overlooked an overgrown valley, thick with trees. A large deck jutted out from the doors leading from the room.

He ignored the view and walked to the other side of the room and into another short hallway. At the end, he withdrew a key from his pocket and opened the door. Standing to one side, he motioned for Ana to enter. He locked the door behind them and pocketed the key.

Eyes wide, Ana walked to the center of the bright room. It had the same sort of floor-to-ceiling windows as the rest of the house with cupboards lining much of the other walls. "This isn't exactly what I thought of when you said dungeon."

It looked too cheerful and downright...*pleasant.*

"Were you thinking a dank, dark, bricked room with chains hanging from the walls?"

"Well...yeah," she admitted reluctantly, pricked by a bit of disappointment. As a girl she'd always wanted to be captured by pirates. Even now, the thought of being tied up excited her more than Christmas. And no one would do it.

With an evil grin, Max flipped open a few cabinet doors, revealing implements that sent goose bumps and excitement flying down her limbs. "I think you'll find this dungeon well-stocked. And since you're determined not to be here long, you'll want to explore everything quickly, won't you?"

*Oh God, yes.* She wanted to try it all.

Her breath caught at the sight of the two pairs of cuffs he plucked from a hook and her heart took off. Did this mean he actually meant to restrain her? Her fingers flexed as a trickle of fear inched down her spine. How well would she endure it, now that her fantasy appeared to be turning into reality?

Coming back to her, he placed one set of bindings at her feet then fastened a cuff around each of her wrists. Quickly, he unbuttoned her shirt and let it drop to her feet. She shivered at the sensation of the silk sliding down her body, her breasts already bare since he'd forbidden her to put her bra back after they'd fucked in his office. Her nipples pebbled as the arousal that had briefly leveled out after her orgasm revved up ten notches. Her body vibrated with need. Max laved his tongue over each tight peak and gave the second a quick bite, drawing a small cry.

"Chilly?" he asked, kneeling before her and sliding her thigh-highs down her legs.

"No." Well, except for the cool air wafting over her damp nipples.

"In a few minutes, you'll notice it's a few degrees cooler in here than the rest of the house." He fastened restraints around either ankle while he talked. She wasn't getting cooler, she was heating up. She wanted him to lean forward and lick her pussy the same way as he had her nipples, maybe even bite her clit. A rush of cream filled her tingling folds.

He lifted her into his arms and carried her to a rectangular, planked table much like she would expect to see in a dungeon or at very least a castle. The grooves where the wood pieces met dug into her ass, although he gave her little time to register it as he laid her along the length.

There was no give in the wood, if Max pounded into her on it, she'd feel every surge through all her limbs. Nothing would cushion her as he drove deep to her womb. She wanted it now. As he pulled her arms over her head, she spread her thighs for him to show him she was ready for his possession.

"Now, did I mention to you earlier that I'm in dire need of a reading?"

"No." He wanted a naked card reading? He didn't need to bring her to his dungeon for that. And he didn't need to tie her up. Not that she was protesting. He captured one of her legs and bent it then fastened her ankle to the corner of the table so her foot was actually suspended over the edge. She knew immediately the position would rob her of any leverage.

"I need the cards to tell me why the hell my sub is thinking of leaving."

"I told you..."

He glowered down at her, his arms over his wide chest. "In this dungeon, you will always refer to me as Master. Do you understand?"

She nodded and he raised an eyebrow at her.

"Yes, Master," she mumbled. It felt weird to call him that, yet right about now she'd do just about anything to get him to fuck her right into the table. Besides, there was no denying the way her body reacted every time she said it. From his position between her knees, Max could probably see what his domination did to her. Her folds probably glistened with it. She felt wet enough.

"We'll work on that." His fingers trailed down the inside of her thigh from her knee. He traced the crease between her leg and pussy, the touch light enough to tickle and make her squirm. Just as lightly, he drew his finger along the crease of her ass. "Ana?"

Her eyes closed as she took deep breaths. "Yes, Master?"

"Has anyone ever fucked you here?"

She shook her head, unable to answer. Reflexively her butt cheeks squeezed together. Hopefully, it wouldn't be as traumatic as when she'd lost her other virginity. Talk about bad sex. It hurt and he was a jerk and she'd cried.

Max wasn't a jerk though.

"This we haven't ever discussed. Are you willing to experiment? There might be a little pain." He drew his knuckles over her compressed muscles. "I promise it will be okay."

"Okay," she answered in a small voice. She wasn't so sure about this anymore. She was tied tightly to a table and unable to get away. Maybe letting him mess with her ass wasn't the wisest decision.

He smiled before she voiced her reservations. "I'll be right back. Stay put."

"Ha. Ha." She rolled her eyes, knowing he was joking to put her at ease. Then remembering his earlier order, added a halfhearted "Master".

"Keep saying it like that and I'll get a complex," he said from across the room where she could see him loading items into a caddy. It seemed like an awful lot of things for the simple act he'd questioned. Didn't he just need lube?

Returning, he set the caddy on a short stool beside the table. Rather than moving between her legs he stood beside her. Carefully, he lifted her hips and placed a folded towel beneath them. "Relax, angel," he whispered. "I'll always take care of you."

He kissed her parted lips, drawing all her attention to his tongue sliding over hers. She moaned, tilting her head to receive him more fully.

She wasn't distracted enough that she didn't notice his slippery finger worming its way along her ass. It disappeared then returned a moment later, even slicker. Slowly, he worked it around her anus. Her breath choked into his mouth as he pressed, gradually sinking the digit deep inside her. Oh, sweet heaven. After her body adjusted, he pulled it almost free and added a second finger, taking his time with the whole process.

His mouth never left hers except to whisper earthy encouragement, his eyes dark with passion as they stared down at her.

"Are you okay?" he asked as he stretched the tiny passage.

"Yes…Master," she answered, the last coming on a sigh as tendrils of pleasure began to override the slight pinch that had heralded the invasion. She never would have imagined…

She protested when his fingers disappeared.

"Hang on, angel. Hang on."

A hard tip pressed to her anus. Immediately, she tensed, trying to lift away from it. It followed.

"Stay still. Relax," he murmured, slowly pushing it against her virgin opening. "Remember. Feels good. You can do this."

"What is it?" she gasped as it stretched her.

"It's a plug. A small one. Just relax."

She felt what seemed to be a slight pop and suddenly she could breathe again. Max brushed his lips over hers. "Good girl. I'm proud of you, angel. I know that wasn't easy."

She stared up at him, blinking back tears. She wanted to leave this? How could she leave him? He was right. What was between them couldn't be replaced. But it was a done deal. She couldn't back out now.

Max molded her breasts, bringing her back to the moment at hand and his command over her body. Her anal muscles contracted around the plug as he tugged at her nipples.

She cried out sharply as pain shot across first one breast then the other. Craning her neck, she saw two clamps holding her nipples, tiny ornaments dangling from them. She glared at him.

Fisting her fingers, she dropped her head back on the table. She could do this. She'd take whatever he doled out. She'd punch him as soon as she was free.

Maybe it was her resolution to get even or maybe it was the sweet calm falling over her but the pain started to recede, becoming pleasure that stole her breath. A heightened sense of well-being swamped her and dulled her senses. At the same time, every touch sent tremors cascading through her.

Distantly, she heard a buzzing noise. That cleared her mind slightly as she saw Max lifting a vibrator toward her vagina. Good lord, he hadn't been joking about the whole nine yards. She bucked as he strapped it against her, placing the device against her clit and leaving her sheath empty and needy. She moaned twisting against the vibrations and the pleasure spiking down her thighs. The more she fought the more her body reacted, winding toward her release.

"You have the prettiest navel," Max said, taking her by surprise while her body contorted. "I think you need a tattoo. A pretty one. Just as lovely as your belly button."

"What? No, Max."

He stood between her legs, a handful of markers in his hand. Pressing an arm over her navel, he opened one pen. "You need to stay still," he instructed as the tip traveled across her skin. "These are permanent markers. You don't want to be walking around for days with ugly squiggles across your belly."

He wanted her to stay still? The vibrations from the toy were rattling into her pussy, tightening the muscles of her womb and ass. Striations of sweet pleasure were reaching up into her aching breasts down to her toes. She couldn't stop the moans rolling from her. And the sensation of his arm holding her down was fulfilling fantasies she'd been afraid to acknowledge.

Her belly quivered against the sensation of Max's markers flying across her skin. He didn't seem to mind. "You know each of the Cress men have tattoos," he said conversationally, while her brain screamed for release and tried to comprehend what the hell that had to do with the price of tea in China.

"Yes?" she gasped. Sweat coated her body, her muscles twitching.

"When we turn eighteen we go to see my uncle and he does them."

Right, right, right already. She'd seen them. They were beautiful scrolling symbols that Max had told her he'd one day explain. He wanted to explain *now*? When she was fighting an explosion with all she had.

"The one around my navel says to control myself during any situation involving my sub. I have to remember to keep control no matter how angry you make me, how hot you make me, how hungry I am for you." He changed markers. "It's very important. I would never want to accidentally harm you. It's essential since we don't use the safe word in my family."

"Master," she begged. "I can't stay still any longer. Please."

"Fight it, Ana. Listen to my voice. Try to separate yourself from it."

He was insane. There was no question.

"My other tattoo," he went on as he drew, "is my charge. It names me as keeper of the temple, owner of the treasure and protector of the spirit."

She lurched but he lifted the tip in time. He capped the pen, tossing it into the basket beside him. Holding both her legs, he blew on her belly.

He climbed on to the table, balancing between her legs. His hands came down beside her shoulders. "Do you know what that means?"

She shook her head, tears forming in the corners of her eyes. She couldn't…she couldn't…take… She had to…

He kissed her. "It's about you. Protecting your spirit. Keeping your temple. You are my treasure."

He reached down to stroke over her folds, sinking his fingers inside her convulsing pussy.

*Too much*. Her torso twisted, ecstasy clamping over her. Her vision blurred as she screamed. Wave after wave cascaded through her. Agony accompanied it, as Max removed the nipple clamps. It twined with the pleasure, becoming one with it until she couldn't separate it from the delight clawing through her.

Max knelt back, holding her knees and watching Ana undulate on the table. He wanted to be inside her, feeling her body clench around him while she screamed. Carefully, he removed the vibrator and dropped it to the side with the clamps he'd already taken off.

Pressing his hand over the delicate vines he'd drawn around her navel, he felt the contractions racking through her. They sank through him and squeezed his painfully aroused cock.

Finally, Ana fell back against the wood. Her fingers flexed as she took ragged breaths, her belly rolling as tremors continued below her glistening flesh. Her legs flopped to the side when he released the restraints. Crawling over her, he unfastened her wrists.

She didn't move.

"Ana?"

"Mmph," she mumbled. Leaving the table, he circled to the side and carefully lifted her into his arms. She was the most precious person in his life. She was his treasure whether she wanted to be or not.

"Wake up, angel. We're not through yet," he murmured. He studied her pale face, marveling at its delicate features. Her sooty eyelashes stood in stark contrast against her skin. He wanted to taste every inch of it until it pinked again with her arousal.

Placing her on a heavily padded mat near the windows, he braced himself over her as she stirred and was immediately surrounded by the adoration and content satisfaction in her bright blue eyes. "Wow," she whispered.

He toyed with the collar around her neck. His collar. Because she was his. He could give her anything she ever wanted, yet she was leaving. Pain tore through his chest and he reminded himself not to demand she stay with him. In the end it would have to be her choice, regardless of what he wanted.

"I'm going to fuck you until you scream again," he whispered in her ear. "I left in the plug. It's gonna feel like there are two men in you, angel." Reaching between them, he switched on the vibrating plug and watched her face contort as the sensations took her over-aroused body.

"No," she moaned. Her lips parted and her eyes closed as she gave herself up to it. He watched her carefully, gauging every reaction. It was rule he'd grown up with. Don't use a safe word, always monitor your sub's status. A good Dom was always in charge—of himself and his slave—and he always recognized his sub's state of mind, recognizing acceptance or stress.

Right now, Ana was in overwhelming bliss. Standing, he unfastened his pants and let them fall. Quickly he went to the toolbox he'd left by the table and retrieved two last items. Protection and a box.

He knelt over her and rolled on the ridged condom he'd selected. His cock prodded her dripping folds, tempting him to plunge inside her molten pussy. Inside her he could lose himself and pretend she'd always be in his arms. He clutched the box in his hand.

"Ana, I want my reading now. I want to know the future."

She stared at him. Her lips formed the word "what" although no sound emerged.

He opened the small card box in his hand, his mind more on his cock bobbing at her entrance than on the stack of cards in his hand. Leaning between her legs, he let his tip slide slightly inside her as he shuffled the cards on her belly.

"Like this, right?" he asked, following the procedure they'd used for all the traditional readings she'd given him over the years.

"Max, I don't know—"

He cut off her words with a kiss.

"Angel, I need to know now."

He cut the cards in three piles that ran from her belly to her breasts. Her accelerated breathing almost knocked the cards right onto the floor. Carefully he gathered stacks into one pile again and dealt out the top three cards facedown across her flat belly. "Are you ready, Ana?" he asked.

She nodded.

He plunged his cock into her deep and hard, bellowing as he possessed her and her tissues clamped around him. Inside her. So perfect. The vibrations from the plug assaulted his balls as they slapped against the end. His body screamed for him to take her as hard and fast as he could, nevertheless he started a slow, measured pace. Balancing on one arm, he reached for the first card. He dragged the edge over her belly then scraped it across her nipple, drawing a harsh gasp.

"Tell me my future, Ana. What's this card mean?"

She stared at it, her eyes barely focused. "An introduction to something new." She panted hard as if speaking was outside her range of ability right now. He pushed her matted hair from her face.

He tossed the card aside. "Something new? I think we might be doing that right now. Everything is new, isn't it, angel."

Making love to her would never grow old.

"Yes." She drew up her knees and he sank deeper into her honeyed recesses. His cock throbbed as his release threatened. He grabbed up the next card before he lost his control. He traced it across her lips before he leaned in and kissed her.

He was losing it quickly. His groin knotted as he fought his release.

"And this one," he grunted, holding up the card so she could see it. "What's this one?"

She squinted at it, then her eyes squeezed closed and her teeth sank into her bottom lip as she struggled to come up with the meaning. He scraped the card over her other nipple.

Her hands gripped his hips, her nails digging into him. Her passion drove him, nearly erasing his goal.

"It…signifies a change," she gasped finally. "Moving to a new position."

"Like this?" He pulled her legs over his shoulders.

"Yes," she cried as he plundered her, driving in and out faster now that completion was near.

He yanked up the last card. "This one. What's this one?"

Her eyes went wide as she stared at it. "Six of Pentacles. Us."

"Us," he repeated, pressing the card over her heart. "Us. The future."

He'd always be there for her. If he had to go to Chicago…

The rest of the cards went flying as he captured her hands and pistoned into her welcoming heat. Ana screamed, convulsing around him. Her hips surged off the mat, slamming into him as her tight sheath milked his tortured flesh. Spirals of pleasure-pain rippled through him until his entire focus centered on the rhythm of their bodies slapping together and the pressure building in his cock. His world at the tip of his penis.

He shuddered and his power drained to his cock. Helpless to his body's demands, he blasted within her, emptying his seed with a strangled yell.

Breathing hard, he stared at the card lying between them on her chest. *Us*. It signified them. Together. He saw it. The damn cards saw it. What would it take for Ana to see it?

# Chapter Four

Ana stared at the outfit Max handed her. "You want me to wear that out of the house?"

"The proper response is 'Yes, Master' and to put it on."

She rolled her eyes, staring at the leather skirt that would barely cover her bare pussy. As if it didn't show enough flesh, a slightly off-center slit ran to the waistband.

"I think you lost your mind when you came this afternoon. Apparently your brain is somewhere in the dungeon."

"Maybe I should try to find it. Want to help me?" He slid his finger through her folds. "I have an idea where it might be."

"How can you possibly want me again?"

"After all the years I've stayed away from you, how could I not?" He pulled her against him, revealing the hard ridge trapped inside the leather pants that matched her outfit—though with a great deal more fabric. She'd never seen anything hotter than Max in those pants. They rode low on his hips, showing off his chiseled six-pack to perfection. Coupled with his wild hair, tattoos and biker boots, he looked like the baddest bad boy to hit town.

Sweet heaven, she wanted to recline back on the bed and invite his badness to do its worst. Unbelievable. They'd spent the better part of the afternoon in the dungeon, until he'd carried her to his bedroom and tucked her into his bed. She wasn't sure how long she'd slept until he'd woken her and taken her again. Afterward, he'd sent her into the shower, telling her to hurry because they were going out.

She glanced at the triangle-cut leather that comprised the top of the outfit. She wasn't sure it would even cover her breasts. Well, maybe she could do a Lady Godiva thing with her hair. It wouldn't cover her past her waist but she could hide her near-naked breasts with it. Of course she'd have to free it. After her shower, Max had pulled her hair back into a ponytail then braided it so it fell in a tight rope down her back.

She tossed the top on the bed and slid on the skirt, unfortunately completely right about how much it covered. It settled low on her hips, leaving the drawing Max had done fully in view. Turning to the mirror, she studied the oval of delicate leaves and tiny purple flowers, all expertly shaded to look like a pastel drawing. How had he done that with markers? She needed to get a picture of it before it faded.

"Like it?" he asked, coming behind her and splaying his hand over her belly.

"Yeah. You're an amazing artist." She grinned. "A master."

He growled and bit her shoulder. Leaving her, he got the top of the outfit and wrapped it around her breasts, fastening it in the back. It covered her breasts adequately, but Ana was sure if she moved funny, she'd pop free. She'd have to be really careful.

"Almost done," he said. Going to the bag he'd pulled the clothes out of earlier, he pulled out a set of cuffs. "Hold out your wrists."

"Yes, Master," she whispered, the cuffs dropping her right into the scene. He fastened them around her wrists. A delicate chain was attached to each and he attached the ends to her collar. He helped her into a pair of shiny black stilettos.

"One last thing."

Her heart lurched as he pulled that item from the bag. Lifting her chin, he attached a black leash to the collar and turned her back to the mirror.

"Dear God, I look like a refugee from BDSM boot camp." And she looked hot. Damn hot. The image of herself kneeling in front of him and sucking his cock while he held the leash sent a rush of arousal to her freshly washed pussy.

"You look like a sub who obeys her master." Wrapping her braid around his hand, he pulled her to kiss him. Her breasts swelled, pushing against their inadequate covering. He slipped his hand beneath the top and palmed a mound while he took his fill of her lips. She moaned, thrusting her hips against him.

"We have to go," he murmured.

"Yes, Master," she replied.

He smiled, drawing his thumb over her swollen lip. "I love when you say that."

Going to the closet, he removed a voluminous black cape and draped it around her shoulders. "Where are we going?" she asked.

"The club."

Panic rushed through her and she nearly dropped to her knees—not in submission. "What? No. Please, no, Max. I can't go there. I can't let—I don't want other men to—"

He pressed two fingers over her lips. His chin tilted down as he stared into her eyes. "Hush. Cresses don't share. Never forget that, angel. I might want to show you off and display my claim but I won't let anyone else take you. Not as long as you're mine," he promised.

She nodded, the action jerky, and looked away from him as he slipped on a jacket. Fear fisted in her middle. This was the full test of her commitment to being a submissive. She didn't want to do this. She didn't want to be seen in public like this. She was worried about what might happen at this club—it was where Tyler had wanted to take her. A cold terror filled her, making her legs tremble as she followed Max to his SUV.

They didn't speak on the way to the club. The security was rigorous and Max showed identification to gain access to the parking ramp. As they navigated the garage, Ana saw other women cloaked as she was. They seemed unworried, even a little excited as they followed their masters. What did they know that she didn't? Maybe they were into group sex with strangers. Some people were.

Max didn't take her hand when they left the SUV. That was unusual, although she figured it was because of the setting. He had to be the Dom with no questions. She followed him quietly, a few steps behind. Near the entrance to the club, she heard strains of Indian music similar to what she'd heard in the single Bollywood movie she'd seen. The blend of woodwinds and drums infiltrated the lower levels of her consciousness, wrapping her with its arousal-heightening sensuality.

At the door, Max again had to show ID and the doorman held the door open. Max ushered her inside with a hand to the small of her back. An attendant removed Ana's cloak. She desperately wanted to clutch it around herself and hide behind its weight. Instead she stood docilely.

The club reminded her of popular dance clubs, the interior dark with multicolored lights blinking on and off. Looking around as her eyes adjusted, she found the similarity ended there. Most obvious was the area that should have been a dance floor. It seemed to be more of a stage of sorts where Doms were having their subs perform sexual acts. Sometimes with other people. At one end a female sub was being flogged—and the woman seemed into it. Ana wasn't sure what to think of that.

Her breathing hitched. Max wouldn't take her down there, would he?

Unable to continue watching, she peeled her gaze away and found the two levels of tables surrounding the floor area were filled with women—and men—in various states of undress. The setup reminded her of posh nightclubs in Vegas. The rest just made her think orgy. The mellow pitch of the

Indian horns barely covered the low moans from the sex taking place throughout the room.

A woman clad only in a black g-string and nipple jewelry approached them and bowed slightly to Max. "Master Cress. May I see you and your slave to your table?"

"Yes, Mirinda," he answered. At his familiarity, Ana eyed the woman, jealousy flaring through her. Mirinda had a phenomenal body. She could easily see Max drawing the woman…or plowing his cock into her barely covered pussy.

Max leaned close to Ana. "Draw back your claws, little cat. I've never fucked her. Although, in all truth, I can't say that about every sub here. After all, I couldn't have what I wanted." Taking the leash hanging between her breasts, he led her as he followed Mirinda. Instinctive revolt rose inside her. How dare he lead her like an animal?

*What did you expect, Ana? It's a leash,* her inner voice chided her. *And doesn't it feel a little hot and naughty?*

It did and if there was any place where she'd let Max do this, it was here. Let? She almost laughed. Like she really let him do anything. He knew her refusal point and she knew he'd do whatever he wanted up to that point. That's what submitting to him was about. She respected that just as he respected her limits. Here of all places, it was of utmost importance to behave. She knew without him telling her so that his position in this D/s community would be questioned if his sub was rebellious or disrespectful. She could mouth off at home but not here.

The hostess stopped at a tiny table and told Max to have an enjoyable evening. She disappeared without ever acknowledging Ana. Ana made a face and turned to the table. It had only one chair. *Why* was there only *one* chair? Confused, she looked askance at Max. With a discreet tilt of his head, he indicated toward the couple at the table beside them. The woman sat on the floor between her master's splayed knees, her legs curled beneath her and her head resting on his thigh. Glancing around the club, Ana saw that many subs were in the same position. The subs didn't appear demeaned by their lowly positions. They appeared...*protected* and even coddled as their Masters petted and fed them.

Okay, if that was the way it was.

She waited for Max to sit then folded herself into the same position as the sub beside them. A slight tug at her collar made her look up at Max. He smiled down at her as he draped the leash over his thigh. He cupped the back of her head and tipped it a little farther back, giving her a lingering kiss. "You're so beautiful."

"I don't know what to do," she whispered. She was totally out of her element.

"Just relax, angel. I'll lead you."

His assurance didn't soothe the butterflies pounding around in her stomach. Not much did, as she furtively glanced around in shell-shocked amazement. The show on the center floor reminded her of a circus. It was a show for all intents and purposes, the actors caught in a frenzy of sexual activity. Each seemed to want to outdo the last and Ana could only watch in horror. Tyler had intended to put her body on display on the floor like the other Doms were doing. He'd intended to give her body up to whatever bidder came forth. Bile rose in her throat as she watched what looked like money exchange hands and flies open.

Idly, Max stroked her hair while she stared in transfixed shock. She barely noticed his brothers Ryan and Theo arriving with their wives, Jessica and Keera. Josh tagged along behind the couples, alone. She worked with all five but had never seen them in this light. The men were dressed identically to Max and she saw for the first time that they had the same tattoos, just as Max had said. How could she have known them all these years, been part of so many of their family functions and not known this?

The women were attired in the same way she was. Though they were married to Theo and Ryan, Max had explained to her earlier that Keera and Jessica were subs too. Together, the seven of them were unmistakably a family—four black-haired, gray-eyed gods and their women. Ana's stomach clenched at the thought. She wanted to belong with this family. She couldn't. It would hurt too much when she said goodbye. She always had to say goodbye. Heck, she'd even said goodbye to her own family when her father had been transferred several years ago. She'd made the decision to stay behind and nothing had ever been the same.

She was alone. Max's hand caressing her said otherwise yet she couldn't forget she was leaving even him in a few more weeks. Turning away from the people who filled the soon-to-be-empty corners of her life, she focused on a sub who'd been led to the floor moments ago. She writhed, moaning loudly over the music while three men took her.

That could have been her.

She buried her face in Max's thigh.

"Come here, angel," Max murmured. He pulled her onto his lap so that she straddled his slightly parted legs with her back pressed to his chest. She gasped in surprise as her skirt hiked up, exposing her to whoever might walk past. He locked an arm around her waist. Slowly he trailed the fingers of his free hand along the inside of her thigh while he murmured calming words to her.

She relaxed in tiny increments while he gentled her. Despite her pussy being exposed, she might as well have been wrapped in a blanket for all anyone cared. She barely jumped as Max's hand left her thigh and slid up into her folds. With a sigh, she closed her eyes and leaned her head back against his shoulder. The sultry Indian music rose around her, its erotic tones bolstered by the moans growing more and more apparent. It was easy to imagine, she and Max alone in his private harem. The Master pleasuring his slave.

She turned her face into his ear, letting him hear her low cries as he spread her lips and gathered her honey on his fingertips. Heat prickled up her neck as he discovered her arousal. What would he think? She couldn't tell him that it wasn't what she watched that brought the reaction in her. It was being in this place with him, surrounded by the blatant sensuality.

"Master me," she whispered, intent on pleasing him as he jabbed two fingers into her weeping folds. She whimpered, unable to contain her shudders as he worked in and out. His body reacted immediately to her husky words and pressed hard to her ass. Contentment worked through her. She knew the words to say to him as her hips rocked into his fingers. "I want you. I want to turn and ride you. With everyone watching. Anyone. I want to show them how you possess me, Master."

Relentlessly, he stroked his fingers into her. He nudged her face up so he could speak in her ear. "You're mine, Ana. Look down there at the floor. See how that sub takes those men. Her name is Felicity. You think her master is cruel to ask this of her, don't you? She loves this. He gives this to her because she loves it. Later, he will take her home. He'll care for her and tell her how proud of her he is. Look at the way she takes those cocks. She's beautiful, isn't she? You'd be just as beautiful with your legs parted, taking those men. With your lips wrapped around their fat cocks."

She quivered, tiny cries escaping as she squeezed his plundering fingers.

"As beautiful as I know it would be, it will never happen, angel," he growled. "It doesn't matter how much you might want it. I'll never share you, not with my brothers, not with my friends and certainly not with strangers."

His thumb rasped over her clit. She closed her eyes, again sinking into the decadent sensations flying through her body. Her whole focus pinpointed on his touch. She pressed her lips together. She couldn't come. Not here. Her body thought otherwise as pleasure coiled inside her, carrying her higher. Reaching behind her, she clung to Max's hips.

"Scream for me, angel," he rasped in her ear. "Scream and let everyone know."

Her breaths came closer together, gasping from her.

"Let go," Max urged.

Suddenly, the tension inside her snapped, ecstasy bubbling over and gushing to her limbs. *Yes. Oh, yes.* Her scream throbbed from her chest as her head pushed back into his shoulder.

A vicious yank on the leash strangled her release with the force of being slammed into wall. Her eyes flew open as Max's hand shot up to knot in the leather and keep her assailant from dragging her off his lap. She stared up at the blond man glowering down at them, his pallid features enraged.

Panic filled her at Tyler's outright attack. She didn't think Max would let her go without a fight but Tyler didn't seem cowed by the power that radiated from her lover. Obviously, Tyler was a raving lunatic. *She'd* be cowed by Max if he wasn't holding her so protectively right now. Instinctively, she pressed back into his chest only to be dragged upright again by the taut leash. Max's hand thankfully diminished the pull on her neck.

"What the fuck are you doing with my property?" Tyler snarled, giving the leash another ineffectual yank. He glared at Ana, sending another shot of pure terror down her spine. "I want you off him and on your knees now, slave."

She twisted sideways on Max's lap and looked up at him. "Master?"

He smiled as his arm tightened almost painfully around her waist. "This sub is not your slave and she never has been. She's been mine for years."

Tyler's eyes narrowed and she saw the distrust in his glare. He didn't believe Max. Great. "She agreed to be mine," he spat. "She signed a contract and I'm holding her to it."

Oh man…she had… Could he hold her to it? Did he have a legal leg to stand on? Max's laugh was mocking. "She was not free to do that. She belongs to me. And only to me."

"But—"

Max's eyes narrowed and Ana buried her face in his neck, ignoring the pull of the leash. He yanked it from Tyler's hands. "It was a grave mistake on her part, a mistake for which she's been severely punished. She bears the bruises."

Tyler's bruises, however Ana certainly wasn't going to point it out. Despite her hopes, Tyler wasn't backing down to Max's dominant stance though it was apparent that Max held the upper hand over the man. Tyler was small in her lover's overwhelming presence.

Gaining strength from Max, she looked back to Tyler and raised her chin, letting him see that she would not submit to him. Since she'd been here at the club, she'd done everything necessary to show her deference to Max. She always would. Now as she stared at Tyler, she straightened her shoulders and gave him her most superior look. He was a worm and unworthy of her submission. She wasn't a weak, spineless woman who would wallow at the altar of his faux power. Tyler was a fraud. And a bully. He didn't know the first thing about being a true Dom.

His lip nearly quivered as he fisted his hands at his hips, a foot stomp away from being an overgrown toddler. "I'm the one she wronged. It's my right to mete out her punishment."

"You will not touch her," Max replied in a confident, matter-of-fact tone. His lack of reaction startled Ana but she carefully gave no sign of it. He stroked his hand, still looped in the leash, down her bare back, both reassuring her and reminding her of her position. She was his. He'd do whatever was necessary to protect her.

Who would protect him?

She'd researched enough to know that each D/s community adhered to strict rules when it came to ownership and behavior. She didn't want to do anything to jeopardize Max's position.

"I demand to see her punished," Tyler snarled loudly. "She must be publicly beaten for lying and misleading me. She will be punished now or I will take my right later."

Ana didn't miss the whispers rising around them. She couldn't make out the words or whether those at the neighboring tables sided with Max or Tyler. Fear curled through her like thick, acrid smoke, filling every pore. Fear for herself. Greater fear for Max. Whatever happened to her, she'd be leaving in a few weeks. Conversely this was his community. Max would still be here, functioning in a society she'd flawed for him.

"I mete out my own punishments. In private," Max said evenly.

"She owes me the lashes."

Lashes?

Max's hand tightened infinitesimally. "No."

The murmurs around them increased.

"Ma-Master, let him do it," Ana said under her breath with more bravado than she'd ever come close to feeling. Terror was more like it. If Max was punishing her, she'd worry about taking the pain. She trusted him. She didn't trust Tyler. She never had. In spite of her fear she couldn't let Max take the fall for her stupid decision. She took a deep breath. "Let him be done with it."

Pain filled his eyes but he showed no weakness to anyone except her. Only she could see the torment inside him. His face hardened to an impenetrable mask. "I will choose the instrument. Seven lashes only. One for each day."

"I want a cane," Tyler replied gleefully as he practically danced about. *Worm.* What the hell had she been thinking? There was nothing remotely exciting or naughty about this sadist. He wanted only pain. And she'd be that sacrifice.

Max gave a single nod, his lips pressed together.

"Stand, slave," he said with an edge to his voice she'd scarcely ever heard. It was the tone he used when he was angry at being forced to do something yet determined not to show it. It was rare for anyone to force Max into anything.

Obediently, she stood and bowed her head to him as he rose, the leash tight in his white-fisted hand. Ill-concealed agitation vibrated off him. Max wanted to kill Tyler. Any fool could see it. Well, any fool except Tyler.

"This way," Max said, leading her deeper into the building with Tyler walking behind them. Ana sucked in a breath when Tyler scraped his nails down her back. Max spun around, his eyes murderous as he glared at Tyler. "Keep your fucking hands to yourself," he growled. "I'm allowing this one concession. You will not take liberties with my tolerance."

Max paused then impatiently waved Tyler in front of them. "You lead the way." He stepped close to Ana. "I should never have brought you here. I don't want to do this," he confided.

"It seems we must, Master. You didn't know this would happen."

"I suspected he'd be here. I wanted to stake my claim." Perversely, his confession sent a burst of pleasure through her. It strengthened her for what was ahead.

"So now you're feeling guilty? Don't. I brought this on myself."

He stroked his thumb along her bottom lip. "So brave."

"Not really but is there way to get out of it?" she added in a whisper. "Without legal entanglements and smearing your name in the community."

"I don't give a rat's ass about my name, Ana."

"*I* care. My father whipped me with a belt and occasionally a switch when I was growing up. I'll survive this." She focused on his sculpted chest so he couldn't see her lie or her fear. Silently, she hoped her father, who'd never even spanked her, would forgive her untruth.

"This is different. I can hardly bear the idea of him hurting you. If it was me administering the cane, I could arouse you sufficiently beforehand. It would ease the sting. You'd actually enjoy it on some levels."

Remembering the warmth that had filled her folds when he'd spanked her, she knew it was true. It was possible for pain to segue into extreme pleasure. She didn't foresee that happening. This wasn't the same as submitting to Max. A scrap of an idea began to form in her head. "Where will you be?" she asked.

"Beside you. I will never leave you alone with him. I'll bind you and remain with you."

She nodded. If he was near her, if she sensed his presence, perhaps she could transfer the pain in her mind. She'd know she was submitting to Max, submitting *for* Max. A surge of power arced through her. Submitting to Max was her strength. Just as the Six of Pentacles had indicated last night, he'd given her so much. He'd patiently taught her and shown her the delight of submitting to him. He was her benefactor and protector.

It was killing him to be powerless to protect her right now.

"Master," she murmured. "My submission to this—it's for you. I would do anything for you."

Emotion boiled in his eyes—pride, tenderness, sorrow…love? He gave her a single nod and led her in the direction Tyler had taken.

Her eyes widened and her knees almost buckled when they stopped before what could only be called The Wall of Punishment. A huge assortment of items was displayed on hooks. All manner of floggers, cat-o'-nine-tails, crops, canes and coiled whips waited ready for a Dom to wield. The heavy whips thankfully looked dusty but the rest appeared clean and well used. Ice splintered through her.

They seemed to be racked by category and Tyler went immediately toward the heavy whips. She'd run before he ever used one of those on her.

"You chose a cane," Max reminded him. "I choose this one."

Tyler's lips pursed in distaste as he glared at the lightweight instrument in Max's hand. "She'll barely feel that," he complained. "I might as well tickle her."

"Turn around. I'll test it on you."

Ana bowed her head and pressed her lips together to suppress her amusement at the thought. Tyler snatched away the rattan cane. "You think it's funny, slave," he sneered. "You won't be laughing in a few minutes. I'll show you how a true Master punishes a disobedient slave."

Beside her Max growled deep in his throat. If Tyler pushed much harder he'd find himself flat on his ass or six feet under, depending on how out of control Max was when he finally retaliated. No matter what he thought, Tyler would not come out of this unscathed. He'd become an outcast or Max would take him out. That in itself gave her comfort.

Still, her legs wobbled like broken toys as she was led to the floor where she'd seen the other sub taken by the three men. The area was deserted now except for the waist-high whipping apparatus. Chilled and terrified, she stared at it, while the club grew silent. Even the music seemed to fade.

"Ana?" Max said, his voice full of concern. "You don't have to do this. I'll take you out of here."

Ignoring him, she walked to the leather-covered bench that looked like a shorter, wider version of a gymnastic horse. There was a bar on the other side for the person being whipped to grasp.

"Ana?" Max repeated. "I can stop this. I'd rather kill him than let him touch you."

Warmth filled her. She looked up at him and smiled. God, she loved him. How could she have been so stupid about fighting it and wanting to leave? And what a dumb time to figure it out. "I'll do it and be done."

His face returned to its inscrutable mask and she knew he was holding back any emotions. Carefully, he bent her over the whipping bench, spreading and securing her ankles in place.

She closed her eyes, sucking in her lips and pressing them together. Her knuckles turned white as she gripped the metal bar. Behind her the cane whistled. She tensed but it never connected.

"He's just testing it," a voice said above her. Craning her head up, she found Theo standing at her head. He settled a hand in the middle of her shoulders. "Keep your head down and relax," he advised.

"Max will keep him under control." This time it was Ryan who spoke. He placed his hand beside Theo's. Josh placed his on the other side, completing the trifecta of support. Looking behind the men, she saw their grim subs. Her family.

"You will not begin until I give the word," Max snapped. "And this is my only warning. If you draw blood, I don't care if it is only one stroke, you're finished."

Blood? Tyler could draw blood? Ana's throat closed and she pressed her face into the bench. Max slowly flipped up her skirt, exposing her bare ass to the entire club. She could do this. It was only seven strokes. She'd be okay. Wouldn't she?

Normally Max's touch calmed her fears. Now there was little comfort when Max placed his hand over her lower back. It was time to begin. An electric current seemed to buzz through the club patrons who watched the activity on the floor.

A whine whirred through the air a moment before the cane slashed diagonally over her ass, the sting exploding across her skin. She tried to contain the resulting scream that howled from her. Tears filled her eyes. Shit.

Suddenly Max was gone along with Josh and Ryan, bellows outside herself surrounded her as another slash fell across her burning flesh. Feminine hands replaced those of Max's brothers.

"Three," Jessica said as another blow came. Her voice trembled. Ana could barely hear her through the blinding, deafening agony slicing through her.

Max struggled against his two brothers as he watched Tyler draw back to deliver a fourth blow. All he could see was the cane flying at the woman he loved and the brutal purple welts lifting on her ass. Tyler was hitting her with every ounce of his strength—far more power than any Dom should ever use on a sub, especially one new to the scene.

Tears flooded down Ana's face as she held the bar with whitened fingers. Valiantly, she tried to contain her cries. Her lip was bloody from the effort. "Let go of me," he demanded as he had since the first blow had fallen. "Get your fucking hands off me and let me help her."

"Every strike is driving him further and further from this community," Ryan pointed out. "Our community will push him from town for this. You know they will."

"You have to let him finish or he'll come after her again. Would you rather he did this without you there to stop him after seven?" Josh reasoned quietly as Max continued to struggle. He had to get to Ana. She was his. He'd promised to protect her.

He'd failed her.

What his brothers said was true but Ana's anguished cries tore through him like a serrated blade. It ripped away every bond he'd thought they'd built between them and left him raw and empty. No matter what she'd claimed before, she'd never forgive him this failure. He didn't deserve her.

"For God's sake, Max," Ryan swore as Max continued to throw himself forward. "Be a freaking Dom and pull out stoic for five seconds."

"You'd let him do this to Jessica?" Max snapped. Ryan's hands loosened.

Max lunged forward as one of the women murmured "seven" and dodged in front of Tyler as the man lifted his arm again. An eighth stroke landed square across Max's legs and he bellowed in rage. He yanked the cane from the man's hand and cracked it over his leg. Tossing it aside, he advanced on Tyler.

Around them, the crowd roared its approval. Max didn't care what the crowd thought. Tyler would pay. Drawing back his arm, he plowed his fist into Tyler's face, satisfaction bursting inside him along with the blood flooding from Tyler's nose. Before the man had a chance to react, Max punched him again and laid him out on the wood-planked floor. It wasn't enough.

Max's hands opened and closed as he stared down at the unconscious man. Tyler would never be allowed at the club again. His family—especially Theo—had enough influence to assure that. As the bastard stirred, Max knelt beside him and pressed a hand to his throat. Tyler's eyes went wide.

"You ever touch her again, you ever come near her and I'll kill you. Do you understand?"

Tyler just stared at him.

Max tightened his hand. "Do you understand?" he demanded.

Tyler nodded slowly.

His fingers relaxed slightly. "If I see you, if I even accidentally run into you, you'd better run the other way. You're no Dom. You're nothing more than a bully and a sadist."

"You might want to leave town, man," Josh commented from behind them. "Max, Ana needs you."

Max jumped and headed back to her, only to come up short at the sight of her behind. Long dark purple welts distorted the beautiful curve of her ass and upper thighs. His eyes burned at the sight. Fear followed. Why was she still bent over the bench? Why hadn't she moved?

Kneeling behind her, he released the cuffs holding her feet in place. Standing, he bent beside her. "Ana," he whispered, wiping her tears with his thumb. She didn't respond. His stomach folded in on itself while his heart thundered in merciless panic. He'd never seen a sub so far gone.

Carefully, he pried her fingers loose from the bar, catching her when she slithered toward the floor. She whimpered as his arm came in contact with her thighs. He shouldn't have let her do this. He should have stopped her, no matter what. They could have dealt with Tyler somehow.

Instead he'd failed her.

Theo stood near the door as Max carried Ana toward the exit. Silently, he handed over her cloak, his face grim as he surveyed the damage. "Tyler's finished," he said, his voice rough with suppressed anger. "Plenty of the Doms and subs here are cops. He's not going to be able to sneeze now without getting a citation for disturbing the peace. He's gonna be too busy with his new friends to bother Ana."

Max nodded, his mind too centered on her to fully comprehend Theo's words. "Call Dr. Manning and have her meet me at Ana's apartment." She'd want to be there after what happened. She sure as hell wouldn't want to stay with him now that Tyler had been dealt with. *Now that I've failed her.*

"Done."

The drive to Ana's seemed to take an eon. There was no way she could sit so he'd laid her across the backseat. She was deathly silent while he cursed himself. How could he have let this happen? Everything he'd been taught since childhood said to protect his sub with everything in him. To treasure her. Not to share her. Yet he'd allowed a sadist to beat the woman he prized more than his own heart. She was his soul.

His emptiness echoed within him, resounding so loudly his bones ached with his sorrow. He'd wagered on the game and lost everything. She'd never forgive him for this.

Dr. Manning stepped from her car as Max pulled to the curb. In leather pants and a V-neck black T-shirt that displayed her hammered-silver metal collar she didn't appear to be a doctor. Along with her Dom, however, Vanessa specialized in tending the D/s community.

She tipped her head as she approached. "Master Cress. How is she?"

He shook his head as he carefully wrapped Ana in her cloak and lifted her from the SUV. He didn't carry her often and right now she seemed as light and fragile as an injured bird.

"Unresponsive?" Vanessa asked, holding open the door for him to enter.

"So far."

The doctor made a noncommittal sound and followed him up the stairs. He wanted to ask her what she meant by that, demand to know Ana would be okay, beg her to make Ana feel better. He mentally shook himself. Vanessa couldn't tell him anything or do anything for Ana until they were inside and she'd had a chance to do an examination.

Using the key Ana had given him when she'd moved in, he let them into the tiny apartment. He didn't bother with lights. The flickering neon from the signs across the street illuminated her apartment sufficiently, giving it the seamy feeling of a B-grade detective flick. It matched his mood. Bleak. Miserable.

He winced as the overhead light snapped on and blinded him.

"It would be best if you lay her on her bed," Vanessa instructed. "That way I can examine her and she won't have to be moved again. Then she can just sleep—unless I find something that will require medical attention I can't provide."

"What are the chances of that?" he demanded.

"She was caned but her skin wasn't broken. It was a fairly lightweight instrument with blows concentrated on the buttocks and thighs."

Max listened intently. Theo had passed on more information than he'd have been cognizant enough to relay.

"I'd say," she continued, "that chances are Ana will be a very sore sub for a while but she won't require a hospital visit." She set down her bag on the table beside the bed, while Max laid Ana on the blankets. Carefully, he peeled away the cloak.

The consummate professional, Vanessa pulled on a pair of latex gloves and turned toward her patient. Professional or not, she couldn't contain her gasp at the sight of Ana's ravaged ass. For a moment, she stood aghast, her lips slightly parted and stared.

Her reaction to the extensive beating sent bile rushing up his throat. He'd known it was bad yet for the damage to stun a woman who routinely worked the emergency room sickened him. If he ever caught Tyler Awkes alone, that bastard was a dead man.

"Sir," she said addressing him by the honorific given Doms in their community. "This is more than I expected. I've seen plenty of patients with injuries from unsafe BDSM but…this is brutal."

"He meant to punish her."

Her brow furrowed. "I'd say he did. Ana is your sub?"

Here it was. The questions about why he hadn't protected her. His throat tightened as guilt closed around him again. "Yes."

Concern not repulsion filled her eyes. "Do you…need a sedative?" she asked tentatively.

Him? He shook his head in disbelief. He deserved to feel the same pain as Ana. Hell if he could take it from her he would. "Just…help her."

Vanessa's face filled with sympathy. Looking away, she pulled a plastic-backed paper napkin from the bag and unfolded it onto the bed beside Ana then placed several items from her bag on it. Quickly, she checked vital signs and responsiveness.

"Mentally, I'd say she's deep in sub-space," she said, mentioning the state of mind many subs entered after an intense experience. "She's fighting the pain and her reactions to it. She'll be okay after some rest and will probably even come out of this enough to talk to you once I give her something for the pain. Now," she focused on the welts, palpating the area as she checked for broken skin and determined the damage, "this looks worse than it is. Thank goodness. It appears she has deep tissue bruising but the welts will lessen by morning. I'm going to give her a shot to help her sleep."

She finished tending Ana, dabbing ointment over the abused flesh then handing him the tube. "Keep this on her. The lanocaine in it will numb the area and reduce the pain. Do you have any questions about her care?"

When he said no, she gathered her things and departed with a reverent inclination of her head. In moments he was alone with Ana and his recriminations. Carefully he worked Ana's skirt off her, wincing at her quiet moans as the leather pulled over her butt. Despite the doctor's assurance that Ana would be more responsive once the pain lessened, he didn't try to wake her. She needed her rest.

He left her on her stomach, her face turned toward him on her pillow. Pain etched across her features. Pain he'd brought on with his stupidity. He should never have taken her to the club. No matter how he looked at it, he couldn't escape the fact that he'd failed her.

Listening to the traffic on the road below her apartment, he sat beside her on the bed and rested his arms on his raised knees. Wearily, he dropped his face onto them. There was no way around it. He'd known Tyler might be at the club. He'd known he might be angry. Max couldn't face her when she woke—and maybe that was part of why he didn't rouse her. How could he look at the woman he loved and admit he'd let this happen to her? She was so precious to him. He loved her.

Emotion welled in his chest as he smoothed the line of pain creasing her forehead and brushed back her hair. She'd never want him after he'd allowed this to happen to her. She wouldn't want any part of the scene either. One day with her as his sub and he'd failed and lost her.

What did that say about him? He was shitty Dom. He understood pain for pleasure, discipline and punishment. How every relationship had degrees of Domination and submission. He even understood that the punishment Ana had endured might be commonplace in some relationships—not in his circle, however. Having all the knowledge in the world meant nothing if he couldn't share it with the one woman with whom he wanted to share it.

She snuggled close to him, whispering his name. The tremor in her voice cut through him. He wanted to run from the emptiness filling him. Run home and drown himself in booze. Anything to dull his reality without Ana. Instead, he stayed beside her all night, aching with what he knew he must do. Ana had promised herself to him—at least until she left. Now that she was safe from Tyler, he wouldn't hold her to it.

At five in the morning, when he knew he had to go home and get ready for work, he smoothed another layer of cream over the welts. Fighting the visceral emotions inside him that told him to do otherwise, he let his brain rule and wrote a note to Ana. He couldn't bring himself to say goodbye—weak-ass bastard that he was. She'd read goodbye between the lines. Carefully, he detailed the instructions Dr. Manning had given and told Ana what the doctor had said about her injuries. Then he promised to have her bags delivered to her.

With shaking hands, he removed the collar he'd locked around her neck, left his key on her kitchen table and let himself out of her apartment. Everything between them had changed.

He'd never be the same.

* * * * *

Ana grimaced as she woke. Her head hurt and as soon as she moved, she realized her head wasn't alone in the pain. Her muscles ached as if she'd been through the workout of her life. In a way she had, she realized as her memory of last night returned.

"Max," she murmured, expecting him to be beside her when she turned over. The other side of the bed was cool and empty. Groaning, she sat up quickly and scanned the room for him. Nothing.

Her brow furrowed as a foreboding knot twisted in her stomach. Why the hell was she here at her apartment instead of at Max's house? And where was he? She didn't even remember him bringing her here. Had she passed out? She wouldn't be surprised. She'd pretty much lost it once the first blow had fallen.

Carefully, she climbed from her bed and felt the twinges of pain shoot through her rear. It wasn't as horrible as she'd thought it would be, but she wondered how she'd sit all day at work. Standing seemed a good option.

Maybe Max would have a better idea that included more time in bed.

"Max," she called, wandering through the house toward the living room. Perhaps he'd decided to sleep on the couch so he wouldn't disturb her. She was more disturbed by his absence. She wanted to be in his arms.

Silence greeted her, while the knot in her stomach grew.

"Max?"

His name cut off in her throat as she spied the key on her table and she lifted her hand to her throat, trying to breathe. Instead of cool metal, her fingers closed on skin. Tears blurred her vision as she dropped to her knees.

Max had removed her collar. She'd failed as a sub after all and lost her Dom just as she realized how much she loved him. Worse, she'd lost her best friend too.

Gathering herself together with the frayed edges of her being, she struggled to her feet. This was no different from all the times she'd been forced to say goodbye in the past, only this time he'd left before she could. Furiously, she scrubbed the tears from her eyes and sniffed, fighting for control.

She'd bury herself in something else. Work would distract her. She could go the whole day without accidentally running into Max, if he was even there. There was plenty to do and she needed to give her notice. Her eyes burned again. One day. That was all it had taken to completely foul up her life.

*Congratulations, Anastasia. I bet this is some kind of record.* She wondered what the record was for the number of pieces a heart could shatter into. She'd probably broken that one too.

* * * * *

Ana stared at her pathetic excuse for a resignation letter and changed two words. It didn't help. She changed them back, deleted a sentence and reinserted it in another spot. It was still pathetic. She might as well write "Goodbye, cruel world, I can't take it anymore". Theo would take one look at this note and think she was joking.

She shifted, trying to find the words to make it at least seem like English wasn't her second language. Her backside didn't feel too bad, unlike this morning. It was a good thing she found the cream and note Max had left behind. She couldn't say her ass wasn't tender by any stretch of the imagination but it wasn't so bad. She'd survive.

The worst part was the knowledge this pain came from Tyler's rage and not from Max's love play. She'd have preferred it to have come from Max. Then she'd think of him and grow warm with every shift.

Thoughts of Max brought tears to her eyes again. All day, she'd waffled between just leaving work or going to his office to demand answers. What had she done to fail him so badly that he'd abandoned her?

Her head jerked up at a knock on her door. Max? A second later Theo and Ryan, not Max, stepped inside her tiny broom closet of an office. Theo quietly shut the door and took a seat in the chair opposite her, while Ryan perched on a filing cabinet.

Their eyes seemed to inspect her, seeing beneath her clothes to her secrets. "How are you?" Theo asked and she felt heat surging up her neck, remembering what he'd seen last night. Anger accompanied her embarrassment. It was pretty damn nice. They were worried about her and Max didn't seem to give a care.

"I'm fine," she answered stiffly. She refrained from moving in her seat to alleviate her discomfort. There was no need to bring their attention to her pain.

"Are you?" Ryan asked in disbelief. "Well, I'm glad someone is. The rest of us are fairly traumatized. Especially Max."

She looked away. Max? Right. He didn't care. And he didn't want her anymore. "I'm sure Max is fine."

"How could he be? It's my understanding, his sub is planning to move to Chicago," Ryan answered.

Well, so much for her resignation letter. She needn't have bothered with the last three hours. Her anger got the better of her. She turned back to the two of them with a glare. "Max doesn't have a sub," she snapped. She clapped her hand over her neck where her collar should be. "I'm apparently free to do whatever the hell I want."

"Ana," Theo started calmly. "I want you to stay and be a project manager. That's the job you're taking at Sissek, right? I'll top what they're offering you and you know the working conditions here are ideal."

They would have been before her incredibly short affair with Max—another world record. She shook her head. Theo went on as if she'd had not answered. "We have quite a few new projects coming in and we're in the position that we'd have to hire another project manager. I'd prefer someone from the inside. Someone I trust."

"And I want Jessica's workload halved," Ryan interjected.

Theo rolled his eyes. "We have a ton of new contracts coming in and he doesn't want her overburdened. Jess isn't happy about it, although she'll do as he says. This morning we were discussing it and your name came up as a possibility."

She frowned, knowing he was talking about the daily Cress meeting of Theo, Max, Ryan and Josh—each reporting on their sector of the business to their father. What a coincidence that her name would suddenly come up, she decided sarcastically. And why had her imminent departure been mentioned. She'd think Max would be eager to get rid of her.

"Just came up, huh?" she said in disbelief.

"Actually, it did. Jess thinks you might be a good addition to that staff. Then Max told us you were leaving. That explained a lot. We were all wondering what the fuck was the matter with him." Theo picked at a piece of nonexistent lint on his suit coat sleeve. "I don't know what went down with the two of you—"

"I'd really like to know too," she retorted.

Theo raised an eyebrow, making it clear she'd crossed the line. Well, whatever. It wasn't like she was a sub—his or anyone else's. What did she care? Her days at Cress were limited and her heart was broken. The funny thing was, if Max hadn't freed her, she would have taken Theo's offer in a second. She wanted to stay here. The Cresses were her family.

"Max renounced our lifestyle," Ryan told her. "That's another reason we're here. We don't think he'll survive it. I don't think he'll survive being apart from you. He looks like shit. I know how I felt for the short time Jessica and I were apart after I'd finally been with her."

"And I know how I felt when Keera ran away."

"You're forgetting. Max chose this. This isn't like what you went through."

Theo shook his head. "Max feels the same."

Her chin quivered as tears filled her eyes. If only they were right. If only Max wanted her the way they wanted their wives. She wanted to believe he did and would have until this morning…

"He loves you," Theo grated, his voice rough with urgency. "Hell, we *all* love you. You've practically been part of our family forever. All of us figured that eventually the two of you would end up together. Look. At least think about my offer."

"Okay," she replied. It wouldn't do any good. She couldn't stay and work in the same place as Max. There was only so much torture a person could take.

Marginally satisfied, both men stood. Theo reached in his pocket and withdrew a folded sheet of paper. "Keera wanted me to give this to you."

"What is it?"

"I don't know. Some of that mystical stuff she does. She was pretty urgent about it."

The only mystical thing Keera did was tarot readings. She didn't do gypsy spells or curses like Ana, not that Ana did them often. As bad as she felt today, she felt a curse coming on. Perhaps something that would keep her from ever falling in love again.

Slowly, she unfolded the paper while the men left her office and found a color photocopy of the Six of Pentacles. Keera had written her a note beside it. "This card keeps coming up in my readings and I know it's about you. Someone's offering you knowledge and some sort of gifts, maybe even love. Would you please take what's being offered, so I can move on?"

Ana stared at the rendering of the card from Keera's tarot deck. In this version, the beggar knelt before the rich man, receiving charity. A supplicant kneeling before the Master. The paper crumpled in her fingers and she balled it up, tossing it into her recycling basket. The Six of Pentacles wasn't her card anymore. Max had given her all he had to give. There was no more. Not even love or his need for her submission.

Leaning back in her chair, she winced, the position pulling at the stripes across her ass. She needed to go into the restroom and apply more ointment. She just didn't have the energy to move. She should just go home and go to bed. Her lonely bed where all she'd think of was Max and what she must have done wrong.

She needed answers. The knot in her middle that had plagued her all day twisted, reminding her of Ryan's words. Max wasn't taking this separation well—or maybe he didn't sleep well. Whichever, she wanted to know what the hell was going through his head. And why would he renounce the lifestyle he enjoyed so much?

Shooting to her feet, she ignored the throb of pain and marched out her door and across the building to Max. He could tell her straight up what he felt, then if a separation was truly what he wanted, she'd never bother him again.

His secretary's eyes went wide when she saw Ana. A flush tinged her cheeks and her hand shook as she removed her headset.

"Hi, Rebecca," Ana greeted, feeling a flood of compassion for the woman who'd heard far more than she'd ever wanted yesterday. "I need to talk to Max, if he's in."

"I'm just going on break. Go on in. I'm sure he'll, uh, be glad to see you."

Watching the woman scurry away, Ana wrapped her arms around her waist and wondered if she shouldn't be the one scurrying away. With a deep breath, she turned toward the door and let herself inside.

It took a moment for her eyes to adjust as she leaned against the door. Max had pulled all the shades in his normally sun-drenched office and now only the barest hint of light filtered inside. The room was so dark and deathly quiet, she almost thought it was empty until she spotted him slouched to one side in his office chair, staring at her like the Big Bad Wolf must have stared down Red Riding Hood.

Reaching behind her, she stealthily slid the bolt into place. Even if she was scared out of her wits of losing the battle she was about to embark upon, neither of them was leaving until her questions were hammered out.

"What do you want, Ana?" he growled.

She took a shuddering breath. She wouldn't let him cow her. She loved him and she was pretty darn sure he loved her too, even if he was being an ass right now. Crossing the room, she rounded his desk until she was beside him and dropped to her knees, letting her skirt ride up her parted thighs.

He didn't look at her as he scrubbed his hand over his face. "Don't do that. You're not my sub anymore."

She dropped her head forward so he couldn't see the way his words hurt her—if he ever managed to look over at her. She bit her lip, taking another breath through her nose. "I'll always be yours, Max. No matter what. Keep me. Send me away. It doesn't matter."

He didn't speak for a moment. His voice sounded odd when he finally did. "Anastasia, I need you to leave."

Something was wrong. Why did he sound so—strangled?

Trying not to wince, she stood and looked down at him again. He still stared the other way. His head snapped up as she clicked on his small desk light. She gasped at his agony-ravaged face. Max was in as much pain as she was. Without a word, she stepped between his splayed knees and pulled him to her. He stiffened, resisting her.

"No, Ana," he whispered.

"I love you, Max."

A deep groan tore up his body and he crushed his arms around her waist, burying his face in her belly. His shoulders shook as he held her. She blinked back tears, stunned by his deep feelings, emotions that wrung through him and dragged the mighty Dom to his knees.

"Please don't make me leave," she begged, stroking her hands through his hair. Her body trembled out of control at the love unfurling inside her, freely shown at last. She'd die if he denied it.

"I failed you," he whispered. "It's my duty to protect you and I let harm come to you."

She shook her head. Held so close in his arms and hearing his rasping voice, she remembered his bellows last night and seeing him struggle against his brothers. If they hadn't held him, he would have leapt on Tyler and the man wouldn't have been able to land more than a blow. Besides, it was her choice to submit to the cane and remove Tyler from their lives.

"You're too hard on yourself," she said gently. "I chose to do it. I choose to submit to you but I still have free will. What Tyler did…it was never something you wanted."

He pulled back. "Let me see it."

Stepping backward, she released her waistband and let her skirt fall. She shivered as it skated down her thighs to her ankles. Naked from the waist down—underwear and hose hadn't been an option—she kicked off her shoes and stepped free of the clothing. Her chiffon shirttails tickled her tender flesh as she returned to the embrace of his spread legs.

"Turn," he ordered.

"Yes, Master," she replied. She couldn't help her grin at the return of her Dom. She wanted his dominance over her for the rest of their lives. Turning, she lifted her shirt. "It's much better," she commented.

He growled, his disagreement clear. "How badly does it hurt?"

"It hurts but it's not terrible. I've kept the ointment on it like you said to in your note." She'd take up that pathetic note with him later when their emotions weren't so high. She sensed any misstep might still send them down separate paths.

His fingers trailed lightly over her bruised skin. A tremble shuddered down her body.

"Hurt?" he asked.

She shook her head. Hurt? No, it felt so good. He continued his ministrations, dragging his fingertips lightly over every part of her ass, down her thighs, up her inner thighs. She desperately wanted him to touch her and sink his fingers into her hungry pussy. Already, tingles engulfed it and her folds filled with cream.

She moaned quietly as his fingers detoured to slide along the underside of her cheeks instead. Her breath left her as his lips touched her tender ass. Good lord, her womb throbbed with need. She desperately wanted to press her legs together to ease some of the clenching desire.

If he tried to make her wait for an orgasm leaving wouldn't be an issue. She'd kill him. "I'm not going to Chicago," she told him.

"Good." His hands slid around her, one flattening on her belly while the other cupped her mound. As he continued to kiss her abused flesh, he slipped a finger inside her folds.

"Yes," she hissed, trying to press into the touch. His hands held her still. Her head dropped backward. Blindly, she reached for his shoulders behind her for support. Slowly, he explored her liquid cleft, drawing shudders from her surrendered body.

"I'm staying with Cress Construction," she panted.

"Even better."

"Max…I don't ever want to leave you."

She heard his desk drawer open but didn't have time to wonder about it before he lifted her into his arms. A crinkle of plastic at her side told her all she needed to know. Carefully, he carried her to the leather couch and placed her on her stomach.

"Max…"

"Hush." He slipped a throw pillow under her hips. Gently, he parted her, dragging his thumbs over her weeping pussy. She needed him. She needed to be fully united with him again, to know the threat of separation had passed.

"Please," she whispered as his fingers slid ever-so slowly in and out of her. He scraped over her clit and she cried out. "Please fuck me, Master."

Relief filled her as he climbed on the couch behind her, pausing only to shove down his pants and yank on a condom. Urgency drove them. There was no time to fully disrobe. No more time to be apart. They needed to be together now.

Despite the force driving them, Max gently probed her folds, parting her with the thick head of his cock. Slowly, he pushed inside her, parting her tight tissues, inch by torturous inch until he was fully seated against her. Violent tremors engulfed her.

"More," she begged as her channel flooded and fisted around him. "You won't hurt me, just please…"

Her entreaties didn't sway him from his slow invasion and even slower retreat. She clawed the couch cushion. Desperately she tried to gain purchase so she could surge backward into him. His hand on the small of her back kept her where she was. "I don't deserve you," he whispered. "But I can't let you go."

His surges grew stronger. It still wasn't enough. She struggled against his restraining hand, the battle raising her arousal to a frenzy. The more she fought the closer her release drew, coiling tighter and tighter.

"Yes," she cried as it dragged him into the furious madness. Mindlessly, he pistoned forward, his balls slapping forward into her clit. A tingle of pain sketched over her ass, immediately replaced by fiery pleasure. It reached down into her pussy, flowing over her. Her orgasm rushed over her and she screamed, overtaken with the joy. A moment later, Max grunted his completion, stiffening deep inside her.

Tenderly, he kissed the back of her neck and slipped to the side, disposing of the condom and pulling her into his arms. He sighed but she heard his amusement in it. He toyed with her spent pussy as he spoke, reigniting the newly extinguished flames. "Not only did I fail you but I've trained you poorly. There is no way I would ever have been able to give you up to another. From the second you agreed to submit to me, you were mine and only mine. You're perfectly made to fill my needs and no other's. You alone are fully able to give me complete pleasure."

She pressed her cheek into his shirt, loving that they'd both been so overcome that they hadn't undressed. She smiled through muzzy happiness. "I see your dilemma. I'm a flawed slave."

"You're perfect for me." His hands abandoned her cleft only to appear in front of her face when she lifted up to protest in an un-submissive-like manner. Her complaint froze on her lips as she saw the gold dangling before her. She shifted her gaze to her tentative gray eyes.

"If I put this on you this time, it stays forever. I wasn't wholly truthful when I gave this to you before. A collar like this is as binding as a wedding ring. My vows to love and protect and cherish you, to always be faithful to you are as binding as wedding vows. And I do love you, Ana. Imagining life without you… I need you beside me. Forever."

She didn't need anything else. Sitting up, she lifted her hair. "I love you, Max. Collar me."

"I love you, my beautiful submissive. Everything I have is yours. I'm everything you need. Everything you've searched for. You never have to search again. You never have to say goodbye."

Happiness exploded to every empty space in her body as he fastened the collar. His. "Yes, Master," she sighed and lost herself in a kiss that promised everything else they hadn't said. But there was plenty of time for words. Later. They had forever.

# GENTLE CONTROL

# Dedication

*To Chuck – the hero of my story*

*Acknowledgements*

Thanks to the great William Shakespeare for letting me borrow a famous line from one of my favorite plays, *The Tempest*. Hearing "we are such stuff as dreams are made on" will never be the same.

# Trademarks Acknowledgement

The author acknowledges the trademarked status and trademark owners of the following wordmarks mentioned in this work of fiction:

Dumpster: Dempster Brothers, Inc.

Grizzly Adams: Sellier, Charles E.

McDonalds: McDonald's Corporation

Oreos: Kraft Foods Holdings, Inc.

Oscar the Grouch: Muppets, Inc.

Pop Tarts: Kellogg Company Corporation

Starbucks: Starbucks U.S. Brands

Styrofoam: Dow Chemical Company

Taco Bell: Taco Bell Corp.

## *Strength*

Dear Reader,

Strength. When some people hear this word, they think of physical power. Given this, a glance at the Strength card can be confusing. In most tarot decks, a maiden is shown with a lion. The lion is not overpowering her. She is gently closing its mouth. This is because the card doesn't represent brute strength—it signifies inner power. When this card comes up in a reading, it means one may face a challenging situation, a family matter or a problem from the past. In *Gentle Control*, the hero, Josh Cress, experiences all three in the prim package of Tempest Montgomery, the challenging submissive from his past.

In this story, we are presented with both aspects of the Strength card. Josh represents the upright manifestation. Throughout the story, he exhibits inner strength. A Dom by nature, he controls Tempest's mind and body though gentle signals, eventually bringing her under his mastery. His quiet compassion breaks through her defenses and in turn gives her strength to face her own challenges.

On the other hand, Tempest's father, John, represents the shadow side of strength. A man full of pride, he prizes appearances and tends to lose his temper. He's an emotional tyrant. He uses manipulation, fear and social power to control others, including his daughter.

Faced with both sides of the Strength card, Tempest must decide in which direction she will bend. Toward inner strength or toward fear and manipulation.

## *Author Note*

This book portrays some aspects of Domination/submission and BDSM but is not intended as a true-to-life account of this lifestyle.

# Chapter One

There he was. The worst mistake of her life and she had to talk to him. Tempest Montgomery looked across the nearly empty restaurant to the area where Josh Cress sat with his family. She recognized his three brothers but not the women with them. Wives, perhaps? None was Josh's wife. She knew that.

She wasn't into stalking but it had taken exactly two phone calls to find out what she needed to know. Josh was still single, unattached and could be found having breakfast at Manolo's on Thursday morning. His brother Max, who remembered her from years ago and apparently was sympathetic to her cause, had provided that information. She hadn't needed him to tell her why the family was gathered. She remembered why. Josh's birthday.

She'd left him on his birthday. Eight years ago.

And she'd never spoken to him again.

She needed to talk with him now.

For a moment she studied his profile. Thick brown hair fell to his wide shoulders framing one of the most masculinely beautiful faces she'd ever seen. A glint of a tiny hoop winked from one of his dark brows. That was new. Her fingers itched to flick over it then trace across his strong forehead and nose. He'd always closed his beautiful gray eyes while she investigated the smooth lines of his cheekbones.

His head tilted to the side as he gave the woman across from him a half-smile.

*Beautiful,* Tempest thought again, remembering how self-conscious she'd been in public with him. Women had fawned over him and she'd gotten the look that said "Why the hell is he with her?". Perhaps it was that condemnation which had made it so easy to walk away. She bit the inside of her lip. It hadn't been easy. At the time it had seemed she'd never recover but she'd had no choice. Her father had seen to that.

With slow steps, she headed toward the party. She would have preferred to speak to Josh alone with no witnesses but she couldn't wait for the opportunity to catch him off-guard and alone. Only Josh could give her the peace of mind and closure she needed before she took the next step of her life. He just didn't know it.

Josh tried not to make faces while his sister-in-law Keera spoke. This was so hokey. Let me spread out these tarot cards and do my woo-woo thing and I'll tell you everything you don't already know about your life. Right. A bunch of useless cards weren't going to answer the burning questions that didn't actually linger in his soul.

Trying not to look bored—his siblings and his three sisters-in-law were watching—he rubbed his tongue piercing on the roof of his mouth and studied the odd cards. Everyone had insisted he should have a birthday reading and as much as he'd tried, he hadn't been able to get out of it.

"This is the most important card in the spread," Keera said as she examined the tarot spread. "It's what all the other cards were leading toward."

"Okay…" he replied slowly. This was a bunch of crap. He needed to get home to finish packing for his trip to the Upper Peninsula and call in to the office to check on his team. Though he was on a two-month sabbatical, he couldn't blithely take off without knowing his second-in-command had figured out the annoying glitch sending all the company's spam into the CEO's inbox. His father—said CEO—wasn't pleased about it. It had caused such a problem that he'd skipped this morning's breakfast in order to sort legitimate business correspondence from junk. He'd insisted that Josh still go with his siblings.

He sighed. He couldn't in good conscience leave town until he knew the email fubar was fixed.

"Oh, look it's the Strength card!" Keera exclaimed.

Big freaking deal. He barely restrained a derisive snort. "Yeah. Cool," he said dryly.

"Josh, don't be a big stick-in-the-mud. This is a great card. It's not about physical power. It's about gentle control and compassion. It's about being freed from fears and discovering love is stronger than fear or hate."

He stiffened, glancing around the table. "I'm not scared of anything, Keera."

She sighed. "Everyone's afraid of something. And even more, this card signifies digging deep inside yourself for inner strength to deal with a situation."

"That's the last card, right?" he asked. Time to leave. The insistence that he'd conquer his fears was beginning to make him uncomfortable. He only had two Achilles' heels and the one that worried him most was far in his past. He'd put his weaknesses far behind him.

He stood. "Well, this has been fun. I need to go."

"This may mean you'll resolve a difficult situation from your past, using your inner strength."

Josh froze, a brand of trepidation he hadn't felt in eight years crawling up his spine. The fingers of one hand fisted and he took a deep breath. All of his brothers were staring at him. It was his oldest brother, Theo, who spoke.

"Tempest."

Josh's teeth ground together. Yeah, she would be that worrisome Achilles' heel. From time to time, thoughts of her still woke him at night with a raging hard-on. It was damned annoying. Tempest was over and done with.

"Who's Tempest?" Keera asked.

"No one," he answered quickly.

"Gee thanks, Josh. It's good to know how you feel right up front."

Josh turned toward the soft voice and looked into a pair of the darkest brown eyes he'd ever seen. Eyes he'd never thought to see again. Hurt eyes.

He was good at hurting her. Well that and being an ass, he acknowledged. Why else would she have taken off and never given him the time of day again? Still, he couldn't stop his next words. "What do you want?"

Behind him, he heard Keera gathering up her cards and chairs sliding back. "I think it's time to get back to the office, don't you think?" Max said. The others agreed and in moments the three couples and his sister were gone, leaving him alone with Tempest. His past. He needed to remember that. Tempest was his past.

"I need to talk to you," she said.

He stared at her in disbelief. *She what?* "You're about eight years too late."

Her eyes momentarily dropped shut as she acknowledged her action. "I know. I had no choice."

"You chose your family—your father—over me. I can't accept that." He swiped his hand through the air. "It doesn't matter. It's all ancient history. Which leads me back to…what do you want?"

She looked around and he suspected she was uncomfortable talking to him about whatever it was she wanted while they stood in the middle of a restaurant. It must be some doozy of a topic.

"Is there somewhere we can talk? Privately?" she asked. "Your car?"

He shook his head. "No. I'm on my way back to my apartment." He lifted an eyebrow. "I'm sure you don't want to go there. Probably the best thing for you to do is to get into whatever sporty car Daddy bought you and go back to your ivory tower. I have things to do."

"I took a cab here."

"You took a cab from Grand Rapids?" Grand Rapids was a good three hours from Brandywine, which was one of the reasons he'd never expected to see her here. Part of him wanted to know why she was here after all this time. Another part wanted to run like hell. The most powerful part of him, however, wanted to grab her into his arms and kiss her until neither of them could breathe.

"No. I'm staying with my brother for a few weeks—in Westfield. I've been doing some company business with Miracles and Hope."

Josh frowned knowing "company business" was her way of describing charity work, which was a euphemism for slave work. Even while he and Tempest had been in college, her father had her chasing all over God's green acre disbursing money and services to needy organizations on behalf of Montgomery Enterprises. Apparently things hadn't changed. According to John Montgomery, her father, caring for the needs of their fellow man was the utmost priority. A worthy goal but Josh would beg to differ. Basic care and nurture of self and one's relationships should rank just as high, if not higher. Sure Tempest always looked perfectly coifed but the business owned her life and soul. It had pushed everything else out—including him.

He shoved aside his irritation. Tempest's dysfunctional family commitments weren't his problem anymore. It unsettled him that she was apparently staying a mere twenty minutes from Brandywine. He'd rested easier knowing she was hours away. That far away, he could pretend she hadn't chosen her family over him. He could pretend someone named Tempest had never existed in his life and had never gouged out the center of his heart.

"And you just thought you'd stop by?" he grated. She shook her head, her light blonde hair brushing her shoulders. For the first time, he let his gaze stray from her face. A mistake.

Immediate reaction grabbed his gut. He shouldn't have allowed the weakness.

She still had those killer curves and he'd bet his best computer that she was still trying to lose them with everything in her. Pudge, she once told him, did not fit the Montgomery image. He lightly ran his hand over his washboard stomach, feeling the ridges through his oxford shirt. If Tempest was pudgy, he was too. God, she was Marilyn Monroe gorgeous. He couldn't understand what she was thinking.

And she was still trying to hide all that loveliness behind those prissy clothes she felt she had to wear. He remembered her in curve-hugging jeans. He almost smiled. He recalled her in *only* jeans and nothing else, her beautiful breasts free for his taking. Those lush breasts pressed against her white silk blouse. The nipples peaked beneath his perusal.

His fingers flexed with his desire to cup the firm mounds.

Tempest shifted and crossed her arms. He glanced at the swivel of her hips.

"Are you about finished?" she snapped.

"It depends on what you want," he replied, wanting to drag her to the nearest deserted place and take her until neither of them could move. His cock concurred as it pressed against the fly of his jeans. He wouldn't succumb. "Are you going to tell me what brought you all the way to Brandywine?"

"Josh, please..."

He looked away remembering the last time she'd uttered those words to him. In a different tone, for a different reason. Minutes later she'd called him Master, begging him to let her find release. Neither of them had known her father had discovered the Dominant/submissive relationship they'd begun. Or that he'd force his way between them by the weekend.

"Do you remember the last time you said that?" he asked quietly.

A rose tinge crawled up her neck and into her cheeks. She looked away and closed her eyes for a second, obviously gathering her thoughts and perhaps courage. "I've been doing a lot of thinking and evaluating lately. I've never set things right with you. It seems like this big festering spot in my past. So I—"

"Festering? Nice." What the hell was this? After eight years, she showed up in the middle of his birthday breakfast, three hours from her home and asked him to give her closure? *Closure*? What about his peace of mind? Tempest was the one woman he'd ever wanted for his own and damn it from the moment he'd turned to see her beside him, his heart had been pounding with that need again.

She made a face.

"Back then, I didn't know how to handle things. There was my father. And you were so…" she trailed off.

*Different,* he finished silently. She'd wanted someone who wouldn't fit Daddy's bill of perfect escort material and he'd been the one. What did that make him? Rebellion?

Hell, this shouldn't bother him after all this time.

"Look, all this time I—"

"I think you've said enough," he interrupted sharply. Steeling himself for the blow of leaving her in the past again, he started for the door. Someone shouldn't have to leave behind their other half twice in a lifetime. But he couldn't not stay.

"Wait. Josh, please," she hissed following him through the heavy glass door to the sidewalk. "Listen to me."

"It seems to me that this is a repeat of a place we've been before. You should probably go inside and call that cab. Go home to your brother's house. Or Grand Rapids."

Her small hand curled around his arm. "Will you listen, please?"

He looked at her, trying to keep his face blank and not show the temptation running through him. "*What*?"

She looked around again as someone brushed past them. The sidewalk was quite busy.

"I'm engaged," she said suddenly. Just as suddenly, he thought he might hurl. She'd come to Brandywine to tell him she was engaged? After eight years? She'd claimed to want closure. Was he supposed to give his blessing?

That wasn't happening.

He started walking toward his bike. *Happy birthday, Josh. This is your life. Do you remember the woman who ripped your heart out? Well she's back for more. Only this time, there's a catch –*

"If you're engaged, what the fuck do you want with me? Does your precious fiancé know you're here?"

Her prissy little heels clattered on the sidewalk as she sprinted along beside him. He was just pissed enough that he didn't slow down. Angrily, he reached in his pocket for his keys. Suddenly, Tempest stopped. "Phillip doesn't know about you."

"Phillip," he repeated, tasting bile in his throat and wishing he didn't know the enemy's name. He turned, glaring at her across the five feet that separated them. Slowly he sized up the battleground. Now that she was here, could he let her merrily walk away with the "closure" she wanted? Not as easily as she might like. The decent thing would be to let bygones be bygones and wave her away with a well-wish.

The hell with decency. There was pain in her eyes again.

"You don't want to marry him?" he guessed.

She shrugged. "It just sort of…happened. He works for Daddy. And everyone thinks it's a great idea. He's a nice guy and I'll be happy enough. He wants kids. I want kids." She shrugged again. "He's supportive of my work. Nice."

Josh fought the overwhelming need to growl. He personally thought it was a horrible idea, but he had no say. The guy was "nice". She made him sound like goddamned Wally Cleaver. Josh knew exactly how happy she'd be with that. Unless she'd dramatically changed, Tempest didn't particularly get off on nice. Not the kind of nice she was describing. Phillip sounded like even more of a submissive than she was.

"So you've found Mr. Right?" he asked dryly. "And then suddenly you were struck with the undeniable need to track down the black mark on your pristine past. Are you still reading those self-help books about thinking yourself to a good future and karma and all that crap?"

She looked away. "If I have, it's not working. Look, it's like this. The closer I get to the wedding, the more you've been in my head not Phillip. That tells me something. I have an unresolved issue and if I want to be happy in my marriage, I'd better figure out what the heck my problem is."

Strange that she'd say that, especially in light of his upcoming trip. The sole reason for his sabbatical was to figure out what the hell was his problem. Funny, he suddenly seemed to have a very good idea why he'd been so unhappy and dissatisfied.

"You've been in my head. Unresolved and waiting. What is that?" she bit out in frustration and stomped her foot.

Josh tried not to laugh at the familiar display of anger. His cock went hard at the delightful jiggle of her breasts. He loved when she vibrated with emotion, tension drawing the lines of her body tight—tension he wanted to relieve. As she'd gotten worked up, her breathing had increased. It reminded him of the rapid-fire rise and fall of her chest after sex. It was enough to kill his minimal restraint, especially with the breeze pressing her skirt to her and outlining her strong thighs.

He'd apparently fucked up in a previous life. His sister-in-law was always spouting about karma and here it was. He put his hands on his hips and dropped his head forward, staring at the ground. There was no way he could share what he was thinking right now. She'd see it in his eyes if he looked at her.

She'd know he wanted to take her home and wrap himself in her body.

"I told everyone I needed more time before the wedding," she continued, unaware of his reaction. "They all think the little bride is nervous. I don't know what the hell little bride they're talking about." She drew a hand in front of her. "This isn't little."

"Tempest…" he warned reflexively. He couldn't help it. He'd always protested when she'd disparaged herself. Something broke inside him and all his carefully contained emotion flooded to his core. It exploded protective, possessive and needy. "You're not marrying him. You're mine."

"What do you mean?" she asked. Josh couldn't mean his statement the way it sounded. Tempest stared at him, sure he'd say more. He didn't. Nevertheless, there had to be something else to this. How could there not be after all this time?

The side of his mouth turned up while his gaze devoured her and spoke of all the things he'd been waiting to do. She couldn't help thinking she'd just jumped straight out of the frying pan and into the fire. And if the flames in Josh's eyes were any indication, she'd be reduced to ashes as soon as he touched her.

And there was no way she'd refuse him, even with Phillip waiting in the wings. She'd tried to break it off with him—something she didn't want to tell Josh. It was enough for him to know no one was listening to her. He didn't need to know that when she went home, she was as good as married. She'd been railroaded to this point. She didn't see that changing no matter how much she protested.

Really, as far as futures went, Phillip wasn't intolerable. He wanted most of the same things she did. He encouraged her "little photography hobby" and wanted a family, just like she did and he was up and coming at Montgomery Enterprises. Everything a woman could want, wasn't it?

Somehow she'd have to convince Phillip it was over. There was no question.

"I mean that you're right. There is something unresolved between us." He paused letting her see all the hunger in his gaze. A shiver ran down her spine before he continued. "I want to explore it and find…*closure*…too."

Her eyes narrowed. "How?"

"I want closure too. I never had a chance to get you out of my system. So…I want submission. Yours. To me. For two weeks."

Two weeks? She had to be back in Grand Rapids in ten days. Yet if they allowed their relationship go its natural course, maybe it wouldn't haunt her anymore and there'd be no more what ifs. Maybe…

It might be too late for them now, but she was willing to test those waters.

She clasped her hands behind her back, realizing afterward what she'd unconsciously done. She didn't suppose Josh had completely changed his sexual preferences. He was a Dominant, and if he wanted her for the next two weeks that would mean he wanted her as his submissive. Now.

She didn't change her position. Let him think what he wanted about her submissive pose.

Josh's lips parted, his eyes growing darker. He swallowed as he backed toward the motorcycle a few feet behind him. "Come here, angel," he growled.

Slowly she walked toward him, drawn by the same magnet that had held her for years. It was stronger now, undeniable. She wanted to be close to him, smell his scent, feel the heat that radiated from him. She'd missed him so much.

As soon as she was within arms' reach, he reached for her and lifted her to sit on the bike without so much as the grunt she expected when he hefted her weight. Without pause, he stepped between her legs, pushing her skirt up over her knees when it would have hindered him getting close. His hand slid into her hair and he brought her mouth to his.

Tempest sighed in pleasure at the taste of the mouth she'd missed so much. His tongue stabbed between her lips in long lazy strokes, a lethal mix of coffee and maple syrup. Agony for a girl on a diet. Arching into him, she wrapped her arms around his waist. Her hands splayed on his strong back. She wished he was wearing one of the soft cotton T-shirts he'd favored when they were together. She'd bunch her hands in it and pull it up so she could feel his smooth, satiny skin under her fingers. Now she contented herself with clasping the stiff fabric of his oxford and dragging him closer.

The spicy cologne he'd always worn enveloped her and filled her with sweet nostalgia as she welcomed his tongue. Being in his arms with his mouth on hers was like coming home. How on earth would she leave this embrace of belonging when the time came? She could only hope he was right about getting this desire out of their systems.

The piercing in the center of his tongue rubbed along the roof of her mouth, sending a decadent shiver down her spine. He hadn't had that before. What would it feel like on her skin? Her nipples? Her clit tingled as she remembered his mouth there and desired the sensation of that little metal ball running over her and driving her mad.

Tears formed in the corners of her eyes as he feasted on her mouth with tender, biting kisses. Every minute that she'd missed him and been without his dominance slammed down on her. The tears slithered down her cheek pooling at their joined lips.

"Hey," he said quietly, pulling back. He slid his thumb through the damp moisture. "What's this?"

"I didn't realize how much I missed you."

He swallowed hard. "The way I see it…we have a two-part problem here."

"Problem?" she echoed.

Her stomach churned while she stared at his shirt buttons. She didn't want to hear about problems, not after a kiss that would have brought her to her knees if she hadn't been sitting on a motorcycle and clinging to him for dear life.

Oh mercy. They were in the middle of a very public parking lot, right beside a very busy street and making out like...like the long-lost lovers they were. It went against every statute of decent behavior that had been pounded into her since childhood but she couldn't bring herself to care much. At one time, he could have stripped her practically naked before she'd have voiced an initial protest. She'd trusted him that much.

"I'm just about to leave on a trip," he replied, tracing her lips with his finger. It was as if they'd been apart forever yet the intimacy remained as strong as if they'd never separated. Shouldn't she feel uncomfortable about this? What she felt wasn't even close.

"Oh," she replied in disappointment. Did he plan to claim his two weeks later, when he returned? Or hadn't he been serious about that? She started to pull back. He halted her progress, dropping his hand to her waist. His thumb massaged her middle, the touch imprinted on her senses.

"I want you to come with me," he told her.

"Okay." That was easy. Just like that. Her family might freak out if she disappeared without prior warning. She'd deal with them.

"And," he continued, "you've always depended on your father for everything. I made the mistake of not seeing that before."

She sighed, seeing his point. Her father and her need of his support had been one of the main issues between them in the end. She tilted her head, waiting.

"I have money, Tempest. When I'm with you I don't want anything to do with your cash. That includes even *you* using it. I will provide for your needs."

She wanted to protest, the thought of total dependence cinching tightly around her. "For two weeks?"

For two weeks? he thought. His gut reaction was to add "or as long as it takes". Good lord, it had already been eight years. "As long as it takes" could take forever. He pushed a burst of hope aside. Determination settled in its place. He'd take the allotted time then somehow convince her to give him more. Somehow.

She bit her lip, sadness flitting through her guileless brown eyes. Her emotions were so easy to read. The sadness kicked him in the ass. Had he read her wrongly? Did she find being with him for two weeks distasteful? Was she upset by his demand? A good man would probably have offered his forgiveness or whatever and sent her on her way. A man like this Phillip. A shocking surge of blind jealousy shot through him. Josh had never claimed to be a good man and he wasn't planning to make a life change now.

Damn it. It didn't matter how much time had passed. Tempest was his and by the time two weeks were over, she'd know it.

She took a deep breath as if strengthening herself for a battle and her lips turned up, all signs of her brief sadness disappearing. "You'll be bored with me before then. Look at you. You probably have hoards of gorgeous woman banging down your door."

His hands tightened on her hips. Apparently, her family had shot to hell her self-esteem while they'd been parted. All the more reason to get her firmly back where she belonged. "You know damned well that I won't get bored with you."

"I'm overweight."

"And I couldn't possibly be attracted to you because of that?" How could she not know how beautiful she was and how much he wanted between her lush thighs again—well more than he was now? Just holding her like this or watching her walk, even watching her breathe, made him hard. He shifted his hips slightly so she'd know exactly how hard. With her position on the bike and all the clothes between them, he couldn't get close enough.

She stared at his shirt to avoid his gaze. Though she dropped occasional jabs about her size, discussing weight made Tempest uncomfortable. He'd learned early on that she made fun of herself as self-protection. If she joked about it, then maybe no one else would. Maybe she wouldn't be hurt. The problem was that her tactics worked on most people, but those closest to her, those who should have treated her best, were often the most hurtful.

As a result, Tempest saw an undesirable woman in the mirror instead of the goddess who could bring him to his knees.

"Why *would* you want me when you can have any woman who looks like a model from a fashion magazine?"

"I'm not particularly into pouting sticks." He stroked his hand over her soft belly, unbelievably turned on to have Tempest in his grasp. "I do however love to have a woman who fills my arms, who feels good against me. A woman who is soft and feminine and makes me feel even more a man." He pulled her close so her full breasts were pressed to him, her mouth inches from his. "How could I get bored exploring these killer curves?"

Her breath feathered across him. "Okay. You can have what you want."

He grinned, knowing he wanted far more than she thought she'd agreed to. This fourteen days was only the beginning. If he had his way, this would last as long as he could make it. He turned to the saddle bags of the motorcycle before she saw his smile fade. He'd claim his time with her but what would he do if she walked away? Prissy socialites just didn't stick with rough-around-the-edges guys like him. He'd learned that the first time around. His family might be wealthy, but hers was far wealthier. She was a goddess and he was a working-class acolyte. That she was a submissive and he was her Dominant, didn't play into it at all—though it should.

He wouldn't let her walk away this time. Not without one hell of a fight. He should have fought last time, yet he'd let her go. He might have been a Dom before, just as he was now, but he'd been young. He hadn't known what to do especially when John Montgomery had threatened his father's company. An idle threat. He recognized it now.

Youth, threats and stupidity made a great recipe for regret. It was time for something new. Wiser and more mature.

He'd spent the last eight years ensuring no one could push him around ever again. Even someone as powerful as John Montgomery.

He pulled a spare helmet from the storage compartment and handed it to Tempest. Fighting the temptation to lose himself in their embrace again, he lifted her from the seat. "Time to go."

"To go?" She trailed off as his meaning sank in. "I can't ride that."

He eyed her, liking the idea of her skirt hiked up while she clung to his back. "You can. And you will. Get on the bike, Tempest."

To an outsider, he knew his words would sound harsh. Not to Tempest. She'd recognize his demand for what it was. The sooner he reasserted his dominance, the sooner they'd return to familiar ground where their desire could again take deep root.

She pursed her lips, a battle warring on her face as she looked away. It was always a battle with them and right now she was deciding whether or not to let him resume his role as her Dominant. It didn't matter that she was a natural submissive, that she'd been his before or that she'd verbally agreed. She was fighting against the mental chains that would soon bind her. They fit her so well, yet she had to decide.

Josh carefully kept his face noncommittal. This was Tempest's battle. He would not persuade. She had to decide without his influence. He didn't want anyone to say she'd been coerced, though her father would likely bellow that accusation loudly.

Tempest considered him, the chin strap of the helmet rolling between her fingers. Uncertainty played over her face. Should she? Shouldn't she? It was all there plainly for him to see. She'd said yes to his earlier dictate, nevertheless until she took this first order, she wasn't his submissive. At least…she didn't think so. He knew the truth. She'd never stopped belonging to him.

He climbed onto the motorcycle while her teeth sank into her plump bottom lip. Slowly she raised her hands and shoved the helmet over her blonde locks. Determination filled her features now that she'd chosen her path. Hiking up her skirt, she climbed behind him. He smiled at the space she left between their bodies. Reaching back, he pulled her flush to him.

"You know how this works, angel," he said, fighting a groan at the feel of her lush thighs bracketing his. Soon they'd be around his hips again while he sank into her. Unable to resist, he slid his palm back over her leg. Her skirt enveloped his hand as he slipped his fingers inside her panties and cupped her smooth ass.

*Happy birthday, Josh.* If he'd taken months to consider what he wanted, he couldn't have thought of a better present. This would be damn perfect.

* * * * *

Tempest tightened her arms around Josh's waist as he took a sharp curve. She squeezed her eyes shut. She hadn't been on a motorcycle since she'd been on his in college. Phillip and the few men she'd dated before him all drove nondescript luxury cars, usually black. She doubted any of them would consider the beast roaring between her legs. It was the perfect match for the beast who'd soon be taking the motorcycle's place between her thighs.

Her clit tingled when she thought of Josh surging inside her. Would her memories of his wide cock match reality? She didn't doubt she'd discover that as soon as they arrived wherever he was taking her. One corner of her mouth turned up as she realized she hadn't bothered to find out where they were going.

She took a deep breath to calm the excitement tearing through her. The butterflies cascading around her stomach would burst free if she didn't get a grip. When she'd come to Josh, she hadn't envisioned she'd end up in his bed. Well, that wasn't exactly true. She'd fantasized about it. Maybe this was part of that visualization thing she'd heard so much about lately. Maybe she'd visualized herself straight into his bed. If that was the case, perhaps she should put more weight in the whole New Age-y thing.

Her father would have a fit when he found out about this, especially in light of the upcoming wedding. There was no manifestation or imagination needed to know that. Of course if Phillip and her father would listen to her, they wouldn't still be counting on her merger with Phillip—in her head that's what it was. A sterile business transaction with each person getting something they wanted.

Perhaps this was the best course of action to make it clear she did not want to go through with the wedding. Lord knew, she'd talked herself blue and they still ignored her decision, segueing from her announcement that she absolutely would not marry Phillip to a discussion of how many guests to invite to the ceremony. After several frustrating minutes of arguing and being ignored, she'd stormed out. No matter what she'd said, her words had been brushed away. The time for words had passed. Now was time for action. Being with Josh would get her point across even if her father had a figurative coronary. The thought seemed coldly calculated except that she wanted this brief time with Josh more than anything.

A temporary liaison.

Even if he suddenly offered forever, she couldn't have it. She knew that. There were too many factors to consider. Her family. Her career. Her freedom. She couldn't see having any of those things if she was with Josh. In the end, she might actually end up married to Phillip but that would be her clear-headed decision. It wouldn't be the result of her father's approval of his hand-picked man and her residual regrets over Josh wouldn't remain over her head.

*You're a complete idiot, Tempest.* Hmm. Nice self talk. She made a face, thinking of the self-help books that told her to speak nicely to herself. *You're the world's greatest idiot,* she revised. How on earth was she supposed to banish her desires for Josh when she had her arms wrapped around his rock-hard belly? The roar of the motorcycle and the brush of his long hair against her cheek reminded her how different he was from her fiancé. Josh had always been a bad boy but now he seemed even rougher around the edges.

Phillip was the polar opposite of Josh. He'd never consider piercings, long hair or a motorcycle. The low-slung jeans stretched over Josh's powerful thighs would have been out of the question, even on cleaning day. Perfect Phillip was John Montgomery's perfect choice for his less-than-perfect daughter. Her father liked Phillip. He didn't like Josh a bit—had never even given him a chance. When she'd been in college, her father had freaked when he'd discovered the BDSM aspect of her relationship with her boyfriend. He'd yanked her from college, telling her he would yank all financial support too, including her tuition, if she didn't cooperate.

At the time, she'd thought she had no choices. Josh was new in comparison to her family. How could she choose him over them? When her father had arrived at her apartment and discovered them in the midst of a tame but nonetheless clearly D/s scene, he'd demanded she get dressed and go to the car immediately.

She'd obeyed him while Josh demanded then begged her not to go. She didn't know what her father had said to him after she'd left. It had been her last contact with Josh. Movers had been hired to get her things.

She'd cried for weeks afterward. As an adult she knew how she would do things differently if she were in the same situation now. But being older and wiser didn't make a difference. That experience was in the past and she couldn't change it. Time hadn't done much to dull the blow she'd dealt to Josh nor his anger at it.

How desperate did it make her that she'd agree to whatever he wanted to gain closure from him—not that she objected much to being under him for the next two weeks. As soon as she'd seen him, she'd known she wanted him again. Maybe she *could* get him out of her system and move on with her plans for her life. They both could move on. Josh needed this too. One look into his red-hot gaze and it was obvious he still battled the same memory demons that haunted her.

She wished she could see his face now. Actually maybe it was good that she couldn't. She was already all melty inside. Her front quivered where they were pressed together and she ached to feel his bare skin against hers even if she wasn't too keen on him seeing her naked.

Josh had always seemed to like her body, but that was when they were younger and he was a horny college student. He'd been gorgeous before as a lanky youth. Now all grown up and filled out in all the right places, he was the hottest thing this side of hell.

Before she was ready, Josh swung into a tree-lined driveway and rolled to a stop in front of a two-stall garage attached to a sprawling two-story house. Silently, he led her into his home. Filtered light slashed across a neat living room.

She barely had time to register it, before he pushed her against the door. His mouth slanted over hers, pressing her lips apart for his invading tongue. The warm little ball in the center of it rubbed sensuously against her.

The urgency…the intimacy…it was everything she'd imagined for years. Heat licked at her core, softening her body for him. Suddenly, her clothes seemed tight over her breasts as her body begged for his attention. Almost as if reading her thoughts, he held her in place with his hips while he insinuated his hands between them. His fingers tore at her shirt. She couldn't bring herself to care that he might rip the fabric or pop off a pearly button.

A tremor racked through her womb. She *wanted* him to wrench them off. She wanted the wild abandon. Her entire life was control and politeness. Josh freed the animal in her. As her cream flooded her cleft, she nipped at his lips, lifting into his kiss and the heady taste of his demanding mouth.

Impatiently, he pulled her shirttails from her waistband. A moment later, he wrenched back his head and growled as he stared down at where his hand splayed over her silk-covered abdomen. Frowning he plucked at the camisole. "You're wearing too many clothes," he complained. Reaching up to where it came to a vee above her breasts, he bunched the fabric in his hands and wrenched them apart. The hiss of tearing material filled the room. Her knees buckled. His body was all that held her up.

Desperately, she tried to regain her strength. If he stepped back, she'd fall into a pudgy lump in his entryway. Unaware of her struggle, he shoved her blouse and destroyed camisole down her shoulders, leaving them hooked on her elbows. His fingers spread over her neck. She swallowed, remembering when she'd worn the mark of his possession there. The sudden vulnerability aroused her as did the slight pressure of his fingertips. His thumb explored the slight hollow at the base of her neck. Josh could do anything to her—his strength surpassed hers and their position left her open to his whim.

With her clothes tangled around her elbows she could barely move her arms let alone fight him.

Her breath shallow, she waited.

"Do you remember?" he asked.

"Yes." The warm cloak of their past wrapped this moment and dragged her back to other times when they'd been like this. Instinctively, her thighs parted so her feet were shoulder width and she was open to him. If he touched her now, he'd find a quivering mass of want.

He raised an eyebrow. The small silver ring there winked at her. "Yes? I don't think you do. You seem to be forgetting..."

"Master," she added. Arching slightly, she pressed her aching nipples against him. The position pressed her neck a little more into his hand. Forbidden excitement stalked her. She shouldn't enjoy what this position did to her, but only Josh understood how much she liked to be physically restrained. Nothing got her off like being tied or held still by his hands. Josh would never choke her, but the danger of his hand on her throat made her wet faster than anything else in the world.

He wanted her right now. That's what this meant.

Never easing the pressure, he took her lips again, mashing her to the molded metal door with his entire body. Tempest gasped into his mouth. A violent storm inside her stole her breath. Desperately, she met his tongue stab for stab, adjusted to every tilt of his head. Surprising him, she sucked her lips around his tongue. She wanted his thick cock surging to her throat and stretching her mouth wide.

His free hand curled into her ass, dragging her tight to his rock-hard arousal. Oh yeah, it would feel so good in her mouth. Almost as good as he felt when he drove inside her pussy, claiming every tender fold as his own.

Suddenly, he stepped back. She nearly slithered down the door before she braced her knees.

"Get undressed but don't move from that spot," he ordered, making the submissive in her shiver in delight. She liked when he stepped into his Dom persona. It fit him so well. He fit her so well.

Her delight, however, turned to icy despair when she realized what he'd said. Undressed. He wanted her naked. With all her layers of clothes stripped away. Josh knew. He knew how she used the layers to disguise the weight she couldn't get rid of. He wanted that disguise peeled away with all her skin showing.

It would have been so much easier if he'd dragged her to the bed, both of them blinded by passion as they ripped their clothes away and fell on each other. It was so much harder when she stood like a slave on the block, waiting for inspection. Every insecurity would assail her. Damn him, he knew that, too. This was part of his asserting the upper hand.

He caught her chin between his thumb and fingers. "All your clothes, Tempest. Understood?"

More than she wanted to. She couldn't turn her face from him, but she shifted her eyes away. Her jaw locked, her teeth clenched together. "Yes, Master," she replied through them. She wanted closure. If he was disgusted by her appearance, that would be that. She straightened her arms and shook free her blouse and camisole.

Josh turned and walked toward the doorway across the room. "Stay there. I'll be back in a few minutes."

She reached for the clasp of her bra. *And I'll be here. Clinging to my shredded pride.*

Too bad it was invisible.

# Chapter Two

The cool metal of the front door chilled Tempest's overheated skin while she waited for Josh at slave-attention position, feet parted and hands tucked behind her back. Her clothes were tossed onto an overstuffed chair several feet away. She eyed them longingly. Josh wouldn't let her go unpunished if she disobeyed him. Some things were never forgotten.

Cream trickled to her thigh. Even punishment aroused her? Was there nothing about him that didn't turn her on? Wryly, she wondered if he still stuffed his socks down the couch. That didn't turn her on. It pissed her off. The recollection, however, lead to thoughts of his perfectly shaped feet.

Her mind raced with questions. How would he react to her nakedness? Would he notice her shaved pussy or her fat? Would he like her shorn folds? What would he do to her?

Her clit itched with the possibilities. Hearing him moving around in the other room, she dropped her hand and trailed her fingers over her thigh. With a sigh, she leaned her shoulders against the door and slipped her palm over her mound. Just a little touch… She'd stop before he returned.

The gentle slide of her fingertips over her clit drew a silent sigh and she dropped her head against the door, closing her eyes. God, she was wet. Opening the dream file where all her fantasies starred Josh, she pretended it was his fingers sliding over her, spreading her folds. Release coiled tightly in her belly. Her other hand slid up to her breast. She pinched and rolled her hard nipples just as Josh always had.

Relentlessly, she worked the peaks while she plunged her fingers into her pussy. Her teeth sank into her bottom lip.

A choked sound shocked her from her play. Eyes wide, she snapped back to her position leaving her needy flesh open to the chill of the room.

Josh stood in the doorway watching her, his own teeth sunk into his bottom lip. Her mouth watered at the sight of his bare chest and feet. His unbuttoned jeans dipped low on his hips, revealing the black tattoo over his navel and an enticing curve of hip bone disappearing into his pants.

"Go ahead," he said. "Finish."

"I—"

His brow raised again cutting her off. Pleasure herself in front of him? *While he watched?* Oh man. Slowly, she returned her hands to where they'd been when he'd re-entered the room. And froze. She couldn't do this. She had to. Her eyes started to close. If she could pretend to be alone—

"No. Look at me," he commanded.

Her eyelids heavy, she gazed at him. He had a tiny gold ring piercing one nipple. Good lord how many other piercings did he have? One in his cock? How would it feel abrading her pussy? Her fingers began to move, gliding over her slippery folds.

"So fucking beautiful," he said. A ribbon of happiness worked through her. Of all the things she'd expected him to say, all the reactions she expected him to have, that wasn't one. Empowered by his admiration, her touch grew more aggressive and she stopped biting back her small cries at the sensations arcing through her body.

He walked toward her. "What do you think about when you touch yourself?"

"You."

"Hmm." He dropped to his knees before her and pulled her hand from her folds. Slowly, he sucked the juice from her fingers.

Tempest's breath hitched in her throat. All the muscles in her pelvis pulled tight as he continued to draw on her fingers. Slowly, he let them slide free. "I've missed the taste of you, Tempest. I want more."

She could only nod as he parted her with his thumbs and pressed his mouth to her. Her palms pressed flat to the door as she widened her stance for him. No one had done this for her since Josh. Certainly not Phillip. She pushed that thought away, focusing on the white-hot sensations Josh elicited as he scraped his teeth lightly over her clit before sucking at it. As the pinnacle of release raced closer, he released the bud and gathered her cream with his tongue, before plunging inside her.

Her whole being quivered, her lips moving in silence as her world dimmed, narrowing on the coming storm. Suddenly, he thrust two fingers into her while his teeth closed around her throbbing clit. Her hips jerked toward him and toward the completion that had waited so many years. She needed him beyond reason. Inside her. Now.

Desperately, she tried to stay still as he drank of her. This position brought back memories of submission she hadn't realized she'd forgotten. The welcome helplessness, the overwhelming pleasure, his effortless control over her…

She'd never forget again.

Josh delved deep inside her, finding the place that jerked her hips forward again. A tiny cry shuddered from her, heralding the start of the orgasm about to boil forth. Immediately, he pulled back. "No, not yet, angel."

The firm command dragged her a few inches from the chasm waiting to engulf her. Release taunted her, dangling in his hand just outside of her grasp. This was her punishment. He wouldn't let her come.

"Please," she begged.

"No." He stood and held out his hand. "Can you walk?"

"Since I was ten months old," she snapped.

Josh sighed and trailed his fingers on the outside of her hip while he held her gaze. He didn't say a word, but he didn't need to. She remembered. The simple touch was a warning—one he'd often used in public places to preserve their privacy and dignity. She knew what it meant. Pull back this behavior or be punished.

She bit her lip and lowered her gaze. She wasn't one who deliberately sought punishment. Josh had a way of turning it into pleasure in the end, but she still avoided it whenever possible.

"I'm sorry."

He gave a single nod. "Come with me."

Josh led the way toward the bedroom, knowing Tempest would be surprised not only by the room but by what awaited her. She likely expected him to fall on her like a ravening beast, and truly that was what he wanted most, but instead he had other plans. Not-so-sexual plans. Sex between them had always been explosive. Her intense reactions to his domination fueled the fire until they both burned out of control. It was outside the bedroom where her submission needed work.

As he'd predicted, she came to an abrupt halt inside his bedroom. Her eyes wide, she surveyed the black and white décor but barely noted the furniture. She gazed transfixed at the black and white vintage prints that banded the room at eye-level. Each print, dating back to the 1950s, showed scenes of BDSM and featured women with the same beautiful physique as Tempest. When he'd first come across them at an auction, he knew he had to have them. How many times had he touched himself and envisioned Tempest as the woman and himself as the Dom?

"Pick one," he rasped. "We'll play it out later."

"There are so many..."

"There are lots of games for us to play then." Perhaps more than they had time for if she insisted on leaving in two weeks. He picked up the shirt he'd tossed on the bed and shrugged into it. He'd been in the process of changing when he heard the suspicious sounds from Tempest earlier. When he'd seen her…it was as if a train had slammed into him. A lust train. "We'll play later. Right now, we're going out. You need clothes for our trip and I want to pick them out."

"I have—"

He pressed a finger over her lips as she started to protest. "Your submission. For two weeks," he reminded.

Tempest sighed, the breath wafting around his finger in a warm caress. Silently, she nodded. The way she'd easily returned to the practices they'd had eight years ago amazed and delighted him. When he'd given her the warning touch earlier, he hadn't been sure she would remember. She had. Instantly. Keera's words returned to him. Gentle control. He shoved aside the thought. He didn't believe in that hocus pocus. It was a coincidence that the card had come up. Just because he preferred to dominate his sub through quiet signals, it didn't mean the card was right.

He followed Tempest's gaze which was fixed on a photo of a submissive draped over an ottoman, her hands tied to the furniture's legs. What the woman awaited was left to the imagination.

He nuzzled Tempest's ear. "Do you want to do that? I bet you want to know what comes next. I do, too. Do you think she's waiting to be punished? Or maybe she's waiting for her Master to return and fuck her. Or maybe there's something we can't see." He reached into his pocket and removed a small egg-shaped vibrator. "Something like this."

"Maybe…" she agreed.

"Shall we find out later?"

She nodded. "I'd like that."

He slid the egg through her molten folds. "I think we should investigate this now."

"How?" she whispered.

He slipped the toy inside her, fighting the urge to bury his fingers there again. "This goes here. The strap I laid out will hold it in place while we shop."

Excitement zipped across her face and he saw Prissy Tempest depart. Burning Hot Tempest was here to stay. "Put it on me," she murmured.

Unable to resist touching his vibrant woman, he stroked her folds while he nibbled the sensitive flesh behind her ear. "I have the control for it in my pocket. I may or may not use it while we're out. You never know. I may just let the feel of it inside you turn you on."

She shuddered, her arousal already taking her.

"You like feeling my possession even when I'm standing away from you, don't you?" he murmured. "It marks you from the inside out. Tell me who owns you?"

She hesitated. It was a moment, a millisecond, but it was a breath too long. "You do," she replied. Next time there would be no faltering. She'd answer immediately without a shadow of a doubt.

Shoving back his irrational irritation, he secured the device then lifted a pair of jeans from the bed. "I want you to wear these."

"They won't fit."

"I think they will. They're yours. The movers your father hired didn't take everything."

"I can't believe you still have them."

God it made him sound obsessive. It wasn't as if he'd created a shrine to her. At first, he'd stuffed them in a box with some of her other things because he'd believed she would come back. Later, he'd forgotten that he had them, the box just moving from home to home as storage items often did. But when he'd seen her today and remembered her in only her jeans…

"Put them on."

"My panties…"

He shook his head, ending the protest. Between the egg and the stiff seam of her jeans rubbing her naked clit, she'd be hard pressed not to come before they returned home. She was so responsive. Playing with her, driving her to the brink of frenzy, had always been a favorite pastime.

For both of them.

He bit the inside of his lip as she bent to put on the jeans, the smooth curve of her rounded ass beckoning him. Tempest wasn't the only one tortured to the edge of frenzy. Maintaining control when they finally hit the bed would be difficult. And he didn't plan relief for either of them until their first stop tonight. God help Tempest. It would probably be fast and hard.

His cock throbbed behind the fly of his jeans, begging him to reconsider, to take her now. Ignoring the arousal, he fished a red T-shirt from his drawer and handed it to Tempest. It would be loose on her, but he didn't necessarily want the world to see her pert nipples.

"Bra?" she asked in a resigned voice.

"No."

She made a face accompanied by an eye roll and yanked the shirt over her head. He almost sighed in relief when her breasts were hidden from view. Almost. The soft cotton draped over the soft mounds, emphasizing them.

They had to get out of here before he lost it. "Where's your purse?" he asked.

"With my clothes."

"Go get it and give me your cash and credit cards."

Her brows drew together.

"Remember," he added. "Dependent on me. You can have them back later. Don't worry, angel. I'll be sure you have everything you need."

"I'm not worried about that."

"Then what?"

She hesitated, then shook her head. "It's nothing."

Josh caught her chin. "Don't hide from me. No secrets. That's always been our rule, remember?"

"It's not my father's money. It's mine. I earn a paycheck. I pay my own bills."

"Doesn't matter."

Her irritation was plain as she padded past him into the living room but she didn't argue. Josh followed, feeling like a modern version of Simon Legree.

So it wasn't her daddy's money. Josh still wanted that crutch out from beneath her. He had nothing against his sub earning her own money and using it as she pleased. He just didn't want that of Tempest. Not right now. Not until he trusted her. She'd left him once—he wouldn't leave the door open for her to leave him again.

It irked him that he couldn't trust her more. He couldn't shake the feeling that he'd spook her and she'd take off faster than a skittish colt. He didn't want to hold back and for that he felt compelled to be sure it would take some doing on her part should she choose to run. Or she'd have to ask him to let her go—and he would.

Tempest had agreed to be his. She wasn't his prisoner.

She was his submissive.

The muscles in his groin tightened. She was his. Period. By the time their allotted agreement was finished, she'd be ready to tell Phillip goodbye forever.

Fishing her purse from the pile of clothes, Tempest dug inside then handed him three major credit cards with a ten-dollar bill. She shrugged. "That's it."

Feeling even more uncomfortable with his demand, he took the offering. He wouldn't back down now. This was for the betterment of their relationship and as a Dom it was his right to place this restriction on her. She knew that.

He shoved the cards and cash in his pants pocket. He'd lock them up in the safe in his bedroom when they returned with their purchases later. First he had to get his keys or they weren't going anywhere. He stifled a sigh. They were in the bedroom…

"Wait here," he told her, already backing toward the hallway. If she followed him, he'd have her on the floor and be in her in five seconds flat.

Damn, he needed to regain some control.

From the corner of his eye, he saw Tempest shift, squeezing her thighs together as he stalked into the other room. He really wanted to stomp and get some of the frustration out of his system. But he wasn't the stomping type.

Behind him she let out a quiet moan and his nerve endings jumped. *Breathe, Josh, breathe.* The egg must have shifted, sliding slightly as her body coated it with her arousal. It wasn't going anywhere with the strap he'd laced around her. The binding fit like an erotic thong and wouldn't allow the vibe to escape.

He fingered the controller. Tempting…but he didn't want her to have her release just yet. Besides, they had to shop for her clothes and get on the road. Practicality took precedence over burning desire. This desire wouldn't go away—it hadn't in eight years. He doubted a few more hours would change that. Check-in at their first stop, a bed and breakfast literally in the middle of Michigan's Upper Peninsula, a.k.a. the middle of nowhere, was at four. If they missed check-in, they'd miss dinner and supposedly there was nowhere, absolutely nowhere, nearby for them to eat. He grinned. They'd better be on time. Tempest would need nourishment to keep up with him.

The outing to get clothes ended up being uneventful despite Tempest's occasional argument about his choices—most stemming from the poor self-image fostered by her family. She seemed to think she couldn't wear anything alluring without looking silly or fat. He didn't understand how she could be upset by the clothes he picked when the thought of her in them made his mouth dry and his cock rock hard.

She'd balked but he knew he was right. His sister was the same size as Tempest and he'd been shopping with her enough times to know the right sizes. That torture had paid off though he didn't want to imagine his sister in most of the clothing he'd purchased for Tempest.

He didn't argue with her. Drawing his fingers lightly over her hip was enough to remind her who was in charge and who had the final say. He didn't allow her anything prissy. Within two hours, the suitcase he'd gotten her was filled with jeans, sexy shirts, scandalous lingerie...anything she'd need for the weekend.

He couldn't believe how much he liked knowing that she wore the panties and bra he'd selected. It fed the Dominant inside him, feeding the beast who'd been without sustenance for too long.

As they drove down the highway in his truck, her head rested on his shoulder, her floral scent filling every breath he took. Being with Tempest changed everything about his vacation. Aside from the bed and breakfast, he'd planned to stop wherever the whim took him. Instead, with the assistance of his cell phone and administrative assistant, he'd made reservations at specific spots along the route. He'd planned to take his bike. Instead they were cruising along in his truck. He'd planned on soul-searching. Instead the soul he'd always wanted was curled up on the seat beside him.

He couldn't be happier.

Well, yes he could. Before this morning, the idea of being with Tempest again hadn't occurred to him in anything other than far-fetched fantasy. So why was it he couldn't fully appreciate this miraculous interlude for what it was? Impending dread crowded in on him. If he couldn't convince her otherwise, she'd leave him again. The thought of the fiancé waiting in the wings filled him with surprising jealousy too. He knew there must have been other men but this one... He had a claim on her. Josh resented it more than he liked to admit.

Tempest was his. There was no way he'd easily let her go again.

His fingers clenched on the steering wheel.

He wouldn't think about that—any of it. He'd focus on the pleasure Tempest brought him. Dropping his hand to his pocket, he flicked on the controller for the egg still lodged inside her.

Tempest sucked in a breath. "Josh..."

"We're almost there, angel." Two miles, in fact. He maneuvered onto a gravel road, canopied by thick trees and edged by wildflowers.

"G-g-good." Her fingernails dug into his thigh, much like they had earlier when they'd crossed the Mackinac Bridge, and distracted him from everything. Driving took all his will. Perhaps switching on the vibe hadn't been such a good idea.

Tempest squirmed making tiny aroused noises that yanked on his cock. The vibrations probably weren't enough to make her come but they'd certainly take her down that path. God, he couldn't wait to be inside her. In his whole life there'd never been anything to compare with being buried deep inside Tempest while she thrashed beneath him, overtaken by her release.

Soon. Very soon.

The trees started to clear and the bed and breakfast came into sight. Josh almost slammed his foot onto the brake. What the hell? His "four star bed and breakfast on wooded grounds" was Four Star Bed—the motel name, he assumed—with breakfast available. There *were* woods surrounding the clustered buildings—however this wasn't what he'd had in mind. Something quiet, relaxing, romantic...not seedy. The place might be off the beaten track, but it looked like a place to take a hooker for an hour.

He really needn't have worried about the four o'clock check in.

"This is it?" Tempest asked.

"Yeah." His irritation sharpened his tone. It pissed him off that his plan had spun awry. How was he going to win her if he brought her to the most redneck hole-in-the-wall on the map?

"It's nice…rustic," she commented.

His head snapped from the abomination before him and he stared at her in disbelief. Her grin told him she knew exactly what he was thinking.

"It's a little…rundown, but it looks clean," she added.

"That's good," he said in a low voice and grinned. "I wouldn't want you kneeling on a dirty floor."

Her eyes went dark, filled with a desire that had nothing to do with the constant rhythm of the toy inside her. "Will you let me suck you off?" she whispered.

"We'll see. You've proven to be a very naughty submissive today." Man, he loved her that way.

Her lips tipped upward. Even with the years that had passed, she knew him too well. She knew how much she'd satisfied him.

"Let me please you then…Master."

Their room had better be ready.

Josh jerked into a parking space and nearly dragged Tempest into the office. It had been a freaking stupid idea to wait until they reached the bed and breakfast before he toppled her to a mattress. He glanced around again. *Really* stupid.

*Way to botch up "romantic", idiot.*

He reached into his pocket and flicked the vibe's switch a notch higher. Tempest jolted, her breath leaving in a hiss. He leaned toward her to whisper in her ear. "Do you think you can keep from coming while we check in?"

Her teeth sank into her bottom lip as she fought to keep control. Damn he wanted to feel those teeth on his cock, lightly scraping upward as she wrapped her lips around him. His balls drew tight in anticipation. On second thought, they'd better wait on that part. It had been too long for them both.

Fighting for the control required of a Dom, he willed his erection to subside. Fat chance of overcoming his body this time. Being aroused by some woman for whom he had marginal feelings and lusting after Tempest were two vastly different things.

She made another strangled noise and he glanced at the man running the reception desk. "Or will you explode right in front to the complete stranger checking us in?"

Why the hell did that thought just about set *him* off?

Tempest's eyes were slightly glazed and her fingertips brushed her thigh, much like his did when he silently reined her in. She was trying to pull herself back from the edge, the same way he did when he disciplined her. It wouldn't work. It wasn't him.

"I'll be okay," she murmured.

He bit back a smile. No, she wouldn't "be okay". She was too close to the edge. Still, he didn't argue as he held open the door to usher her inside. She waited just inside the door then trailed behind him as he approached the clerk. Josh wasn't stupid. She sought to hide her wobbling steps as her release overtook her. Each rapid breath taunted him. He should have fucked her before. If he didn't come in his pants now he'd be lucky. Chances of restraint were fifty-fifty with his odds rapidly decreasing. A sudden vision of shoving her against the counter and taking her for the world to see almost undid him.

Especially when he considered that Tempest probably wouldn't protest.

Damn it. He needed to get a grip—and not of her. Doms didn't act this way. He was in control, *not* his hormones. Redoubling his efforts to will his erection down, somewhat unsuccessfully, he thought about ice-cold water and big, hairy spiders as he approached the counter and the clerk behind it.

The man appeared perfectly matched to the outback surroundings. Grizzly Adams couldn't have done a better one-with-the-wilderness impression. Of course Adams wouldn't have leered at Tempest the way this man had. His ire rising, Josh watched as the man's blue eyes scanned up and down her frame while he licked his bottom lip. The gaze lingered on her taut breasts and the hard nipples showing through her T-shirt.

"I have a reservation," Josh ground out as he shoved Tempest behind him, barely overcoming an instinctive need to growl, "Mine". The man seemed unaffected by Josh's territorial move.

"Cress?"

"Yes." Apparently, there weren't a lot of reservations. Josh wasn't surprised. This didn't exactly seem like the hub of upper Michigan. The fact that the board behind the desk was nearly full of keys confirmed his suspicion. "Your internet listing called this a bed and breakfast. I'm guessing it's not… Where can we eat around here?"

"There's a McDonald's and a Taco Bell about a mile north of here. Fischer's Grocery and Bait is a few minutes' walk." Fast food and a grocery-bait shop. Romantic. Not. This is what he got for being in such a hurry to make reservations. A little investigation would have served him well.

They'd make do. It was only for one night. They'd probably be too busy in bed to worry about where their food came from. If they got around to eating at all.

Behind him, Tempest made a strangled sound and buried her face between his shoulder blades. Her breathing caught, heralding her release as her fingers dug into his sides. It swelled through him, bringing him unexpected pleasure. He fought back his response as she continued to arch into his back, her teeth clenched in his shirt.

Josh fisted his fingers. If this guy didn't hurry with their room, they'd go back to the truck and he'd nail her against the front seat. As her orgasm flattened her against him, the need to be in her—*now*—drove all reason from his mind.

Eyeing her, the clerk shoved a wad of papers at Josh to sign along with the room key. Silently, he pointed to the signature space, more interested in Tempest than whether or not Josh signed John Doe instead of his name. The lust written on the man's craggy face made Josh uneasy and renewed anger surged through him as he scrawled his signature across the line. Who did this guy think he was to stare at a woman who was so obviously taken? If the man so much as touched her… Josh snaked a hand behind himself and cupped Tempest's ass, pulling her flush to him. He'd allow no question as to her availability.

Damn, where the hell had this predatory nature come from? He didn't like being this out of control. It had always been this way with her, though. Some guy would say hi and Josh wanted to pulverize him. He'd thought he'd outgrown this, but apparently not. There was just something about Tempest that shot past any control or maturity he'd gained over the years and manifested into primal territorialism. This new strain of base jealousy had been building all day, ever since she'd mentioned the fiancé.

He snatched up the key. Turning, he lifted Tempest into his arms, just as another release spasmed through her. She lurched, pressing her face into his shoulder. "Please," she moaned. "Oh God, stop it, please."

He brushed his lips against her temple, tasting a salty trickle of sweat. "Hang on, angel. Almost there."

"Is she okay?" the clerk asked.

"Not feeling well," Josh lied. He carried her outside as fast as he could, considering his throbbing arousal. He didn't bother to move his truck in front of their room, instead carrying her the short distance to the out-building labeled four. Tempest was so far gone she didn't protest for him to put her down because she was supposedly too heavy. A bunch of bull that was. She'd never been too heavy for him to carry and he liked having her in his arms like this. This move was worth repeating. He'd keep her in a sexual haze if need be. Anything to keep her from berating her weight.

Her body was perfect and right now he couldn't think of another place he'd rather be than between her supple thighs.

His hand shook as he fit the key into the lock.

Tempest began to writhe and he almost dropped her. *Open, you goddamn door!* Suddenly, it slammed open. He rushed inside, kicking the door shut, and tossed Tempest on the bed. There would be no waiting, no more foreplay—hell, their entire day had been foreplay. Frantically, he worked at the closure of her jeans. He shoved them down to her knees. Her folds dripped with her cream as he ripped away the egg and the restraints holding it in her. A growl rose in his throat. He wanted to taste her, he wanted to fuck her, he wanted to slide his fingers through the slippery honey and he wanted to tie her up and torment her. The need to be inside her took precedence over everything.

"Please," she rasped. Her hips lifted toward him, like a supplication to the god of lust. In the shadowy room he couldn't see her aroused flesh, but her heady scent surrounded him. He had to taste her.

He shoved up her shirt, trapping her arms in the fabric above her head as he kissed a path from her shoulder to the deep valley between her breasts. Agilely, he unfastened the front of the scanty bra they'd purchased on their shopping spree. He peeled back the lacy cups from the firm mounds. He latched onto a pert nipple, pressing the hard peak to the roof of his mouth as he ripped open his fly. She tasted of vanilla and smelled of every dream he'd had for the last eight years. Hungrily, he ate at her breast, sucking, nipping, licking.

Nearly mindless with the need that drove him, he barely remembered to pull the condom from his pocket and roll it on. He'd known it would be like this. Hot and out of control.

Thank God, he'd shoved the packet in his jeans earlier. Unable to wait even a second longer he positioned the head of his cock at her fiery opening.

The gate to heaven.

Tempest screamed out as Josh drove inside her, parting her swollen tissues with his wide cock. Her body protested the invasion, unaccustomed to his girth and length. It had been so long since she'd been with anyone—even Phillip. Sex wasn't part of their relationship and she hadn't wanted another guy. Every other man had fallen short of Josh. She just hadn't bothered.

Desperate need clawed into her womb as he pistoned in and out and her body began to swell in welcome around his shaft. She'd never been so sensitive. So ready for a man to fill her. After hours of waiting followed by the orgasms that had rocked relentlessly through her body, feeling Josh moving in her sent her immediately rocketing toward another release. She arched into his frenzied thrusts. Need for him twisted tight in her belly, driving her as she rode the wild storm he built inside her.

She bent her knees higher and opened wide for his thrusts as he laved her breast. The small silver ball in the center of his tongue drove her mad as he flicked it over her tight nipples. She flooded around him in a hot surge. "Yes," she moaned. "Yes…"

He plowed forward, each drive growing harder yet eased by the cream surrounding him.

"God, angel, you feel so good. Yeah, like that," he groaned as she ground her hips into him. Her cries punctuated the darkness of the room, arousing her further. She was his. His slave. Restrained beneath him yet giving him pleasure. Her fingers flexed in the fabric twisted around her wrists. She longed to investigate the tiny ring pierced through his nipple.

Her pussy clenched around him. Every ridge, every inch of his cock taunted her frantic nerve endings. The nipple piercing wasn't the only piercing he had below his neck. She moaned as the extra ridges in his penis stimulated her sheath, touching her most sensitive spots. The sensations blurred together in a mass of pleasure but she knew he had some sort of modification there. More piercings. She ceased to care as he drove wildly inside her.

Suddenly, his teeth sank into her upper breast, hard enough to stake his possession. Not enough to really hurt. She wanted more.

"Yes," she cried and then he was there at her mouth, kissing her as if he'd breathed his last breath and he needed hers to survive. It was desperate and as needy as she felt, taking everything she could give. His tongue plunged between her lips. There was nothing civil in this mating. It was all consuming—wild. They'd left civil hours behind them in the restaurant where they'd reunited.

In this dark, stuffy room their flesh melded, sticking as rivulets of sweat marked their desperation. She struggled to get the jeans off the bottom of her legs so she could wrap her legs around him and draw him even closer. She only managed one leg but it didn't matter as her thighs embraced his waist and her ankles crossed behind his pistoning hips.

Her release tingled in her core while she met him, stroke for stroke. Slowly it seeped outward into her limbs while her center screamed to release lightning throughout her.

"Now Tempest," Josh growled. "God, now."

At his word, the golden warmth mutated into a desperate beast. It suddenly clawed to her extremities, obedient to his word as it had always been. She arched beneath him. Exquisite pleasure held her frozen while he continued to pound into her clenching pussy. Each thrust shoved her orgasm higher and deeper. So deep. She'd never experienced this bone-melting rush with anyone but him. Squeezing her eyes shut, she took gasping breaths between choked cries and unintelligible utterances.

Josh grunted, muttering her name so harshly it seemed half curse. He grasped her hips dragging her tight to his groin as he came and waves of pleasure poured over her. It went on and on, tearing a scream from her until spent, she collapsed onto the mattress and he let her go. His mouth brushed her ear while his fingers feathered over her inner elbow.

"We are such stuff as dreams are made on," he murmured.

*What?* Tempest squinted at him through the inky darkness. He was quoting *Shakespeare*? His fingers traced down her raised arms to her shoulder until he splayed one hand over her neck. Another shudder tore through her. She understood this. His fingers like this, mimicking a wide collar. *His. His dream.*

The silent signals had been an integral part of their relationship before. Josh didn't believe in ruling his submissive with the flogger, whips or spanking. Those things had been an active element in their bedroom but not as punishment. He'd always said she was perfect for him because it took so little for her to obey him and bring him pleasure. She'd rather have had the flogger sometimes. Instead, her Master punished by withholding her release.

His fingers moved slightly and she pushed into them, answering his unspoken statement of ownership.

*His.* For so long, she'd shared the same dream he had. Living as they wished. A life together. She'd wanted to be his… She almost sighed as regret began to needle her. She only had ten days to erase him from her system. Then finally she'd move on, with her life and her career. Most of her things were already packed and she had the money to support herself while she got her business off the ground.

Being with Josh today had cemented in her head that no matter what, she couldn't be with Phillip. What she felt with him didn't come close to what she felt with Josh. Every moment with Josh was intense yet she had an easy camaraderie with him.

She'd been lying to herself to think she could expunge him from her system in a few days. Josh would always own a part of her. But he could only have these few days—not even the fourteen he'd demanded.

She couldn't tell him. He'd be furious when he discovered but there was little she could do for it. If she hadn't agreed to the two weeks, she wouldn't be here in his arms. Guilt ate at her. What would he do if she told him now? She couldn't risk it. As mercenary as it might seem, she wanted as much time with him as she could get before she had to say goodbye forever.

"What is it?" he asked, stroking her sweaty hair back from her temples. He stared down into her eyes, his gaze concerned as he seemed to search inside her soul.

She glanced away, uncomfortable with his scrutiny. She licked her lips. "Nothing."

"Tempest. Don't lie to me."

She shook her head. She couldn't tell him what she was thinking, so she struck upon another truth. "This is so…unexpected. When I got up this morning, I never thought I'd be in bed with you by dinner."

He nipped her neck. "But what a delightful dinner it is."

Distracting him with sex was a very good idea. If only she could forget her deception…

He buried his nose in her hair. His hips shifted, rubbing into her clit. "It feels so good inside you."

"Mmm, yes," she sighed, temporarily forgetting her worries. They ceased to matter much when he moved over her, his cock still firm and growing harder by the moment. His hand crept up her torso to cup her over-sensitive breast, gently twisting the pearled nipple. Tempest moaned as the heat built in her center once again. How many times would it take before her body was sated? She'd orgasmed countless times. And she still needed more. And more. And more.

It was always this way with Josh. It didn't matter if it had been three minutes since she'd found release or three hours. He could rebuild the fire within her with the slightest of touches.

"That's right, angel," he murmured as she arched beneath him, moaning for more. "Whose are you?"

"Yours, Master," she gasped, her hips jerking. "Yours."

"Always."

She shuddered around him, her pussy squeezing around his ridged cock. She struggled to hold on to reality, turning her head and staring at the slit of late afternoon light fighting its way through the heavy curtains. If she lost herself in his embrace whenever Josh plowed into her, she'd never break free. The tenderness, the mind-blowing emotions and corresponding physical reactions would bind her to him more tightly than chains. He'd haunt her every breath.

Her heart lurching, she disconnected. This was just some guy fucking her. Nothing special…a horny guy in a seedy motel room where hundreds of couples had probably fucked before. Tomorrow, he'd move on… She'd move on… Nothing special.

Fingers turned her face from the light. "Don't do that," Josh rasped, dragging her back to reality. "Stay with me."

She sobbed as starbursts exploded before her eyes, blinding her to the desperation in his eyes. *Stay with him.* If only he knew…

# Chapter Three

ℵ

Josh held Tempest as he stared at the faint light breaking through the curtains he'd cracked open last night when they'd finally settled into sleep. They'd never stopped to eat, each being content to "live on love". He smiled as he remembered Tempest giggling that sometime yesterday evening. As her stomach rumbled beneath his hand, he suspected she wouldn't feel the same this morning. Finding food would be high on their agenda, right after checking out of this place.

With a contented sound, Tempest turned in his arms and snuggled into his chest. Her lips closed around his nipple and tugged at the small gold ring.

"Morning, angel," he gasped.

"Hungry," she murmured. "Need coffee."

She gave the ring another gentle pull, sending a spark straight to his groin. "Tempest..." His fingers dug into her ass, dragging her tight to him. "Keep that up and it will be noon before we eat. And—" Her stomach growled in support of his statement. "I think we need to feed you."

"I'm fine," she grumbled, slipping from his arms and swinging her legs from the bed. She wrenched the sheet up with her, like a shroud to hide her ivory perfection.

She didn't say anything, but he knew. He'd hurt her feelings with his insistence that she needed to eat. For God's sake, she was human, wasn't she? He grabbed her, yanking her back and burying his face in the crook of her neck. He growled, biting her shoulder. "I'm *starving* and before I fall into a faint over your luscious body, I need some serious protein. What kind of a Dom would I be if I couldn't keep up with my lusty wench?"

"I guess we'd better find that McDonald's," she replied. A spark of mirth danced in her eyes when she turned her head toward him. "Do I get to put on some clothes?"

He pretended to consider her question. "I suppose," he teased with a dramatic sigh. Settling her back on the pillows, he straddled her body and kissed her until their moans echoed in the room. "Stay right there," he told her, reluctantly climbing from the bed, then tucking the sheet around her. Her eyes followed his every move as he reached for his jeans. Carefully, he pulled them on, adjusting himself so that he didn't have a zipper mishap. He grabbed the room and truck keys from the floor where he'd dropped them. "I'll be back in a sec with our suitcases."

The birds sang merrily as he slipped outside and headed for his truck. The sun peeked through the leaves to dapple the ground, giving the area an overall peaceful feeling. Despite the rundown motel, it was nice here. He could almost believe he was at the heart of nature primeval. Until he looked behind him at the shabby structures with their peeling paint and torn screens. He kept his gaze on the thick woods, unwilling to let his mood be tarnished by the glaring reminder of how he'd been misled.

He climbed into the truck to pull it around in front of the room. Still deep in thought, he turned the key…and was met with silence. What on earth? He had gas. He kept the vehicle in tiptop condition. He'd just had it in for its regular maintenance and inspection, in fact. Frowning, he turned the key again. He could not be stranded here. *Please, no…*

Nothing.

Squeezing his eyes shut he dropped his forehead onto the steering wheel. Somewhere, for some reason, one of the minions of fate hated him. This could not be happening. For good measure, he turned the key again.

It was happening. Damn it!

Just great. The birds seemed to change their tune, chirping their ridicule in his direction. The dappling turned slightly sinister.

Such a wonderful interlude he had going on here...crappy motel, broken down truck. He shoved a hand through his unruly hair and took a deep breath. This could all be fixed. He'd call a mechanic, get the truck repaired and they'd be on their merry way. In the meantime, Grizzly Adams had mentioned the grocery-bait shop was nearby. Surely they'd have something to eat if the McDonalds was too far to walk.

Right. Okay. So he had a plan. This wasn't so bad. Call a mechanic. Get some food. Be on their way to his favorite place on Lake Superior, a secluded cove untouched by civilization. God, he couldn't wait to make love to Tempest there.

He pulled his cell phone from where it was clipped to his waistband. Flipping it open, he pressed the speed dial for his secretary. Emma was brilliant. She'd find help with a few clicks of her manicured nails on the keyboard. Three beeps let him know it wouldn't be as easy as that. Incredulous, he stared down at his phone.

No service.

He was in hell.

Reluctantly, he turned toward the main building and scowled at the dented metal trashcan. Someone had painted the wretched thing white and emblazoned it with large black letters spelling *Office*. Perfect. Perhaps Oscar the Grouch was in residence and could point him to a payphone and the nearest mechanic.

* * * * *

Tempest leapt back in bed when she heard the key rattle in the lock. She'd waited forever for Josh to return. When minutes had dragged to a half hour, she'd gotten up and peeked out the window. Not seeing him but figuring he was probably in the office taking care of their checkout, she'd made coffee in the complimentary pot on the dresser.

It would be a dead giveaway that she'd strayed from the bed, but she was willing to deal with the consequences. She needed her coffee.

Josh shouldered into the room, carrying a scrap of paper, a white, wax-coated bag and their suitcases. The luggage dropped to the floor with a thunk as he shut the door. One look at him and instant worry filled her. This wasn't the ebullient man who'd left the room earlier. Strain pulled at his eyes, filling them with shadows that had nothing to do with their lack of sleep last night. He gave her a half smile that barely reached beyond his upturned lip.

"What is it?" she asked as he crossed the room and sat on the bed beside her. Ignoring the sheet that dropped away as she rose, she knelt beside him and wrapped her arms around his shoulders. She sighed inwardly as her bare breasts and belly flattened against his warm, hard side and her body revved up for a replay of last night. She steadfastly ignored it, her only thought to giving him comfort for whatever had upset him.

"Truck's dead."

Well, that *was* worth being upset. He hadn't been pleased when he'd seen the motel and now to be stuck here…

He turned and dropped a kiss on her shoulder, distracting her. He smoothed his thumb over her forehead. "It will be okay."

Tempest smiled. Josh was so adorable when he was trying to reassure her. When she was younger, she'd occasionally acted worried, just to see his soothing in action. Silly. But back then she'd been a silly girl, unaware of much of the world and its workings. Josh had been her world and she'd liked the way his attention warmed her. Even now his comforting turned her on, warming up the dusty places inside her that nobody else touched. He'd tried to shelter her from everything when she was with him—physical and emotional.

No one else had ever protected her as Josh did.

But she wasn't the one who needed consoling. He was upset and she really didn't care *how* or *where* they spent their scant time as long as they were together.

He shoved the white bag toward her. "There are a couple of doughnuts in here. from the hotel's continental breakfast. I can't vouch for their freshness, but they're something to hold us over until we can walk to the grocery and get a few things."

She sat back on her heels while he stared at the curtained window and they both ignored the bag he dropped on the bed. He shoved a hand through his wild hair and she fought back a grin as a pleasant sensation of déjà vu prickled over her. He'd always done that and it always made things worse. It would be so easy to slide back into the memories of what had been and forget everything that had happened since they'd last been together.

Absently, she smoothed the long strands, wondering if he'd let her brush his hair later. It seemed an appropriate gesture of a submissive to her Dom. She wanted his comfort and pleasure. She needed it.

His fingers clenched beside his thigh and she drew back her hand. Had she angered him when she'd touched him? As if sensing her worry, he turned to her, again sharing the partial smile that tore at her heart. Lifting her hand, he pressed a hand to the center of her palm.

"You please me, angel. Don't fret."

"Thank you." She bowed her head, hiding her irrational relief. How had she fallen so easily back into the Master and slave routine? As much as she desired to be dominated, she knew deep inside that she'd kneel to no other man. Somehow, Josh had claimed her soul way back when, and she'd never gotten it back. "If I please you," she asked carefully, "then what's wrong? The truck can be fixed. Can't it?"

"We're stuck in this..." He stopped to look around the room, his face crinkling with distaste, "*hovel* until at least tomorrow. I called from the office. That's the soonest the garage can get someone to come out." He chuffed out a breath. "This isn't exactly what I had in mind."

"Okay...so we'll find something to do," she offered. "Remember how we explored when we were in college?"

"Yeah." He smiled, his eyes growing dark as he remembered. His gaze wandered over her, taking in her nakedness and her position. Purposely, she slid her arms behind her and lowered her focus to the rumpled sheets between her parted thighs. Her slave pose had always turned him on. And he seemed to need distracting right about now. Wasn't that the first precept of submission? See to the Master's wellbeing, whether physical or emotional.

His happiness always led to hers.

As he stared at her, her body responded, growing soft and hot and wet in all the places clamoring for his touch. Her nipples tightened, aching for him. She didn't even care that she was naked with all her flaws visible. Josh didn't seem to care. He even seemed to like her generous curves her clean-shaven pussy. And, man, how she liked his hard-plated muscles.

She bit back a groan as she eyed his belly and the curve of his hipbone disappearing beneath his low-cut jeans. Her center clenched sending a flood to her cleft. God, how she wanted him. She peeked at his face through her lashes. Would this longing ever stop, or would it go on long after they'd parted once again? He hadn't come after her before. He certainly wouldn't chase her this time.

She shoved the thought away, unwilling to taint the moment with the inevitable.

His lids heavy with need, Josh leaned toward her while she fought the urge to arch her chest into him and rub her breasts against his lightly furred body.

"You're so responsive," he murmured. "Even without me touching you...but I wonder...what would happen if I did this?" His fingers stroked down the inside of her elbow, grazing the slightly raised veins.

"We are such stuff as dreams are made on," he whispered.

A shudder riffled through her and her body spasmed with the force of a tiny orgasm, threading its way along her languid limbs. *Where the hell did that come from?*

She struggled to breathe and make reason out of her reaction. How had he done that? She'd always thought Shakespeare was okay, but it had never had this kind of an effect on her before. He'd quoted this line every time she came, every time stroking her inner elbow. Goose bumps rose as he trailed the backs of his bent fingers between her breasts and over her quivering belly. Slowly, he slipped one long finger between her folds. "Hmmm...all warmed up."

"Yes," she whispered.

He cupped her chin, lifting her gaze to his. "You're mine, Tempest."

They both startled at the sound of his cell phone ringing. His head dropped to her shoulder. "I can't get service to call out, but someone can call me..." he muttered, reaching for the holder on his belt. "I better answer it. Might be Marv's Garage. Maybe we can still get out of here today."

"Hurry," she whispered as he answered. She leaned back and raised her hands over her head, looping her fingers through the rungs on the headboard. Deliberately, she raised her knees and parted them. "Master..." she mouthed.

"Ryan..." Josh greeted his brother as his chin lowered and he stared at her. Ire mixed with the desire swirling through his eyes, a heady mix that strengthened her arousal. She was in trouble as soon as he got off his call, but she liked it.

"No, I'm not going to Superior today," he said.

She sighed, shifting her body to show him her need. She bit her lip, closing her eyes and tipping back her head.

"The truck died." His voice sounded choked and she heard him moving away from her. What the heck? He wasn't supposed to be walking away from her obvious display. She sighed and reached down for the sheet.

"Don't move."

Her eyes flew open and she returned to her former position, gripping the headboard.

"No not you," he told his brother. "Who? My sub… What is this? Twenty questions? It's Tempest, okay?"

He frowned as Ryan apparently said something he didn't like.

"Yes, I know what I'm doing. Look, lay off the baby brother routine. We're fine. *I'm* fine. Is there a reason you're calling other than to check up on your errant sibling?" He sighed as his suspicion must have been confirmed. "No, we're not in St. Ignace. Do you think I'd be stranded if the truck had died in St. Ignace? We're north of that. Off one twenty three, on the way to Tahquamenon. In the middle of nowhere…"

Propping the phone on his shoulder, he lifted a small, black carryall from the group of luggage he'd dropped at the door and set it on the end of the bed.

"Well, yeah it's pretty here," he licked his bottom lip, eyeing Tempest in a way that made her think perhaps he was talking about her. No man had ever made her feel so good…so confident.

*Touch me now,* she wanted to scream. *I need you.*

The sound of the bag's zipper tensed her nerve endings. His gaze told of surprises inside and a moment later, he confirmed the promise. Excitement winged through her as he withdrew two long strips of red fabric and smiling an evil grin, walked toward the head of the bed. Her cleft flooded as he bound her hands in place, ensuring that she wouldn't move from her position. She was his, helpless to escape. Like she'd even want to.

He splayed his fingers over her neck, claiming her silently. She whimpered unable to stop as she pressed into him in answer. "Please," she mouthed.

He raised an eyebrow, reminding her she was not in charge. He was the Dom. He was in charge. She was his pleasure. At his command. His knuckles dragged down her arm and over the slope of her breast. Slowly, he rolled her erect nipple between his fingers. Bending forward, he flattened his tongue over it, catching the tip with his piercing. Tempest fought back a moan. She could hear the indistinct rumble of Ryan's voice as he continued to talk and she knew he'd hear any sound she made.

Josh molded her other breast, taunting the flesh as he continued to answer his brother noncommittally and torment her with his mouth. Tremors flew through her, amplified by her battle to remain silent. Still, her tormented gasps seemed to explode around her.

Her teeth sank into her bottom lip and she squeezed her eyes closed. It made no difference. His sharp, masculine scent filled her senses. The ring in his nipple scuffed her belly as he played her. She wanted to feel the tiny barbells on the underside of his cock as he drove into her again. Hell, she wanted to investigate them with her tongue.

He chuckled at something Ryan said—or was it at her struggle? The wood spindles bit into her hands as she clutched them. Each draw of his mouth seemed to tug at an invisible line between her breasts and her pussy. He sucked and her body clenched. He nipped and her body clenched. He…*breathed* and her body clenched.

She started to shudder as her release reached its pinnacle. One "step" and she'd be there, careening to the valley of satiation.

"I need to go," he told his brother and snapped shut the phone.

Finally. She parted her thighs a bit further.

"You're very naughty," he chastised. "Naughty subs don't get rewarded."

"Josh…no," she pleaded. Oh God, she couldn't stand it if he left her like this.

"What should I do with you, naughty sub?"

"Fuck me," she offered.

"I don't think so." He stood over her, his muscular arms crossed over his magnificent chest. "I have a flogger with me, but I think you'd enjoy that too much." Opening his pants, he stroked his large hand over his cock. With firm strokes, he drew a glistening droplet to the tip.

Tempest licked her lips, wanting nothing more than to taste him. Okay, that wasn't true. She wanted him deep inside her.

He smoothed his thumb over the tip. "You want this?"

She nodded, almost unable to speak past the "Yes," she managed.

"Hmm, that's too bad. I'd like that, you know. But since you've been so naughty."

"Please, Master," she begged falling into the play. "Let me please you. I'm sorry."

He chuckled. "I doubt that."

Frantically, she shifted on the bed, the inner walls of her pussy contracting wildly. She loved him like this. Controlling the scene. Dominating her. Her gaze blurred slightly as she stared at his hand moving over his erection and her own hand restlessly stroked the wood spindle she held. He'd be as hard as the wood, yet softer. Her fingers itched to encircle him Damn it she needed him and he knew it. He knew what sweet torture this was for her.

Moisture dripped from her cleft, trickling along the crease of her ass. He'd slide so easily into her, even with the metal posts tracking the length of his cock. She shifted, drawing her knees together to relieve some of her arousal.

More of his fluid escaped the tiny slit on his cock, getting on his fingers. He rubbed it on her belly. "I love watching your muscles roll as you fight your need," he told her, trailing the pad of his thumb around her navel. She groaned as his touch trailed to her pussy, slowly he rubbed her clit.

"Oh God, Josh," she cried.

"Who?" he asked.

Confused, she stared at him. "Master," she said, finally. "Please."

He slipped a finger inside her and she almost came from relief. Her aching tissues closed around it, begging for more. Agitated, she thrust her hips toward him, but he pulled back before she found any true reprieve from the desire pulling taut her nerve-endings.

Slowly, he traced the path of moisture to her ass. "When was the last time you were fucked here, Tempest?" he asked hoarsely.

Her bottom instinctively clenched. There? Forever ago. She wasn't even sure she could. But for him, she'd try. She needed him anyway she could get him. "When was the last time you were there?" she asked. Sudden shyness fell over her. How boring and unsophisticated would he find her now?

Josh almost lost it right then and there. He'd been the last one to slide into her tight passage. Not just the last, but the only. It was his, completely his. He gazed at her flushed cheeks, the pink staining down her neck and on to her chest. Her tousled blonde hair spread around her head like a damaged halo. Her eyes glazed, her arms tied over her head, she waited for his pleasure.

He dipped his finger into her cunt again and dragged away her lubricant. Slowly, he pushed it against her puckered hole. Slowly, ever so slowly, he gained entrance. Fiery heat surrounded his fingertip, tempting him to rush. He knew better. If either of them was to gain pleasure here, he couldn't hurry. Tempest moaned, her mouth moving with incoherent words as she squeezed shut her eyes.

"Feels…good," she gasped. "Let me go so I can get in the right position."

"No, like this," he insisted. He liked taking a woman from behind as much as the next guy, but he wanted—no needed—to see Tempest's face as he sank inside her to the balls. Reaching to the head of the bed, he grabbed two of the fat pillows and slid them beneath her hips.

The case where he'd stowed some of his gear, still lay on the end of the bed. Less than an arm's length away. Quickly, he retrieved a tube of lube and a condom. In a moment, he was ready and perched at the entrance to her nether passage. A single quiver shot down his thighs as tension held him tight. He needed in.

"If you want me to stop," he said, "Say—"

"I won't. Please J-Master. I need you. Please."

"Fuck, Tempest," he swore.

"Please," she whispered, lifting her hips slightly and pressing her opening to his tip. Her movement forced him inside. The initial band of muscles cinched around the head, taking him to hell. Or was it heaven? At times like this, the line between was too thin. His body was a miasma of pure sensation.

"More," she panted.

"Wait. I don't want to hurt you," he answered through gritted teeth. How humiliating would it be to come when he'd barely gotten inside her?

"Don't care. Need all of you. Please."

Driven by her need, he shoved forward while she screamed. It was as if his body wasn't his. It was hers. A machine reacting to her need. But he wasn't. He knew better. Desperately, he clutched for his retreating control.

"Sorry, sorry, sorry," he muttered. Tears streamed down her cheeks. Horrified guilt tore at him. What had he done?

"No. Good. It's good," she told him. Unbelievably, she arched. "More. Again. Please, Master, please..."

She was so tight. The squeeze was almost too much. He waited, breathing shallowly, praying, counting the gouges in the wall above the headboard... Bit by infinitesimal bit she relaxed around him.

And he moved. Drugging pleasure clutched him while her body clutched his cock so tightly he might never get it back. He didn't want it back. She felt too good. Grasping her hips, he drove into her. His thumbs pulled at the fleshy lips hiding her cleft and opened her to him. The dark, sensual scent of her filled him while he rubbed against her clit with every thrust.

Tempest writhed. Screaming, begging, Oh-my-Godding, she stiffened. Her tight nipples pushed toward the ceiling as her orgasm claimed them and her nails added more gouges to the wall. Her passage clamped down on his shaft. He couldn't hold back. With two violent thrusts, he came.

Nothing. *Nothing* would ever come close to Tempest beneath him.

* * * * *

Tempest woke to the smell of coffee. The room smelled of sex too though they'd showered sometime in the night. A moment later, the sensation of her stomach eating its way to her backbone attacked. How late was it? They must have slept for a while if her gnawing hunger was any indication. Well, lack of food wouldn't hurt her. Still she needed something soon or she'd take a bite out of the hunk stretched beside her.

She grinned. She might anyway… He looked so good.

Content in the moment, she rolled toward him, curling her arm over his chest and resting her chin on her hand. Idly, she reached out and traced the black tribal tattoo banding his arm with her fingertip. All the Doms in his family had a similar band. And while most people—like her—would consider it merely tribal symbols, it was actually some ancient language she couldn't dream of comprehending.

"Keeper of the temple," he murmured, signaling he'd woken just before his arm looped around her waist. Her finger moved again and he continued reciting the meaning of the symbols. "Owner of the treasure. Protector of the spirit."

Toying with the tiny, gold ring in the nipple beside his tattoo, she turned her cheek to her hand and gazed up at him. "You're not keeping the temple very well. Your treasure is starving."

He snorted and smacked her behind. "But the spirit is obviously fine."

She made a dramatic sound of suffering, as shimmering heat flooded to every part of her. "For now… Much longer and I may sink into a decline."

"Oh we can't have that." He shifted from beneath her and climbed out of the bed. "Okay, up with you. Since Marv's in no hurry to fix the truck, let's see what we can find in town. Grizzly Adams told me how to take the shortcut through the woods."

"Who?" She bit her lip as she watched the muscles contract in Josh's ass while he moved. The man was perfection walking. Why would he want her? Disgusted with herself, she shoved the thought away. Obviously, he did and that should be good enough for her. He'd never once mentioned a problem with her appearance. It was always her obsession.

Maybe it was time to figure out how to get over that. It would certainly make her happier.

"The desk guy," he said as he pulled on his jeans. "I think he actually owns this place. When I went to the office this morning, he was wearing his pajamas behind the desk. Hey!" He turned, crossing his arms over his chest. "I thought you were starving. Aren't you getting up?"

"I'm enjoying the view. Turn around again."

His brows drew together but his stern look was ruined by his amused smile. Returning to the bed, he knelt over her and bracketed her body with his arms and legs. "You're a very naughty sub. *Still.* I should have punished you earlier. Get up or I'll spank you and put you in a corner."

"Promise?" she giggled as he got up again. She hadn't felt this sort of euphoria in…eight years. Despite her teasing, she too got up and crossed to her luggage, acutely aware of the new aches in her body. She couldn't help her smile. Each twinge marked her as his. And she liked it.

Quickly, she grabbed a pair of jeans and a T-shirt along with some of the sinful lingerie he'd picked out for her. What had he said? *You have no idea what it does to me to know you're wearing the bra and panties I selected for you.* It did a little something for her too. Her womb gave a little quiver at the remembered words.

"No time for a shower. We'll take one when we get back."

"I really need one to wake up. I feel like I've done nothing but have sex for hours," she protested.

"Haven't you?"

True, but she didn't want the world to know it. She had to look completely debauched. Oh, who cared? It wasn't like she'd see these people again after tomorrow. If Josh said no, it was no. He was in charge. "I've done more than that. I made coffee," she offered weakly.

"You weren't supposed to get out of bed," he gently reminded.

There was that… Without another word, she slipped into her clothes, acutely aware of his eyes on her. If she'd had a little more confidence, she might have tried to be sexy. Instead she put on the garments as quickly as possible. She tugged at the hem of her shirt which crept up to show a sliver of her belly every time she moved. "This shirt's too small."

"It's perfect. You really do need to eat. You're crabby."

Her lips pressed together. She wouldn't argue with him. She'd only lose—particularly since she was starting to feel a bit crabby. Looking away, she tugged at her shirt.

"Stop," he said, stepping close to her. He closed his fingers around her wrists and pulled them behind her. Carefully he slipped her fingers in her back pockets. "Just like that. Don't move them."

Don't move? Like this, her breasts thrust forward, her nipples no doubt poking against the thin cotton. The position lifted the hem of the top, exposing a few inches of flesh.

Josh circled her navel with his thumb and shook his head. His tender gaze pierced her. "You have no idea… It amazes me how unaware you are. This softness… What more could a man ask for?"

She could think of a whole lot of things.

His fingers splayed and slipped beneath her waistband to graze the upper slope of her mound. "Don't you dare say what you're thinking or I'll force feed you Oreos."

"Oh the torture," she quipped, a little worried that he might actually do that.

What would it take for Tempest to understand how attractive she was? Her family had done some number on her self-image. Her stomach growled loudly, dragging him from his thoughts. Maybe he would feed her those Oreos. He'd love to taste them on her lips. The sugar buzz would keep her going through their next session in bed until it wore off and she collapsed into his arms. In the deep sleep to follow, she wouldn't question her presence here or ridicule her perfectly healthy body.

Holding her took him to a heaven he hadn't visited in years.

Going to the door, he held it open for her. "C'mon, slave. We need to find food and the general store. We have one condom left."

Her eyes widened in surprised, then a sultry smile curved her lips. Obviously, Miss Smarty Pants had mentally calculated and realized that yes, they had fucked enough times to run through the modest box he'd brought. He should have planned better. He couldn't get enough of her.

"I'd guess we'd better hurry then," she conceded. "I'm feeling kinda needy."

His cock jerked back to attention. He'd only just gotten the thing to relax. Tempest was out of control. Purposely angling for punishment.

"Your hands don't come out of your pocket unless you're in danger of being snapped by a branch or you trip and must catch yourself. Understand?"

She lowered her gaze, appearing appropriately submissive, even though he knew she was anything but. "Yes, Master."

He gritted his teeth. She sidled past him to the pitted, crumbling sidewalk outside the cabin. Was it his imagination or were her hips swaying more than usual? She smiled at Grizzly Adams who happened to be crossing the parking lot, presumably on the way to the Dumpster judging from the black trash bag in his hand. He stopped dead in the middle of the pavement, ogling Tempest. Obviously, he didn't see hot women out here in the wilderness. If she didn't watch it, she'd find herself kidnapped and married by some backwoods minister.

Damn it! Josh caught her elbow and guided her toward the path through the woods just as she winked at the man. Obviously at the hands of her Dom her self-confidence was improving, at least a little, and that pleased him. However he was not impressed with the way the Four Star proprietor consumed her with his eyes.

"Who do you belong to?" Josh growled near her ear.

She smiled serenely. "You, Master."

"You like being punished," he accused.

She gave him a "duh" look that had him hard in less than a breath. "Yes, Master," she replied, her voice husky. Her eyes darkened, obviously, remembering the last time he'd disciplined her. He'd failed there. There was something about Tempest that sent him to his limits and destroyed his control. Yet he needed to dominate her and feel her submission. He swallowed against the tightness in his throat. It didn't matter how much Tempest misbehaved when it came right down to it—she obeyed him. It didn't matter if they were parted eight years or eight minutes. It was as if she was programmed to be everything he wanted in a woman. Sassy yet compliant. Subservient yet as naughty as hell.

And strong. The image of the Strength card Keera had shown him on his birthday flashed through his mind. Tempest could easily be the woman pictured closing the lion's mouth. She had inner strength she'd never recognized. It pleased him that with his guidance, she seemed to be coming into her power.

She swayed seductively as they walked through the woods to the general store. He frowned knowing she was teasing him, yet she didn't so much as slide her fingers a centimeter from her pockets. Any of his three brothers would turn their sub over their knee for the behavior Tempest displayed. He suspected his sisters-in-law would enjoy it too. That wasn't the way he operated. He'd always been the rebel in the family. He had a different way, even in the way he lived the D/s lifestyle.

Without a word, he brushed the backs of his fingers in a deliberate line down her hip. She couldn't mistake it was an intentional touch. She stopped, looking askance at him.

"Behave," he ordered quietly. "Taunting me won't get you anywhere. I left the only condom back in the room." He held up a finger when she opened her mouth. "And don't suggest something else either."

She blinked slowly then nodded.

Leaning toward her, he cupped the back of her neck and gently kissed her. "Not that I wouldn't really like to have you on your knees, bringing me off."

She bit her lip making a small sound in her throat. Oh yeah, he felt the same way.

Splaying his hand on the small of her back, he guided her in what he hoped was the right direction. There did seem to be a distinct dirt path through this densely wooded stretch. White pine and maple towered over them while unseen birds twittered merrily. As they continued, they passed a secluded waterfall. Josh was tempted to stop. He could easily envision Tempest naked beneath the modest fall, water sluicing over her while he explored her body.

His steps quickened. Food… He needed to feed his woman before surrendering again to the desire zipping between them. There was a lot more to their relationship than sex, but right now when reuniting was so fresh, nothing else really seemed to matter. He needed the reassurance of her body connected with his—and she wanted him just as much. That knowledge only served to incite his drive.

A good ten minutes later, they exited the woods onto the main street of Trent, the only town for miles according to the Four Star owner. It was actually bigger than Josh had imagined. Directly to his right stood Fischer's Grocery and Bait. A small hand-painted placard below the store's sign declared there to be a pharmacy on site, as well.

*Condoms*, he thought, thankful the pharmacy would be easy to find. A bakery-restaurant was at the end of the street with a Chinese restaurant two doors down. Chinese? He wouldn't have expected something so specialized in such a small place. He glanced at Tempest knowing her fondness for crab rangoon and saw a bright spot in this vacation disaster.

A gas station, the Trent church, a post office and Marv's garage rounded out the town. To the north, a smattering of white houses with peeling paint had sprouted up along the main road leading to and from the main drag.

Josh guided Tempest toward the store. "Snacks," he said.

"Condoms," she retorted, knowing his mind.

He leered at her, sliding his hand down to give her ass a squeeze. "Like I said…snacks."

A blast of stale, cold air hit them as they stepped into the musty store. Except for the long counter doubling as a pharmacy station near the door, the set-up of the place vaguely reminded Josh of the convenience store around the corner from his house. Ignoring the couple standing near the soft drink cooler, he headed down the nearest aisle. It didn't take long to find what they needed. Between the sleep aids and the prenatal vitamins, a sole row of boxed condoms had been slotted.

"Don't people use birth control around here?" Tempest asked as he wiped a thin layer of dust off the box. Considering this was the only store in town, there seemed to be dust on everything. Where did people shop if not here? "Check the expiration date," she suggested. He squinted at the date imprinted on the side, deciphering the garble to the proper numbers.

"We're good," he confirmed, noting the date was still months off. They shouldn't have any mishaps.

"Can I help you two?" the man at the counter called.

"Got what I need, thanks." Heading down the next aisle, Josh grabbed a box of strawberry Pop Tarts and a few juice boxes. It wasn't exactly the fare he'd wanted to provide Tempest on their trip, but it would do for now.

"You all staying at the Four Star?" the clerk asked when Josh set the supplies on the counter a moment later.

"Yeah. We were supposed to be here a night, but this morning my truck wouldn't start."

The couple exchanged a glance. "I'll see what I can do to get Marv over to help you sooner than he may have told you." The man held out his hand. "Tom and Maggie Fischer. I run the store and she's one of the local rangers."

They chatted with the couple for a few minutes while Tom rang up the order and Josh paid. Tom promised once again to speak with Marv, who happened to be his brother, about getting over to the Four Star to check out Josh's truck.

Feeling better about the situation, Josh led Tempest from the store. "Chinese?" he asked. Her eyes lit up and he knew her hunger would override her inner voice, which would chide her to diet. He'd squelch that voice as quickly as possible. He wanted it to be his voice she heard in her head, telling her how beautiful she was and how much he loved her.

He froze, right in the middle of the street stunned by his revelation. Tempest turned to him. "What is it?"

Could he tell her how he felt? Was it too soon? Probably. "Nothing. I'll talk to you about it later." He shrugged and smiled. "Nothing to worry about, angel. Come on." He laced his fingers through hers. "I'm starving."

* * * * *

"I hope the rangoon isn't cold," Tempest commented as they entered their room, although she didn't care if it was cold. She was starving and for some reason. Josh had insisted that they come back to the Four Star to eat their meal.

He constantly surprised her. Even after all this time, he remembered her favorite foods and made sure that they'd ordered them. She honestly wondered what else he remembered. It seemed to be an awful lot.

Sliding a hand to its favorite position on her waist, he led her to the small table in the corner of the room. Setting the grocery and take-out bags on the surface, he started to remove the white take-out boxes. The scent of orange chicken and stir-fried vegetables saturated the air. Her stomach rumbled.

Methodically, he handed her the bottled water and plates the restaurant had provided with their meal. Then he handed her the containers and she took a bit of each. She noticed that Josh took even less. He had to be starving, too.

"I'm not very hungry," he lied when she raised her eyebrows at him. "Saving room for dessert."

"What's for dessert? Pop Tarts?" she asked, putting a bite of chicken in her mouth. The sharp taste exploded across her tongue and she groaned.

"You," he replied.

"What?" she choked. He handed her the bottle of water she'd set near her plate. As she recovered, he took a few bites of his food. Had she imagined what he'd said? He seemed so nonchalant.

"Full already?" he asked.

She shook her head. "What happened to the rangoon?"

He pushed back the food he'd barely touched. "You know, I think I'm ready for dessert."

"But—"

"C'mon, slave...I'm hungry for something sweet. I need you to feed me." He rose, pulling her to her feet. His eyes shone with the devil. Grinning, he removed another white box from the take-out bag along with the jar of sweet and sour sauce he'd purchased at the restaurant. He threaded the metal spoon he'd insisted on needing between two of his fingers.

Good lord, did he intend her to feed him like a Roman prince? No, he'd said *she* was dessert. Her belly clenched and cream flooded her lacy panties. Any desire that had temporarily subsided came rushing back. A bite of Josh was way better than orange chicken.

"Come with me," he directed.

"Come with me," she mimicked in a deep voice, giggling. Josh worked hard, just like the other men she knew—her research had revealed that. But he liked to play, something she'd always valued about him. Her father, her brother, *Phillip*...none of them knew the meaning of play, beyond a rousing round of golf to talk business.

Josh set the food on the table beside the bed and turned to her. His eyes darkened, turning the gray almost black as he drew her toward him and slipped her T-shirt over her head.

"Tempest," he whispered. Her barely there green lace bra revealed more than it hid and he tweaked her nipples, tormenting them with the fabric until she moaned and her head dropped back. A storm of need lashed at her pelvis, electrified by his touch. Lightning surged through her limbs.

She shivered as he skimmed his fingers over her skin to the clasp of her bra. They shook slightly as he released each of the hooks. A moment later, he cupped her freed breasts in his large hands and scraped his thumbs over the hard peaks. Her pussy tightened. She wanted him now. Naked. Beneath *her* this time.

She almost giggled manically at that thought. The likelihood of riding him was slim in his current state of mind if the tension vibrating from him was any indication. He needed her pliant body undulating beneath him. She was happy to comply.

Urgency washing over her, she shoved off his shirt. Leaning forward, she pressed her mouth to his warm chest and tasted his slight saltiness. He grasped her hips and pulled her tight to him while she trailed kisses over his chest. His nipples were tight beneath her mouth. She took the pierced one between her lips. Humming with pleasure, she flicked the tiny ring with her tongue all the while sucking and pulling.

"Jesus, angel," Josh swore. His cock thrust against her, hampered by their clothes. Hurriedly, she reached for his fly, but he stilled her hands. "Not yet."

"I need you."

"You'll have me."

Her world tilted as Josh lowered her onto the mattress but she barely noticed. Josh was her world right now. Nothing else mattered when he sprawled over her. Hungrily, he feasted at her mouth, capturing her gasping breaths. Her fingers threaded into his hair, holding him as her lips widened for his questing tongue. Playfully, she prodded his piercing while he thrust inside.

After a moment he slid a trail of open-mouth kisses across her jaw and down her neck. She whimpered as he sat up, straddling her thighs, and reached for the clasp at her jeans. Her temperature inched up as her zipper inched down. He lost no time pushing her clothing from her body. She reached for his pants as he tossed aside her clothes and returned to straddle her hips. Again, he pushed her hands away.

"Not yet," he said. Reaching over to the table, he lifted the spoon and the sweet and sour sauce off the table. The lid popped as he twisted it off.

"What are you doing?" she asked.

He dipped the spoon into the apricot-colored liquid. "Eating lunch." He lifted the utensil and drizzled the sauce between her breasts. She shivered as the cold puddle spread and crept toward her stomach. A moment later, he scraped a rangoon through the trail. He lifted it to her lips and popped it into her mouth.

"Some for you," he murmured and leaned forward, laving his tongue through the sauce. "And some for me."

She couldn't help the "oh" that whispered past her lips. He lifted the spoon again.

"We're gonna make a mess," she gasped as he dribbled a twisting design down to her navel.

"I'll make sure you're not sticky," Josh promised. He swirled his tongue over her. "So sweet," he murmured.

"I'm sure it's the sugar in that stuff," Tempest panted, the final words coming as a squeak when he smoothed the cool bowl of the spoon over one of her erect nipples. Sauce drifted down the sides of her breast, looking like topping on a sundae. This time he didn't bother with a fried morsel before his mouth dived on her.

He didn't stop her this time when she worked on the clasp of his pants. His erection sprang forth into her hand. She encircled him, gently squeezing the heat. Her thumb smoothed over the ridges on the bottom, counting five barbells through the skin on the bottom of the shaft. No wonder he felt so good thrusting in and out of her. Who needed ribbed condoms when they had this?

Josh pushed against her fingers, a movement that seemed somewhat involuntary as he lapped at her. She wasn't the only one sighing in pleasure. He murmured her name. He tossed the spoon to the side and poured sauce along the indentation of muscle leading to her belly. The sticky condiment coated her stomach, pooling in her belly button. She'd definitely need a shower. Hopefully, he'd join her.

Josh reached for a rangoon. "Still hungry?"

Hungry? What?

She nodded, watching as he split one open and squeezed so that the filling oozed from the opening. Grasping the end between his teeth, he dipped it in the sauce at her navel and dragged it lightly over her skin on the way to her mouth. He teased her with it before she snatched it away with her teeth. A moment later, her tongue darted out to lick away the remnants of sauce from his lips and chin.

"There's another half," he rasped, holding it up for her to see. The remaining two points of the rangoon rested in his palm. Taking it in his other hand, Josh scratched the points over her shoulder, then her arm to her hand but snapped it away before she could take it. Dragging it over her torso, he bent and lapped away some of the sweet and sour.

"You're gonna have a huge sugar buzz," Tempest laughed, as a tingle zinged to her toes.

"I already have a Tempest buzz, so I guess that's okay."

She bit her lip. Yeah, she had a Josh buzz, too. Coming down from it in a few days was going to be hell. God, it would hurt.

Josh stalled her thought by continuing the path of the rangoon to her hip then to her sensitive inner thigh. When she thought he'd stop, he teased the back of her knee and then he popped the morsel into his mouth, wagging his eyebrows playfully.

Reaching for another piece, he pushed the cream cheese filling out onto two of his fingers. "Want some?" he whispered, holding it up to her lips.

She opened and darted her tongue over his fingers as he slowly moved them inside. Her teeth came down, firm but gentle, holding him still as she flicked at his fingertips. Josh's eyes widened in surprise before darkening on a new rush of desire. Relishing her power, Tempest sucked at the digits, pulling and releasing while he stared, entranced, at his hand and her mouth. His erection throbbed against the top of her mound and begged for her attention. She smiled smugly as she pulled away and freed him.

Now it was time. Now. Tempest held out her arms to him. "Josh, please…" she whispered.

He shook his head, his gaze intense.

"I haven't finished yet." Reaching up, he covered his fingers in the sauce remaining on her stomach and painted lines on her legs. His fingers arrowed toward her pussy, never quite touching. He reached for the spoon beside them. Tempest closed her eyes, wondering where he'd dollop the sweet next. She jolted in surprise when the cool of the metal patted her clit and sent streams of wild sensation jolting through her.

Her fingers clenched the sheets as she arched into the Morse code he tapped out against the aroused bud. Small, choked cries erupted from her lips, a mix of pleasure and torture as she burned for deliverance and completion. His mouth closing on her was sweet relief.

"Yes," she sighed. This new game, however, was worse than the last. Josh brought her to the edge of release over and over but never allowed her to tumble into her orgasm. Her entire being desired him and cried out for fulfillment.

Pushing Josh from her, she sat up and slid her hands through the remainder of the condiment on her stomach. If he wouldn't complete her voluntarily, she'd make him wild enough to do it. She scrambled to the end of the bed on her knees while Josh sat up, a confused look on his face. Before he could question her, she leapt to the floor. He swung around to follow, freezing when she knelt between his spread knees. Slowly, she pushed her coated hands over his legs and up his cock. He reared up, grunting when she covered him with her mouth. His sticky fingers pushed into her hair. Clamping her lips tighter, she worked up and down his thick shaft.

"Take it," he said through his teeth. "Yeah, take it." He shoved toward the back of her throat while she massaged his heavy balls, pressing her thumb into the base of his cock. "God, your mouth feels good."

His fingertips dug into her scalp as he neared his peak. Finally, when she suspected he couldn't take more, she sat back on her heels and looked up at him. Very slowly, she leaned forward, watching him and lapped a droplet of cum from him.

Josh immediately clasped her upper arms and dragged her onto the bed with him, rolling over her. The head of his cock poised against the opening of her channel.

"Vixen," he rasped.

"Master," she whispered, batting her eyelashes at him while he jerked on a condom. "Don't punish me..."

"You'd like it too much. I have better ideas."

Her retort died on her lips as he surged inside her. Her cries filled the room. The world shrank to just the two of them, their pulsing heartbeats, their bodies rocking together. Problems, imperfections, faults…they all ceased to exist. In Josh's arms, she was perfection. He was perfection.

She grasped his shoulders, holding on while he drove inside her. Josh cupped the back of her head, drawing her up for a mind-numbing kiss. Almost at once, her body began to tremble beneath his as their personal universe exploded into a world of color before her eyes. She went soaring and with a gruff cry, he went with her.

He collapsed on top of her. He stroked the inside of her elbow, whispering Shakespeare to her while she smoothed her fingers in a lazy motion over his sweat-slicked back. She could get used to this. A sudden need to cry wrung through her and her stomach dropped. This would be gone before she knew it. She pressed her cheek to his damp shoulder, looking away from him, and blinked back the tears burning her eyes.

"I think we're stuck together," she sniffled, hoping she sounded more breathless than sad. Josh's chest shuddered above her as he silently laughed.

"Well, I did promise that I would make sure you're not sticky. Maybe we should shower."

"We?"

He got up, lifted her into his arms and dropped a kiss onto her shoulder. "Of course we." His eyes traveled over her naked body covered only by what remained of the sweet and sour sauce. "You know, you're a messy eater."

"Take a look at yourself."

"I'd rather look at you."

The ringing of her cell phone interrupted her response. A very familiar ring tone split the air. Tempted as she was to ignore it, she knew she couldn't.

"Let me down," she said. Her father beckoned.

# Chapter Four

"Dad…" she answered while Josh stared at her. She couldn't ignore the call, as much as she wanted to. She hadn't told her father she was going away or told anyone where she planned to travel. If she didn't explain her whereabouts her father, the head of a powerful conglomerate would have an APB put out on her.

"Where are you?" he demanded. She crossed her arms over her chest as she faced the wall, her back to Josh's anger. The voice across the line brought back all her insecurities. She wanted to pull the blanket from the bed over herself, but it was already sticky enough.

"I'm with a friend. On a trip," she hedged. Behind her Josh grunted. What did he want from her? Her father would go ballistic if he knew who she was with. Eventually, she'd have to deal with his reaction to Josh, but she didn't want to taint her time with Josh any more than this phone call already would.

"Where? How dare you disappear without telling anyone," her father railed.

"Dad…"

"Where are you? I'll come and get you."

"No," she exclaimed. She'd been through that before. She wouldn't be dragged from Josh's presence by her father again. No one needed to live through a scene like that more than once. Besides, she wasn't a teenager anymore. She'd outgrown the necessity of obeying him. He just didn't get that.

"Why not? Who are you with?"

"It's…Dad, it's not really your business."

"Not my business?" he repeated, his tone taking on a lethal edge that could cut his adversaries to the bone. "Young lady—"

Oh great…

"What has gotten into you—"

She almost giggled hysterically at the thought of what exactly had gotten into her.

"You haven't behaved this way since…that boy," he continued, unaware of her irreverent thoughts. "Tempest, who exactly are you with?"

Uh-oh.

"You're with him, aren't you?" her father continued before she could answer.

Bingo.

"It doesn't matter," she defended herself. She turned back to Josh. He leaned against the headboard of the bed, one leg bent up, the other dangling to the floor. He'd thrown an arm across his eye. His displeasure over this call couldn't be any more evident. His silence spoke to her far louder than if he had a fit right now. Strength and confidence emanated from him. He knew that eventually he'd win this battle.

"Look, I'm a grown up, not a kid," she muttered into the phone.

"How could you? You're marrying Phillip—"

"No, I'm not," she protested vehemently. "I've told you both that. Over and over. I'm not marrying him."

Josh's arm dropped from his face and his eyes narrowed. Tension revved within him, evident from the suddenly taut cords in his neck and the throb of a tiny muscle high on his cheekbone. His lips turned white around the edges. He didn't like the talk of another man. The hand on the arm draped over his thigh fisted. He looked away without a word.

She had a feeling she'd hear a whole lot of words about this later. Or perhaps just one. Mine.

"Tempest—"

"No! I'm safe. I'm healthy. I'll call you when I get home-"

"I need you home now," her father interrupted.

"What?"

"The Miracles and Hope benefit is the day after tomorrow. You're the company's liaison. I need you home. I need you to be there."

She sighed, irritated with his apparent helplessness when it came to the company's charity work. He'd agreed to field anything that came up until she returned later this month. "Dad, we've talked about this."

"This last time, Tempest. Please."

She sighed, some of her anger dissipating. She wasn't returning to Grand Rapids early. "You'll need to do it."

"I need you to," he insisted, taking on a much softer tone.

Her brows drew together at his about-face. "Why?"

"I don't want to worry you while you're away from home." He cleared his throat. "It's a little thing. I'm sure my doctor will schedule some sort of procedure and…" His voice cracked and he trailed off, too emotional to go on. "Just…I need you to do this."

"Fine. Fine. Okay." Guilt racked her. He'd told her he was going to the cardiologist and she'd never thought another thing about it, sure he was fine. She'd been wrong and now he needed her. His health wasn't a reason for him to run her life, but she'd do this charity thing for him. Afterward, she'd gently set him straight about her plans and his unwelcome control over her life.

"You'll be there?"

She glanced at Josh. A different guilt resonated in her middle, a dull, insidious emptiness that grew as realization of what she had to do grew. "Yes."

Her father heaved a relieved breath. "Shall I come to get you?" he asked in a brighter voice.

"No. I'll talk to you later." She flipped the phone shut then turned off the power. She wouldn't have her father hustling her away from Josh again. It was bad enough she'd have to leave before they'd even really started.

"Josh—"

"I don't want to hear about it," he snapped.

"But—"

"But nothing. That man stole years from us, Tempest. I don't care what he said. He's your father so you need to talk to him, but I don't want to hear what he has to say."

"But I have to—"

"You don't have to do anything but be with me, Tempest." Scooping her into his arms, he drowned her protests with his mouth. He had her almost mindless by the time he reached the bathroom with her. Beneath the shower's prickling spray, Josh reminded her of all the reasons she didn't want to leave him. Thankfully, the water cascading over her hid her tears.

* * * * *

Dread plagued Tempest until the next morning when she woke. What could be mocked her as she imagined waking in his arms every morning for the rest of her life. If only… But "if only" only made things worse. How many times had she thought that in her head? If only her mother hadn't died. If only her father hadn't remarried that woman who hated Tempest. If only she could lose those stupid extra pounds clinging to her. If only she'd spoken her mind. If only she hadn't let her father drag her from Josh… That wondering had never served her. It had opened big gaping holes in her psyche.

Slipping free of Josh's grasp around her wrist, she got up to make coffee. The caffeine might ease the ache throbbing in her head. Nothing would help her throbbing heart.

If only he'd listen to her and she could explain. If only…those damned words again. There was no if only. There was just reality. And her reality said she had to leave. Today.

Standing before the untouched coffeepot on the dresser, she curled her arms under her breasts and stared in the mirror. Signs of Josh's loving marked her body. She smiled faintly touching a red mark on her shoulder. She liked his mark. It would be permanently on her soul marking her as his even when they parted. Staring at the inky circles beneath her eyes, she momentarily considered dealing with her father then returning to Josh. She immediately shoved the idea away. It wouldn't work. Josh wouldn't forgive her for choosing her family over him again.

Despair roiled in her stomach. What had happened to her plans and the independence she'd so desperately wanted when she'd come to Josh to obliterate him from her mind? She'd wanted to be free. To be independent. Now she just wanted to be his.

With Josh, she would be free.

He'd encourage her dreams. He'd support her as no one else ever had. With him, she felt desirable and confident. She belonged because she was his.

Then why, dear God, did she have to leave him? She took a wobbling breath. She'd always second guess her independence if she left things as they were with her father. She needed to deal with him before she could truly be free. Otherwise she'd always feel she had run away. He'd retain control over her complete freedom. He might never understand, but at least she'd know she'd tried and she'd had her say. He'd know where she stood.

She shifted her gaze to the man lying in the bed behind her. He was so strong and determined. He had overcome a lot. As he moved seamlessly through life, few knew the battles he'd fought and conquered. She knew. As the baby brother of the Cress family, he'd fought for respect from his three older brothers. He'd had to prove himself and claim his place as an equal. He'd had to gain respect. He had even overcome dyslexia.

And she was worried about confronting her father?

Josh stirred, sitting up anxiously when he realized she wasn't with him. She smiled at him in the mirror. His hair tangled wildly around his head and a mark from the pillow creased his cheek. He rubbed a hand over his face as he met her gaze in the mirror, relief filling his eyes.

"Hi," she whispered around the knot in her throat.

"Come back to bed," he urged in a rough morning voice.

Banging on the door stopped her. Her eyes went wide as the sound startled her. Her father couldn't possibly have found her. This was too much like last time.

"Mr. Cress," a voice called. "I'm here about your truck."

Josh jumped out of bed while relief filled her. "I'll be right there," he called. "Thank God," he said to Tempest, giving her a quick kiss before yanking on his pants. "We'll be able to get out of here today."

She nodded mutely. She was going home today. He just didn't know it.

Josh dashed out to meet the mechanic while she mulled over her situation. She rushed into the bathroom for some essential hygiene. Afterward, she pulled on another set of the lacy lingerie Josh had gotten her, promising herself she'd buy herself some when she got home. She liked the way they made her feel. Feminine and desirable. Josh sure liked her in them. She dressed in a cropped blouse that ended just above her waist and another pair of jeans, then pulled out the purse she'd shoved in her suitcase when they'd packed at Josh's home.

After dragging a brush through her hair, she opened the curtains to let in sunlight then sat at the table. A holder near the window held a pad of paper and a pen. Removing them, she stared out the window at Josh talking to the mechanic next to the open hood of the truck.

*I'm sorry,* she wrote. *I have to go home. I'll never regret my time with you. I don't want it to end, but it must.*

She frowned at the inadequate and wholly pathetic note. She couldn't do better, not without succumbing to the ache inside her and breaking down. She stared at the words.

*All my love, Tempest,* she added. Quickly, she folded it and shoved it in her purse. When they went to town later, she'd hire a car and go home. She glanced again at Josh. If only he would listen to her. If only… if only, if only, if only! She didn't have time for it.

Getting up, she straightened the room so Josh wouldn't have to after she was gone. She stowed her dirty clothes in a laundry bag in her luggage and picked up their food boxes. She flushed as she picked up the sauce container. She'd never think of sweet and sour sauce the same way again. The jar thunked into the trashcan. Picking up the nearby spoon, she tucked it into her purse.

She shook her head. A spoon…her only reminder of this trip.

Her fingers splayed over her neck. Being able to take Josh's collar would have been better. He hadn't given it to her though. She sighed. It was a good thing he hadn't. She would have needed to leave that behind, too.

She jumped as he came into the room. "Marv says he can have the truck done tonight."

"You're back," she said. Lame, Tempest. Lame.

Josh cocked his head. "Yeah…" His arms slipped around her and he kissed her. "It was life and death. I almost didn't make it. Just about got eaten by a squirrel."

"Oh no," she replied, her words indistinct as he covered her lips again. Immediately, her body leapt to attention. Desire settled low in her belly and she wished for one more time in his arms. Once more at his command.

"Let's go get breakfast," he murmured. "I think I saw that the bakery actually has Starbucks and I'm dying for a doughnut. I need some sustenance for what I have in mind for you this afternoon."

She blushed thinking of last night. "You have a serious sweet tooth." She trailed her fingers over his hard belly. "Better be careful."

"With you around, I'll burn off the calories and more," he laughed. "Trust me, no worries."

She drew back. She wouldn't be here. He talked like they had forever. They had hours.

"What is it?" he asked.

She shook her head. "Nothing. Starbucks you say? I never had my coffee this morning. I really need some." She touched her forehead. "A bit of a headache."

"Oh angel, I'm sorry. Let me get on a shirt and we can get going." He rubbed his thumbs over her brow. "It's probably this musty room."

"Probably," she agreed, giving him a half-smile to hide her lie. Careful of any sticky spots, she sat on the bed and watched him as he finished dressing and brushed his hair. Quickly, he pulled it back, securing it with a rubber band at the back of his neck.

He held her hand as they left the room and headed for the woods. She adjusted the strap of her purse on her shoulder and glanced at his left hand where he'd stuck his fingers in his pocket. She could almost imagine rings on their left hands. If they'd been given the opportunity to stay together, it would have happened. They would have married. She had no doubt.

Despite their sexual preferences, they were very much like a normal couple. No one looking at them would know she liked to be tied up and he liked to dominate her. They were just a pair of people who wanted to be together and share their lives.

Just inside the tree line, she turned to him and curved the hand behind his neck. "I love you," she whispered. Her throat constricted. She couldn't stop the tears that flooded down her cheeks as she realized, she'd never tell him that again.

"Angel," he exclaimed, pulling her into his arms. "Don't cry. I'm so—oh angel..." Speechless from the emotion filling him, he covered her lips with his. Desperate to show her what he hadn't said, he pushed her lips apart, delving inside her mouth. Lifting her into his arms, he walked deeper into the woods, stopping only when he reached the secluded waterfall they'd come across the day before. Ribbons of water gushed over a ledge several feet above his head, dropping into the shallow river below.

Thankfully, it was hot for a fall day.

He set her on her feet on one of the stone slabs bordering the small river running from the waterfall. "Clothes. Off," he said, already sliding the strap of her purse from her shoulder.

Taking deep breaths, she wiped away her tears with her fingers. "I'm fine, Josh. You don't need to—"

"I'm not. My sub just told me she loves me. I want to be inside her when she says it again."

"Oh..."

Need jumped in his belly at her quiet response. Already his blood began to fill his shaft. He wanted to be in her as she screamed her declaration in rhythm with his thrusting cock. She toed off her shoes then quickly pulled off the rest of her clothes while he did the same.

"Kneel down," he told her when he was naked. She followed his order without hesitation, instinctively placing her hands over her tailbone.

God, she was beautiful. Submissive and kneeling before him. Her knees were parted enough he could see her pink inner lips and damn if they didn't look slick. It didn't take discipline beyond the quiet, mental control he had over her to arouse her. This sort of subjugation alone brought that glistening cream to her folds. His mouth watered at the remembered taste.

Digging in the pocket of his pants, he pulled out a condom packet, which he set beside them on the rock along with a length of thick, gold links.

Tempest's brows pulled together but she didn't speak. Instead, her teeth sank into her bottom lip.

"Do you know what this is?" he asked.

She shook her head.

"It's a collar. Every Cress woman—every one who's a committed sub, anyway—wears one just like it." The chain appeared purely decorative, but wasn't. Loops for bondage and submission were hidden in the design. He shifted the links. "I want you to wear mine."

"Okay."

"It has hidden loops," he told her. "For bondage."

"Useful," she whispered, her voice taking on a husky quality that wrapped around his dick and yanked him to full attention. Her shuddering breath fanned across his groin as he stepped close.

Lifting her hair to the side, he slipped the collar into place and turned the locks on the clasp that would keep her from easily removing it. She was his. Forever.

The pleasant weight of the collar around her neck nearly brought her to tears again. She shouldn't have said yes, but just once she wanted to feel it and know he'd placed his claim on her. Josh ran his fingers over it.

"Beautiful."

Reaching for his jeans, he removed the belt. Tempest's eyes went wide. He intended to whip her?

"Lie on your side," he instructed.

Immediately, she complied. He put their clothes in front of her. Carefully he looped the leather belt around her ankles and pulled it tight through the buckle. Drawing it upward he pulled until her legs were bent behind her then wrapped the other end of the strip around her wrists. He pressed the remainder into her fingers. "Hold on with both hands."

She closed her eyes, wondering why he'd trussed her up. Like this her ankles were a mere foot from her wrists. "Turn onto your belly and lie on the clothes."

The garments partially padded the surface, but the hard surface was still firm beneath her. Josh ran his hands over her ass. "You please me, Tempest," he said.

"Thank you, Master."

She dropped her head onto the clothes. He'd placed his shirt there and his scent filled her senses. Spicy and masculine.

Her fingers clenched on the leather she held.

"Part your legs, angel."

Hampered by her position, she complied as well as she could, feeling open and exposed and incredibly sensual. She shivered as Josh dripped cold river water over her and it trickled over her ass. She screeched a moment later when he slipped an icy-cold rock along her folds. Smooth from tumbling in the river, it slid easily into her, a long, wide oval. She groaned as he worked it in and out while he flicked her clit with an extended finger.

"Oh God," she moaned, unable to tilt into it. She was helpless to do anything but experience this.

"Oh yeah, angel," he answered. Pulling the rock free, he dipped it in the water. A moment later, he was back, working it into the crease in her ass. She trembled as the frigid surface pressed to her anus. He didn't try to gain entrance. In fact, he turned the stone so it lay lengthwise in her crease. Parting her. Tormenting her with the cold. She squirmed against it. Turned on. Tortured. Against any notion she might have had about the cold, her body flooded heat between her thighs. She was so wet. It could have been the water or her juices. It didn't matter.

The erotic feel punctuated her desire. She needed Josh inside her. Now.

He drove his fingers in and out of her sheath, massaging the swollen tissues. Bumping her clit. Rubbing her g-spot. He knew she needed him—there was no disguising it in the silky slide she provided him. She jerked, screaming as her body contracted and flung her into an almost painful orgasm. The violence shook her as her muscles clenched. It drew her body taut, squeezing the stone, squeezing his fingers which continued to work nonstop, driving her higher and prolonging the spasms.

Finally, she collapsed on the slab. The leather slipped free of her grasp. Josh unlooped it and freed her feet. Gently, he lifted her into his arms and carried her into the river. Water sluiced over her body. It invigorated her from her lethargy and turned her nipples to rigid points.

He turned her to straddle him. His cock poised at the entrance to her pussy and she realized he had pulled on a condom while he tortured her. "Say it," he murmured against her lips.

"Master," she groaned as he slowly prodded inside her. So big, so wide, so hot. He outrivaled the rock by three thousand percent.

"Tell me how you feel."

"Perfect. Wonderful." She kissed his neck, sucking at the pulse throbbing there. "I love you—"

"Yes. That," he exclaimed, driving to the hilt. "Oh, angel, take me… You have all of me."

Their cries echoed around them as he took her to the sky again. She would have stayed there forever if she could have. But the sadness looming ahead of her was insidious. As she pressed her face to his neck, safe in his embrace, misery stabbed through her.

He stroked her arm and whispered in her ear, the words now familiar.

She'd never experience this again. Desperately, she kissed him. Silently, she told him she loved him. Would always love him. She would miss him and this was goodbye.

* * * * *

Tempest glanced around the restaurant attached to the bakery, surprised at how busy it was. Apparently, farmers came from miles around to drink coffee, chat about crops and unless she'd misheard, black bears. That didn't instill any confidence in her, considering the time they'd spent in the woods.

Unaware of Tempest's furtive examination of the place, Josh studied the menu. A waitress came around and filled their coffee cups. Despite her earlier declaration of need, Tempest hadn't touched hers other than to add creamer.

Idly, she fingered the new decoration around her neck.

This was it. This was where she'd step into Josh's past, leaving him alone to find a woman who'd fit into his future. She swallowed back her jealousy. This was the way it would be. The irony of the moment didn't escape her. She had returned to him during breakfast in a restaurant and now she would leave him in almost the same way.

"I'm going to go to the restroom," she murmured. "I need to, um, clean up."

He grinned, a naughty dimple in his right cheek touching her heart. "Hurry back or I'll order you the baked goods breakfast. Doughnuts and muffins and pie." He took a deep breath as she stood. "Doesn't it smell good?"

"Delicious." Without a care for their fellow diners, she bent over him and kissed him. His eyes grew dark.

"Hurry back."

Chains seemed to weigh her down as she headed for the front of the restaurant. She could stop now. She could stay. She took a deep breath. No, she had to get her freedom from her father before she could step forward.

She headed toward the bakery counter, which was out of sight from the restaurant's eating area, to ask the hostess where she could hire a car.

"Tempest?"

Her head jerked up. Maggie stood at the counter, a white bag in one hand and a Styrofoam to-go cup in the other. "Why so gloomy?" the woman asked.

"I have to leave," Tempest admitted. "My dad called and needs me at home. His health isn't good. Josh has to wait for his truck to be fixed so I was just coming to ask where I can hire a car to take me to the airport."

Maggie snorted. "Nowhere around this place."

"Oh..." Well that clinched it. A burst of happiness went through her as she realized she'd have to turn around and return to the table.

"I could take you."

Her stomach fell.

"The Chippewa Airport is about an hour or hour and fifteen minutes from here. There are only a few flights every day. If we hurry, we might be able to get you there in time for the next one."

"Are you sure you have the time?"

Maggie shrugged. "It's my day off. It'll give me a reason to escape my husband for a few hours."

Tempest nodded wanting to tell the woman how lucky she was to have a guy who loved her and wanted to be with her. How lucky she was that she *could* be with him.

She pulled the note to Josh from her purse. Then tried to remove the collar. Try as she might, it wouldn't release. She sighed. She'd mail it to him after she figured out the puzzle release.

Catching the hostess, she gave her the note and asked her to deliver it to him. Tempest brushed away a tear. Had to be like this. Josh wouldn't listen. He wouldn't let her go without a fight—a fight she knew he'd win, too. This wasn't something she wanted to do. It was something she had to do. For her freedom.

She'd call her father. He'd have a ticket waiting. A bitter taste filled her mouth. She hated depending on him. She hated letting him have even this much control over her life. If she knew him—and she knew his MO way too well—he'd try to make the airline ticket an opening for suppressing her independence.

*Last time, Tempest,* she promised. If her father wanted her home, he could pay for it.

Funny, she'd never felt that way about Josh. He dominated. He didn't oppress. He didn't bully her. He didn't steal her independence. In fact he seemed to like it.

She almost turned around and went back in the restaurant. The man she wanted to be with for the rest of her life was sitting in there.

"Let's go," she told Maggie. She had to deal with her father or she wouldn't have a whole rest of her life. It would be a rest of "their" life and unfortunately, the other half of her "their" wouldn't be Josh—it would be her father.

* * * * *

Josh stared at the note in his hand, sure he was reading the words incorrectly. The paper trembled as realization riffled through him. She'd left him again. Ten minutes ago, if what the hostess said was correct.

No. Denial filled him, along with image after image of the last few days. They'd been so happy together. Tempest couldn't have done this.

He stood and tossed a few bills on the table to cover their coffee.

As he rushed toward the front of the restaurant, determination filled him. He'd stop her. They'd talk about this. *You didn't listen last night.*

She'd said she loved him, for God's sake. That had to mean something.

There was no sign of Tempest as he reached the glass doors leading to the street. She'd left him again. Just like before. He took a deep breath. This time would be different. He'd been heartbroken before. He'd suffered.

That wasn't happening. He wouldn't suffer like he did before. Not this time.

* * * * *

Tempest stood at the far side of the ballroom, trying to keep a pleasant expression on her face when all she really wanted was to find a dark corner and cry. With her luck, she'd find the dark corner occupied by an amorous couple. Wouldn't *that* make her feel better.

"You should dance. Mingle a little."

"Hi, Dad," she replied without looking his direction. She really didn't want to see his debonair tuxedo and tanned good looks. Make that his tanned, picture-of-perfect-health, good looks, she corrected.

The bastard had lied to her.

"Still angry with me?" he asked.

She glared at him. "What do you think?" Turning on her heel, she marched from the ballroom. She'd stop at a party store for booze and a bakery for the most fat-laden, sugar-coated doughnuts she could find. Perhaps a dozen.

"Tempest, stop. This minute."

She spun on him in the quiet foyer outside. "No more, Dad. Not anymore. You lied to me again to manipulate me into doing what you want. I told you how I felt, last night and again this morning. I'm tired of you controlling my life. I'm tired of being told who I will see. Who I will *marry*. What I will look like."

"You would look better if you'd lose weight. You wouldn't have to settle for Phillip. You'd be a knockout."

She glared at him. The condemnation hurt just like it always had. Surprisingly, though, it made her more angry than anything else. The only thing she'd ever wanted from him was acceptance. She'd fought for it her whole life, never quite meeting his expectations no matter what she did.

She straightened her shoulders. Wonder filled her. She didn't feel small and he couldn't make her feel that way. She was a beautiful, desirable woman. She smiled, knowing he'd lost that power over her. *Thank you, Josh.*

"I'm not settling for Phillip or anyone else. You're not controlling my life anymore."

"I suppose you want that boy."

"He's a man. Not a boy. And yes, if he'd have me, I'd go with him in a second. I love him." As much as it hurt to know Josh was lost to her, it was pretty damned spectacular to admit her feelings to someone else.

Her father's lips pursed and he pushed a disgusted breath through his nose. "Fine. I'm going back in there." He glanced at his watch. "I need you for another hour, then you're free to do whatever the hell you want to with your life."

He took a few steps then spun on her. "What do you expect to do without my support? Without a job or prospects…and apparently without a family since you're writing us off."

Realization opened wide inside her. For the first time, she saw the emotionally needy man who'd used his control as a path to affection. "Dad, I'm not writing off my family."

Misguided triumph flared in his eyes. He held out his hand. "Are you coming back inside with me?"

Ignoring his outstretched arm, she headed back into the ballroom. Oblivion at the feet of baked goods would still be there in an hour. So would this problem with her father. She fingered her collar, thinking of Josh. Somehow she would draw on the strength he'd shared with her.

* * * * *

Josh stepped from the shadows, watching his woman disappear into the party. Her father needed the crap kicked out of him. Josh's fist clenched. How dare John insult her like he had?

Despite his irritation at having to chase after her, Josh was proud of her. Not many people would stand strong against their parent like she had. He couldn't believe she meant to leave everything behind. It was more than he'd expected, but it worried him. Would she want what he offered…a life bound with his? Bound to him. Bound *by* him.

If he had his way, she'd be back in his arms and beneath him before the night was over. Especially since she loved him. His stomach knotted. He might not have his way.

She wanted independence. That wasn't his plan. As his submissive, she'd be cherished as his ultimate treasure. All her needs would be met. But she'd also be his to command. He almost laughed when he thought of the sassy woman who'd shared most of last few days with him. She liked it when he dominated her and she would obey him, but he wasn't fooled into thinking his feisty mate would be forced into something she didn't want to do. She was too strong for that.

Straightening the jacket of his black tuxedo, he followed Tempest's path into the ballroom. Unusual unease assaulted him. He wanted their paths to join.

What if she said no?

She wouldn't. At least, he hoped not. When he'd gotten back yesterday, Keera had given him a crash course on the Strength card—more from her insistence than his desire. He doubted he'd ever be a tarot believer—it was all still hocus pocus to him—but what she'd said made sense. He had inner strength and gentle control, which was signified by the upright card. Tempest's father thrived on the shadow aspects of the card—manipulation and tyrannical behavior. Josh feared he might be assigning values based on what he wanted to see but Keera assured him that if he kept in mind that love would conquer antagonism he'd succeed.

Josh wasn't so sure.

The room was crowded, filled to capacity with men dressed as he was and women wearing gowns in every color of the rainbow. Scanning the sea of bodies, he found John chatting with a group of men near the far wall. John's eyes met his and Josh saw recognition and dread in them. It was the man's furtive glance that directed the way to the one Josh sought.

Tempest stood, near the glass doors leading to a stone balcony that overlooked downtown Grand Rapids and its Grand River. Fairy lights reflected on the dark water below, giving it a magical twinkle.

Josh was far more captivated by Tempest's voluptuous curves and the way her fire-engine-red dress hugged her in all the right places. Her hair was lifted into an upswept twisty thing that exposed her slim neck and the collar he'd placed there. She fingered the links while she stared outside.

He was lucky she didn't have a horde of men knocking each other down to get to her. Approaching her silently, he stood behind her and breathed in her floral scent. His cock grew hard…and decidedly hopeful…at being so close to her again. It shoved against his fly wanting to claim her now.

Gently, he skimmed his finger tips along her inner elbow, knowing the reaction that would come. He'd fostered it in her.

"We are such stuff as dreams are made on," he murmured close to her ear. Tempest trembled, her breath arresting in her throat. Smug satisfaction filled him. Unless he missed his guess, her panties had just gotten very wet.

Tempest's gaze flew up to meet his in the window. She panted as the aftermath of an unexpected orgasm continued to vibrate through her. How *did* he do that? How had he made it so her body recognized him? Her knees wobbled, but Josh pulled her against him to give her support. His hand splayed over her wildly contracting belly while she leaned weakly on him and waited for the room to stop spinning.

"I'm here, angel," he whispered. "Don't fight it. Your body remembers the pleasure between us. You know me. You know what is between us. Even with a touch. Even with a phrase."

"Josh," she gasped, unable to believe he was here and holding her. What was he doing here? How on earth had he found her? Did she really care? For the first time since she'd left him in the restaurant, she didn't feel like crying. Her heart was in one piece, at least temporarily. Judging from the tremors rolling through her like gentle waves, the rest of her body was thrilled as well. He was right. She knew him. Instinctively.

His cock pressed to her back, proving he wanted her too. He held her upright as he guided her through the double doors and into the chill of the autumn night. No one else had braved the sudden cold snap, leaving the balcony deserted.

Turning, she buried her face in the front of Josh's shirt. "You're here. You're *here*."

Relief filled her. This was right. Being in his arms. Being with him.

"I'll never let you go, angel. Not if I have a choice."

"But…I left…" That guilt might never leave her.

He lifted her chin and brushed a kiss over her trembling lips. "And I'm angry. We'll deal with that later." His knowing gaze searched hers. "You'll feel better afterward."

"I'm sorry."

"I know."

She blinked at him. Why wasn't he raging at her? He seemed downright…saintly. It was his eyes that told her. Worry rimmed them, yet determination filled the gray depths. He had every intention of fighting whatever battle he must to claim her. The rest would come later.

Her guilt shifted and a glimmer of happiness started to burn away the emptiness inside her. He might find the battle easier than he thought.

"Your hair," she exclaimed, suddenly realizing he'd changed his appearance.

He sheepishly ran his fingers through the newly shorn locks, the shorter strands curling without the extra weight pulling them down. A few errant curls fell toward his eye. "I hope it's not a deal breaker. It looks like grown-up hair, don't you think?"

He'd done this for her. The thick, wavy strands begged for her fingers. She ran her thumb over his naked eyebrow. He'd removed the ring there and all but a single stud in one of his ears. He'd seemed dangerous before. A good girl's lust-filled dream. Now, with this new, clean-cut appearance, danger hid behind a guise of drop-dead sexy and waited to lure in his woman and capture her.

"I like it," she admitted. "But I liked your long hair too. And the earrings. You don't have to change for me."

"The piercings aren't all gone," he confessed, telling her clearly that her favorites remained.

"Thank goodness for *that*."

"Mmm, yes," he agreed as he waltzed her toward the shadowy corner of the balcony. He scraped his teeth on the sensitive flesh behind her ear. "My brothers flew up in the company chopper when you left. Ryan stayed with my truck and dealt with the motel. He suggested I flog you. I'm not going to."

She could just imagine what his three siblings, Ryan, Max and Theo, had to say about her departure. They'd probably been irate that any woman would dare leave their baby brother—twice. She wasn't surprised Ryan had suggested the flogger. It was mild compared to what they probably thought she deserved.

"I wouldn't mind." She didn't prefer that but if it was what Josh wanted, she'd concede.

"I know. On the way to the airport, Max suggested spanking you." He raised an eyebrow at her. A flutter flew through her belly and her panties grew more damp. She knew how heat flew through her on the few times he'd ever done that in the past.

He palmed her ass. "I might. Anyway, I missed you at the airport by five minutes. That's when Theo suggested, and I quote, that I 'drag Tempest's ass home and chain her' in my dungeon. That's not all he said, but I'll keep his assessment of my Dom qualities to myself."

She winced. He'd dealt with that because of her. "I don't deserve for you to trust me—I've left you twice—but…oh God, Josh. I'm sorry. I'm miserable without you. I knew I would be, but I had to…deal with things. I-I don't ever want to be apart from you."

"What about the independence and freedom you want so badly?"

"I am free with you." She didn't have to hide behind appearances or her fears. With Josh the real Tempest stopped hiding and stood boldly in the sun. "Please believe me. I promise you. I *want* to be with you."

"I guess I could keep you chained up like Theo suggested."

"If you must," she answered, slipping her fingers inside his shirt. He'd never do it. She knew him too well. He preferred mental chains to the physical type.

Pulling her tightly to him, he pressed open her lips, claiming them as fully as she knew he intended to claim the rest of her body when they were alone. She groaned, meeting his thrusting tongue and sucking it into her mouth. Josh's fingers dug into her intricate twist. She didn't care. If she had her way, it would be a disaster within an hour.

"I trust you, Tempest," he admitted against her lips when they were both breathing heavily. "I know why you went and I should have listened to you. If I had, you wouldn't have felt it was necessary to sneak away. I would have come with you."

"So I'm not in trouble."

He nipped her bottom lip. "Don't count on that. I've made lots of plans for you. My sweet tooth has gone completely unfed since you left. I need a lot of Tempest to feed me."

Lifting her onto the stone wall, he shielded her with his body and pushed his hand beneath her dress. He eased aside her panties and thrust his fingers into her with no preliminary. She whimpered. Her body immediately squeezed around him.

"So slick. So hot and ready for me," he said, nuzzling her neck. "You want me to take you right here. Don't you, Tempest? It excites you."

"Yes. I'd let you take me anywhere."

"Mine," he grated through his teeth as he plunged his fingers forward.

"Tempest!"

She jumped at the sound of her father's harsh admonition as it echoed across the balcony. She knew he couldn't see what they'd been doing, but a blush burned up her neck anyway. Josh withdrew his hand and stepped back. His other arm remained tightly around her as he stared into her eyes. Slowly, he lifted his hand to his mouth and sucked away her essence.

She licked her lips.

"What the hell are you doing with my daughter, Cress?" her father demanded.

Josh turned and pulled her close to his side. "Taking her home."

Her father's face turned red in the moonlight bathing the area where he stood. If he'd truly had a health problem, she might have worried. "I'll have you arrested for trespassing," he exclaimed.

"I don't think so, sir. Upon investigation, you'd find I own a great deal of stock in both Montgomery Enterprises and the Hartley Foundation who sponsor Miracles and Hope. I have every right to be here." His chin lowered, the only indication, outside his sparkling eyes, that fury burned inside him. "I don't take chances. Not when it entails my future. I paid the price for that lesson years ago. This time I don't intend lose." His arm tightened around Tempest but she shifted.

She was a prize? His words made her uneasy until he continued. "I love your daughter. I won't lose her again."

"Something you could have told me privately," she murmured for his ears only.

He leaned down and kissed her. "I thought I did. I've been feeling it long enough."

"You're lying," her father accused.

They both stared at him. Josh deciphered his meaning first. "No, sir, I'm not." He looked at Tempest. "I bought the Montgomery stock a week after you left me last time. I just picked up the Hartley stocks yesterday. I knew you were arguing with him about attending something. After you left I put two and two together and took a chance. This is one of the biggest functions of the year for shareholders."

"It doesn't matter. Owning shares doesn't make you any less of a freak. Tempest, if you go with him now, that's it. I'll disown you. You'll get none of the company. You don't want that. I know you don't." He held out his hand. "Come with me now."

Josh's arm dropped and she knew he was giving her a choice. She also heard his intake of breath when she crossed to her father. *I'm sorry Josh,* she thought, knowing this must pain him. She stopped when she was even her father and kissed him on the cheek. "I love you, Dad. Someday you'll realize that."

She backed away until she was flat against Josh's chest. "I'm staying with Josh."

"He'll destroy you," her father bellowed. "You'll have nothing. You'll have nowhere to go."

"Yes, she will," Josh growled. His arms closed around her. His support bolstered her.

"I'll have everything," she choked, her heart breaking that she had to make this choice. This time she knew she was making the right decision. It didn't make the pain any less.

"That freak will tie you up and treat you like a slave."

She crossed her arms over Josh's. "What we do is none of your business, Dad."

"You're no better than he is."

She glanced up at her Dom. "Nope. No better."

Her father spluttered.

"If you'll excuse me, sir," Josh said. "I'm taking Tempest home." He pulled a card from his pocket. "This is where you can contact her. I won't keep her from seeing you, but I warn you… You'd better treat her well. I will not allow you to insult and degrade her."

Her father's bitter laugh scraped the air around them. "Oh that's rich coming from you."

Josh stiffened, and his voice was razor sharp as he spoke. "I don't expect you to understand, but know this well. I value Tempest more than my life. Don't cross me. I will protect her."

Leaving her father speechless, he guided her from the balcony and through the ballroom to the elevator in the foyer. He pushed the call button for an elevator to take them to the upper floors where the hotel rooms were located. "You don't mind if we don't go home until tomorrow, do you?"

She shrugged. "No. I need to get some of my things from my apartment anyway." She sighed. "I wish it didn't have to be like this. You know, with my dad."

Josh kissed her temple. "He'll come around. He does love you. In his way. When he sees we're happy, things will change."

"I hope you're right." They stood silently, waiting. "It doesn't change my mind," she finally said. "This is what I want."

"Tempest..."

"No. Don't let him put a pall over this. You're right. He will come around. In the meantime I want to start living my life. With you."

He smiled. "Have you ever had a tarot reading?"

"Well, yeah," she replied, looking surprised by the apparent change in conversation. "You know me—self-help books, karma and all that. Why?"

"I had a reading right before you came back. I don't know if I want to believe it... I mean, the metaphysical isn't really my thing. But the Strength card came up. My sister-in-law insists that it's about us. You and me."

She knew the Strength card. "And my father," she added. "I'm surprised," she teased. "A big, tough Dom resorting to tarot cards. My image of you is shattered."

"It solved our problems, didn't it?" he grumbled. His fingers stroked over her hip and she sighed leaning into him. Yeah, Josh was all about gentle control and she was all about complying.

"I like when you do that."

He shook his head. "I love you. You know that?"

The bell over the elevator doors rang and the doors slid open. A moment later, they were enclosed in silence. He pushed the code that would take them directly to the penthouse without any stops. Leaning against the wall, he played with a lock of her hair that had escaped her twist. "I was thinking…maybe you'd like to continue our vacation. Go back to the Four Star. Bob—Grizzly Adams—promised not to disable my car again."

"Disable your car?" she asked, confused.

"That's what happened this time… Bob, Marv and some of the other townspeople like to detain visitors. Marv would have even given me the repair 'on the house'. They're harmless and just want more people to see their town. I should press charges, but I have a bit of an attachment to the place—thanks to you."

"I think I have a bit of an attachment too."

"I thought maybe this time you'd like to bring your camera and take pictures."

She stared at him, mouth open, and suddenly realized he'd had her so distracted while they'd been marooned that she hadn't thought of missed photo opportunities. Yeah, she'd like to have a re-do on that. "I hear there's a good Chinese place," she laughed.

Linking his finger through her collar, he pulled her toward him and nibbled her bottom lip. "There might just be some good Chinese food upstairs, too. That and a whole lot of love."

Mountains of love. Her hands went to his fly as she knelt. "That's good. I'm starving." She looked up at him. "I don't know if I'll ever get enough."

# Also by Brynn Paulin

ꟹ

Wedding Jitters

# About the Author

ꟹ

When it comes to books and movies, Brynn Paulin has one rule: There must be a happy ending. After that one requirement, anything else goes. And it just might in any of her books.

Brynn lives in Michigan with her husband and two children who love her despite her occasional threats to smite them. They humor her and let her think she's a goddess... as long as she provides homemade chocolate chip cookies on a regular basis.

She attributes her writing success to 70's music, her local road construction crews, a trusty notebook, and of course, her husband and willing research subject, AKA Mr. Inspiration.

Brynn welcomes comments from readers. You can find her website and email address on her author bio page at www.ellorascave.com.

*Tell Us What You Think*

We appreciate hearing reader opinions about our books. You can email us at Comments@EllorasCave.com.

## Why an electronic book?

We live in the Information Age—an exciting time in the history of human civilization, in which technology rules supreme and continues to progress in leaps and bounds every minute of every day. For a multitude of reasons, more and more avid literary fans are opting to purchase e-books instead of paper books. The question from those not yet initiated into the world of electronic reading is simply: *Why?*

1. ***Price.*** An electronic title at Ellora's Cave Publishing and Cerridwen Press runs anywhere from 40% to 75% less than the cover price of the exact same title in paperback format. Why? Basic mathematics and cost. It is less expensive to publish an e-book (no paper and printing, no warehousing and shipping) than it is to publish a paperback, so the savings are passed along to the consumer.
2. ***Space.*** Running out of room in your house for your books? That is one worry you will never have with electronic books. For a low one-time cost, you can purchase a handheld device specifically designed for e-reading. Many e-readers have large, convenient screens for viewing. Better yet, hundreds of titles can be stored within your new library—on a single microchip. There are a variety of e-readers from different manufacturers. You can also read e-books on your PC or laptop computer. (Please note that Ellora's Cave does not endorse any specific brands.

You can check our websites at www.ellorascave.com or www.cerridwenpress.com for information we make available to new consumers.)

3. ***Mobility***. Because your new e-library consists of only a microchip within a small, easily transportable e-reader, your entire cache of books can be taken with you wherever you go.
4. ***Personal Viewing Preferences.*** Are the words you are currently reading too small? Too large? Too... *ANNOYING*? Paperback books cannot be modified according to personal preferences, but e-books can.
5. ***Instant Gratification.*** Is it the middle of the night and all the bookstores near you are closed? Are you tired of waiting days, sometimes weeks, for bookstores to ship the novels you bought? Ellora's Cave Publishing sells instantaneous downloads twenty-four hours a day, seven days a week, every day of the year. Our webstore is never closed. Our e-book delivery system is 100% automated, meaning your order is filled as soon as you pay for it.

Those are a few of the top reasons why electronic books are replacing paperbacks for many avid readers.

As always, Ellora's Cave and Cerridwen Press welcome your questions and comments. We invite you to email us at Comments@ellorascave.com or write to us directly at Ellora's Cave Publishing Inc., 1056 Home Avenue, Akron, OH 44310-3502.

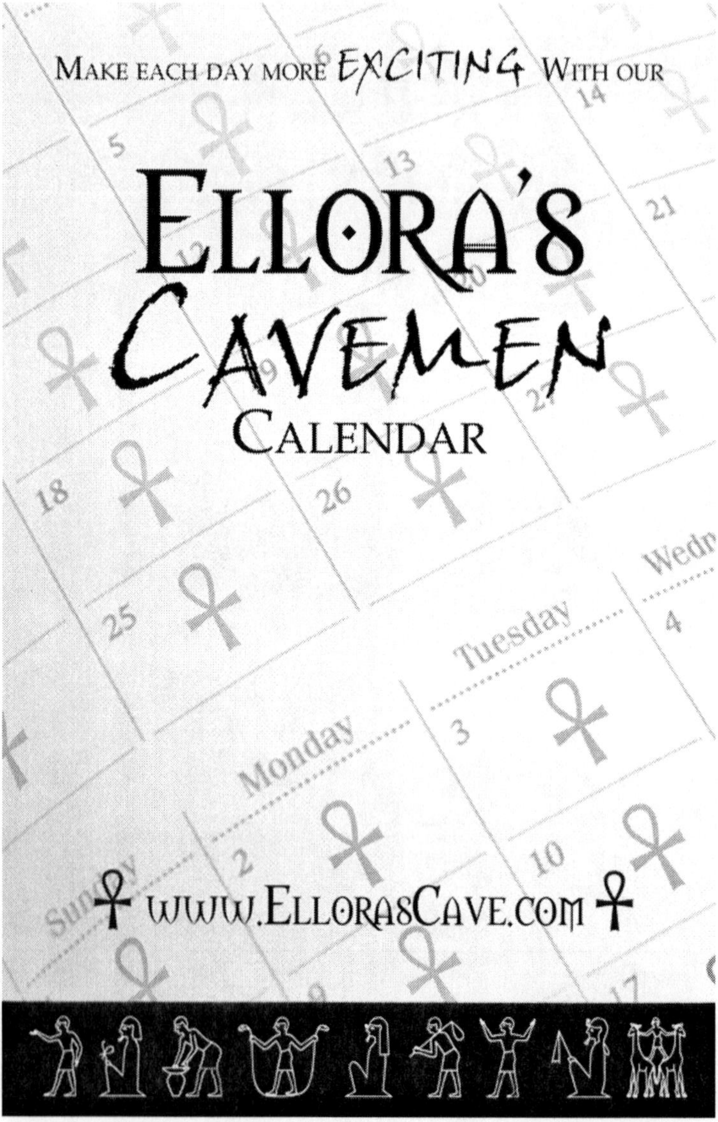
MAKE EACH DAY MORE EXCITING WITH OUR
ELLORA'S
CAVEMEN
CALENDAR
WWW.ELLORASCAVE.COM